I0638286

DARK TARGET

DARK TARGET

MICK WILLIAMS

Copyright © 2021 by Mick Williams

All rights reserved.

No part of this book may be reproduced in any form or by any electronic or mechanical means, including information storage and retrieval systems, without written permission from the author, except for the use of brief quotations in a book review.

ISBN: 978-1-948374-67-5

First Edition

Enigma House Press

Goshen, Ky 40026

www.enigmahousepress.com

Dedicated to the selfless and fearless work of healthcare professionals and first responders who have kept the world turning during crazy times…in the midst of uncertain panic, you stepped up.

Thank you.

Chapter One

Reflected streetlights glinted starlight bursts of orange off the cobbled, mosaic-like road as John 'Macca' MacIntyre and Jason Knowles turned a corner and began the slippery downhill trek into Old Town, Edinburgh. A full and round setting sun burned off the last of a short rainfall and held enough heat to warm their backs as they made their way down Grassmarket toward the shade.

"Feels weird, what with us being out like this, Macca. Especially weird it being the two of us here. And the streets seem quiet tonight. Just me, you, and him." He gestured to a homeless guy huddled inside a store doorway. Buried under a fleecy blue blanket, he played with a large, expensive-looking cell phone.

Macca turned to his friend and colleague. "Big football game on tonight, pal, Hibernian verses Hearts. Local rivalry. Most folks will be indoors or in the pubs to watch it. And, regardless of what we do, or even what we find while we do it, life must go on. Especially since you just created a new one.

Well, Marcy did," he smiled. "Your part probably lasted about ten seconds. Give or take five."

"Hey, come on, credit where credit's due. He's a beautiful wee lad."

"Can't argue with that. Great effort for ten seconds of work."

"Aye, you're funny, all right. Thought you might have invited your twin lads out tonight. It's been a while since all four of us got together. I miss them."

"I mentioned it. Archie's staying with his girlfriend, and Cameron is finishing up at Uni. There's always next time."

Against the force of tourism, the city's architecture tried hard to maintain its medieval look, with Georgian buildings built from huge slabs of stone butted alongside more up to date pubs and clubs. The small stones underfoot caught out many a visitor in slick footwear, but Macca knew each street intimately. After his military service, he didn't hesitate to return to his birth town, despite repeated and insistent requests from his wife to move to a warmer place.

There's no place like home, he told her in his thick Scottish brogue. I'll be happy to die here and be buried alongside the many generations of other MacIntyres.

The street sloped away from the front of St. Giles's cathedral and curved past the clubs and Harry Potter trinket stores down into the Old Town center, where the two were on a rare night out to wet the head of Jason's newborn son.

Macca looked up in time to see a flash that seemed out of sequence with the disco dance of sparkling stone ahead of them. In the distance, the Church of St. Almus rose above the tiled roofs, its tallest parts wrapped in scaffold as the city renovated the centuries old building.

Old instincts kicked in instantly, and he tensed as well-trained senses snapped awake.

"You see that?"

"See what?"

"A flash over the church. The sun's just high enough to catch the peak. It could be that reflected off sunglasses but, these days, they don't allow people into the bell tower. Something or someone's up there."

He turned to one side as Knowles stepped forward to look. The whine of a supersonic bullet buzzed his ear a millisecond before he spoke again, and Knowles staggered backwards in a cloud of pink spray. Macca dropped to the ground and rolled sideways into a doorway.

In the street, a stream of blood gained momentum and zigged and zagged through the cobbled cracks from the remains of Knowles' head.

Macca cursed and scrambled to his feet. He knew their work was dangerous but, since Knowles was a silent researcher, Macca also knew the sniper's bullet would have been meant for him.

The church was a five-minute run away, enough time for the most amateur sniper to break down his weapon, stow it, clean the scene and move on.

Remorse could be dealt with later. Retribution and revenge were instant.

He broke into a sprint and ran a random course down the street to the center, until the lower buildings gave cover from the church. A pizza store offered a corner to peek around.

The building was swathed in shadow, derelict of tourists, but the threat still lay somewhere inside, hidden behind stained-glass windows.

From the store, it was a straight dash to the church, yards of dangerous, wide open space. Full, lethal exposure, like running through a minefield, until he could dive for cover behind a moss-covered headstone or a well-tended tree. Had the sniper given up on his main target, content to try again another time, or was he still crouched, hidden in shadow at the top of the church? Waiting for his prey to wander into the line of fire.

A few tourists milled around, oblivious to the carnage farther up the road. Macca sprinted again, weaving in and out of them as a distraction. Moments later, he thumped into the thick wall at the base of the church, breathed deeply, and listened.

Other than a faint bustle from the street and the waft of green netting that covered some of the scaffold, the only sound was the thump of his heart rate returning to normal. He edged around the wall, cursing Scottish law that banned the carrying of handguns. The thick, oak door which formed the main entrance to the church stood ajar by less than an inch. A shifting darkness waited through the crack. Flat against the wall, he moved closer until he was able to nudge it wider with his foot. Still nothing.

Inside, rows of wooden pews lined up under a kaleidoscope of color that washed across them through the stained glass. Hours old incense and the musty smell of old paper wafted over him as he stooped, edged through the doorway, and crouched behind the rear pew.

Macca waited until his eyes adjusted to the unusual light, took another breath, and then raised his head.

The tops of the benches fanned out across the church in orderly rows and stopped at an altar at the end of the main aisle. An ornate, wooden confessional booth took up a section of the wall to the left. An open door at one side revealed nothing but a padded knee rest, while the other had a closed panel door, the perfect hiding place for an assassin. Overhead, and to his right, thick stone pillars supported a balcony that stretched the length of the room. Beneath it, to the right of the altar, was the vestibule door.

He shuffled, crablike, to the edge of the aisle using the solid wood benches as cover and ducked beneath the balcony and down the side of the pews, checking each row for company.

The vestibule door near the altar lay open. Again, nothing of substance moved in the darkness beyond it, just an inky black that moved with the changing outside light. The altar itself was a solid slab of marble with ornate carvings across its front. A red cloth covered the top, held in place by a heavy-looking silver candle holder at each corner. With a glance toward the confessional, he edged out into the open and closed the distance to the rear of the altar in seconds. When the echo of his footsteps faded, he risked another look around.

A row of windows left no shadows on the balcony, and he cleared it at a glance. He reached overhead, grabbed a candle holder from the altar, and hefted the weight in his hand. He levered the candle free and turned the holder upside down, gripped the narrow stem, and shimmied across to the confessional. Breath held, he peered into the open section and studied the lattice that separated the two sides. When nothing moved, he raised the makeshift club and flung open the door. Empty.

With the balcony still clear, he rushed back to the safety of the altar and crouched. The entire search had taken twenty seconds. Macca mentally patted himself on the back. A few years out of the military and the old house-to-house search skills were as sharp as ever.

Moving to the opposite side, he pressed himself against the wall and edged open the door to the vestibule. Again, outside light offered a dim view through multi-colored windows, this time of a long bench and row of coat hooks draped with small gowns. As the door swung farther open, he saw a desk that took up another wall. To its side, a stone staircase disappeared upwards into the gloom.

Macca moved toward it. He paused when a rustle broke the silence. Well-trained senses filtered out the background noise from the street, and he waited for a repeat to give a bearing or sense of position. The bell tower was perhaps sixty feet above and, if the sniper wasn't professional enough, there was a slim chance he could still be in the building. Or he'd researched his quarry and figured he'd come to investigate.

After a brief pause, he moved toward the staircase and mounted the first step. As was the style with a lot of old churches, the staircase wound around in a spiral to save space. He leaned out and glanced up into the void above, but nothing moved in the shadow.

One step at a time, he climbed the stairs, ever alert to any movement or sound. Patience and concentration.

Memories of the old job stabbed at his thoughts. One wrong move was the difference between life or death.

The smooth, worn-down concrete edges of each step brushed against his shins as he inched upwards until he grew level with the balcony. From this angle, fading sunlight shot through the windows in pure, angelic fans of light without even floating dust motes to break it. All the windows were sealed units, with none opening out onto the street, which confirmed his suspicion. The sniper took his shot from the bell tower.

Macca continued his climb until he reached the top.

A huge bell hung in the opening, the brass mottled green and brown with age. It had no rope or means to move it, presumably either rotted and not replaced, or the bell was rendered useless to obey local noise laws.

As he leaned to check the tower, a flurry of movement

blurred in his peripheral vision. His head hummed as a fist struck him from the side, and he toppled into the wall. Before he could recover, a boot slammed into his chin, cracking his head against the brick. Lights danced as his teeth rattled, and Macca dove to one side to avoid the next blow.

A heavily accented voice scoffed above him. "I knew you'd come looking. Your profile was accurate, you are arrogant. I also knew I'd be the first to reach you. Sorry about your friend, by the way. Honest mistake. Wrong place, wrong time."

Macca spotted a rifle-sized kit bag leaned up against the side wall as the tell-tale, metallic click of an opening switchblade focused his attention. As the sniper advanced, he put every ounce of energy into an arm swing, ensuring the solid candle holder connected with the side of the assassin's knee.

The resulting howl of pain drew a tiny hum of vibration from the huge bell as the man dropped with a thump to his good knee. Macca slammed the metal into his face then rolled to the other side of the bell to regain his senses.

The sniper was quicker and stronger than expected.

As he pushed up off one arm, a kick took it away, and Macca tumbled to the concrete.

In a second, the man sat astride him and pinned his arms with his shins.

Macca looked up into cold blue eyes and cheekbones sharp enough to cut paper. Two trails of blood ran from a shattered nose. Speech was difficult, as the sniper's weight centered on his chest, but Macca took a shallow breath. "Whatever you want, we can sort something out."

The man smiled. "I have all I need and, anyway, this is nothing to do with me or you. I don't even know why you have to die. All I know is it pays well. It's nothing personal."

Macca breathed again and tried to stall to give his swimming head time to clear. "At least tell me who sent you. And what do you mean, you knew you'd be the first?"

As he spoke, he hitched his back and inched across the concrete to drag them closer to the wall. The man winced as he dug in his knees. "I recognize your tactics, but I'm not here to enjoy the view." The steel blade glinted over Macca's face. "I'm sorry, but it's time to join your friend."

Macca waited for the man to lean forward then used his momentum against him and, with a thrust of the hips, lifted him airborne.

Instinctively, the assassin held out his hands and shifted his weight.

Macca took the cue, clutched fistfuls of clothing and, with a twist of the body, heaved him up and over the top of the wall. Other than the clatter of steel against concrete, he toppled out of sight in silence.

With his chest free, Macca sucked in gulps of precious oxygen then looked around the bell tower. Other than the bagged rifle, the only other thing in the tower space was the silver candle holder. He picked it up then leaned out to see where the sniper had landed. Instinct and reflexes arched him backwards as a fist swung inches from his face.

He'd landed three feet below the edge of the tower on solid scaffolding boards. With the advantage of height, Macca vaulted the wall and used his weight to push back the man. The whole assembly shook when they crashed into the nearest aluminum pole, and the man cursed in a foreign tongue as a rib cracked. Despite the pain, he pushed back. His palm pressed against Macca's nose, aggravating his already aching face. At the limit of his pain threshold, Macca relaxed enough to let the man ease forward then dropped to his knees, grabbed his ankles, and heaved him up, over his shoulder and over the edge.

This time, he watched while the body free fell almost sixty feet. It bounced with a dull clang against a protruding piece of scaffold about halfway down and cartwheeled wildly until it landed with a heavy thump to the ground below.

As blue lights flashed in the distance and the wail of sirens grew louder, Macca retrieved the rifle, cleared the scene, and edged down the stairs and out of the church.

Chapter Two

English padded down the steps to his basement, paused at the first hint of sound, and sat at the halfway point to survey the room. It reflected in a wall of monitors that lined the side wall, connected to a powerful system that ran software equal to that in most military outposts. The people in the reflection caught his attention; a ragtag group of pensioners sitting with a set of beaten-up identical twins.

A wry smile crossed his face as he slid down another step, pulled a mouthful of beer from a cold bottle, and studied each man in turn. Perched on the arm of the sofa, far left, was Sarge. After a hair-raising adventure in Jamaica, it was clear that Sarge took the lead in what the group did. He'd served multiple tours in some of the most hellish places on Earth, yet still sat with the group and listened to the conversation with nothing but humility and the cool glint of experience in his eyes.

It occurred to English that, even after fighting side by side with the man, he still didn't know his name.

Sitting next to Sarge was Marbles. After first meeting the group in a local fast-food restaurant, and before an initiation ceremony that rivaled any hazing he'd experienced in the military, English was convinced that the wiry man on his sofa was named Marbles because he'd lost most of them. Then, Marbles had pulled out a canvas pouch and emptied its contents onto the table. A collection of painted glass eyeballs clicked and rolled in a tight-knit pack and, only then, did Keith 'English' Watson figure out why the man's gaze was unnerving. A sliver of shrapnel had flown into one of his eyes, and a generous ex father-in-law had furnished him with a set of glass eyeballs to fill the void, painted in different designs to cover his differing moods. Right now, after a successful mission, he still wore the smiley emoji he'd flown home with.

It turned out that Lucas Durrant would find a way to operate an engine of any kind, and he'd ferried them from Jamaica to Columbia through the toughest of tests using multiple vehicles.

A sentence, spoken in a strong Scottish brogue, shocked English out of his study.

"Aye, and that's when Dad said he saw Uncle Jason's head vaporize."

He stood to complete the trek downstairs to join the others.

"Sorry, guys," he said. "Food'll be ten minutes. Pizza, if that's okay? Been a little busy to go shopping. Had to raid the freezer."

The group nodded; a group which had affectionately been dubbed The Old Farts Club.

"And sorry for interrupting, Cameron. Go on, mate."

The younger lad nodded a head of ginger hair and continued. "He wasn't really our uncle, so to speak, but we'd known him long enough that we just thought of him that way. Took us fishing and to footy matches. Even bought us our first legal pint. He was Uncle Jase." The boy raised a bandaged arm and massaged the back of his neck while he dipped his head to hide his expression. His voice still cracked with emotion. "Now he's dead and Dad's in hiding."

"Any idea who's responsible?"

English looked at Dud when he spoke. Of the whole group, Dud was the one he knew the least about, simply because their first mission together was to travel to Jamaica to help Dud find his missing wife. He knew where the nickname came from, and that Dud battled PTSD, a condition that he'd at least learned to tolerate. Almost.

Average height and build betrayed the fact that Danny 'Dud' Wilkerson put any life before his own and, so far, had faced everything with a bravery that left English humbled.

He was also blunt but to the point.

"No, but we don't think it's just the one person."

The other twin, Archie MacIntyre, spoke in a calm, steady voice. The shock of ginger hair on his head matched his brother's, but his demeanor was the polar opposite. Deep-set, steely blue eyes didn't flinch as he continued.

"Dad pitched the bloke a fair way over some scaffolding. I imagine he made a grim sound when he hit the ground. Kind of a damp splat, I reckon. No loss there. It was by the church, too, so at least they didn't have to move him far to bury what was left of him. He bounced off the scaffolding on the way down, so the police think all the damage was caused by him jumping. But, before he went, he told Dad he knew he'd be first to reach him."

English smiled at the way Archie pronounced 'first' as 'fost'.

"So he's part of a kill team," said Sarge.

"No clue. There's been nothing since. Having said that, Dad's taking no chances. He sent Mam packing to my nan's and moved around at night to different hotels and B&Bs, staying hard to pin down, until he found a safe location. He's good at that kind of stuff."

"He certainly is," said English. "I remember it well. I owe your dad, big time."

Dud stroked his thin chin and spoke again. "Do we have a motive? I gather it's rare for snipers to operate in Scottish towns, so there must be a reason. They don't just turn up out of thin air and take pot shots at the tourists. What did Dad do to earn a visit from a bad guy?"

Cameron winced as he edged forward.

"Sorry about that," said Numbers. "Again."

The oldest man of the group looked genuinely remorseful as the young lad perched on the edge of the sofa. At sixty-six, Ron Cole had built up a formidable network of contacts and knowledge to earn his nickname. Planning and logistics were as comfortable to him as breathing.

He continued. "If I'd known your reason for breaking into English's house, I might have gone easier on you. Jenny and I saw a genuine threat, and we reacted accordingly. Again, sorry."

Cameron nodded while English contained a rush of pride that flushed his face. While the Old Farts had been in action in Jamaica, Numbers had used the technology in the basement to coordinate the mission while Jenny, English's wife, had kept him watered and fed. Thinking the twins had broken in, the two had shot Cameron with buckshot and broken Archie's nose with a sock filled with pool balls. Then, they trussed them up with duct tape and kept them quiet in a closet until the mission was complete.

"Not your fault, we should've spoken sooner," said

Cameron. "It looks worse than it is, and I don't blame you. As for motive, Dad and Uncle Jase were investigating something. He hasn't told us much, need to know and all that, but it's ruffled a few feathers, and now some bastard wants them silenced. They got Uncle Jase, but Dad reckons the bullet was meant for him since he's the one doing the serious digging."

"Digging for what?" said English.

"He won't say, but I've never seen him this nervous. He cannae relax. At some point, he'll have to stop looking over his shoulder, but right now, he cannae trust a soul. That's why he sent us to get you. We weren't expecting the A-Team, to be fair, but I'm sure he'd welcome as much help as he can get."

"As old as the team might be," smiled Archie before he winced as the bandage on his face twisted.

"That's karma," said English with a smile. He paused before sitting on the arm of the sofa. "It goes without saying, I'm in. I was in before you spoke. As for everyone else, that would be up to them. I'd tell you about what we just went through but, if your dad's waiting, I'll tell you in the transport. These guys can make up their own minds."

The room fell silent as English's words sank in. Hours back from a harrowing time in Jamaica, some of the group clearly still hadn't found their land legs.

Numbers spoke first. "I gather this trip involves a flight to Scotland?"

The twins nodded in time with English.

"My passport's expired," he continued, "although if I make the right contacts, that won't be needed. But, once again, you'll have to count me out, guys. I'm in no shape. Having heard about your last trip, I'm convinced I'd have slowed you down. Still, I can sort out the flight for you. Might not land in a legitimate airport, but I'll get you close. It also goes without saying that you can count on my support from this end. Again."

"You can do that?" said Cameron. "Get us a flight home?"

Numbers smiled. "I have lots of friends in sky-high places. And a few in places low enough to require digging pretty deep. I hate to be missing out on the action again but, to be honest, this body's not up to it. Then, there's dealing with the wife. She's meaner than a month-hungry bear. And that's on a good day."

"No one faults your commitment to the cause, mate," said English, "but easy and discreet flights would be great."

He glanced at the others.

Marbles shrugged. "I'll check with Joy but, heck, if I never see the wife, I'll be married forever. No time to fall out. You guys have any interesting machinery a dude could play with?"

The twins looked non-plussed as Sarge spun the bill of his cap to the back of his neck.

English smiled and recognized it as a sign that the man was thinking.

When Sarge spoke, the group listened. "I formed The Old Farts Club as a means for us all to get together and offer support, and to retain a link to our military roots. Folks have come and gone, but the group has always been strong. I must admit, I didn't envisage it becoming what it already has; men ready to lay down their lives for one another. Still, given our pasts, it shouldn't surprise me. When Dud's call came in, no one wavered. Each of us, to a man, got involved. I don't see why this should be any different."

He stood and wandered across the room, then squatted on his haunches between the twins. "If your father served with my buddy, English, and saved his life…"

"A few times," said English.

"…then, as far as I'm concerned, he's already in The Club." He first shook Cameron's hand and then Archie's.

"Count me in. I'll always be there for a brother."

English chugged the rest of his beer. "We don't know the severity of the situation in Scotland. Us plus Macca and the twins is one hell of a squad. And we owe it to our fallen. Every time. Numbers, can you get us to Scotland on the quiet?"

Numbers nodded.

"And, there are plenty of CCTV cameras in Edinburgh. Most of the streets are covered. It'll be easier to move around without any heavy-duty weaponry. Sarge, you got anything light and quiet we could use?"

"Sure do, buddy. Would a few silenced nine millimeters get the job done?"

"One each would be great," smiled English. "I'll update the tech down here and get Numbers up to speed so he can watch our backs. Dud, you've been quiet, mate. What's your take on all of this?"

Dud ran a hand through his close-cropped hair. "Me? Guys, I know Evie is beat. After what she's just been through, the best thing for her is a proper vacation. Only, this time, forget tropical sunshine. She can stay here in the States and visit her sister in Ohio. The pair of them together is like an uncensored comedy duo. And I've never been to Scotland. I hear it's an amazing place, with or without flying bullets." He glanced at the twins. "I'm in if you'll have me."

Cameron nodded. "You look like a weathered Liam Neeson. Consider yourself taken."

"Weathered?" smirked Dud. "Every one of these lines is hard won and well-earned, son. And let me tell you, chicks dig 'em."

"And I'm up for a quality single malt," said Marbles.

"It's decided, then," said English. "It's us and the boys

against whatever the best or worst Scotland has to offer. And it at least offers incredible single malt whisky and haggis."

Dud stood and clapped his hands then looked at the twins. "Damn, repaying The Club already. Kinda glad I didn't have to wait too long to clear my debt, to be honest. Still, there's not much that worries me, but there is one thing I need to ask. What the hell is haggis and how concerned should I be?"

Chapter Three

The man in black narrowly missed an expensive laptop and slammed his palms onto the table in frustration. His colleague, perched on a sill, blew cigarette smoke through an open window and smiled.

"Hudson, you can't blame shitty hotel Wi-Fi this time. He's well trained, that's all it is but, don't worry, everyone slips up. No one is perfect. Keep looking at that screen and he shall appear, as if by magic. Then, we'll make our move."

"I'm running everything through this. CCTV footage from streets and stores, traffic cams, social media. I always said social media would be humanity's downfall. Jeez, Cox, I thought New York was bad for tourists. Edinburgh might have a cool castle, but it seems people come here from everywhere to celebrate everything under the sun and just drink themselves crazy. And, since I've never had an issue with facial recognition tech, you're probably right. But, if nothing else, he must be getting low on toilet paper by now. He has to move."

A furtive glance at the ceiling-mounted smoke detector, and another billow of cigarette smoke escaped through the window. "Maybe he's not alone and he has a runner. I would if we were after me. We're exceptional and he might know that."

"I doubt he knows that. But look what happened to the other guy. That's what happens when clients get paranoid and book more than one solution. The cream rises to the top and the crap gets taken out early. MacIntyre might think someone else is coming to follow up, but we're not exactly two minutes from Boston. I doubt he'd think they were already here. Unless someone tipped him off."

Cox shrugged. "He could have turned the screws on our Russian friend. Got info from him. The morgue report said he was really messed up. The cops think he jumped, but we know different. What if he knew there was competition and there was an element of torture before he went flying over the edge?"

No expression showed as cold eyes studied the screen while Hudson spoke. "He's useful with his hands, Cox, but there's nothing in the dude's file to say he's capable of that. We are but, like you said, we're exceptional. It stands to reason we'd go the extra mile. You get what you pay for, right?"

Cox took one more deep pull on the cigarette and stubbed what was left out on a brown stained window frame and tossed it into the street. "Desperate times call for desperate measures. Who knows? Maybe he took a big story to the 'papers and they've got him in protective custody and that's why he hasn't surfaced."

"And what would his story be? They didn't tell us that."

"For this much money, could be anything. Your guess is as good as mine, but I'll bet it's big. With lots of chapters and subplots. That's why they called us. The small fish don't call us."

"Yeah, but the big fish also don't pit us against sub-standard competition. We don't need to be kept on our toes. We're alert. Primed. Ready for action. That's why we walk this way."

As the words were spoken, Cox slid off the window ledge and sashayed toward the bathroom, whistling a well-known Aerosmith song.

The bathroom door closed with a click, and as a stream of water splashed noisily into the pan, Hudson looked once more at the screen. To one side, a highlighted square flashed image after image with dots appearing over certain ones at odd intervals. The blurred images moved so fast they were impossible to study and moved in a flurry of vision. To the right, different feeds scrolled by; supermarket names, pubs and clubs, bars, streets, parking lots; each location checked over and over for a match to the image that sat at the top right of the screen.

Hudson rubbed his tired eyes, pushed away from the table, and stretched out his legs. Blood flowed into his cramped calves and tingled at his feet while, in the background, Cox continued to empty his bladder of an alarming amount of liquid.

As the deluge lessened, Hudson shouted through the door. "What the hell did you drink, a lake? And what do you know about our employer? You accepted this job, so I'm still in the dark. The money shines a light bright enough to make it acceptable, but I'm still curious."

Cox coughed and spat into the pan then flushed and opened the door.

"You're not going to wash your hands?" said Hudson with his lip curled in disgust.

Cox popped his head through the opening. "Jesus, give me a minute, you prissy bitch. I've opened the door so we don't have to shout. Who knows how good the insulation is in this building?"

He disappeared and ran the basin faucet. "To answer your

first question, while you ate a burger, fries, and two apple pies, I ate a solitary burger and washed it down with three Cokes. I get thirsty when I eat starch. As for your second question, I have no clue. I did the usual checks, but the data from the mission details bounced off enough servers to make a juggler dizzy. All that matters is the funds will hit our respective accounts and, if we don't complete the job, or if the job doesn't kill us like it did our Russian friend, then it's safe to assume that he or they will kill us, anyway."

Hudson pressed his lips together and nodded. "Okay. I like it when they keep it simple. Kill or be killed. It's like high school all over again."

———

"Do you remember the rock singer who wore assless chaps? I reckon I look like him."

Evie Wilkerson collapsed backwards into a pile of plush cushions and let a raucous laugh rip the air. It was so good to hear the voice that lifted over the other side of the changing room curtain.

"Oh, come on. I can't wait any longer. Let me see."

With a machine gun rat-a-tat-tat of metal on metal, Evie's sister flung back the curtain and stepped forward, arms stretched wide.

"Ta-da!"

Evie collapsed again. "Oh my God, Sam. You can't take those home. I've never seen your hubby blush, but I reckon those would do the trick. He wouldn't know where to put himself, in any sense of the word."

Brown faux-leather tassels shimmered as Sam shook a leg. "It's only fancy dress but, hey, these would totally put some spice back into the nights, wouldn't they? God knows they need it."

"They'll certainly make his eyes water. Especially if he wore them. Come on, if you're not a hundred percent, we have plenty more stores to check out. The best thing you could do is decide what you want to dress as. At least, that way, we can look for an outfit to do the job. So far, you've played cowboys and Indians, been a doctor and a car mechanic. It's like an audition for The Village People. Why can't you just have a normal birthday party like everyone else?"

Sam stuck out a bottom lip. "Because, this time, I'll reach the big five-oh. I, like, refuse point blank to do it in an adult fashion. This girl's growing old disgracefully."

Evie laughed again and relaxed while Sam drew back the curtain to change into her own clothing. She glanced around the store, at its paper thin and unrealistic mannequins, at the fall colors that splashed through the window displays, and at the normalcy of it all. People browsed and chatted, unaware of the dangers that lay outside.

Dud was right. She needed this break. After their nightmare vacation in Jamaica, it felt good, no, scratch that, safe, to be here on home turf. In America. With family.

After a tearful goodbye, he'd joined the others and boarded a plane on a small side airstrip at Louisville's Muhammad Ali International Airport, and she'd watched as the plane picked up speed before tilting and cutting into the air.

She was still waving, knowing full well he couldn't see her, when it banked and turned into a tiny dot that disappeared without a sound through the cloud base.

Evie had never been there to see him off to war, having met him at the end of his Army career, but she imagined having to feel this, over and over, knowing that he'd signed up for multiple tours in scarier places than Scotland. Scotland was a world away from the horrors of Afghanistan and Iraq, but that didn't calm the nerves.

Jamaica was supposed to be a Caribbean paradise and look what happened there.

And now she sat in a shopping mall, like a spectator on 'Say Yes to the Dress', waiting for a younger sister who loved to have fun, despite her husband.

She held a hand before her face. It still shook, although now she could at least hold a cup of coffee without the drink slopping over the edges of the mug. A slight tremor had replaced the uncontrolled and jarring shiver that followed her home from their vacation.

She jumped when a deep voice spoke behind her.

"Is everything okay, ma'am?"

Evie turned to face the store assistant.

"I couldn't help but notice you studying your hand. I just wanted to make sure that everything was okay. We have policies here. And stupid expensive liability insurance."

"Yes. Yes, everything's fine. Just waiting for my crazy sister."

Sam took that moment to reappear in faded denim jeans and a plain shirt. She handed a selection of clothes to the assistant.

"I might have found what I'm looking for, but I have a couple more places to check first. Appreciate your help, though. Thanks."

They stopped at two more stores without success before grumbling stomachs dragged them to a bustling food court.

Evie scanned the line of restaurants and eateries. "Reckon we should call home? See if the guys are hungry? We could get something to go."

"See? That's why they say you're the favorite sister."

"I'm the only sister," laughed Evie.

Sam dug into her purse. "Yeah, but you're still the favorite. Where did I put my phone? I normally slip it into this little side pouch, but..."

She dropped the purse onto a table, pulled wide the zipper, and dug deeper. Then, she patted down her pockets. "Shit. Evie, I can't find my phone."

"Hang on." Evie dug out her cell. "I'll call you. Even if it's really buried, you'll still hear it."

"Don't bother. When we went into the first store, I put it on silent so we wouldn't be disturbed."

"Okay, so think back to where you had it last."

"That is such a dumb statement. If I knew that I'd just march over there and pick it up."

"Sorry, Sis. It's not in the car?"

"No. I called Daryl as we walked in here, and I definitely put it back into my purse."

Evie glanced around the bustling food court and at the constant procession of shoppers that milled around the mall. Hundreds of people going about their business. And some of them doing their business. She shook away the notion of pick-pockets.

"You've tried on a load of clothes. Did you put it on a bench in one of the changing rooms?"

Panic began to paint rosy circles on Sam's cheeks. "I don't know. God, Evie, everything is on my phone. All my pictures and contacts. Shit, and all my bank details and payment apps. They're totally password protected, but how good is that? They can probably hack it easily."

"Okay, stay calm. I think I might have a solution. We have resources we can call upon."

She opened her phone, highlighted a contact, and tapped the screen. The call burred through the speaker, connected, and was answered by a puzzled voice.

"Evie?"

"Yes," said Evie. "Hi, Numbers. Sorry to bother you, but we have a problem and I'm hoping you can help."

"Absolutely. The guys haven't landed in Scotland yet, not that I'm saying the guys are more important than the girls but, you know, they're trusting me to…"

"Numbers. Focus. Can you track a phone? Surely English has the tech there to do that?"

She could hear the glee in his voice. "Oh, yes. Phone tracking's easy. I'm almost an expert. But, Evie, you're on your phone."

"Not mine. My sister, Sam's. Can I give you her number? It might have been stolen."

"Of course. Shoot."

She waited while Numbers inputted the information.

"It goes without saying that if they've turned off the phone or removed the sim card…"

"Not anymore," said another voice in the background.

"Is that Penny?" said Evie.

"Hi, Evie. Yep, it's me."

"Who's Penny?" asked Sam.

"Later. Penny, it's so good to hear your voice. Now, what were you saying?"

Penny's voice grew clearer as she, presumably, got closer to the phone. "A dead phone is no longer necessarily dead. There are still ways to track it. It's high-end tech, obviously, but I have a high-end husband. And…"

She paused for a moment, as if she was checking information.

"…yep. Got it. Found your missing phone."

Evie turned to Sam and slapped a high five. "Great. Where is it?"

"Right now? It's headed west on I-480 at about fifty miles

per hour."

————

English pressed the buckle release, and his lap belt keeled to one side. As the small plane's door hissed open, he leaned out and took a deep breath.

"Damn, you can feel it in the air, can't you? It's good to be back on British soil. I'll bet there's no humidity, no ozone, or diesel smog. Just the intoxicating, sinus-clearing aroma of cow and sheep shit."

"I resent that remark," shouted Archie from the back of the plane. "That's Dad's aftershave."

Dud, Marbles, and Sarge shuffled down the narrow aisle and pressed in behind him. Ahead of them, over the top of the runway building, sprawled a blanket of orange and white lights.

"Welcome to Scotland, I guess," said Marbles as he looked out into the darkness. "Would've been here in half the time if I'd flown, but kudos to the pilot. Smooth take-off and landing. And his ignorance of his passengers was second to none."

Dud slapped his back. "We like it that way, bud. No passport or gun control. No security with rubber gloves and an excess of lube."

"Numbers could have come after all."

"Nah, he was right. These bodies of ours wear out after enough abuse. It sucks, but it comes to us all eventually. He'd have struggled in Jamaica. And, anyway, Numbers hates lube."

English turned in the doorway. "Mate, it puts the fear in me, too. I remember this one covert mission during Desert Storm where I had to hide a package up my—"

"Looks nice out there," said Marbles. "Let's get to where

we need to be. I'm itching to see Scotland in the daylight and try some of the local produce."

"You mean Scotch," said Sarge.

"Bread and milk," said Marbles, showing his best shocked expression.

A small metal staircase trundled up to the side of the plane, and the men disembarked and walked past an empty makeshift terminal building to a small entrance shrouded in darkness.

Archie waved as a shadow moved.

"There's Dad," he said and broke into a jog, followed by the others.

The tug of familiarity put a spring in English's step, and he powered past the Farts then waited patiently as his old friend greeted his sons.

Then, Macca looked up and caught his eye. In a blink, years of shared horrors and experience passed between them. English held out a hand, ready for a firm shake, and instead found himself pulled into a tight hug.

The Scotsman pushed him away and held him by the shoulders. "It's good to see you, mate. I'm sorry it's in such shitty circumstances. Introduce me to the other guys and then tell me what you did to my boys? I can't imagine you lot played rugby, but I've never seen them so handsomely disfigured."

English turned to the team. "Macca, this fella here is Dud. To be fair, I've not known him long, but I already trust him with my life."

Macca leaned forward and took Dud's hand in his. "Pleased to meet you, mate. And eternally grateful. Any mate of Keith's is a mate of mine."

"Pleasure's all mine," said Dud. "I've heard enough about you to know you'd do the same. And likewise, any mate of English's is a mate of mine. I owe him a big debt."

Macca barked out a cynical laugh. "Seems like this is the day for paying debts. I just wish it was for a few quid from gambling and not this life-or-death shit. And English? What's that about?"

"Nicknames. And life and death shit seems to be how we roll," said English before he gestured again.

"This here is Sarge. He's our unofficial leader."

Sarge held out a hand. "Pleasure to be here, buddy. I'm not sure about the leader part, but I've got enough experience to make sure the right things happen at the right time."

"It's good to have you here, mate. It's really appreciated."

"And finally," said English, "this fella's Marbles. If it's machinery, and moves, might move, or moved in a previous life, he can operate it."

"A handy skill to have," said Macca as he returned another handshake. "And what's with these nicknames? What would you call me? Scottish?"

English laughed. "I could reel off a list, but it might make your ears bleed. The nicknames are all part of the club, mate. All earned or suitable. Either works."

"The club?"

"The Old Farts Club. Get us out of here and I'll tell you the gory details on the move. And, before we get into it, your boys are a credit to you." He looked at them and smiled. "We'll just have to train them to be stealthier."

Thirty minutes later, Macca pulled his Jeep Grand Cherokee into a pitch-black entry and killed the engine.

"What's with turning off the lights early?" asked Dud. "We must have driven the last half mile in the dark. And that was the half mile that wasn't scary countryside. Talk about narrow ass roads. Don't you guys pay taxes to keep the streetlights on?"

Macca pointed through the windshield and across the

entry to the corner of the opposite building. A tiny red light blinked under the cloudy shadow of a night sky.

"CCTV. Closed circuit television. There are cameras everywhere, mate. I only have to get clocked on one of those and I'll have bad guys all over me."

Cameron leaned forward from the back seat. "Is it really that bad, Dad? You're not being paranoid?"

"Wish I was, Cam. Remember, our Russian friend said he got there first. That means there's at least one other person who wants to get there second. And cameras are not necessarily a bad guy's enemy. Not when you can use them to your benefit." He thumbed to the other passengers. "I've not worked with these guys yet, but I know English, and you'll see how handy he can be. If the others are the same, we're blessed. Make no mistake, I need them here."

Cameron pointed to his bandaged shoulder and then to English. "That bloke's wife did this. I dread to think what he can do."

"I've seen it firsthand. And you're right to dread it. But he's on our side, along with these other Farts." Macca laughed. "Cannae see me ever getting used to saying that."

He opened the car door and gestured to a small door in the side wall of the adjacent building.

"That's where I'm staying this week. It's not the penthouse, but it is the room at the top of the building. Excellent view of the surrounding area, with a fire escape to one side and stairs at the other for movement. No good being hemmed in with one means of escape."

English glanced up the side of the building. In the dark entry, the only thing visible on the tall side wall was the door and a window at the apex of the roof canopy. He knew the type of building well. The room at the top would be a converted loft, with two steep sloping walls and a window at either end.

Whoever converted this loft added one more window at the side that looked out over the city.

"Looks perfect. The important thing is, does it have a kettle? A few minutes here and I already fancy a cup of tea."

Macca stepped out into the alley with his head lowered then walked behind the Jeep. "What kind of dumb question is that? Boys, come and give your old dad another hug, then you'd best get back to your Mam."

The boys each took a turn to embrace their father.

"Thank you for fetching these guys. I hated to send you. And tell your Mam not to worry about those injuries. Tell her you suffered worse playing rugby at school."

"I don't recall getting shot at school, Dad," said Cameron.

"Aye, fair point. You didn't go to my school. Ah, just wing it, you'll be fine. Love you boys. Be safe and…"

"We know," said Archie. "Keep our heads down. Love you too, Dad."

As the boys jogged out of sight, Macca turned back, his face stern and focused.

"Come on and follow me. I'll get us all a brew and then tell you exactly what's going on."

Chapter Four

Marte Dahl glanced around the room at the gathered digni-
taries and celebrities. Enough bling-covered wealth sat within a
twenty-yard radius to pay off a small country's national debt.
And provide indefinite funding for vital research.

Sports personalities, actors, politicians, and famous scientists all gathered around linen-covered tables littered with
frosted bottles of top shelf champagne and ridiculously over-
priced canapes. Dahl grimaced in disgust.

The food bill alone would pay for a new laboratory or fund
a six-month supply of medicine for a third world country. The
very people who rubbed shoulders here to pay tribute to the
greats in science added to the machine that could easily
provide a means to make massive breakthroughs.

On Dahl's table, LaShawyne Dupray sat to the left. All
seven feet of him. The athlete arrived at the event fresh from
signing a five-year contract with a Los Angeles basketball team
that guaranteed him one hundred and ninety-five million
dollars. On the right was Dante LaVerne, linebacker for a
Midwest NFL team. Ten inches shorter than the baller,

LaVerne made up for it in width and probably matched him pound for pound. And, with his four-year contract for one hundred and fifty million dollars, he almost matched him dollar for dollar, too.

Dahl did the math. Dupray made thirty-nine million per year, LaVerne thirty-seven and a half million. For playing sports.

More math brought up an average hourly wage for a forty-hour week; the athletes made around thirty-six thousand, seven hundred and seventy-eight dollars an hour.

Dahl forced another guilty sip of the expensive champagne, swallowed it hard, and looked around again.

At the front of the room, a vast screen all but filled the wall and displayed a glittering banner that now read, *Award for contribution to scientific research*.

The audience broke into loud applause as a popular chat show host walked like a model across the stage beneath the banner, her sequined dress shimmering under the lights along with her million-dollar smile, with an envelope clutched tightly to her even more expensive chest.

She stopped at a podium and angled down a microphone until it almost reached her mouth.

"Ladies and gentlemen," she started, "any one of us could be involved in a serious accident at any time. We see it on the news every day. Should that happen, we'd rely on the emergency services to get us to a hospital as quickly as possible. Once there, we'd then also rely on the resident professionals to diagnose our injuries and carry out potentially life-saving surgery." She paused while the autocue caught up.

"As a country, we are all aware of the importance of blood donation but, in busy times and despite of our population, that supply can still run short. In that instance, it's down to courier services to deliver those much-needed supplies in as short a time frame as possible. However, say that your blood group is AB negative, one of the rarest types and, by an even rarer stroke of awful luck, multiple casualties need units of the same type, units the hospital doesn't have? Then what happens?" She paused again to let the crowd speculate.

"There are blood banks around our country that hold those much-needed supplies, but red blood cells can only be refrigerated for around a month and a half. Even with regular donations, supplies of rare blood types often run low. Thankfully, important research is ongoing to find a way to determine blood type faster and prolong the shelf life of our most precious liquid; and I'm not talking about bourbon."

A titter rippled through the room.

"This research is vital and, thanks to your donations, will continue until, hopefully, we're able to store blood indefinitely. Which brings me to the final award of the evening. In this envelope, I have the names of the four nominees for the award for 'contribution to scientific research', the award every scientist dreams of winning. Only the top people in this field are nominated and, as always, each year we drill down this award to a certain area. This year, it's the storage and transport of blood supplies. The following nominees are all at the forefront of this research, each working toward a unique and dynamic vision to make our world a better and healthier place. And they are, in no particular order..."

She lifted the envelope and read from a list of names on the front.

Dahl felt a tiny flutter and smoothed out the front of an expensive suit at the mention of the family name.

The air felt oppressive, charged by the cloying anticipation of the announcement.

"And the winner is..."

The chat-show host fumbled, smiled, and then ripped open the envelope and leaned up to the microphone. "Marte Dahl."

The room erupted into a white noise blast of applause.

Events like this not only brought extra funding but increased notoriety.

Dahl hated notoriety. They could lift no radar high enough to fly under when your name appeared in newspapers and society magazines.

As the clapping continued, Dahl stood, turned and raised an appreciative hand then wound through a maze of tables to the stage.

At a table by the stage, American millionaire, Thomas Fraine, grudgingly pushed back his chair and finally stood and clapped.

Dahl offered him a dazzling smile and nodded a discreet thank you.

As the leader in his field, Fraine chaired the board at California's leading plasma research center. Earlier in the evening, he'd picked up two awards, the only person to ever scoop two trophies in one night.

He also remained the only person to have ever terminated Dahl's employment. An event never forgotten.

Dahl took one confident step after another toward recognition. Now look at me. Remember what you did and never forget. This is karma, bitch.

———

Marbles tipped his steaming mug toward the group.

"What the hell is this crap? I thought we were having tea?"

"We are," said English.

"But it's hot. I've never needed oven mitts to drink tea.

And it's got milk in it. It's supposed to be black and have ice and piles of sugar in it."

"That's your bastardized version. This is proper tea. Made the way it's meant to be made."

"Yeah, well if you had proper weather, with sun, you'd have the need to make proper tea," said Marbles.

Dud clapped his hands to silence the chatter. "Ladies, enough debating over who has the best drinks. Before we start, why don't we do one of those 'introduce yourself' things they do every time you attend a course? Name and skills. That way, Macca will know exactly who he's got on his side and what he can call on."

"Excellent idea," said Macca. "I figured the nicknames were callsigns, like Silver Fox or Grey Goose."

"That's a vodka," said Dud.

"And a fine one at that." Macca moved to the center of the room. "Okay, I'll go first. I'm John MacIntyre. I guess my boring nickname is Macca, even though some Liverpudlian bloke stole it."

"I think that Beatles guy McCartney might have been there first," said Marbles, "but I reckon you could take him in a fight, so have at it."

"Thanks, I think. From my sexy accent, you can probably tell that I'm a proud, born and bred Scot. As for skills, I can deal with any type of bomb, at least the ones I've come across so far. I can also build them, too. Traps are my specialty, though. And I'm a decent shot, pretty handy with my fists and I'm loyal to a fault." He pointed to English.

"I've served a few campaigns with that fella where I defused my fair share of roadside bombs and landmines and saved his arse as many times as I've served. He knows me as well as my wife. Just, you know, dressed."

Marbles spoke again. "This is so weird. I half expected you

to say that your favorite movie is *Cape Fear*, the original not the remake, and that you want to work with underprivileged children."

"I feel like I'm in a room with some right now," smiled Macca. "Go on then, fella, spill it. Who are you and what's your story?"

Marbles cleared his throat. "Well, my wife knows me as Kevin Durrant, but everyone else calls me Marbles."

"On account of the fact that?"

Marbles leaned forward, bent his head, scrambled at his face with his fingertips, then sat upright with a gaping hole where his left eye was.

Macca recoiled. "Bloody hell, mate, that's quite a scratch. Let me get you a plaster."

Marbles smiled and held up a glass eyeball that bore a smiley emoji. "I have a set of six of these, one for most occasions, that was made for me by an ex-father-in-law to replace the one that got torn up with shrapnel."

"Much respect. Must make hand to eye coordination difficult."

"On the contrary, it seems to focus my concentration. If it has an engine, wheels or wings, I can handle it better than most. If it's a piece of kit I've not seen before, give me a few minutes and I can probably work it out."

"Even more respect."

Macca turned to Dud. "I know your nickname, mate, but I'm intrigued to know where it came from."

Dud flushed and fidgeted in his seat, then smiled. "It's nothing, really. I'm Danny Wilkerson, forty-nine years old, and I'm an Aquarian."

"A water carrier. You'll do well in the pubs over here."

Dud smiled. "Why am I called Dud? That goes back to a tour I did a while ago. Some bastard tossed a grenade into a group of children. I did what any of us would do and dived on it."

"You dived on a live grenade? Jesus Christ, mate, at least the shit I dealt with had fuses and wires and gave me a decent crack at defusing it."

"That's just it, though. It turned out to be dead."

"A dud."

"Yep, and the name stuck. My skills? When I'm not being an Old Fart, I run a garage back in Kentucky. Whereas Marbles can operate anything mechanical, I can fix it." He glanced at Marbles. "Guess that makes us a good team."

Dud held out a fist, which Marbles bumped with a 'hell, yeah'.

"And, like yourself, I can take care of myself and I know my way around pretty much anything that fires a projectile or makes a bang sound. Not that I like the noise."

Macca glanced at English.

English shook his head.

"Really? You all know me."

"We need the info for your dating profile, sweetheart," said Macca with a grin.

"Whatever. Okay, I'm Keith Watson, English, and now that I'm back on British soil, I'll probably turn into an alcoholic."

"You've grown out of that," said Macca, "and we're all proud of you, son. Do continue."

"I'm known as English to these guys on account of me being, well, English. I'm the new guy to the Club. Met them, had a burger and, as you do, got involved in a hostage situation in Jamaica. Served multiple tours in the Middle East, first one when I was eighteen. Had a nasty habit of stepping on mines and IEDs, which is where you came in. Saved me twice."

"You didn't learn the first time?" said Dud.

"Nope, I'm stubborn. He also bailed me out of a few bar fights and one potential and probably fatal marriage. And if anyone mentions that to the wife, I swear to God there will be bloodshed. These days, I'm an IT specialist. If it has code, beeps or processes, I can work it out and, more importantly, make it work for me. Or us."

"And I guess that leaves me," said Sarge. "My nickname came from me being the founder of the group. Can't quite remember who gave it to me, might have been Walt Zimmerman, but it stuck. I've served all over and done it all. I'm a crack-shot through a scope and, if you need a plan, I'm your man."

"Genuinely appreciate you being here," said Macca. "All of you."

English took a breath. "Okay, does that cover everything?"

"I reckon so," said Macca.

"Good. In that case, now we've exposed our souls, why don't you tell us why we're here?"

Macca stepped into the center of the group and leaned his back against the side window. "You guys are here because of fishing activity."

Marbles carefully laid his mug on the floor. "You should have said that earlier. We've got the best lakes, too."

"I'm not talking about a bloke with a rod and a six pack, I'm talking massive scale, miles wide, under the radar, illegal fishing. With fleets of boats in international waters. Hundreds of men. And an organization controlling the unauthorized movement of those fleets and those men."

"Which organization?" said Dud.

"No clue."

"Okay, which fleet?"

"Couldn't tell you."

"What can you tell us, mate?" said English. "These boys are used to direct info and, since Knowles died because of this, you must have something concrete."

"That's just it, I've got something that vaguely resembles sludge but nothing concrete. And they've already killed a man because of it. And I reckon the bullet was meant for me. Which is why I called you."

"Okay, so they mean business. Tell us what you do know."

Macca sipped his tea and then perched on the edge of the sofa. "I doubt you guys know much about overfishing, but it's big business and bad news. There are voluntary and paid organizations that monitor the volume of fish caught, and the movement and whereabouts of the fleets on the ocean. The actual amount of fish caught yearly makes me wonder how we have any left, since some companies ignore the agreed limits and fish for as much as they can carry."

Dud held up a hand.

"It's not school, mate," said Macca. "You can speak when you like."

"You were on a roll and I didn't want to break your flow," said Dud. "If they fish for as much as they can carry, there's only so much storage space on a boat, right? Surely, once these boats are filled, they have to return to land to offload. Are there no measures in place to check how much sea life gets moved from ship to storage? And, if a boat reached its quota, wouldn't they keep it docked until the next shift arrived?"

"Like the way you think and, ethically, the way to go, but there are thousands of ships. Plus, companies have a system in place to ensure the boats are working around the clock. That was our first red flag. You need lots of manpower to do that. Folks have to sleep. So to ensure they make maximum profit, some use cheap labor or, more to the point, slave labor."

"Cutthroat business," said Sarge. "We've recently had first-hand experience of that."

"And I'm sure that's involved, but it's not what Knowles found. The ships don't return to land because once full or low on fuel, they meet up with a larger ship called a reefer."

"That means something entirely different where I come from," said Marbles.

"Same here," said Macca, "and they both smell like shit, but this type is huge and doesn't burn as easily. The smaller ships offload their catch onto massive vessels, or reefers, refuel from them, and then head back out to sea to carry on."

"Other than too many fish," said English, "this doesn't seem dodgy enough to be life threatening."

"I'm getting there. As you know, there are no streetlights at sea and, if the moon's hidden by the cloud base, it gets very dark at night. Any ship in international waters with a gross tonnage of three hundred or more must have a beacon that lets other ships know its location. It's called the AIS, Automatic Identification System. Boat folks don't seem to go for fancy acronyms like us military types. It's important to let everyone know your whereabouts, to avoid collisions, and make search and rescue easier should you fall into trouble. And, as with any money-making activity, to allow authorities to keep an eye on you. And, if it were a permanent thing, we wouldn't be sitting here."

"But it's not. And Knowles found something."

"Correct. We were investigating illegal fishing, but there's more going on than that. The ships can turn off their transponders. They call it 'going dark'. Basically, the ship drops off the map."

"I trust myself to handle any transport," said Marbles, "but I sure don't trust the other guy. There's no knowing how good he is. Sounds risky. Huge risk of accidents if you're traveling blind and not knowing who's around you."

Macca took another sip of tea. "It is risky, but it outweighs the risk of being caught. Once the signal is off, the ship becomes what's known as a 'dark target'. Allegedly, while dark, the Iranians move oil on the sly, and the Chinese mine the seas for a crazy amount of fish. Since they're no longer on the radar, it's all hidden from prying eyes."

Dud spoke. "Surely, if an agency is watching a fleet of ships and it suddenly turns off its transponders, wouldn't it be cause for concern and investigation? Here one minute and gone the next? That's Bermuda Triangle type stuff."

"Absolutely, but other than shipping lanes the ocean has no roads. By the time any investigative team arrived, the fleet could be miles away in any direction. Satellites can get close, but we're talking about searching over seventy percent of the earth's surface. Too much ground to cover with no landmarks. And this is where we come to what Knowles found; what if some ships turned off their transponders, but not all of them? Remember that movie where a car tucks in between a few semi-trucks, kind of gets hemmed in, so the police drive right by?"

"Wasn't that *Smokey and the Bandit?*" said Marbles.

"I don't remember now, but it was a cool film, and the principle's the same. What if there's a vessel, or vessels, piggybacking their way into international waters camouflaged in the middle of a fleet to meet up with something? Maybe a reefer, maybe something altogether different? Knowles noticed that, once a week, a ship in the cluster of suspects he was watching switched off its transponder; then turned it back on again later, always at a certain point. Someone was meeting up with someone or something else at a pre-determined location."

"Hate to ask the obvious," said English, "but why would they do that, knowing they'd be seen?"

"No clue. In the grand scheme of things, they were a tiny blip against everything else monitored on the ocean, and it probably didn't worry them. It's their bad luck it just happened to be in the few square miles of ocean that Knowles was watching. I'm guessing they had to let someone know they were there, to trade or hand over something, but I don't know what. Don't have the resources. Knowles contacted local authority to get the ship registration so we could track it to its owner."

Dud stood and stretched his back. "Well, you have the resources now, buddy. You've got a tech wizard, a shit-hot mechanic, a guy that can move anything, and a guy to plan it all. We'll get to the bottom of it. So you got the registration. What happened next?"

"We hit a brick wall. We got the location; it's in the middle of watery nowhere, but that's as far as we got. We didn't get the registration. Three days after the request, Knowles' brains decorated the cobbles on Grassmarket."

The group sat in silence for a moment, until Marbles walked into the kitchen, dumped his tea and returned. "No offense, but . . ."

"None taken," said Macca. "Acquired taste, I guess."

Marbles shrugged. "So inside job, then? Seems like local authority is compromised. Reckon we should start there?"

"I have Knowles' paperwork. We could go through it and see who he contacted, although it might not necessarily be that person. They might have had to pass the request up the chain, and it didn't raise any concerns until someone entered that ship's particular reference."

"Still," said Dud, "you know how chains work. Grab the first link and pull. The links are all connected, we just have to shake until we rattle the right one. I reckon that, if we can work out what's going on, it'll probably lead us to whoever killed your buddy."

"Sounds like a plan." Macca glanced at his watch. "Guys, I've been stuck indoors for so long, I'm going stir crazy. It might sound careless, but I could murder a beer. I say we start in the morning. For now, since I have some back-up, you guys fancy a wee pint?"

"Is that wise?" said Marbles. He gestured toward the kitchen. "Don't get me wrong, after that attempt at tea I'm thirsty, too, but didn't you mention there are cameras everywhere."

"Aye, but I know where they are. The place I'm thinking of has one at the entrance and nothing inside. It's run by an ex-squaddie and he, er, likes to keep the brothers in arms, if you know what I mean."

"Doesn't your country frown upon the brothers carrying arms?" said Dud.

"It does." Macca reached around and into his waistband and pulled out a matt black pistol. "That's why we don't wave them around or wear them John Wayne style."

English patted his pocket. "Sarge hooked us up on that score."

"Still, I do feel thirsty," said Marbles as he licked his lips, "and I did want to try the local produce. I'm game."

Macca moved toward the door. "Cool. Then, I guess we're going for a pint."

Chapter Five

After a ninja-like trek through Edinburgh's wet backstreets, the group emerged into an alleyway lined with small craft shops that sandwiched a single pub. In the slight breeze, a wooden sign swayed above it which read, *The Billet*.

Macca looked around to find the alley deserted, except for one person outside the pub's entrance, a huge guy with his hands thrust deep into the pockets of a heavy black overcoat. His thick beard seemed to be level with the top of the door frame.

"That's Clarence."

"Clarence?" said English. "Damn, I've seen some doormen but, damn. He looks more like a Ripper."

"Well, I wouldn't knock his beer over, but he's okay. His mates call him Bruiser. He keeps an eye on things from out here."

Macca pointed across the alley. "Okay, guys, there's a camera at the end to our left that covers this entire area, and you can see another one over the door. Huddle up, keep your heads down, and follow me. I know Clarence."

"Thank God for that," said English.

The men formed a tight-packed crowd and hustled toward the pub.

As they reached the door, Macca whispered a few words, and Clarence stepped aside to let them through a small entrance and into a room the size of two houses.

Once inside, the noise level increased significantly. A busy mahogany bar stretched across half the space, stopping at a wall that separated the main bar from a smaller area that contained a dart board and two occupied pool tables. The green baize glowed like a couple of small lawns beneath harsh lighting, while two men sent red and yellow balls ricocheting around the tables in silence, lost in the bustle of chatter.

The bulk of the noise came from a group of around a dozen women that took up one corner, all of them dressed in white lace and wearing glittering tiaras with 'Single days are over' splashed across them in gaudy pink. Tall glasses and empty bottles littered the area and gleamed in a barrage of phone camera flashes.

Two muscled guys moved behind the bar. The nearest lifted a hand in acknowledgment.

Macca smiled and waved a greeting.

English nodded toward the women and shouted over the noise. "What the hell are they doing in a place like this? Let's avoid them and find somewhere we can hold a conversation. And remind me to call the wife when we get a moment."

"Agreed," said Marbles. "If I'd wanted to listen to that racket, I'd have stayed home."

The group moved to a table at the side of the room.

Macca took a drinks order and went to the bar.

Marbles followed him.

"It's time I tried a drop of your best Scotch. I'll pick up the tab, just in case it's priced like our best bourbon."

"No need for that, mate. You've come to help; the least I can do is buy a brother a drink."

Marbles scanned the row of shining optics that lined the back bar as two women from the corner table bundled into them.

"Sorry, love," said the first as she turned to Marbles, "we're celebrating our Sheila finally getting married."

Sheila landed a playful punch against her friend's arm. "Cheeky sod, I've just been waiting for the right...oh, bloody hell, Maxine, look at him. He's got a smiley face where his eye should be."

Marbles cringed as the girls pointed then braced himself as they backed into him.

Maxine held up her phone. "Selfie!"

The phone's light flashed, and the girls staggered off toward the pool tables, bundled over with laughter.

Marbles turned back toward the bar with spots in his vision as the barman ambled over.

"Sorry about that, lads."

"Not your usual clientele, mate," said Macca.

"No, but they're spending so much money I can't kick them out. And they're causing no trouble. Plus, it's a rare display of eye candy for the locals."

"Fair play. This fella here needs to try a good Scotch." Macca turned to Marbles and pointed to the rear of the bar. "The best stuff will be on the top shelf. We're surrounded by distilleries. They don't want their quality drink mixing with the likes of gin and brandy, so it doesn't hang from the wall."

"How about I follow your lead?"

"Can't stand the stuff, mate, nothing but beer for me, but Tony loves it."

"Tony?"

Macca smiled and thumbed toward the barman.

"Macca, it's been a while since you've been in. I figured we'd given you a hangover to put you off beer forever. Everything good with you and yours, mate?"

"A few things going on, Tone, but nothing I cannae handle."

Marbles caught a slight tremor in the Scotsman's voice. So far, Macca had shown no emotion over the death of his colleague.

"Marbles, this here's Tony Bright. He's worked in similar places to us. And Tone, meet Marbles. I've got friends over from The States, and this one likes his bourbon."

Tony offered another hand. "Can't fault your priorities, my friend, but I hope you've brought your checkbook. If you buy two, along with what the girls are drinking, I might be able to close early tonight. Buy three and I'm retiring."

"He's messing with you," said Macca. "What do you normally drink?"

Marbles didn't hesitate. "Maker's Mark."

"The one with the red wax collar," said Tony. "I've got a bottle of that in the storeroom for occasions like this. I get a few American visitors. Our boys have always fought well together." He turned and grabbed a clear glass bottle from the top shelf. "But the good news is you'll only need a small mortgage. If it's smoky stuff you like, try this. Lagavulin sixteen-year-old. Comes from the wee island of Islay, as does a lot of the good stuff. Not cheap, but you won't need to sell the wife. Just a kidney."

Muscles rippled beneath dark tattoo sleeves that tipped a nod to football teams as Tony pulled off the cap and handed over the bottle. "Here you go, get your nose into that."

Marbles took one sniff and passed it back with a contented nod. "Sign me up."

Tony poured a measure into a whisky glass with a reverence normally reserved for communion wine then filled another small glass with water.

Macca gave him the rest of the order and leaned against the bar.

"I don't have to tell you how much I appreciate you guys coming over to help, but I'm going to, anyway. Cannae say I've known anything like it, though. An Old Farts Club. You couldn't make it up."

"Blame Sarge. It wasn't until his wife passed away that he realized he missed the banter. There's something shared between military men that no one else would understand. Most groups are about talking through feelings and working through issues. Ours is about friendship, although recently it seems to have developed into something more physically and tactically demanding, too."

"Hopefully, to my benefit," said Macca as Tony reappeared with a full drink tray. Each glass was filled to the brim, with not a single drop of liquid wasted.

"Here you go, mate. Want to open a tab?"

"Better not, as tempting as that is. Need a clear head."

Tony slid the tray across the bar to Marbles while Macca reached for his wallet.

"It's good to meet you, mate," said Tony, "and I love the glass eye by the way, although you need one with a pint glass on it. A smiley face is okay for a regular situation, but there comes a time when a man fancies a pint. Your eye could be great stress relief for a lot of needy people."

Marbles laughed and grabbed the tray. "Now that would be a good conversation starter. And I appreciate the whisky advice; I'm guessing I'll find out what the water's for."

Tony gave a wise wink. "That you will. It's not a palate cleanser. Enjoy Edinburgh, my strange-eyed friend."

———

"You should get one of those vape things, instead of inhaling all that shit into your lungs."

Cox tossed a still flaming match through a crack in the window and followed its path to watch it burn out before it reached a patch of damp grass littered with cigarette stubs. He took a huge pull on the last of his pack and slowly blew out the smoke. A slight breeze blew some of it back into the room. "Chemical shit."

Hudson waved his arms to waft it back toward the window. "Whatever. And I'll be pissed if you set off the smoke alarm. We've got work to do."

Behind him, a laptop whirred away, its internal fan cooling processors that scanned pictures at a near impossible rate and that, so far, had come up with nothing.

"Can tell you don't smoke." Cox held the cigarette before his face and studied the glowing orange tip.

Hudson wafted again as a thin wisp of burned tobacco drifted over his head. "In a passive sense, I reckon I get through twenty a day tagging along with you but, personally, I wouldn't touch one. They take years off your life."

"A bullet to the head does a quicker job. I'll take my chances. And this shit I'm inhaling is naturally grown, give or take the odd additive. Do you know what's in those vape things? Just because they smell like a State Fair food stall doesn't make them any healthier."

"Don't know, don't care," said Hudson. "Either will kill you."

"And cigarettes don't explode in your hand. Well, unless you smoke something like the cigar we made in Uganda, but that was designed to do that. I consider it a success, too, when they can't even use dental records to identify the target."

"It's nice to team up with a guy who takes such a huge amount of pleasure in his work."

Hudson beamed a huge grin. "What can I say, I'm committed to it."

"Let's say 'should be committed' and leave it at that."

"And we all have vices. Mine's smoking, yours is torture. My passive smoking might harm a few civilians or colleagues, but nowhere near as many, or quite as painfully, as your torture."

"You couldn't call my vice passive, I'll grant you that," said Cox with a fake coy look.

"Yeah, but you do enjoy it. You've turned it into an art form."

The laptop beeped, and Cox held up a finger and spun in his seat. "Hello, what do we have here?"

A button press cleared the screen and brought up a photograph.

"Well, would you look at that. What did I tell you about social media? Facebook to the rescue. Maxine Burns is celebrating with Sheila Whittle and ten others at The Billet public house. Someone's getting married."

Hudson leaned in to study the screen. A camera flash whitewashed the girls in a picture of them leaning back against a guy with weird eyes. Next to them, another guy had tried to turn his head, but the camera had snapped enough features for the facial recognition program to pick out a match.

A picture of John MacIntyre flashed up to the side of it.

Cox smiled. "He's still here in Edinburgh. Got him."

Hudson stubbed out his cigarette on a plastic window frame already stained brown to black with applied heat. "Cool. I need more cigarettes, anyway. And you won't need your GPS, I remember that place. It's only a couple of blocks away."

Chapter Six

The front wheels of Sam's Chevy Malibu momentarily left the asphalt before crashing back to Earth with a shriek of rubber and a thump that shook the entire car. Evie's phone bounced off the dash and into the passenger footwell.

Sam gripped her seatbelt as if her life depended on it. "Holy crap, Evie, I'm still making payments on this car. Please, don't let us be those people on TV who try to make a claim after they wreck. I'll be fifty next week. I never thought I'd say this, but please let me be fifty."

Clear of the parking lot, Evie wrenched on the wheel and slid the car sideways onto I-480 before she slammed the accelerator into the carpet. She braced herself for whiplash and, instead, remained content as the small engine dragged the car up to sixty.

"Put my phone back on that cradle thing, Sam. It makes it much easier to follow the bad guys when I can see where they're headed."

Sam fumbled beneath her seat, retrieved the phone, and secured it into a plastic holder on the dash. On the screen, a small red dot flashed against the jumbled background of Ohio's roads. And the small red dot was still moving away from them.

"We shouldn't automatically assume that they're bad guys. Perhaps they picked up my phone by mistake."

Evie let out a rush of air through her lips. "Really? Come on, Sam. You think they whistled, and your phone just leaped into their possession because it felt all warm and fuzzy?"

Sam flushed. "I'm just saying that there might be a totally reasonable explanation for this."

"There is," said Evie. "Someone stole your phone and we're going to catch them before they sell it or strip it for parts. Or whatever it is they do with phones these days."

They sat in silence for a moment as Evie concentrated and wound through the roads. Bit by bit, they gained on the red dot.

At one point, it was mere yards in front, but a light stopped them, and they sat shouting with frustration as the dot regained its lead.

"What lies this way?" asked Evie. "Assuming we follow this to the end, which we damn well are."

Sam's face creased to send tears trickling down her cheeks. "Crap, I don't know, Indiana? Evie, I stay home and make sure Daryl's shirts are crease free. I don't race around the state chasing bad guys. Shit, this is giving me hives. At this rate I'm going to need my inhaler. Evie, I'm scared. How the hell are you even coping with what's gone on?"

For precious seconds, the words hung in the air. The car's cabin seemed to fill with pressure and the red dot disappeared.

Sam shrunk back into the passenger seat, afraid of her own words, while Evie gripped the wheel even harder.

None of the guys had mentioned Jamaica. The kidnapping. The murder.

She assumed that Dud would do what she assumed military men do and, when asked, make a joke of it and play down the whole event as nothing more than a blip on the road of life. Another event to deal with and move on.

No one had asked her how she felt.

The air rushed out through the dashboard vents and the dot reappeared.

"I just get on with it," she said through gritted teeth. "Life throws curveballs, Sam, and I try to catch them and throw them back twice as hard. What I've seen doesn't begin to compare with what Dud's been through. And you know why we're still together? We're a team. And, damn it, Sam, so are we. Now, stop getting emotional and watch that dot. This started as something basic, to get your phone. But it's more now. I'm sick of people thinking they can run roughshod over me. I'm not military. I'm not an Old Fart. But, dammit, I can look after me and my own."

They sat in silence again as Evie's words sunk in.

Sam spoke first. "An Old Fart? Aren't you one of those cradle snatchers? Isn't Dud your Boy Toy?"

Evie fought the smile that tugged at her lips. Damn her crazy sister and her warped sense of humor.

"Maybe. Why?"

"Well, because he's forty-nine, right?"

"I'm not sure I like where you're going with this."

"And you're five years older than him."

Evie risked a glance at her sister as I-480 tore beneath them, a black ribbon threading beneath the car. "And your point is?"

"Sorry, Sis," said Sam with a smile, "but you are an Old Fart. There's no denying it."

Before she could respond, Evie noticed the GPS's red dot leave the highway and double back onto I-71.

"What the heck? Are they heading to the water?"

The water was Lake Erie, which lay a few districts north, separated by Tremont and Ohio City.

"What if they've got a boat waiting and we lose them forever?"

"I think you might have had a few too many adventures, Sis," said Sam. "There's not much on my phone but a dodgy picture of the hubby in his briefs. Nothing worth scooting down Erie on a speedboat for."

"Your phone might be a drop in the ocean," said Evie. "Pardon the pun. What if this is a huge thieving ring, or organized crime? Who knows what else is going on?"

She floored the accelerator, and the small car lurched forward. Tree-lined roads flew by as the dot left I-71 and headed directly north through a series of smaller roads.

Sam leaned forward as if her angle gave her a better view of the road ahead. "Do you think they're trying to lose us?"

"I doubt that very much," said Evie. "I can just about drive Miss Daisy in this piece of crap. But perhaps it's not only us following them. You just keep an eye on that dot and make sure we don't lose it."

They meandered through side roads and took turn after turn until, without warning, the dot stopped.

Evie applied the brakes and pulled over to the side of the road. "Sis, what's there?"

Sam shrugged as Evie yanked on the parking brake, grabbed her phone, and used her fingers to zoom in on the screen's map.

"Well," she said as she frowned at the screen, "at least now we know where they've taken your phone. The only question is, why the heck would they take it there?"

———

The crisp tips of well-pressed, pin-striped trouser creases brushed a whisper against the top of gleaming black dress shoes as Marte Dahl strode through the slightly swaying corridor that separated the main building from the research area of the complex. On either side, droplets of water spattered against small square windows of inch-thick glass and ran like tears to gather at the bottom until they trailed away in rivulets. Clinical, white-tiled walls emphasized vibrant green eyes and reflected off cheekbones just as sharp as the trouser creases.

An airtight door unlocked with a faint click when Dahl swiped a laminated card against a discreet panel in the wall and opened with a whisper into a room filled with half a dozen glass-topped desks and the bustle of white-coated people. In the far corner, a woman with horn-rimmed glasses beckoned with a wave.

Dahl had always found her attractive but remained professional and swept up beside her.

"I'm busy. Talk to me."

In such a secretive business, only a select few had access to the research area. Anneka Ergström earned her right to be there by supplying ultra-fast DNA readings to the maximum six frames, using technology she began to design in a home lab in her hometown of Oslo, Norway. Born in the same town, Dahl's wealthy parents funded her move to a custom-built facility, hidden high in the Glittertind mountain range, for a percentage of any profit she made from the research. When their car left the mountain during a descent in a freak windstorm, the young and newly orphaned Dahl used inherited money to continue the research.

Their bodies were never recovered. Dahl never mourned.

Ergström replied in perfect English. "For our latest requirements, I'm unable to find anything in our inventory that won't be at least one identifying marker short."

"How is that possible?" said Dahl. "I thought we had the ability to fulfill any request?"

"Me, too. The latest client seems to be quite unique. I can get the required parts, I'm sure, but at short notice, it will cost more. Our foreign facility will have to acquire new product quickly."

Dahl drummed trimmed fingernails against his pale red lips. "What is our time frame?"

"Two weeks."

"Location?"

"Home," said Ergström with a smile. "Oslo."

At the sight of Ergström's perfect teeth, a flutter bounced inside Dahl's stomach. It was dampened instantly. "Do it. Failure to complete any contract will appear as weakness and inefficiency on our part. We must be seen to be totally reliable."

Ergström nodded as Dahl adjusted and tightened the knot of a striped tie, turned toward the door and marched away.

"Of course. I will see to it."

———

Marbles waved his empty glass in mid-air. "Gorgeous. It's weird how the water brings out the flavor. I could get used to drinking that."

"Water?" said English. "Bloody hell, it must have a different flavor in Scotland."

Macca smiled and clinked a half-empty pint glass against its edge. "Get saving, mate, it's about fifty quid a bottle."

"I've paid my dues with the cheaper stuff," said Marbles. "Fifty's a small price to pay for that quality."

The noise level in the pub dropped as the party of women filtered out into the street.

Tony waved off the last one and gave an exaggerated sigh of relief.

Sarge leaned forward and adjusted his cap. "Now, we can hear ourselves think; let's get back to business. Macca, just in case the paper trail goes cold, you mentioned that Knowles worked out the location of where whatever's happening happens. Did you guys get to check it out yet?"

Macca shook his head. "No. Like I said, no resources. Plus, it's an area, not a location. I do know it's in the North Sea, quite a way out. Not somewhere we'd be swimming to."

"We have a man in Kentucky who can see where the coordinates would put us. Could we reach it with a small boat?" said Marbles. "You know, if we were to acquire one?"

"I'm all about acquisition but, from what I can work out, we're talking eighty to a hundred miles off the Scottish coast. And it wouldn't be the distance that concerned me most, it'd be the conditions. Not only would that put us smack bang in the middle of high traffic shipping lanes with huge vessels, but the water there is deep, cold, unpredictable and unforgiving. The weather can go from cold to 'fuck me, my nuts have frozen off' in a matter of minutes. One mistake and hypothermia would take you before you could say a shivering goodbye to no one that could hear you. Now, we could acquire a helicopter. That might work."

"Wouldn't be the first time, but it'd have to be a decent size to accommodate us all. I can handle the machine easily enough, but do you know a man?"

Macca shook his head again. "Nope, but I'm sure there are plenty of air-ferry services up there to the oil rigs. We could hire one, but how would we explain why we were flying? And how would we proceed if we came across something nefarious? We'd be involving civilians. We'd have to borrow one."

"Nice word, buddy," said Sarge. "Nefarious. Guys, this beer and talk of water is making this old man need to empty his overactive bladder. Where's the bathroom in here?"

"There's no bathroom in here," smiled Macca, "but there is a Gents. Head past the pool tables and take a left."

Sarge stood and excused himself as the main door opened then watched as two men walked in and ambled across to the bar.

Tony marched up to them as Marbles continued.

"How about the registration office? Is that reachable?"

"Easily. That's based in Southampton. On the south coast. We can get there by train."

"But isn't registering a boat like registering a car over here?" said English. "Can't you do that online? If so, that makes it hackable."

"Never thought of that. Knowles didn't have the necessary skills."

"No, but I do. Perhaps we should start there. Shake some trees and see what falls out."

One of the guys at the bar glanced over as the other ordered drinks.

English caught his eye and nodded.

The guy nodded back.

"Before we take a trip into the unknown," he continued, "it would be better to have as much information as possible about any potential target. If we could work out exactly what Knowles found, we could kill three birds with one stone. Finish off your investigation, put any bad guys out of business, and find out who might be looking for you."

———

Cox glanced across the room and spoke under his breath. "There's the weird-eyed guy and MacIntyre. Still, I didn't expect a crowd."

"Me neither. This might not be the best place to do this." Hudson scanned the room and pulled his jacket tighter to hide the silenced Glock nine-millimeter which nestled against his chest. "Good news is I don't see any cameras. And while I don't care about collateral damage, there might be more here than we can handle without automatic firepower. Pistols might not be quick enough. Maybe we should use this as a reconnaissance mission. See where they're staying."

He paused as a tattoo-covered bartender approached. The phrase, *I'm forever blowing bubbles* stretched across his arm in fancy scroll.

"Evening, guys. What'll it be?"

"Couple of Buds," said Cox. "And do you sell cigarettes?"

"No, mate, just alcohol. There's a Tesco down the road that can get those for you."

Hudson nodded as the bartender continued.

"Americans?"

Hudson nodded again.

"Weird. You guys are like buses. Already got some of your guys over there. Don't imagine you're from the same party?"

"No," said Cox. "America is a big place with lots of people. We're here for the castle. Beautiful city."

"That it is, on both counts. And the city has much more than a castle. Lots to do in Edinburgh."

"Oh, we already have a full itinerary. Got no need to kill time. What's with the bubbles tattoo?"

"That? It's a West Ham song. Best football team in London, mate. Well, when I say best, I mean mine. Most years, they frustrate the crap out of me, but you should feel the atmosphere when the fans start singing 'We're Forever Blowing Bubbles'."

"Blowing bubbles? Wasn't that Michael Jackson's monkey? Seems like a sexual statement. Can't see that inciting a riot or motivating a team."

The bartender ignored the comment and placed two filled and frosted glasses on a mat that had an Innis and Gunn logo splashed across it.

"And I thought you didn't have guns here," grinned Hudson as he pointed to the mat.

The bartender's eyes widened in surprise, and then he laughed. "Funny, wise guy. That type won't kill you quite as quickly. That'll be seven pounds dead."

Hudson laughed back. "Dead. Touché. I like that." He placed a ten-pound note on the mat. "Keep the change, man."

"Cheers. Enjoy the drinks."

The money disappeared with the bartender as, across the room, the oldest guy in the group stood and threaded between tables to the back of the room.

Hudson nodded toward the guy behind the bar. "Something going on with him. Make sure no one else leaves that table. I'll follow grandad over there and see what's up with him. Maybe we can reduce the numbers and still make this work. I'm already sick of this place, and I didn't even try the beer yet."

Cox took a deep pull of his drink. "At least the lagers are cold. You go do what you do. And if he has cigarettes in his pocket, hide the body but bring those back with you."

Hudson mumbled, "Slave to the drugs" under his breath and weaved through a set of round oak tables and between two well-lit pool tables until he spotted a door labeled, *Gents*. The thick, wooden door was just closing as he jabbed a foot against it and entered the room.

The old guy was hustling up to a squeaky-clean urinal, the brim of his cap almost touching the white-tiled wall in front of him. His feet were spread either side of the porcelain to avoid any drunken splashes, which made him flat-footed and vulnerable.

Hudson checked the stalls were empty and then shuffled up alongside him. "Heard you talking in there. Sounds like we're from the same part of the world. Seems like a nice bar."

The old guy continued to stare down as if the break in concentration might ruin his flow. "You've got good hearing, buddy, but don't let the locals hear you say 'bar'. It's a nice pub, that's for sure. Local and friendly. No trouble and decent beer."

"Yep, just the way I like 'em."

Hudson unzipped his jeans then reached beneath the back of his jacket for his pistol.

———

The pressure on Sarge's bladder was enough to make him stand, but the two guys entering the pub bothered him more. The first guy, tall and wiry, walked upright and confident. Walking upright stretched the whole wardrobe. Sarge spotted the bulge of a shoulder holster before the doors had closed. There was no open carry law in Scotland.

The second guy gave off an air of confidence and had roving eyes that scanned the room quickly and professionally and checked all their faces but settled on Macca and then looked away with a 'job done' detachment.

When they walked to the bar, everything seemed stilted and forced. And when Tony bit his tongue and didn't leap over the bar to batter an obnoxious customer, he knew something was off.

The bathroom was easy to find. It was where all bathrooms were in well-designed pubs and bars. In a corner, where men instinctively go to relieve themselves if there are no bathrooms available.

When one of the guys entered the room behind him, Sarge switched modes and shuffled his feet so that the stranger's reflection moved in the mirror he could see reflected in the shiny steel hand dryer beside him.

After small talk, when the guy's reflection reached for its gun, Sarge zipped up, crowded him, and pressed himself shoulder to shoulder.

"Weird isn't it, how, even while you're holding your pecker, men come into places like this and strike up a conversation based on geography and equal sex?"

While the guy still had one hand occupied, Sarge reached up and clutched a fistful of hair. Before another word was spoken, he drove the man's head forward into the wall. Tiles cracked and red splashed against white as the guy bounced away with a yelp. Sarge reached out again and repeated the action.

As the guy slid down the tile, Sarge slammed his head into the urinal for good measure and then let the limp body drop to the ground.

He slipped the gun into his waistband and, after a quick check of the guy's pockets, headed back to the bar.

Everyone appeared calm as he retook his seat.

He leaned into the group and whispered. "Guys, we have trouble. I think whoever's looking for Macca might have found him. Just had a tender moment in the bathroom with that guy's colleague."

Sarge glanced toward the bar, where the other guy sipped at his beer.

"Do we reckon there are just the two of them? Any calls on a cell to suggest he might have called reinforcements?"

"Other than drinking his beer, he's not moved a muscle," said English. "Perhaps he's waiting for his pal to get back from the loo. And when you say a tender moment, you don't mean..."

"They're both carrying. Bathroom boy pulled his pistol during a vulnerable moment, so I had to put him to sleep. You'll have to apologize to Tony about the state of his facilities."

Macca leaned forward, pulled his own pistol, and stowed it beneath the front of his shirt. "Shit, Sarge. I'm sorry you got into that. You okay?"

"Yessir, freshly relieved and ready for action, although I'd prefer to not have to kill anyone. I'm trying to be done with those days. Guys, I don't know how long his buddy will be out, probably a while based on the sound the porcelain made."

"Eh?" said Marbles.

"His face bounced off the urinal."

"Ouch."

"After it bounced twice off the wall."

"Jeez, Sarge..."

"He's still alive. And a little naked. I wasn't going to spare his blushes. The guy at the bar doesn't look like a boss to me, he looks like hired help. And, unless his buddy was constipated, he's going to wonder where he is. I have an idea that might get us out of here and allow us to find out who they are. Then, we can also find out if they're hired and, if so, by whom?"

"I'm game for a non-violent solution," said Macca. "This is my local. I'd hate to shoot up my mate's pub. What are you thinking?"

Sarge stood and stepped away from the table. "Give me a sec. Let me have a quick chat with Tony."

Tony met Sarge at the service hatch at the rear of the bar.

"Be discreet," said Sarge as Tony leaned in. "There's been a little trouble in your pub. Is there another way out to avoid any more?"

Tony didn't bat an eyelid, walked through the hatch, and sidled up alongside Sarge. "The guys that came in after you are packing. And I did notice the geezer that followed you hasn't returned yet. Did you leave me a big clean-up job?"

"No, other than maybe a tile or two. He'll be around soon, but I do apologize for the spatter in the bathroom."

"You mean the gents. Yeah, I hoped they'd just have a beer and leave. Do I need to be prepared?"

"Possibly not. Is there a back door out of here? I wouldn't mind waiting outside for them. Then, since I assume they're tourists like us, we can follow them home and see exactly what's going on."

Tony smiled. "I like that. The hunters become the hunted. There is a back door, mate, but it might be more prudent to use the other way."

"The other way? You might have Clarence out front, but I'd still rather avoid any bloodshed. At least here. I like this place."

Tony smiled again. "Appreciated, mate, but this is Edinburgh. We don't need to worry about front or back. We can go under."

Chapter Seven

Even zoomed close on the phone's small screen, Wendy Park seemed to be a whole lot of nothing, acres of woodland and greenery sandwiched between Lake Erie, and a twin train track that crossed a bridge by the coast guard station and ran a parallel route to the lake's coast.

From what Evie could tell, its best feature was that it lay off Whiskey Island, a name that would have brought a smile from Dud.

"I know this place," said Sam. "Twenty-two acres of wildlife and not much else. I saw the commercial on TV. Really boring. No stores at all. It's totally a bird watcher's paradise."

"So why would they come here? I'm sure they could find something better than your piece of crap phone to take bird pictures with."

"No clue. How far away are we? And, hey, about my phone."

Evie snatched hers from the dashboard cradle, activated the speakerphone, and dialed a number.

The ring tone burred once.

"Hi, Evie. Numbers here."

"I'm guessing you can see what I can see?"

"Just like your husband, right to the point. Yep, got you on one of the monitors here. Penny's been watching your every move while I've been keeping an eye on the guys."

"So she sees where we are?"

"Yep."

"And? What do you think?"

After a brief silence, Penny's voice boomed crystal clear through the speaker. "Hi, Evie. I don't know what to think, to be honest, but if Keith was here...sorry, English was here, I know he'd go to infra-red and see how many bad guys we were dealing with. You know, heat signatures and all."

"Of course," said Evie. "Penny?"

"Yeah?"

"Can we go to infra-red and see how many bad guys we're dealing with?"

Another brief silence.

"We're still learning," said Penny. "Bear with me. Just applying the filters."

Evie took a deep breath and let it out slowly between her teeth.

"I hear that, young lady," said Penny. "Okay, well it looks like it took more than one guy to steal your phone."

"Come again?" said Sam with a blush. "It's just a regular phone. I barely put security on it."

"Yep, I've got three toasty red signatures glowing onscreen. Looks like they drove through Wendy Park, I can't help thinking that sounds like a porn star, and have stopped at the slips by a marina on Lake Erie."

Evie cursed. In the time she held her phone the bad guys had moved again.

"Can you direct us and get us close if we keep you on speaker? How far away are we?"

"I can," said Penny. "You're only a few minutes away. You guys are packing, right? I mean, if I direct you to the bad guys, you have the means to disable them and take control, right?"

Sam turned to Evie with a frown. "Disable them? Do all you military wives talk like you've just stepped off the Discovery Channel?"

Evie ignored her with a wave. "We'll work it out. Sam has some pretty offensive lipstick that could disable a dude."

"Seriously. If I sent you into a firefight without sufficient prep, the guys would never speak to me again."

Evie took her foot off the brake, slid up the leg of her jeans, pulled a slim 9mm pistol from an ankle holster, and dropped the firearm into the door's side pocket.

"Holy fucking shit," said Sam. "Pardon my French, but shit, Evie."

Evie ignored her sister. "We're covered, Penny. You reckon Dud would leave me hanging with all the crap we've had going on?"

"Never in a million years," said Penny. "Okay, it looks like there are three of them, presumably one of them is your purse thief. They're moving slowly from a secluded parking lot and are headed toward the slips of the marina."

"Slowly, like they're struggling?"

"No clue. I just see three slow moving dots as opposed to three faster moving dots. They're just dots. Moving. How about I switch the view and use a satellite image to see them as people. Would that help?"

"Probably not. If it's like Google Maps, there'll be more jumble with the background and all. Stick to thermal. Can we park closer?"

A pause, and then, "Yep. Drive north while we talk."

Evie gunned the engine as best she could. The temperature in the car seemed to rise the closer they got, as anticipation caused her skin to crawl.

"Okay," said Penny. "Pull over and park."

Evie spun the wheel and skidded the small car until it bumped and juddered against a curb.

"They're yards away. Can you run?"

Evie glanced at her sister.

"I didn't buy any heels," said Sam with a pout, "so, yes, I can run."

"Yes, we can run."

"Okay, well then, run. These dots are merging with the water, which might mean they're boarding a boat of some sort. You should at least get eyes on them."

Evie didn't think to lock the car doors as she and Sam raced through a parking lot filled with binocular wielding anoraks and powered toward the marina.

Birds took to the air in a blur of feathers as they rounded a row of dense bushes.

In the distance, two men wrestled a younger woman onto a small speedboat.

"There," she pointed. "Do you recognize her?"

Sam followed her finger. "Yes. Bitch! She was in the changing room next to mine. We even talked for a while through the wall. She doesn't look happy, though."

"But that's her," said Evie. "I don't think she's happy about getting onto that boat."

The two men forced the girl onto the rear seat, and one stood over her as the other fired up the boat's engine.

Evie glanced across the slips until her eyes settled on a boat that bobbed innocently on the current. The throttle from the speedboat rumbled and rose in volume until the boat turned from the jetty and pulled away.

"We'll take that one."

"Say what?" said Sam.

Evie spoke into her phone again. "You guys still seeing us okay?"

"Got you right here," said Penny.

"Right here," said Numbers in the background. "What are you doing, Evie? The others are moving east."

"I see them. Keep an eye on them and direct us. We're going to play follow the leader."

———

Cox drained the remaining beer from his glass and glanced at Hudson's untouched pint. His alarm level raised from one to two when the old man returned from the bathroom, unscathed, and casually wandered through the tables and retook his seat.

It went from two to three when he stood again and wandered across the room to chat with the bartender, and from three to four when the old man stepped behind the bar and disappeared through a door.

The bartender looked over. "Need a refill for that empty glass?"

"I'm good, thanks. If my pussy of a friend doesn't get back here soon, I'll start on his. I hate to waste."

"No problem. Like your attitude."

Cox nodded an acknowledgement before the bartender shouted across the room.

"You guys give me a hand with something out back?"

His alarm level shot off the scale when MacIntyre and his group stood and walked through the same door.

"Be right back." The bartender paused at the door. "Need to do a bit of heavy lifting."

"Nothing I can help with?" said Cox.

"Appreciated, mate, but I know these lads. They owe me. And if you pulled a muscle, I'd be liable." He gestured to the other guy behind the bar. "My colleague here can help if you change your mind about that refill."

Once the door clicked shut, Cox barged into the bathroom. Hudson lay on his stomach beneath a urinal in a small halo of blood. A telltale streak of red ran down the cracked tiled wall above him.

"Shit! Jesus, Hudson. Vicious old bastard."

Cox knelt beside Hudson's prone body, found a thready pulse, then checked the vertebrae down the back of his neck. Satisfied there was no serious damage, he carefully rolled him over. A deep gash above his eyebrow signaled where most of the blood had come from. Breath came in ragged gasps.

A peripheral glance of skin stopped him from glancing any lower than chest height, and he scooped water from the faucet and drenched Hudson's face. At the second attempt, his colleague's eyes twitched and then snapped open.

"What the…"

"Can you move?" said Cox.

Hudson used an elbow to raise himself, groaned, and paused for a moment and then rolled onto his side.

"Gimme a sec, the room's spinning."

Each word came out flat and sent tiny sprays of blood across the floor. Hudson's airways were crushed.

"Sorry, bud, but we don't have a sec. They're leaving through the rear of the bar. Come on, zip up and get up."

Cox looped an arm beneath Hudson's armpit and yanked him to his feet as his colleague fumbled with his zipper.

"Can't believe you let a fossil got the better of you. The guy's so old he probably still sees in black and white. Come on, let's go."

He half-walked, half-carried Hudson past glaring eyes and hushed whispers, leaned him against the wall, and summoned the other guy behind the bar.

"What's through that door?"

The barman frowned and pointed to a sign pinned halfway up it. "Says right there, mate. Employees only. I don't think it's any of your business, to be fair. Your business is on that side of the bar where you can enjoy a beer. Let the professionals take care of back here."

Cox looked back at Hudson. His arms hung loosely at his sides, and he shuddered with each breath. Bubbles of blood formed at his nostrils then popped like small balloons.

Cox opened his jacket to show off his pistol's handgrip and watched the barman's eyes widen.

"That's right, and I have no qualms about killing every person in this place. But what I'm after went through that door. You don't want to be on tomorrow's news, right? How about you show me what's back there and save a significant amount of bloodshed?"

The door opened onto a small hallway. A tidy office to the left was empty but for a desk covered in paperwork, as was the storeroom to the right. Farther on back, the hall opened into a larger room with kegs lined up along one side. The other side had a hatch door formed into the floor.

Cox pulled the pistol and gestured toward the hatch.

"Open it."

The barman said nothing but walked forward, gripped a handle in the door, and levered it open. A waft of cool air drifted up carrying a sharp, hoppy smell. Wooden steps disappeared into darkness.

"It's the cellar," he said. "There's nothing down there but the kegs we use for the pumps on the bar. Folks like their beer to be served at cellar temperature."

Cox gestured again. "Turn on a light and lead the way. Try anything stupid and I'll warm things up."

They passed a thermometer on the wall which read twelve degrees. He tried to translate it into Fahrenheit as the droning hum of an air conditioner grew louder with each step.

The staircase stopped at a concrete floor. One side of the cellar had rows of beer kegs lined up like soldiers against the wall, the other an elaborate metal racking system that held the kegs in use. A hose snaked from each into chrome piping mounted on the wall that disappeared through the ceiling. Between the two rows, a ramp ran from a hatch down to the cellar floor.

Cox studied the room in a matter of seconds. There were no hiding places. The twin doors of the ceiling hatch were padlocked shut from the inside.

He raised the pistol. "Where are they? I saw them come back here."

"Where's who? Mate, I've been working all night. I didn't see where anyone went."

"What's your name?"

"Say what?"

"It's an easy question. What's your name?"

"Ken."

"Okay, Ken. Last chance. Where did they go?"

The barman shrugged. "Don't know what you're talking about."

Cox fired a single shot from the hip, which ripped a perfect hole dead center between Ken's eyes then stepped over his crumpled body and tugged at the padlock. It remained locked.

After one more cursory glance around, Cox picked up the shell casing and climbed the staircase.

Chapter Eight

Li Jing Chen rattled her slick, warm handcuffs against the metal siderails and screamed again. The sound tore at her throat and finished in a croaking dry rasp.

Like every time before, no one responded.

Scratches that looked like tiny gates on her cell wall indicated it had been a month since she'd woken to find her right eye gone, the gaping and tender hole covered with a cheap fabric eyepatch. Its elastic strap irritated the side of her head, but the passing weeks had made it bearable.

Then, they came for her again.

She swallowed down bile and used her remaining eye to take a scared look at her new surroundings.

The coppery scent of her own blood mingled with the sharp smell of disinfectant. Various banks of machinery crowded her table like curious spectators, with wires and cables hanging and waiting to find her tender skin. All of it was enclosed in a small space surrounded with the vertical plastic strips Uncle Jian used to maintain the temperature in his meat locker at the restaurant. Each overlapped the next like an almost see-through skin to either keep her hidden from sight or to prevent her seeing her location.

The time of taking food orders and serving hot dishes seemed a distant and beloved memory. After a passionate celebration at the temple, she and her fellow Falun Gong worshippers filed carefully along a side street to the restaurant. Their yellow T-shirts did little to hide them and, when the State's soldiers came, only she was left alive. The others were shot in front of her. They lay, motionless, their blood seeping into the concrete.

Her friend, Li Wei, tried to crawl away until a soldier stepped over him. His body jerked when another shot pierced the back of his head.

The bodies were left in the street while she was bundled into a waiting van which sped away with no fanfare or sirens. No one looked up as they dragged her, teary-eyed and screaming, through the blood-soaked entry to the vehicle, the street's commotion and bustle uninterrupted.

She had no way of knowing what had become of her friends' bodies.

The wall of plastic straps parted and slapped a dull smack, and the man with the clipboard stepped before her. The same man had looked her up and down when her eye was taken.

Her stomach churned as he checked the machines, gave her a cursory glance, and scratched something on his papers with a pen before he nodded and moved away.

Men and women in white coats replaced him and began to move the machinery around the table.

She screamed again, a useless cry for help, and writhed and turned as a tall man tried to force a thick needle into her arm.

He shook his head, reached to a side table, and returned

with a zip tie which he used to secure her arm to the bed's siderail.

The tie cut off the circulation to her hand. Pins and needles danced in her fingers and, after one more scream, her voice broke into pitiful sobs as the needle was pushed through her skin, jarring its way through a white dimple, before he turned to a machine and pressed a button.

In tired stages, the room went from vivid terror, to blurry jumbles, to black.

———

"This is like something from an Indiana Jones film," said Macca as Tony led the group along a cold, damp tunnel.

The first surprise had been when their host marched behind them into a small storeroom and asked them to step aside. They stood over a small hatch door as Tony gripped the handhole of one of the kegs on the opposite wall and pulled. The keg was empty, joined to two others and fixed to a small trap door in the floor that raised easily to reveal the tips of an aluminum ladder. A motion sensor blinked a fluorescent light into life, and he gestured for them to descend.

The second surprise was at the bottom of the ladder. It ended at an ancient and uneven floor that led into a musty corridor lit by small wall sconces that painted the entire area a muted orange.

English held out his arms and trailed his fingers against the wall on either side. "Tony, what is this place? And how the hell did I not know about it?"

"You're in the vaults, mate. And if you didn't know, you either weren't educated in Scottish history or you never took a tour here. Oh, and mind your head."

"My head?" said Marbles. "I'm concerned about my allergies. Jesus, this place smells damp."

"Well, of course, it does," said Tony, "but it's drier than you'd expect, thanks to some conditioning work from some friends of mine. Still, you're underground. And these tunnels were built in the seventeen-hundreds. You might be surprised to know that they didn't have air-conditioning back then. People lived down here in shocking conditions, isolated from the people above."

They walked farther, following Tony's every step. Occasionally, wooden beams shot across the ceiling overhead to support crumbling brickwork. The musty smell increased the farther they walked.

"How did they cope?" said Sarge. "It feels like a prison. Not that I'm speaking from experience."

Tony pointed to hollowed-out sections in the walls. "Of course not, Sarge, but you know how it is. We've all been in less than cozy accommodations. You just do, don't you? Those used to be beds. Imagine them covered in straw and filled with families. You know they're still finding bits and pieces of ancient crap down here? Tiny, hand-made toys or fragments of tableware. The affluent folks lived up top. The others, the grafters who worked themselves to the bone, lived down here. Other than the locations, I don't think we've really changed that much, have we? Same differences, same division only, other than penthouses, we all mostly live above ground now."

Surprise number three came as the group ducked under another low doorway and into a larger room, where the hollowed-out wall sections were lined with modern wooden racking that held an impressive collection of firearms and equipment.

"Did I just see an office?" said Macca.

"Keep on walking, people," said Tony with the wave of a hand and a wry smile. "Nothing to see here."

"How did you get to be down here?" asked English as the group filed through the room behind him.

"Tourism. These vaults were abandoned in the eighteen-hundreds, probably riddled with disease or crime or lack of West Ham games on television and weren't rediscovered until the nineteen-eighties. You know how consumerism takes over. I can hear them now; there's a whole labyrinth of tunnels beneath the city, anyone want to own a section? It was probably a bidding war. When I took over the pub, the vaults came as part of the package. A lot of them owned by tour companies, but I figured I could put my section to better use. I made a few modifications, added some security, haggled with the neighbors, and here we are."

"Fair play to you, mate. I can imagine the modifications. Where does this lead? Do we come out to anywhere I know?"

"Yep. You'll know it."

When they reached a solid metal door, Tony raised his hands to stop the group.

"Okay, guys, listen up. When you get out there, pretend to be a stag party."

English translated for the Americans. "He means bachelor party."

"Whatever. Behave like a bunch of pissheads wandering around Edinburgh. You won't need to explain pisshead, mate, that's a universal language. You'll step out onto a main road. This door is rarely used, so it might be a surprise for the locals to see a stream of military-looking types deposited onto the street.

"Luckily, I know a man in the local council who's redirected the camera opposite to miss this entrance. Still, CCTV will pick you up farther on. Be careful. Go down the bank and around the corner and you'll find yourselves at the entry that opens out onto the front of the pub. There are a few places a bloke could hide if you want to scope out the place and wait for the bad guys. Hopefully, Ken has kept them occupied long enough to give you time to get into position."

Macca pulled Tony into a hug. "I'm gobsmacked, mate. And eternally grateful."

"Always up for helping out a brother," said Tony, "although I'd better be getting back. Those yanks might be better than they seemed. I'd hate to leave Ken with them on his own for too long."

"Understood. I owe you."

"Duly noted. Now, go deal with your crap."

Tony entered a code into a small panel on the wall and the metal door clicked and swung open on silent hinges. He turned to face the group once more. "The beautiful city awaits, guys. Get out there, watch each other's backs, and good hunting. Anything else I can do; you know where to find me."

Macca led the way as the group filed out onto a cobbled street. He looked across the city and then across at the church, its bell tower silhouetted in the evening light, with its downlit walls still wrapped in a hazy, plastic gauze. He looked back to see the vaults door click shut then marched with solemn purpose once again down Grassmarket and headed back toward the entrance of The Billet.

———

"I can't believe you're making me do this, it's totally illegal."

Evie tried to tune out Sam's whining voice as she fiddled with the wires beneath the small boat's console.

"Daryl would have an absolute fit. And have you seen

Orange Is the New Black? I can't get arrested. I wouldn't last a day in prison."

"I'm not making you do anything," said Evie, "and you won't go to prison. If it'll shut you up, I'll take the rap. Now, let me do this. You want to find out what's going on and get your phone back, right?"

Evie twisted a combination of wires together and forced the ignition. The boat's engine chugged and belched into life and sent a plume of black smoke into the air.

"Of course, I do. Wait, did you really just do that?" said Sam. "Oh, my God, you just hotwired a boat. Does Mom know you can do this? She'd totally have a cow."

"If this boat was big enough to have a brig, I swear I'd put you in it." Evie stood and eased the throttle lever forward to send the boat out into the marina. "Will you please just shut up and check the phone? Where did they go?"

Sam swiped the screen, then pointed a finger. "That way. To the right."

"Or east, as most folks call it," said Evie. She clutched the chrome rail that topped the boat's windshield when the vessel lurched forward. The tip of the boat lifted as the engine powered it out of the marina and into the main body of the lake, and they bounced and tilted in ripples of wake.

"Are you sure you can drive this?" shouted Sam.

Evie grimaced. "I can drive it just fine, Sis. You keep an eye on what we're following and be sure to direct me. If they move off course, let me know. Call me superstitious, but something about this whole thing is wrong. I have a feeling this is about more than your phone."

"Okay, superstitious, but it's a cool phone. I'll be totally bummed if she gets away with it, but I'll be even more bummed if they have to fish us from the bottom of the lake."

As they rounded the curve of a bay, the other boat came

into view. In the distance, it was tiny and bounced and crested waves just like theirs.

"Are you going to shoot them?"

Evie's mind snapped from the boat's progress to Sam's words. She glanced at the boat's instrument panel to find the fuel tank full. At some point, the other boat would stop, and they would have to stop behind it and face a possible confrontation. Then what?

"Over a phone? Of course not. But if it's more? Who knows? Your new friend didn't look entirely happy to be forced into that boat. Like I said, this may be about more than your phone. This could be kidnapping."

Sam didn't reply, until the lead boat stopped bouncing in the water and grew closer much quicker.

"They're turning right toward land," she said.

Evie eased back the throttle and the boat's engine changed from a guttural roar to a steady chug. Ahead, the other boat coasted up to a slip before someone jumped out and lashed a rope from the boat to a pier.

She killed the engine and angled toward the shore.

"Okay. Let's give them a minute and then we'll see where they are. Does that screen show anything?"

"Blue water and green land," said Sam. "Same as before."

Evie held out a hand, and Sam passed the phone.

She scrolled through to contacts and dialed.

Penny answered after the first ring. "They stopped."

"Yes, they did," said Evie. "Any idea where they might be headed?"

"They didn't travel far, so perhaps this is a waypoint. Maybe they need to refuel or meet someone else. Closest place to you of any decent size is called Euclid. Ironically, the cordless phone was invented there. Other than that, it's a regular town. Nothing stands out. At least, nothing any closer than the highway."

"I don't think they're looking to reinvent Sam's phone, it's as good as they get. Okay, they've tied off the boat, but no one's disembarked yet. Keep an eye on us, if you would. And them. I'll coast closer and see what we can uncover."

"Will do. Be careful, Evie."

The phone chirped as Penny disconnected and Evie laid it on the seat behind her and steered the boat to the shoreline.

"Ready to play some hide and seek?" she said as its prow ground into a grass bank to stop them. "It's a good thing you're wearing flats. We'll circle around and see what they're up to."

They followed the edge of the water for five minutes before they came to a cluster of large storage units clad in red corrugated metal. Evie led the way and sprinted until they ducked behind the closest building.

A yellow forklift sat idle beside a large open doorway, sandwiched between huge steel containers. To its left, the boat they'd chased bobbed gently against a wooden pier.

"Okay," whispered Evie. "Let's get closer and see what's going on. Stay behind me."

"You don't have to worry about that," said Sam. "I'd be totally fine on the boat, but then I'd be on my own. I hate being on my own."

Evie listened for sounds and heard nothing but the lapping of water against the grass bank and the hum of the distant highway. In a crouch, she crept forward to the side of the first building and pressed her ear to the metal.

Sam pushed against her moments later.

Evie held up a finger to shush her. "Nothing. With these open spaces, even regular conversation would be audible."

"Have you always spoken like this," whispered Sam, "or do

you flick a switch when you go into G.I. Jane mode? Who are you and what have you done with my sister?"

Evie scowled and pointed across the empty yard. "I'll bet they're in one of the buildings on the far side. Come on, we'll creep up and check them out one by one."

She glanced inside the first building as they moved past it. Steel racking lined the walls, sat on smooth, dusty concrete. Other than a tall, multi-drawered tool chest and a collection of oil spills, the building was empty.

The next two were locked, with huge brass padlocks hooked through thick steel loops. As they approached the next, Evie finally heard the dull rumble of conversation.

"Okay, we're in business. Let's get close enough to hear what they're saying and find out how many we're dealing with."

Sam gripped Evie's shoulder before she could move. "Dealing with? Evie, what are you planning? All I want to do is get my phone back, I don't want to start a damned turf war." She fanned a hand in front of her face. "Gosh darn, my anxiety is kicking in. It's just a phone. I've changed my mind. Let's go back, I can always get another. This is totally crazy."

"I thought your life was on that phone?" said Evie.

Sam said nothing.

"Look, chances are it's a huge misunderstanding. We'll get your phone, make sure everything is okay, and then we'll head home."

"Bullcrap. You don't believe a word of that," hissed Sam. "And do you even watch films? It never works that way. We're probably in the middle of a huge drug deal and, if they find us, there'll be nothing left, and the authorities will have to identify us by our dental records. Come on, let's go."

"Sam, like I said, this may be about more than your phone. What if that woman is innocent and got caught up in something dangerous? If I saw her on the news, I'd never forgive myself. I'll go alone if need be, you can wait on the boat."

"Innocent? She stole my phone. And damn, Evie, that's no choice! Head into potential death or sit alone on a stolen boat?" Sam fanned her face again. "Shit, I just realized I prefer potential death to being alone. Oh, my God, what happened to my life, it's all gone haywire."

"And I just realized my sister is a drama queen. Wait here, then. I'll go see what's going on."

Evie moved before Sam could respond and ran in a crouch to the last building. The voices grew louder as she grew closer, but the building's steel walls muffled the words enough to drown out any meaning.

Sam hustled up behind her.

"I'm going to sneak around front and use my phone to video through the door," said Evie, "then we can see what's in there. Wait here."

"I'm not a dog," said Sam. "I'll be right behind you."

Evie tutted and edged around the corner until she could peer through the huge entrance. A car with tinted windows filled a quarter of the width of the opening, its trunk and rear doors open. She rushed across and ducked behind it.

She pulled out her phone, fumbled with the camera settings, and videoed the room while Sam waited behind the door.

"I don't care what she says," said a deep voice, "he reckons she saw something. Until he knows who she's spoken to, she's valuable. There can be no witnesses."

"I swear I saw nothing," said a woman's voice. Each word trembled with fear. "You don't have to hurt me."

"That's not my call. Come on, we need to be sure. Let's get her in the trunk and we can take a quick break before we head out."

Another voice grunted, and the woman screamed as Evie scurried back to the door. Ten seconds of shuffling and shouting ended with the slam of the trunk lid.

When the heavy footsteps receded, Evie chanced a peek around the entrance in time to see two men disappear through a side door.

"Shit. Okay, forget watching video, I'm going to have a quick scout around the side of the building. Maybe there's a window; it might give us a clue what they're up to. You let your friend out of the trunk and I'll meet both of you back at the boat. Think you can handle that?"

Sam gulped, nodded, and crept toward the car while Evie slipped past her, hugged the wall, and moved forward.

A reinforced four by four window sat at chest height on the side wall. Through it, she could see the two men seated at a table, taking turns smoking a hand-rolled cigarette. Before she could check out the rest of the room, the larger of the men took a phone call, listened for a moment, then tapped the screen and cursed. He stubbed out the cigarette, stood, and stormed back to the main room.

His colleague followed.

Evie's stomach lurched. She raced back to the entrance and almost collided with a younger woman crouched against the wall.

The woman recoiled and clutched a red purse to her side.

"You must be the phone thief," said Evie. "Where's Sam?"

The woman stared. It took a moment for the panic in her eyes to fade.

"You're not with them. Thank God. Listen, I'm guessing Sam is your friend? She…"

The rest of her words were lost in the roar of an engine. She rose and raced around the side of the building.

Evie followed as the rear of the car appeared in the

entrance, its reverse lights glowing grey in a haze of exhaust smoke.

Together, they watched the car brake, turn, and meander along a small road until it paused again, then accelerated off onto the main highway.

"Sam!" Evie shouted and ran back into the main building.

The other woman followed.

"Sam! Come out, they're gone!"

The woman tapped Evie's arm. "Lady, I hate to say it, but your friend isn't here."

"That's not my friend, that's my sister."

"Oh, okay. My bad. Well, anyway, your sister's not here."

Evie glanced around inside the main building. Other than scattered mechanic's equipment, the room was empty. She then pointed in the direction of the highway. "She's not . . ."

"In the car? Yep. They must have done something to the trunk release; she had to pop it from beneath the driver's console. By the time I climbed out, we could hear those guys coming back. As I got out here, she froze. When they got close, she climbed in and pulled the trunk shut."

Bile rose in Evie's throat before she forced herself to think.

Sam had her phone now. Penny and Numbers could track it. All they needed to do was get to a car.

"Shit. She's in the trunk. Okay, do you have a car? Sam's got our car keys. I assume you didn't manage to steal my sister's purse as you crept out?"

"What? No! Why the hell would I do that? I do have a car, but it's back at the mall."

"That's okay, I have a boat."

The woman stared, glassy-eyed.

Evie turned and shouted over her shoulder as she ran along the shore.

The woman followed.

"Never mind, long story. I can get us to the mall. Then, we can go after my sister."

"Whoa, what's with all this 'we' shit? She's your sister."

Evie stopped, turned, and slammed a hand against the woman's chest. "What's your name?"

The woman paused for a second. Her face flushed as Evie glared.

"Carina. Carina Harrigan."

"Listen up, Carina Harrigan. My sister is the most chicken-shit person I know, she freaks out if she breaks a nail, but she just crept into that room to get you out of what looks like a life-or-death situation. Because of that, she's now in the same situation. Do you know the people who grabbed you?"

Carina shrunk into herself. "No."

"You sure?"

"I kind of know the type of person they work for."

"And is he a nice guy?"

"No. Most definitely not."

"So what will happen to my sister when those guys open that trunk and find her inside instead of you?"

"I guess they'll be very confused."

"Carina," said Evie, "I have a gun and I'm not afraid to use it."

Carina spat out words like bullets. "They'll probably torture her to find me."

Evie placed a hand on her shoulder to calm her. "That's not going to happen. We're going to get to her before then. We. You hear? We are. After all this shit, you're indebted. Deal with it or I'll do the job for them and dump your body in the river."

Carina flushed white. "Well, when you put it like that."

"And I heard them say you saw something."

Carina nodded.

"Was it bad?"

She nodded again.

"And I guess you really saw it?"

She nodded again.

"How bad?"

"Bad" she said. "Life or death bad. And, yes, I saw everything."

Chapter Nine

Macca turned the final corner to find the entrance to The Billet deserted. The street was empty, with no sign of Clarence.

Marbles pulled up behind him. "You reckon we've missed them?"

Sarge joined them and peered around the corner. "They shouldn't be moving too quickly. One of them will be baggage. He'll be dizzy with breathing difficulties."

Macca cringed. "Remind me not to piss you off, Sarge. Although it's okay to kill the bad guys, they won't hesitate to do the same thing to you, given the chance."

"Sorry," said Sarge, "but everyone is someone's son. If it's all the same to you, I'll leave them out of action but barely breathing."

"Sarge found God," said English with a resigned shrug. "Don't worry, he can still take care of business. It's just business with a conscience."

Macca nodded. "Clearly. Hang on here, guys. I'll go check out the lay of the land."

He hid in the shadows, avoided the glassy eye of the street CCTV, and sidled up to the first window. Through the misted glass, nothing moved inside. The bar had emptied in a hurry, leaving upturned tables lying like dead spiders, with a carpet of sparkling glass diamonds surrounded by random pools of liquid.

The main door wedged open to cast a shaft of light into the street. As he grew closer, Macca noticed red flowers of dripped blood leading from the entrance mat into the street and found Clarence, face down, his head holding open the door.

The others joined him before he'd lowered his gesturing arm.

"Someone left here in a bad way," he said, pointing to the blood drops.

Sarge stepped forward. "Like I said, crushed nose and battered face. I destroyed a lot of blood vessels. How about two of us track the blood before they get too far or it dries, the others check out the pub and catch up? Split resources and join up later."

English yanked open the door while Macca pulled Clarence free. The big man groaned as he moved and curled into a fetal ball.

"Yep, I agree with Sarge. How about you and Marbles do the tracking? Macca knows the pub. I'll stick with him. Check in when you find something."

With a nod, Sarge moved off to follow the trail.

Macca pulled his handgun and ducked inside the door with English behind him. "It's too quiet, mate," he whispered. "Looks like everyone panicked and ran. We need to find Tony."

Macca dropped into a crouch, used the bar as cover, and tried to avoid crunching glass as he moved into the center of the pub. He turned through the bar hatch and stopped when the cold barrel of a pistol pressed against his forehead.

Breath left him in a hiss when Tony lowered the gun. "Shit. Don't do that to me, mate. I'm still learning stuff. I've got kids to keep up with, I need these brains."

"Understood, although I appreciate me not having to pull the trigger; there's enough mess to clean up in here. Relax, mate. I know every squeak and whisper of this floor. Heard you coming a mile off. I've already cleared the place. Looks like your boys have gone."

"They're not my boys, but they're definitely professionals. Sarge did a proper job on one of them. Clarence will be okay, but he's taken a decent whack to the head. You might want to help him to get it checked. You know a man, right?"

Tony nodded, his face clouded with grief.

Macca looked around the empty bar. "Where's your help?"

Tony dropped his head. "They got Ken in the cellar. Looks like it was quick, but it won't be long until he's the same temperature as the beer. I'm with you now, Macca. No one comes into my place and takes out one of mine without there being a retribution of sorts. An eye for an eye and all that."

Macca glanced at Sarge and clasped his shoulder before replying. "Jesus. Sorry, mate. Seemed like a decent bloke." He let out a deep breath. "Hang tight for a bit and take care of yours, okay? I'm sure we'll call on you, but you have responsibilities here, too. There's enough of us to sort this out; we just have to find the bastards and see what they're up to. Don't worry, we'll make sure they pay. An eye for an eye."

"I know a few folks who can make this look like something else, pal. In the meantime, be sure they do. Make sure they pay."

Tony flinched when English's phone chirped.

"Got them," said Sarge through the speaker. "Bottom of

the road, turn right and go two blocks. They're right around the corner in a shitty hotel with more cigarette butts littering the grass than you'll find in a dive bar's trashcan."

"Can't fault your tracking abilities," said English. "Hold the fort, Sarge, and we'll see you in a few."

"A few what?"

"Minutes, mate. Modern lingo. Sit tight, we'll be right there."

———

The earlier five-minute walk from the pub to the hotel took fifteen on the way back, as Cox half dragged, half carried the slumped Hudson through every step.

Hudson's chest heaved when he took sharp breaths, each gulp sucked in desperately through his mouth like he was breathing through a puddle.

"Drank too much and fell," said Cox to the alarmed hotel receptionist as they cleared the entrance. "Don't worry. I'll get him cleaned up. He'll be fine in the morning."

In the room, he lowered Hudson into the burgundy wraparound armchair which filled the corner. Even with support, his colleague still slumped to one side with his head rested against the chair's arm. Purple bruising already spread from his forehead to his upper lip, and blood still seeped from his crushed nose.

"You gonna make it, buddy?"

With no reply, Cox pulled back the curtains and considered lighting another cigarette until Hudson sneezed to release a shower of blood droplets. The sneeze peppered the beige carpet like a barrage of gunshot wounds.

"Well, at least that cleared your airways." He slapped

Hudson's face. "Time to rejoin the real world, man. We need to work out how to take care of business."

Hudson's head lolled while pink drool ran from his mouth.

Cox leaned in closer and pulled up Hudson's eyelids. Brown irises swam drunkenly from left to right as functions failed.

"Shit, he did a good job on you. You're in a bad way, dude. Damned if I know where to get medical help in a foreign country. Sure as hell can't go to the hospital. Way too many questions and too much paperwork."

Hudson slunk deeper into the armchair.

"You're the brains of the operation," said Cox. "Without you, all this tech shit is useless." He slapped Hudson's face again.

Hudson lolled, and more drool rolled and dripped from his chin.

"And it looks like the brains are out of action."

Cox stood and moved toward the window. He yanked open the sash, lit a cigarette, and blew the smoke out into the Edinburgh night.

Hudson's laptop held all the information they had; the target's profile, the mission parameters, payment instructions, dead-drop destinations. It was all on the equipment Hudson used.

Cox was the muscle. The trigger puller. Still, he did know the password.

He glanced again at the chair.

Hudson sagged into the cushions, his head hung low. Drool ran from his open mouth and dripped from his chin in pink spots. His mouth was open simply because his nose didn't work anymore.

In their six years together, both had dealt with gunshot

wounds, stabbings and beatings, but neither had suffered injuries that weren't treatable. Until now.

Cox flicked away the cigarette, swallowed hard, and walked into the bathroom. To the side of a gleaming mirror were four towels, two hand size and two bath size, folded neatly over a heated rail.

He turned on the hot faucet then held his hands beneath the warm water before covering them with soap. He twisted and turned his hands until they were spotlessly clean, rinsed off the soap, and then towel dried.

When he was sure his hands were as clean as possible, he scooped up the towel and took it into the room.

Hudson said nothing as Cox lifted his head and whispered, "Sorry." He complained and groaned when Cox forced the towel into his mouth and covered his nose, and he thrashed when his airway became blocked with the thick material.

Cox held on tightly as Hudson fought for air when his lungs protested. It only took a minute or so before the struggling stopped.

Cox hung the stained towel over the shower rail then reconsidered, folded it, and bundled it into a backpack. He closed Hudson's wide, bloodshot eyes with his palm and put his lifeless body into the bed. Room service could deal with it in the morning.

Forensics would find material fibers in his mouth, but that's all they'd find. Hudson didn't exist in any records the authorities would use. The real Hudson died years ago.

For a second, Cox considered what his colleague's real name might be before he slumped onto the bed, levered open the laptop, pressed his dead colleague's thumb against a small pad, and then keyed in the password. The screen flickered to life, and he clicked on a text box and told their employer about the new situation.

A reply came back immediately.

Complete the mission.

Need tech help, replied Cox.

The cursor blinked while he waited. And waited.

Complete the mission.

"Miserable fuckers," said Cox. He sat in the chair and reached for another cigarette.

———

"Third floor up, second window from the left."

From their spot behind a low wall fifty feet away, the view of the hotel lived up to its bad reputation. Cheap floodlights over the entrance were the only bright spot to break up a concrete block with windows arranged in rows of eight stacked over six floors.

Boring, predictable, and cheap. Six of the windows had narrow shafts of light shooting out from behind the edges of heavy curtains.

English followed Sarge's pointing finger and nodded while the older man continued.

"Our man likes a cigarette. I could smell it on his colleague in the bathroom. He pushed open a window to let out his smoke a few minutes ago."

"Well spotted, Sarge," said Macca. "We need a plan of action. You might think there are cameras out here, but the hotel will have one on every corner. And a person manning reception."

"Well, we're dealing with an unknown bad guy," said Marbles. "He's holed up in an unknown location where we can't really be seen, and we have no clue what kind of weaponry he's got. We can't kill him because we need to know what he knows, but we can't exactly tickle his feet until he talks, otherwise he'll kill us."

"That just about sums it up," said Macca.

"I say we go to plan 'B-Dubs'," said Marbles.

Sarge nodded. "Wing it."

Macca shook his head as English grinned and translated. "B-Dubs. It's a restaurant chain in the States that's known for its chicken wings. Except they're not wings, they're nuggets. And they come from an entirely different part of the bird. But I digress. When all else fails and time is of the essence, it's what we do; we wing it."

"Crazy Americans," said Macca. "Just say 'we'll wing it' and move on. We can't waltz right through the entrance; reception won't recognize us from checking in earlier, and they'll ask questions. We need a distraction, so we'll need to go inside in pairs, not a group. Less conspicuous and we won't look like a stag party."

"Bachelor party," said English.

"We can't get in through the fire escapes; there are no handles on the outside. So while it would be cool to B-Dub it, let's at least come up with an entrance strategy. We can wing the exit strategy."

"Agreed," said Marbles. "How about the British guys wander in and pretend to be looking for someone? We'll follow and distract the front desk while you make your way up to the room. If we can follow, we will. Push comes to shove, and we get kicked out, we'll wait close by and come running if need be."

Sarge spun his cap, thought for a moment, then spun it back and cleared his throat. "Too many ways that can fail. I've read that there've been a few nasty incidents involving fire and tower blocks on this island. How about the Brits spring the fire alarm and wait for the compulsory evacuation? Most times, hotel reception staff work on eight-hour shifts. Stagger in, tell them you checked in first thing this morning and wave something that resembles a keycard. Then, when they clear the rooms, a couple of us can watch out here in the street, while the others can head up to their room and see what's going on."

"What's with the cap-spinning thing?" said Macca.

"Dunno, just kind of engages the brain, I guess."

"Seems to work. I prefer Sarge's plan," said Macca. "Cleary, that's why they call you Sarge. It's all falling into place now."

Sarge dismissed him with a flap of a hand.

"So how do we do this? And what's plan B if the bad guy spots us?"

"We whack him," said Macca. "That's plan B, simple as that. Although it would be beneficial to find out who sent them first. It would be nice for this to stop. Are you guys okay with mild torture?"

"Left my blowtorch in the States," said English. "Let's not do that and just say we did."

Sarge stood upright and moved toward the hotel. "Agreed. Macca, you and English head inside and pretend to find the bathroom."

"Gents," said Macca.

"Whatever. See the fire door on the left corner of the building?"

The group looked and spotted a door with a fluorescent green sign above it.

"Hard to miss when you see it," said Macca.

"Get inside, find the alarm panel, and activate it. Marbles and I will wait here. If you're able, pop it open and we'll run upstairs while you go back through reception as if you just got spooked."

"What about CCTV?"

"Screw it," said Sarge. "CCTV's already recorded an almost dead guy get checked in. By the time they play back the tapes and get past that, we'll be long gone and in the clear."

Macca wrapped an arm around Sarge's shoulder. "Glad you're on our side, buddy. But what about getting into the room?"

"Don't worry about that," said English, "I've got that covered."

"I know you're good, but this is an 'on the spot' situation. You seem confident."

English smiled. "I am."

"Very well. Let's get to it."

Chapter Ten

A privileged education in London ensured that Marte Dahl's English accent was as perfect as Anneka Ergström's, but each word carried a huskiness borne from too many strong cigarettes. An affair with an older married woman in Essex that came with justified complaints of 'smelling like an ashtray' put an end to that habit. And the affair.

The husky voice still managed to purr into the phone. "I'm aware of your schedule, Mr. Lee, and also of the need to get our product to you in good time . . ."

A pause while Lee interrupted and continued his rant. Dahl tuned it out and waited for him to finish.

"Yes. I understand. I don't recall letting you down before, and let's be blunt and to the point, Mr. Lee, can you get our product from anywhere else within your current timeframe? You don't want a random amateur ripping off parts in a dark alley, do you? I'm sure you've done your research and you'll know that I guarantee quality."

Dahl smirked at the silence.

"I'll take that as a 'yes'. I'm aware that you have a team in place and the equipment organized to switch the parts, and I won't let you down. Am I correct in thinking I have two weeks to supply?"

A timid 'yes' filtered through the phone's speaker.

"Then, that gives me more time than I'll need to work this out. With our advanced storage and transportation system, the product will reach you in perfect condition and in plenty of time. And yes, I'm also aware that you'd normally need to arrange delivery much further in advance, but I have access to plenty of product and the team to ensure it matches your requirements perfectly. Relax, finalize your own preparations, and leave the rest to me. You're not a million miles away; everything will arrive checked and ready to go."

Dahl didn't wait for a reply but tapped the phone's screen to end the call, reclined into a wrap-around chair, and picked up a framed picture from the desk.

The black-and-white photograph of an older couple came supplied with the frame, but their blonde, swept back hair and pale skin gave the appearance of family and shared genes and diverted more questions than it answered.

Dahl ran fingers through the same short haircut and slid open a desk drawer to reveal a sealed pack of Camel cigarettes.

Discipline was important. Without it, efficiency stalled and died.

The same hand slid the desk drawer closed, picked up the phone, and called the supply depot in China.

———

Evie hit a speed-dial button as they reached the boat.

"Numbers. You hear me?"

"I do," said a concerned voice. "I'm right here, Evie; is everything okay?"

"Can you track a phone?"

"Of course," said Numbers, "but you sound stressed. What do you need?"

"Bad guys have kidnapped Sam. We have to track her phone."

"Kidnapped Sam?" said Numbers. "And what bad guys? Hell, Evie, where are you? Shouldn't we call the police? And your husband?"

"I'm in Ohio, Numbers, and no, don't call Dud. He has enough to deal with. And we can't call the police. Not yet. There are too many things I don't know. Numbers, please, track Sam's phone. She's in serious trouble."

"Can't you call her?"

"No, I daren't. She's trapped in someone's trunk, and the longer they're not aware it's her, the better. If her phone rings, it'll only give up her position. Right now, they think she's someone else."

"Sounds to me like we should be calling someone else but, okay, give me the number."

Evie read Sam's number from her own screen.

"Got it," said Numbers. "Give me a second to find it."

The line went silent for a moment, and then, "Evie, at the moment she's stationary, somewhere near the river in Ohio."

"That's impossible. I just watched the car she's in merge onto a highway. How accurate is that program?"

"It's one of English's, so I'm going to guess very accurate."

Carina tapped Evie's shoulder. "Get him to track your phone, then he can place hers in relation to yours."

"That's a great idea. Numbers…"

"Already on it," said Numbers. "One moment. While this program's running, who's that I'm hearing?"

"Time's ticking," said Evie, "but long story short, someone stole Sam's phone and now I'm lumbered with her while Sam is in big trouble."

"Hey," said Carina, "I'll have you know…"

Numbers hummed down the line. "That's weird. Evie, according to this screen, Sam is right beside you."

"What? That's also impossible."

She turned to Carina. "You're certain you don't have my sister's phone?"

"Positive," said Carina as she rooted in her purse. She pulled out a phone. "See? This is my phone. Everyone gives me crap because the case is so sparkly."

The high-end phone glittered in a gaudy, jeweled case.

"Carina, that's Sam's phone."

"No, it isn't. This is my phone."

"Open it. Check the home screen."

Carina huffed and pressed a button to show a picture of Daryl relaxing on Sam's sofa.

"What the hell?" Her eyebrows raised. "First off, he's hot as all get out, but she should really use screen security and, honestly, I'd swear this was my phone. Hang on."

She rummaged again and produced another phone in an identical case.

"Well, I'll be damned. What are the odds of that? She has the same phone. And case. And, apparently, terrible taste in phone cases. The question is, how did her phone get into…" Carina's mouth made an *O* shape.

"The changing room. I tried on a dress and, when I picked up my own clothes to put back on, this phone was on the bench beneath them. I assumed it was mine and dropped it into my purse."

"So you didn't steal it?" said Evie.

"What? No. What do you take me for? I've never stolen a thing in my life. I feel guilty signing on to someone else's Wi-Fi."

"Shit." Evie slumped against the side of the boat. "Numbers, Sam doesn't have her phone. What are our options?"

"I could see if the car's plates show up on any cameras. Did you manage to get the number?"

"No. The trunk lid was up, so the tags were out of sight."

"If you can send me a picture of Sam, I could link it to facial recognition software. It might take a while, but she might surface that way."

"As much as it pains me to say, I don't think Sam will be out in public anytime soon."

"Penny will be back any minute now," said Numbers. "I could check with her and see if English has anything here that could help?"

"Do it." Evie swallowed and blinked quickly to wash away tears. "Call me as soon as you get something, Numbers."

"Will do, Evie. Stay cool and trust in the team. I'm due to check in with them soon. You know the guys have a way of coming through."

Evie disconnected the call and clambered aboard the boat.

Carina followed. "This situation sucks," she said. "Listen, I have nothing to do and all day to do it and, since this is kind of my fault, though not intentionally I hasten to add, I'll tag along and try to help out."

"It's appreciated," said Evie, "and I'm sorry for the accusations."

Carina nodded as Evie gunned the boat's engine then switched it off again.

"No idea why I did that. Not much point in moving." She

dropped onto a seat and put her head in her hands. "Sam's useless in a stressful situation. She'll go mental if she smudges her make up. And she's in the wind, in the company of bad guys, and we have no way to find her."

Carina sat on the opposite seat and stared at the floor-boards. "Hate that you guys got dragged into this. Talk about wrong place and wrong time."

They sat in silence while Evie willed the phone to ring.

Carina clasped her hands together and then shuffled upright. "Okay. Well, since we're here with not much to do, I suppose I'd better tell you what I saw."

———

English shouldered heavily through the hotel entrance and staggered into a glossy-tiled foyer with Macca trailing a few feet behind.

Before the door whispered closed, the concierge behind reception looked up. Her eyes widened before Macca threw an arm around his colleague, beamed his widest smile, and pretended to hold him upright.

"Sorry about this. I swear he'll be no trouble. Just need to get him to our room." One-handed, he fished a credit card from his pocket and wafted the back of it toward reception.

"Checked in first thing. Second floor. He's got a conference tomorrow. Key speaker. He's ultra-nervous and had a glass too many, but I reckon he'll be okay. Early start, though, so I'd better get him to bed. Say a prayer for him, would you, and hope he wakes with a clear head."

The receptionist opened her mouth to voice a protest, but the phone rang and, instead, she picked up the receiver and waved them forward.

Macca steered English around the corner and pointed to the elevators. "Third floor, then to the left once we get up there. There's a fire alarm on every level, so we should get in position and pull it once we know we have the right room."

"Agreed," said English. "And 'conference'? Where the hell did that come from?"

"Hey, come on," said Macca, "you cannae tell me you weren't convinced. I should get an Oscar for that performance. At least a nomination. Pacino would be jealous."

English shook his head and pushed an arrowed button to summon the elevator.

The two men stared at the carpet, aware of a camera mounted in the ceiling to their right.

"I don't know why we're trying to hide our faces," said English, "they'll have clocked us every step of the way. And, like Sarge said, there's plenty worse on tape around here. Chances are, it's not going to get any better, either."

"I get the impression Sarge doesn't like the darker side of our work, but his eyes show too much experience for him to be a pacifist. He's been places and done things that a regular guy hasn't."

"Maybe," said English, "but Sarge found God. I'm not sure why, or what happened, but he'd be happier if we can avoid killing."

Macca shrugged as the display over the elevator door began to count down from six. "Can't say that I'm comfortable with it, either but, push comes to shove, and it's him or me? He's punching the clock. Every time."

"Agreed," said English, "but we can at least try. Sarge is a good man and, if needed, he'll step up and do what needs to be done. He'd just prefer not to."

A bell pinged, and the elevator doors slid open.

English caught a glimpse of himself reflected off the

mirrored back wall of the small space. Five o'clock stubble shrouded his face in shadow and gave him a ninja-like appearance. The flashing red light in the corner of the elevator ruined the image.

They stepped inside and pushed the button for the third floor.

Macca nodded his approval as the car reached floor three in an instant. "Nice lift. Never even felt it move."

The doors opened onto plush red carpet dotted with a random pattern.

"Jeez, you could kill a man on this floor and CSI would never know. The cleaning service must go home with a pounding migraine."

A brass plaque on the facing wall had an arrow pointed left and stated that rooms twenty-one to thirty lay that way.

English stepped out first.

"Okay, it's along here," he whispered, "second door from the end. I'll go see if I can hear anything. You find the alarm panel. It's probably just inside the stairwell at the end of the corridor."

Macca gave a thumbs up, brushed past him and sauntered along the corridor. English followed and stopped at door twenty-eight as Macca disappeared through the last door and into the stairwell.

He pressed his ear to the wood and heard nothing until the stairwell door hissed open and Macca reappeared.

"Got it," he whispered. "Say when."

English joined him. "No clue if our guys are in there, can't hear a thing. Not even a TV. I guess there's only one way to find out."

"On it," said Macca as he ducked out of sight.

For a moment, the silence remained until the shrill scream of the fire alarm shrieked along the corridor. Macca followed

English back to the elevators and watched around the corner until the door to room twenty-eight opened and a man stepped out with a gym bag. Once he disappeared into the stairwell, they weaved past rushing people and made their way back to the room.

Chapter Eleven

Sam cursed as the car hit a sudden dip in the road and the spare wheel bucked and punched an instant bruise into her thigh.

As the trunk lid had closed, plunging her into total darkness, her first thought was that she felt naked without her purse, and assumed it was still beneath the driver's seat, where she'd shoved it as the bad guys strolled into the garage.

After a hasty 'thanks', the phone thief made short time of leaving her alone, ducking out of sight behind the garage doors seconds before the men reappeared.

The engine roared and the car rolled over bumpy ground, and her second thought was that there was nothing in her purse that would help her right now, anyway.

So think like Evie. What could help?

The bumping stopped and the noise level dropped as the car turned onto smooth road. Thumps of heavy bass vibrated against the rear seats as someone up front turned on the radio. Sam fumbled around the tight space but felt nothing but the vicious circular imprint of the spare tire.

Kids locked themselves in trunks all the time. Didn't the manufacturers make something foolproof to allow them to escape? A fluorescent handle to operate a manual release?

She scrambled around the trunk lid but, other than a faint red glow where the plastic from the brake lights hugged the watertight metal body of the car, the trunk was jet black. A blind person would see the same things.

Sam took a deep breath and thought again of Evie. What would Evie do in this situation?

For one, she'd tear open the trunk and kick some bad guy ass. At this moment, she couldn't do that.

Then, for two, take pictures of said bad guys, bloodied and battered, and share them all over social media. Except her purse was in the front of the car beneath the passenger seat and, even then, her phone wasn't in it. Thief lady had taken care of that.

Three, chipped nail varnish wouldn't be a concern or even, heaven forbid, a broken nail, and she'd tear the shit out of her surroundings to find a way out. Okay. That was an option.

Sam chewed her bottom lip and started at the bottom of the trunk lid where its edge met the car body. She slid her fingertips along the material. It felt surprisingly smooth for durable fabric, and she reached the glow of the brake light with no bumps or interruption to the cloth.

Then, she moved down to where the rear of the trunk met the floor and found a crack. She rolled back as far as she could and wedged her fingers beneath the base. Her acrylic finger-nails bent and flexed but held and, with a grunt, she managed to lever it up and against her body. Beneath it, her fingers felt the imprint of the solid rubber tire of the spare wheel, the source of the dull ache in her leg.

She took a deeper breath when she remembered a movie that she and Daryl watched, where the hero reached into the wheel-well, grabbed the metal bar thing that took the wheels off, and saved the day with a lot of swinging and clanging.

What did they call that thing, a tire lever? Sam squeezed her eyes closed to contain a flood of frustrated tears. Daryl would know.

In a few hours from now, he'd panic and call her phone. When she didn't answer, he'd call Evie.

It wasn't a tire lever. What the hell was it? She gave herself the faintest slap across the cheek. Why did it matter? Who gives a shit about its name? Just grab the damned thing and be ready to inflict as much Evie-type damage as possible on whoever was closest when the trunk lid lifted.

She felt a rush of pride as she ran her hand across the spare wheel and found a loose nut that barely held it in place. The tire iron, that was its name, was normally secured beneath the wheel itself. All she had to do was unscrew the nut, lift the spare wheel, and grab hold of the iron.

Then, she could unleash all kinds of retribution as soon as she saw daylight.

Initially, the nut wouldn't budge, held in place by a sharp layer of rust, but after a two-handed effort that resulted in a broken nail and a sob, it gave and twisted for what seemed like a thousand turns until it fell free and dropped inside the wheel.

Another nail snapped as she lifted the wheel and scrambled around inside the cold, metal well until she found the tire iron recessed into a foam base. She fumbled it loose and placed it behind her, before dropping the trunk mat back into place.

Sam patted her eyes dry with the back of her hands and imagined the filth that must be all over them. By now, she probably resembled a panda.

The car continued at a steady speed, with the constant, jarring rumble interrupted by an occasional bump in the road.

Each time the car jerked, a brief flash of daylight flared around one of the lights and lit up the trunk.

She leaned closer and felt around the rough edges. To one side, her fingertips rubbed across a slight seam and traced the shape of a plastic panel. In the corner, against the beginnings of a wheel arch, she finally found the latch that opened it.

Daylight flooded her tiny prison, and tears flowed again.

In the light, she followed a cluster of wires that fed into the light space from somewhere beneath the floor. Beyond them was another section that held a few bulbs. With a pinch, the bulb section came away to reveal the flimsy-looking red plastic that gave the clear bulbs color on the outside each time the brake pedal was pressed.

Every bump opened a tiny crack that flared like a light-house beacon around the light fixture.

Sam took the tire iron, braced herself, and slammed it into the plastic to the rhythm of the radio's music.

———

"Counterfeit money," said Carina.

Evie leaned back against the boat's wheel. "You saw counterfeit money, and now the bad guys want to kill you? Seems a bit extreme unless you saw where they locked their billion-dollar stash and you stole the only key."

Carina slid along the plastic seat and stopped beside her. "Did you know that US bills are the easiest form of currency to forge?"

"What is this, a game show?" said Evie, "No, although if I'd known there'd be a test, I'd have studied harder. That doesn't surprise me, but if there's a point anywhere near, could you please get to it?"

"I need to give you a little background to put things in perspective, so bear with me."

Evie sighed and nodded. "Sorry. I'm a little tense."

Carina didn't skip a beat. "The reason they're easy to forge is that they don't print US bills on polymer, like most currency. In the grand scheme of things, printing on paper is easy as long as you have the correct ink—"

"And the right printer?" interrupted Evie.

"Kind of. They use plates to print counterfeit money. It's not done by a group of spotty interns, sitting in an office, sending files to an inkjet printer from Best Buy. It's a huge concern. Very professional. The process is called offset printing, and it not only needs the correct ink, but heavy machinery and very, very precisely produced printing plates."

"Okay," said Evie, "I'm on the hook. Reel me in. What are printing plates?"

For the first time, Carina smiled. "Glad you asked. They're usually made from aluminum, since it's easier to manipulate, and contain a mirror image of the image you want to print. They're the most important part of a complicated process that goes into printing the actual bills, since they have the image of the president you're used to seeing. And, since you see Benjamin every day, you'd spot a dodgy portrait from a mile away."

"And you saw the process?" said Evie. "Don't tell me, it's a mafia thing, and now the dons are after you to shut you up?"

"Nice imagination," said Carina, "but no. They're nasty people, without a doubt, but I won't find a horse's head in my bed, hopefully. Imagine having a few hundred thousand in counterfeit bills hanging around . . ."

"I could cope with that."

"Yes, but you've got to get rid of them in bulk. Even at a basic level, there are pens that highlight forgeries. And, sure, you could launder them, but you'd need either a legitimate business to pass them through, or other people, professional people, to do it for you. So imagine that, instead of sitting on piles of fake cash, you had the key to the process of producing as much of it as you'd like, when you liked. Why mess about with something like this street level stuff? Too risky for the big guys. Own the means to print your own to order. And then, imagine you were holding those means to ransom to some very nasty people to get them to up their already extortionate bid for them."

"That's a lot of greedy, big, prominent, very nasty people in one scenario. I'm not sure I'd like to be a part of that."

"In the real world, you wouldn't," said Carina, "not in a heartbeat. Unfortunately, thanks to this crazy mix up, you are."

Evie shivered and rubbed the goosebumps from her arms. "Okay, now you have my undivided attention. Go on."

"A gang in Pittsburgh stole a complete set of plates that could produce an unlimited amount of twenty-dollar bills and has them hidden. Another gang in New York, the one they were intended for, is tearing buildings and families apart to find them, and is killing people for the location."

"That's bad business," said Evie.

"That's big business," said Carina, "and the thing that makes it scary is that the gang members who knew where they were all died in a shootout."

"And you're not talking about the gangs, are you?"

"No. The plates. And the thing that makes it nothing short of terrifying for us?" Carina paused to let her question sink in.

Against her will and dreading her next words, Evie felt herself lean forward in anticipation, until Carina finished.

"I'm the only person who knows where the plates are. And the big guys know that I know."

———

Macca shouted over the sound of an alarm that bounced around the walls of the long corridor as they strolled back to the room.

"Don't you think it's strange that only one bloke came out? I know Sarge did a great job on the other guy, but we should assume that the healthy fella has at least a few morals. Injured comrades and all, I know we'd never leave a man behind. So where is he? Still here?"

English shrugged as they stopped at the door to room twenty-eight. He fiddled inside his jacket and pulled out a fountain pen.

"No clue, but I guess there's only one way to find out."

English pulled a cap off the pen and bent to look beneath the door handle.

"What's that for? Are you going to write them to death?" said Macca.

"You know those key cards they give you in hotels? They're nothing but a magnetic strip on a piece of plastic. The door reads the strip and, if it likes what it reads, it'll let you in. If it doesn't, you don't get to see that sexy green light that says, 'Come on in, boys'."

"I hop between bedsits," said Macca. "I rarely get the luxury of a decent hotel room. Shit, I rarely get the luxury of a decent mattress. Right now, I'm in a penthouse."

"Well, this is a magnetic scrambler. It might look like an old school pen, but it's a Jack of all trades where access is concerned. If I click this tiny button like this . . ." English pushed the pen into a slot beneath the handle and pressed a small nib on its side. The light on the door handle flashed green. ". . . it confuses the reader enough to open the door." He pushed down on the handle and nudged open the door.

"Abracadabra. Let's see if our resident nutjobs stole the bathrobes."

The glow from the outside sign bled around the thick curtain edges enough to light up most of the room. The space inside looked like any other hotel room; a bed split into two halves, a basic TV, the curtains, which were heavy enough to block out a solar blast, and enough furniture to hold pocket change, the TV remote, and a bundle of travel leaflets.

Other than the remote, nothing stood out in the room but a hump, hidden under the sheets at the far end of the bed.

Macca peeled away into the bathroom, returned, and mouthed "Clear."

"No point whispering, here's our other guy," said English as he pulled back the bed covers. A battered face, already pale with the lack of pumping blood, lay against a blood-smeared pillow.

"Remind me to not piss off Sarge," said Macca. "Stupid question, but I'm assuming no sign of life?"

English rested his hand against the sheets to lean closer, then shook his head.

"He's gone. No chest rise, and nothing from his airways. I could check his eyes, but I hate touching eyes. I reckon they'll be either stone-cold blank or bloodshot."

"So Sarge sorted him good and proper at the pub, or our guy doesn't want any baggage and finished off business himself. Since we know this guy at least staggered from the pub, I'm going with our guy's a vicious bastard. Cold, but it fits the skill set of the guys in my life, lately."

"Then, you should definitely steer clear of dating apps, mate," said English.

Macca grimaced. "Don't tell the wife. So now what? We're no closer to finding out who's who or what's going on."

"They're clearly professional, but we should still toss the room on the off chance they left something."

"That should take all of two minutes, my toilet's bigger." Macca pulled a tissue from the bathroom and used it to open the closet door. He strained to look inside. "Empty. Room safe's open and cleaned out, too. Here, take this. No fingerprints."

While Macca wandered into the bathroom, English took the tissue and opened and closed each drawer in order. "Same here. And it's a solid ceiling, so that's out. Come and support our flat-nosed friend while I check under the mattress and pillows."

"Bathroom's clear, too," said Macca as he braced the corpse.

After a thorough search, Macca gestured 'all clear' through the curtains while English wiped down the door handle.

"Dead end. Other than a mountain of empty cigarette packets in the bin, they've kept a clean site. Sorry, mate. Let's join the others and take it from there. Hopefully, they've tagged the other guy."

———

Hidden across the road, Sarge and Marbles watched a steady stream of people thread through the doors of the hotel entrance and gather at a designated area in the parking lot. Some were fully dressed, while others stood and clutched at bathrobes that glowed in the dull light.

"No sign of our guy," said Sarge, "from either the main entrance or the side fire escape." He raised his gaze and studied the shadows that danced through a crack in the hotel room curtains. "But I see movement upstairs. Someone's definitely in the room."

"Let's hope it's our boys, then," said Marbles. "Benefit of the doubt, though, we'd better get prepped for action. They'll either deal with the bad guys themselves, or they'll send them our way. I know you don't like it, but we should be ready to do bad things."

"I can do justified bad things," said Sarge with a firm nod.

The hotel room curtains parted long enough to show Macca's face. After a shake of the head, he disappeared again.

"They're not in there."

He glanced sideways and saw Dud leaning against a bus stop farther down the road. The position offered a perfect view of the small fire door built into the other side wall of the hotel. A small wave got Dud's attention, and Sarge relayed the message. Dud nodded, then dropped his head and pointed discreetly to the side of the building.

Moments later, a dark-clad figure paced across the lawn, ducked into shadows and strolled at speed toward the town lights.

Dud pushed himself off the bus stop and followed.

Sarge nudged Marbles. "There's our guy. He's on the move."

"He's motoring," said Marbles. "We'd better get after him. Still, where's your buddy?"

"I left him in a pretty bad way. Hopefully, his colleague radioed for help and left him in the room."

English and Macca pushed through the fire escape and joined them in the road as the guy crossed a street, picked up his pace, and rounded the far corner out of sight.

"We're losing him," said Sarge.

Dud broke into a jog.

Chapter Twelve

Marte Dahl leaned against a lab bench and watched Anneka Ergström fan out a matchbook of lemon-yellow paper slips. Her fingers slid across each perforated piece with a smooth grace that tied a knot in Dahl's stomach.

"It's like a litmus test."

Damn this woman.

The room swayed a fraction of an inch as a strong gust lashed water against the thick glass windows. Dahl moved closer to rest on the opposite bench

"Talk to me like I'm a first-year student. Layman's terms."

Ergström held back an impatient sigh that still managed to crease her lips.

Dahl smiled. Ergström's levels of experience and knowledge were much lower, and she knew it, but it was good to retain power. Employees needed to know their place.

Ergström tipped her head then swallowed hard and continued. "Very well. You know how people use litmus paper to determine whether a substance is an acid or an alkaline?"

"Blue and red," said Dahl.

"Yes, red reads acidic, blue reads alkaline. Obviously, in testing blood samples, it would be inconvenient if one of the results was red, because blood is…"

"Red. Yes, I'm aware of that. Okay, maybe continue to explain but not in total layman's terms. We'll be here all day and I'm already getting hungry."

Ergström batted her eyelashes, a familiar tell that her composure was faltering. "Sorry. We've managed to perfect the readings for the common blood groups, especially both O- and A-positive, the strip turns a clear color, but we're really struggling to get a result with AB-negative. The research is valid and holds up against all arguments, but we just can't seem to identify AB-negative blood with the strips. Regardless of chemical composition, the paper won't change. We're missing something."

Dahl pushed off the bench and wandered slowly across the lab to stop behind Ergström's shoulder.

"And would that be down to the chemical coding of the strip, its production quality, or . . ."

Dahl paused and soaked in the tension that flowed from Ergström like a scalding summer breeze.

". . . the fact that we simply haven't managed to find a test to identify that blood group yet?" Ergström tried to hide the tiniest of shudders.

"I suspect Option C, I'm afraid. The combination of protein and antigens in AB-negative blood is significantly more complicated than in any of the others. And the raw product is so rare that we can't get it in the quantities we need to really get to work on it. We've cracked the others but, so far, everything we try with this group falls short."

"So far," said Dahl. "And it's the one we want the most. Rare is always good. Elusive and expensive. Always remember, nothing good ever came easy."

Ergström nodded as Dahl continued. "The O- and A-positive strips have meant that we can identify donors for those blood types immediately. Our Chinese supplier has found them invaluable. The demand for AB-negative organs will never be as high but when the time comes and, at some point it will, finding a suitable donor is time sensitive since they're in such short supply. Our storage solutions do mean that we're able to transport organs over greater distances without loss of integrity, but too much time is lost looking for the organs in the first place. A small nick and swab with a paper strip would be so convenient to avoid having to test multiple donors and could potentially save life after life."

"I couldn't agree more," said Ergström. "As much as I know about breaking down DNA and proteins, perhaps it's time to bring in outside help. Someone with a specific specialty."

Dahl sauntered to the window and looked out over the expanse of water. Waves rolled and crashed against the side of the structure, sending fishtails of spray into the air. A small dot floated along the line where the sea met the sky, its movement so slow that it was barely perceptible.

Up close, the cruiser would be as tall as ten bi-level houses. From here it was a pinhead rolling along a countertop.

"There's a reason that we are where we are. And size does matter. We keep our team small to keep our findings close. You and I, a few technicians and a basic security team. Plus, you know that I don't enjoy company. Not here. Still, we need to make progress. Do you have someone in mind?"

Ergström shifted her feet and blinked again. Dahl rarely asked for advice and the request threw her.

She thought for a moment and, put on the spot, drew a blank. "A specialist," she laughed.

Dahl smiled back. "Is that all? You know that our funding allows us to approach anyone."

"You know that circle better than me," said Ergström. "I would trust your judgement."

"Very well. I will give it some thought and put out some feelers."

"Thank you."

"And that would push us through this roadblock?"

Ergström wrung her hands.

Dahl waited and soaked in the moment of discomfort.

"With the right person, I'm sure. We are also running low on certain supplies, but I'm aware that they're hard to come by."

"Such as?"

"Critically, AB-negative blood."

"I can get that. How much do you need?"

"To be able to relax testing and take chances? Lots of it."

Dahl laughed and sauntered toward the door. "I can't guarantee lots of it, but let me make some calls. As they say, I do know a man. A few, actually. I did say that I'd keep you happy out here, didn't I?"

The door opened with a whisper as Ergström flushed.

"Leave it with me."

———

"So now what?"

Evie raked shaking fingers through her hair, then clenched her fists in frustration.

"You're on the run from serious, death-dealing gangsters, and my sister is holed up in the bad guys' trunk. They think they have you, and we have no idea where they are."

Carina nodded. "That's pretty much it."

"And when they get to wherever they're going and open the trunk, they're probably going to do nasty things to her. Even though they know she's not you, they might still think that she knows something about these plates. Or where you are."

Carina nodded again. "I'm so sorry, Evie. If only she had her phone."

"But she doesn't, does she?" snapped Evie. "You have it."

At the sight of Carina's wide eyes, Evie stood and paced the boat. She turned her back while she dabbed her eyes. "Carina, I'm sorry. Again. I know it was a genuine mix-up, I get that. I'm just not used to feeling helpless."

"Come on, we have our phones. Other than the dishes, they can do everything now. There must be something we can do, a radar or car tracker or something. Ring that guy again. He seemed pretty switched on. Maybe he'll look at it from a fresh angle."

Evie shrugged. "It can't hurt. Hang on."

Numbers answered immediately. She couldn't help but smile at the warm wash of comfort that the sound of his voice spread through her.

Evie pressed the speakerphone button. "Numbers. Anything?"

"Sorry, Evie. Without something to latch on to, it doesn't matter how many programs we have access to; none of them work without something to look for. Think back. Did you see anything that could help, no matter how trivial it may seem?"

She stared at the boat's wooden floor and replayed the previous events. With the other boat now moored, that was useless. There were no identifying marks or names at the garage area and, since the guys had moved so quickly, she'd barely seen their faces. In fact, all she'd done was swept her phone's camera around a corner to record a useless video of a crude chop shop.

"Nothing. I took a stupid video so I could see into a room, but the car's tags were hidden."

"Play it again," said Numbers, "and double check to see if there's anything, even the smallest thing, that we could use. Penny's back now, she knows a lot more about English's programs."

"All right," shrugged Evie. "For what it's worth."

She shuffled next to Carina and hit play.

The image started at the edge of the door and swept along a side wall of rusting, corrugated metal, over tool boxes and a ramp, then past a corner and over a workbench that glinted with welding equipment and a Budweiser sign, then across the side of the car, its open doors, raised trunk, and tinted windows and, finally, the other side of the entrance door.

"No. Still nothing."

"Play it again," said Carina. "I think I spotted something."

Evie hit play once more and watched the shaky image until it reached the bench.

"Pause." Carina pointed to the screen. "Can you enlarge it? Look above the workbench, I'm sure that Budweiser sign's a mirror. Check it out."

Evie squinted at the screen and parted two fingers to stretch the picture.

"Well, I'll be damned."

Below the scratchy color of the car's hood, and lower, beneath a gleaming silver grille, a small band of yellow, bordered in black, reflected in the mirror.

"Carina, you're a genius."

"True," said Carina. "Just because we don't have tags on the front of our cars in Kentucky doesn't mean that other states don't, either. New York requires all of its vehicles to display them front and back."

Evie studied the screen again. "Except it's too blurry. I can't make out the letters or numbers."

"Send me the video," said Penny, "and I can run it through an image enhancement program."

Penny read out her cell phone number, and Evie keyed it in then sat back to wait. She pressed a hand to her stomach to calm the swarming butterflies and turned to Carina.

"Looks like you're already paying back your debt."

"I wasn't aware I had a debt, but I'm here to help. This isn't your fault, but it's not entirely mine, either. Please, remember that."

"I know," said Evie. "Let me know when you get tired of hearing me apologize."

"Hate to break up the bonding session," said Penny, "but I've got the image. That's it cleaned up. Now, all I need to do is flip it..."

The line went silent as Evie crossed her fingers.

"...and there we have it. A nice, shiny New York tag. Okay, hang on a sec. Numbers, if you click that bar right there, it'll open a tracking program."

"Got it," said Numbers.

"Okay, switch places."

"You guys are a well-oiled machine," said Evie.

"We're getting more and more practice," said Numbers. "I'm thinking of changing my name."

"Don't you dare. I've only just got used to the ones I know."

"I've inputted the tags," said Penny. "Now to mobilize cameras, but you may have to be patient. It'll slow down the program, but I'll utilize everything available. Let's hope our bad guys aren't paranoid or camera shy."

Evie heard the keypresses through the phone's speaker. "I can't thank you enough for this, guys. If anything happened to Sam, I'd never forgive myself."

"Don't mention it," said Penny. "If I've learned anything being married to a military man, it's that we look after our own. Some would say we don't really have a choice."

"But that's another conversation," said Numbers. "When we find them, and we will, what's the plan, Evie?"

"I've only got a plan A, to get in front of them. After that, we'll see what opportunities present themselves."

"Well, that chance might come sooner than we thought," said Penny. "Our bad guys are not shy at all. I've already picked them up on a traffic cam heading east on I-80. Get after them, team. And, Evie, please consider calling law enforcement. As much as I wouldn't like to cross you, you could be in way over your head."

"I'll consider it," said Evie, "when the time comes. Right now, this is close and personal. So I guess the next thing we need to do is obtain a vehicle."

"And, when you say obtain you mean steal, right?" said Carina. "Like what you accused me of?"

Numbers piped up over the speaker. "Cool your jets, girls. You don't need a car. You have a boat. How's the fuel looking?"

"It's pretty much full," said Evie, "but, last time I checked, they really don't like it when you drive a boat down I-80."

"Tut tut," said Numbers. "O' Ye of little faith. Don't forget I've traveled, Evie. The river network you're on will take you from there to New York, and with no lights or traffic stops. There's no chatter from the guys, so it seems like they have everything under control in Scotland. We can monitor the car's progress and guide you at the same time. If your fuel lasts, you can get there by boat. And, if the car deviates or stops, you can find a slip and tie off and, er, obtain a vehicle."

"Love you, guys," said Evie.

The boat started with a chug and belch of smoke, and then the engine settled into a steady purr as Evie tipped back her head and shouted.

"Hang tight, Sam. We're coming for you."

She glanced at the expanse of water through the boat's small windscreen.

"Okay," she said. "Numbers? Lead the way."

———

Macca pulled up a mental map of the area as the guy disappeared around a corner.

Small cut-throughs and alleyways riddled the medieval old town, most dating back to the eighteen-hundreds, and provided short cuts to and from the main streets. A lifetime of trawling them, both sober and drunk, gave him extensive knowledge of their layout.

The guy had turned onto North Meadow Walk, a sprawling road that bordered a green area of lawns and walkways.

During the day, the area bustled with tourists and visitors. Locals played sport on the courts by the tennis club, kids laughed and screamed at the play park, watched by attentive parents, and students from the local universities wandered the lawns, oblivious to the scenery with books in hand.

Tonight, it would be deserted, with plenty of secluded areas and tree-lined walks to hide amongst.

A nightmare area to search.

Their quarry had either done his research or had just got lucky.

"Keep following, guys. I'm going to get ahead of him and try to cut him off. If we fall too far behind, the chase is over."

Before anyone could respond, Macca ducked into an alley and broke into a sprint.

Adrenaline coursed through him. A potential link to Knowles' death walked just feet away on a parallel street. As good as it was to have help, the idea of bringing down the guy personally added extra fuel to Macca's pumping legs.

Familiar pubs, coffee shops, and the odd neck-craning tourist passed in a blur until he reached the first corner, paused, and chanced a peek into the next street. With the coast clear, he took a left and jogged to the next corner that turned onto North Meadow Walk and stopped at the sound of fast, padding footsteps.

The timing was perfect.

Moments later, the overhead lights of the tennis club cast a bouncing shadow that danced on the sidewalk.

He tensed and waited as it grew larger.

Chapter Thirteen

At the sound of the fire alarm, Cox barked a cynical laugh, lit a cigarette, and blew smoke at the small alarm that flashed a reassuring green light in the corner of the room.

"Deal with that, bitch."

The light quickly switched to a blinking angry red as his smoky breath covered it, and the unit issued a shrill beep that blended into the noise outside.

He keyed a code into the wall safe and took out two pistols and a bundle of fake passports.

Hudson lay silent and calm under the bedsheets, arms relaxed at his sides. Blood had finally congealed and blocked his nostrils. He didn't need those anymore.

Cox slapped shut the laptop, pulled the cable, and shoved it all into a padded backpack.

He paused for a second then tore a piece of clear tape from a roll in the bag, part of Hudson's 'back-up plan' supplies, pressed it to his deceased colleague's thumb, then stuck it to the back of the hotel key card and slipped it into his pocket.

He patted the bedclothes. "Sorry, but no hard feelings, dude. Hope you'd have done the same for me. Trust me, I'll finish the job and I'll be sure he hears your name before he punches out. This won't all be for nothing, I promise."

After a quick check of the rooms, he swung the pack over his shoulder and stepped into the corridor.

Doors buzzed open and clicked shut as people followed directions like lemmings. Cox paused to consider the human mentality; the first sound of an alarm, and all common sense went out the window.

Every man for himself and fuck the others. So much for Christian values and looking out for your fellow man.

Standard procedure locked down the elevators in the event of a fire, so he moved into the stairwell, took the steps two at a time, and landed at the fire exit that opened at the side of the building.

With a quick sweep of the outside area, he patted the pistol in his back pocket for comfort, barged open the door, and stepped from the hotel warmth into the cool night.

As the door slipped shut behind him, he took in his surroundings.

A grass lawn led to a decent-sized street that would lead into the maze of the city. A lone guy slumped at a bus stop across the road, head bowed, probably drunk or drugged. Nothing else.

This was as good a time as ever. Retreat, regroup, find a new place, and come up with a new strategy.

The powers that be didn't seem to care, and there would be no reinforcements or additional firepower sent to tackle the problem. They paid their money and expected results. That was the job.

Cox hitched the backpack between his shoulders and strode out onto the lawn.

Edinburgh was a beautiful city but, in the current situation, it might as well have been Afghanistan. Danger. Decisions. Cause and effect.

As he pushed off from the door, a vivid memory broke through his concentration.

A unit of eight, torn apart by a lucky rocket launcher strike that took out six of his men. Cox and the other survivor, Perry, dragged themselves in a snail trail of blood, to the roadside and radioed for help.

When the radio crackled a garbled reply of static, Cox pulled Perry by his blood-soaked shirt along a dusty side road to a small town and tried again.

This time, the signal connected.

Cox and Perry made it back to a US base in a whir of dust and Blackhawk helicopter blades.

Cox received a commendation.

Months later, the military cut back and released him, and he sold his commendation on eBay to cover two month's rent.

He snapped back to the present.

To his left, a swathe of green lay dormant and quiet. Tennis courts washed a deeper green in the overhead glare of sodium lights, and he dipped into the sides of the path to try to find security in the shadows.

The lights lit up everything, and Cox regretted leaving the hotel. Three in the morning was designated as the best time to move. Most people slept deeply by then and the streets would be deserted. Nothing about but emergency services and people with something to hide.

The sensible option would have been to join the crowd in the parking lot and wait until the alarm ran its course. Safety in numbers. Or the reluctance of others to open fire into a group of innocent civilians.

But then, a cursory search of the room would have revealed a dead guy in the bed. And questions.

He looked back to see the bus shelter empty, the lone drunk missing, and the road ahead lit up like a party. Drunks couldn't move that fast and no buses drove by.

He broke into a sprint. Ignoring the jarring bounce of the backpack, he planted one foot after the other onto smooth concrete and moved steadily to the safety of the city and its maze of streets.

He barely noticed as he reached a street corner at full pace when a thick, outstretched arm shot out, locked, and caught him just beneath the chin.

There was a split second where he considered a formula from college, something about a fast-moving object meeting a solid obstruction.

At pace, the arm might as well have been a steel bar.

His throat flattened under the impact.

His airway closed with a grunt and the lights grew brighter. Then, he was airborne, and he had a millisecond to curse his carelessness before his skull cracked against the ground and all the lights went out.

———

Sam rolled forward and peered through the hole she'd created in the rear light cluster.

A two-lane road stretched out into darkness. The flashes of light that flared through the plastic earlier were gone, along with any remaining sunlight. At intervals, two tiny pinpricks rose and fell in the far distance, a lone vehicle that shared the road.

Other than that, barring any cars in front, they seemed to be alone.

The spare wheel dug into the small of her back as Sam rocked back and tried to stretch. A painful calf cramp had stopped her light-smashing progress at one point, just as the plastic began to crack, and she cried out and pulled her toes as hard as she could to relieve the pain.

It wouldn't do to have her body seize; when the time came, she'd need to be awake, alert and ready to move.

And while she enjoyed the earlier food court stop with Evie, now the pressure of a large caramel macchiato, combined with two morning cups of coffee, pushed against the walls of her bladder.

Time no longer had meaning. With a clock on her phone, Sam quit wearing watches years ago. How long had they been driving? Where were they going, and how long would it take to get there?

For a while, she counted songs. Daryl said that radio songs were around three and a half minutes long. Rounded up to five, since that was easier to count and to allow for DJ chat and commercials, twelve songs equaled roughly an hour. Somewhere in the early twenties, the cramp kicked in and, in the distraction, she lost count. Still, that was at least two hours.

She kicked against the side of the trunk. Damn that phone. If not for that, she'd be home now, snuggled on the sofa next to Daryl with a glass of wine, watching a good reality show. Tears teased the corners of her eyes again, and she bit hard on her tongue and willed them to stay put.

Be strong. Be Evie.

She felt a shoulder gently pop as she reached and stretched her arms behind her. Her fingers slid up the smooth fabric at the back of the rear seats and then brushed against hard plastic, the release lever to drop the seats.

Her stomach somersaulted as she rolled to face them. With no light bleeding through the cracked plastic cluster, she traced the outline. Only part of the lever was in the trunk. The rest disappeared behind the hard edge of the parcel shelf but, with a grimace and a firm push, Sam managed to force her fingers between the edges to grasp the tip of the lever.

As she prepared to pull, a wash of green light spilled into the trunk space and the car rolled to a halt.

The music stopped, the engine died, and the car bounced and then lifted on one side as the driver climbed out.

———

Evie rested one arm against the side of the cabin and gripped the ship's wheel with the other.

"Since it looks like we're stuck together for the time being, tell me a bit about you."

Carina sat in a small seat to the side and gazed out over the water. Wind whipped her hair back to show a clear face with the beginnings of crow's feet forming at the eyes.

"There's not much to tell, to be honest. Approaching middle age, divorced, no children and no pets. Shit, I sound lonely."

"You must have something. And what do you do, you know, when you're not in a boat chasing bad guys?"

"I have a nice enough house in Kentucky, mostly paid for thanks to the divorce. And, unfortunately, I seem to have too many phones."

Evie managed a tight smile.

"And I'm currently between jobs. I worked as a corporate trainer for a utility company, but I must have done too good a job. They're content with the standard of their employees now and so disbanded the training division. Bastards."

"Ironic," said Evie. "Still, they must need someone to take care of new recruits?"

"Yep, department managers now have that duty added to their job description."

"Shame. That must affect their roles, too, surely?"

"Absolutely, but utility companies are pretty much monopolies. They don't care about service as long as the dollars keep rolling in. Enough about me and boring work talk, what about you? What's your story? If you don't mind me saying, you seem to be very hands on. You didn't bat an eyelid hot-wiring this boat."

Evie turned the wheel to steer the boat around a gentle curve. Now and then, lights from the highway appeared to the sides but, with little light on the river, she maintained a steady speed and watched the way ahead closely. It wouldn't do to hit a small fishing boat. Loss of life would be awful. The loss of their boat would be catastrophic.

"Didn't have a choice. And it's only a small boat. Believe it or not, but I know exactly what Sam is going through. We've just come back from a vacation in Jamaica…"

"I've always wanted to go there," said Carina.

"…where I was abducted."

"But not there. Jesus, what is your family, a trouble magnet?"

"We've had better times, for sure. My husband was a military man. What am I saying? He'll always be a military man. I'm hoping these bad guys aren't as bad as the bad guys I've already come across, if that makes sense."

Carina nodded. "Barely."

"I've come across some pretty awful bad guys and barely got out with my life. And a lot of other people died."

Carina turned in the seat. "How come I didn't see this in the news? It sounds like international headline stuff."

"It was, without a doubt, but the ones who died were high profile people who the local government wanted gone for a long time. My husband and some of his friends helped to make that happen then removed all trace of their being there. I'm sure the authorities had great pleasure in just rolling in and dealing with the clean-up."

"And you were involved in this?"

"Yes."

Carina smiled. "I feel better already."

"You'd feel better still if my husband and his friends were here to help us."

"If they can help, why don't you call them?"

"Can't. They're in Scotland, helping another friend. Something to do with a sniper."

"Okay, I'm quickly learning to just listen and not to ask too many questions," said Carina, "although I can't help feeling like I've landed in the middle of an *A-Team* episode."

Evie banked the boat to take a bend in the other direction. "Something like that. The good news is we have Penny and Numbers on the end of the phone."

"Numbers?"

"Yep, he's one of Dud's mates. Penny is English's wife."

"And Dud is?"

"My husband."

"And English?"

"Another one of his mates."

"Do any of them have real names?"

"Sure, I think. At least Dud does. I honestly can't comment on the others."

"What, is it bathed in secrecy? Like a 'need to know' type thing? Official Secrets Act?"

"No, it's an 'I don't really know' type thing. I don't know them as well as Dud, but I know they'll lay down their lives for one another. Hence, he's in Scotland. I think Numbers is the oldest of the group, so he doesn't travel or do the hands-on stuff. He manned the phones last time. In English's basement."

Carina rubbed her eyes. "Okay, this is giving me a headache. How about you keep the names to yourself, I just offer my services as best I can, and I'll follow your lead?"

"Can't fault you," said Evie. "Way less complicated."

The girls enjoyed the fleeting scenery for a while until the boat buzzed under a bridge. The phone lit up and rang as it came out the other side.

Evie answered and pressed the speakerphone button.

"Hi, girls, it's Penny."

"The only one with a normal name," said Carina.

"What's going on, Penny?" said Evie. "Everything okay?"

"Not sure. Travel another two miles or so and then pull over to the bank on your left."

"Penny, did they…"

"Yep. They stopped. Not sure if that's good news or bad but, either way, it's time to head inland."

Chapter Fourteen

Cox woke to the musty smell of damp concrete.

The surrounding silence was broken only by the rhythmic pounding of drums that played a powerhouse rock solo at the base of his skull. Each breath forced its way through a bruised windpipe as if it passed over a speedhump. He kept his eyes closed, focused his listening, and waited for the rest of his senses to catch up.

Each wrist and ankle chaffed, probably secured with zip-ties. His lower back throbbed from sitting in a rigid chair for too long. And his feet were cold. His shoes were missing.

He remembered the 'drunk' and the scramble to get to a safer position. Everything after was a blank but, without unwanted and outside help, it took a while for strong muscles to ache and cramp. So how long had he been here?

One of his senses pricked. Was that a breath drawn a few feet away?

Cox fought the urge to swallow, but the dryness and pain at the back of his throat kicked in a reflex and, as the saliva passed through the tight bruising, he flinched.

"Well, there you are, sweetheart. Welcome back."

An English accent. Close.

"Wakey, wakey, bitch. You've been busted."

Cox opened his eyes to see the pub landlord seated before him. Two other men walked into the room behind him.

"Now that you're with us…"

The guy stood, swung a tattooed arm, and crashed a fist into the side of his jaw.

Lights flashed, his aching head hummed and screamed as it snapped sideways, and warmth flowed into his mouth. He swallowed blood and grimaced again.

"…that's for Ken."

Another blow rocked him in the other direction. More pain. More blood.

"And that's for being a bastard."

MacIntyre stepped forward and grabbed his arm.

"He's no good to us asleep, mate. Let me take over."

Cox tried to speak but managed nothing but a dry rasp. He swallowed, grimaced, and tried again as the landlord stepped back. "Don't suppose you guys have any painkillers? I'd kill for some Ibuprofen. Shit, I've killed for less."

MacIntyre dropped into the seat. "Funny. I'm not in the mood to mess around, so let's make this as quick and painless as possible. Simple question first. Who are you?"

Cox smiled and looked around. His tongue brushed against a sticky sheen of blood that coated his teeth. "Where am I? And what is this place? It smells like a library. Feels like we're underground, and you guys don't seem to me to be the intellectual type."

Beige stone formed the walls of a compact room, with the only light coming from a bright orange sconce set into the wall at the side of the opening.

"Ah, I reckon I know where we are. Under the bar, right?"

MacIntyre leaned closer. "Pub. Who are you?"

"Well," said Cox, "I'm not the guy who killed your buddy in the street. Someone beat us to that."

"I know about him, and he's dead. Unless you want to be next, be more specific next time you open your mouth. Who are you?"

Cox stared at the stone floor then screamed when MacIntyre stood and slammed a booted heel into his toes.

Tiny bones snapped and nails protested as the heel twisted and ground. The room swam as Cox drew on all his training to temper the pain.

"Since we're currently taking eyes for eyes, that's for my buddy. I'm only going to ask you once more," said MacIntyre. He gestured over his shoulder. "Then, I'll go get a drink and leave you with him. Last time. Who are you?"

Cox waited for the throbbing to dull. The back of his throat felt slashed and crushed.

With no hint of street noise and no dull rumble of chatter from above, this location was probably soundproof. No one would come to rescue him, and no one would miss him. Just the way he wanted it.

On a small table to the side lay the laptop and his wallet.

"Only name you need to know is Cox. But you already know that since you have my driver's license. Look, we both seem to be professionals, so we know how this works. You torture me, I tell you what you want to hear, and you still don't know if it's the truth. That's how torture works, right?"

"Maybe, but it would make me feel better."

"What you should be asking is who sent me? Who's paying the bill? Who wants you dead so badly they'd pay more than one person to get the job done?"

MacIntyre nodded. "That could go two ways. Either someone very concerned about what my friend found with more than a little to lose, or someone who couldn't trust one person to do the job properly. I'm going to assume this is a 'paid when the job is done' kind of deal. And I'm also going to assume your employer didn't expect to be paying multiple people by the end of play. Which, thanks to violent intervention, is how it turned out. But okay, I'll play the game. Go ahead. Enlighten me. Who's paying the bill?"

"Honest answer and torture aside?" shrugged Cox. "I don't know. The guy who might have had a clue is dead, and we all share responsibility for that. I'm not proud, but he'd have done the same for me. Anything you need is on that laptop and I don't have the password. And, even if you got it, you'd need his thumbprint and I'm guessing that, by now, the hotel fire alarm is silent and they've found his body. You going to break into the morgue and chop off a thumb?"

"I've done worse," said MacIntyre, "but I hope we won't need to. So what you're saying is you're of no use to us now?"

Cox studied the floor again. "You know they'll keep coming, don't you?"

"Who, porn stars?"

"Bad guys. Whoever sent us won't stop when we do; they'll just send someone else."

"Not if we work out who it is and then have a conversation."

"What, like this one? Good luck with that. Like I said, we're both professionals. We know how this'll end. Just do me a favor and make it quick. I'd do the same for you."

MacIntyre stood. "Would you, really? I seriously doubt that. Left to me, you can sit there, and we'll take bets on how long it takes for you to rot. Fortunately for you, one of our party doesn't roll that way. Ironically, it's the same guy who started the job on your partner who you probably finished. No, the bad news is you're not going anywhere yet. The good news is you're not going anywhere yet."

The other guy sighed, stepped forward and picked up the laptop and wallet.

Another English accent.

"Come on, Macca. That's what I expected. Let's see what we can get from this. Since you have nothing to lose, do you know the password?"

Cox fixed his gaze. "Dude, I still have my pride. And it hurts to talk. If I knew the password, you know I wouldn't tell you. But no, I don't know the password."

"Expected that, too, but it can't hurt to be civil. Come on, guys. I can work it out."

————

Thomas Fraine waved a cheery goodbye to the receptionist and carded through shining double glass doors that opened onto a busy Rodeo Drive.

Even at night, the two-mile street bustled with the needy and privileged, rubbing shoulders with tourists and working girls. He thought back to the *Pretty Woman* movie and gave himself a stern reminder.

Don't assume someone's appearance tells their entire story. You guys work on commission, right? Big mistake. Huge.

The scene summed up this entire area.

He clutched the briefcase tighter and turned to walk toward the private parking garage.

The approval of any new drug required clearance at the highest levels before the FDA would even consider testing, and Fraine's signature was priceless in the world of blood-related medication.

After taking a percentage of the profits from a bidding war

to produce the latest anti-coagulant drug, Fraine then offered his services to the winning bidder to clear the next-to-last hurdle, approval for testing.

While he expected an approach for his signature, he didn't expect someone with the appearance of a homeless man to deliver a case containing six hundred thousand dollars for it. As a down payment.

He pulled the case into his body and turned along a well-lit walkway that led from the famous street into a not so famous parking garage.

Each building on this side of the street shared the first level for private parking. At thirty-five fifty a night to park at the Beverly Wilshire, the ten-thousand-dollar annual fee this garage charged was small change.

Especially small to park a one point seven million-dollar Bugatti Veyron in safety.

Fraine barged open the garage's entrance door and stepped past the private elevator, through more doors, and into the garage.

Graffiti ruined the wall to his right, with a crudely drawn logo sprayed across it. That would have to be reported to the management company.

Still, cold fluorescent light flooded the space and lit every single car in dazzling color. He played his usual game of identifying each vehicle as he walked the distance to his personal space halfway down the far wall.

A vivid red Lamborghini Countach. A gleaming black Porsche Carrera. He sneered; they were common as medical contracts in California. A midnight blue Rolls Royce Dawn. Nice.

His eye twitched as he took in another Bugatti Veyron. The nerve of some people. And parked on the same level, too.

The other wall didn't seem quite so opulent, with an array

of what he considered to be 'regular' cars, and a ghostly gray panel van parked against the far wall.

Fraine reached into his pocket and pressed the key fob to open the Bugatti's doors. Its twin red lights flashed a disco beat, and he leaned to open the trunk and dropped the case inside.

He slid into the driver's seat and, as he clicked on the safety of the seat belt, a shadow passed across the rear window. The tiny side mirrors showed nothing, and he started the engine, put the vehicle in reverse, and edged out of his space.

Even over the guttural chug of the engine, the sound of both rear tires popping and then hissing air bounced off the garage walls.

Fraine jumped, cursed, then put the car in neutral, pulled on the parking brake and climbed out.

As he rounded the rear corner of the car, a coarse fabric hood dropped over his face and the world went black.

A punch took the panicked breath from his lungs, and he dropped to his knees with a painful thud.

His three hundred-dollar Testoni shoes dragged and scuffed a ragged trail across the concrete. He couldn't help but hopelessly wonder how much the security cameras would pick up and how he'd look on TV, until he heard the doors of the panel van slide open.

He was bundled inside, and then another punch rattled his teeth and put him to sleep.

———

With Cox left alone and strapped to the chair, they moved deeper into the tunnel network.

"How far back does this go?" said English. "I've seen an equipment room, you've got Sarge, Dud, and Marbles napping in a small billet, and you've got the room back there holding our friend. I'm assuming there's a supply room somewhere, and another that holds generators to power all of this? And something to deal with the damp."

"All assumptions correct," said Tony. "Normally, I wouldn't have this much space. I'm fortunate that the folks either side of me traded some of their space for use of the facilities in the event of, shall we say, an unpleasant situation."

"Like this one."

"This situation is pretty unique to be fair but, yeah, I guess anything goes."

English ducked his head to enter another room with the same floor and walls as the others, but the lighting clashed with its calm surroundings. Buzzing fluorescents splashed a cool blue white across a wall filled with humming equipment.

A large monitor took pride of place in the center, surrounded by an array of machinery lit up like an airport. A swirling image of the pub's emblem bounced around the screen. Below it, a black desk stretched from one rack to another but looked bare by contrast, with nothing but a wireless mouse, a keyboard, a scanner and an elaborate, glass-boxed printer.

"Bloody hell, Tone, do you land planes from in here or just contact alien life forms? I've got a decent set up at home, but I don't recognize half this stuff. You could be sending messages to Mars."

"Welcome to the Situation Room. Perks of previous jobs, my friend. I don't just equip the brothers with things that go bang. That would be limiting. I like to think of myself as a jack of all trades but master of none. If you need something, chances are I can sort it. And, if I can't, I'll know a man who can."

Macca dropped onto a small sofa as English gestured to the desk area. "Mind if I jump in?"

"Be my guest. What's the technical equivalent of *mi casa es su casa?*"

"I think it's 'dive in, mate'."

"Very well," said Tony. "Dive in, mate."

English pulled out the chair, sat, and tapped the keyboard. The monitor cleared and flashed a single prompt requesting a password.

"That changes often," said Tony, "like a random generator but, at the minute, it's under the bar."

"Can't fault your security. Be a pal and go get it, would you?"

"No, mate, the password is 'under the Bar'. Capital B, the rest lower case."

"Oh. Okay."

English entered the words, and the monitor lit up with an image of a purple shield with two crossed hammers in its center. Bubbles drifted up the screen on either side.

"Really? The nerve center for the supply of dodgy paperwork and arms to Scotland has a football badge and bubbles on its screen?"

"West Ham," said Tony. "Mate, if I've got it tattooed on my body, it's sure as hell going on my monitor. I'm forever blowing bubbles."

"So much to say and so little time. Sounds like you eat too much broccoli, but I admire your loyalty."

English pulled out his phone. Something in the cave system ensured he had a full signal.

"I need to link in with a few things at home. You okay if I network?"

"Whatever you need to do to get the job done. Everything

is ultra-secure. I'm going to see what I can do upstairs. Call me if you need anything."

"Cables. I'll need to connect their laptop to your system."

Tony pointed to a small cabinet beneath the desk.

"Everything you need should be in there. Help yourself, mate. I'll see you later."

Macca stepped up to the desk and handed over the laptop as Tony left.

"Here you go. Do your best, would you? This seems to be the only way forward. We're running out of options."

English looked through the cloud of bubbles at the icons arranged on the left of the monitor.

"Wow. Tony has some high-end stuff here. When we're done, I'll have to ask if I can borrow some of this. There are classified NSA programs here I've never managed to obtain. I wouldn't know where to start with half of them."

"And when you say obtain…" said Macca.

"Exactly. First things first, though, I know my programs. I need the IP address for my system so I can log in. I use a few VPNs and they change all the time."

"Yeah, you lost me at IP. Hell, you lost me at exactly. Crack on, fella."

English tapped his phone's screen. "Trust me. If it can be done, I'll do it. Give me a sec."

He activated the phone's speaker and laid it on the desk as the dial tone chirped.

Numbers answered. "Isn't it past your bedtime? Thought you guys would be tucked up by now."

"Some of us are," said English, "but we're on a mission, bud. I need your help with a few things."

Penny shouted in the background. "Hi, honey."

English smiled. "Hi, babe. It's good to hear your voice. Are you keeping Numbers under control?"

"It's tough, but yeah. Beneath that rugged exterior, he's a pussy cat. Just have to keep him watered and fed, you know? Are you guys staying safe over there? I worry about you."

"As safe as can be. And don't worry, babe, we've got some excellent help. The Old Farts Club got some new recruits, and it's working well. I need your help to patch into my network, though."

"We can do that. What do you need?"

English spat out a list of commands, until Penny read back a series of digits. He keyed them into Tony's system and, moments later, a mirror image of his screen appeared on the monitor.

"Okay, I'm in. Hate to cut and run, babe, but I'd better get to this. Talk soon, okay? Love you. You too, Numbers."

Penny laughed. "Hey, don't put me in a competition. Love you, too, babe. Stay safe."

English disconnected the call.

"Now to link our friend's laptop to this."

He rummaged through the cabinet and came back with a cable. With one end plugged into an open port, he flipped open the laptop, powered it up, and plugged the other end of the cable into a slot on its side.

The laptop screen remained black, except for a single, flashing cursor in the top corner.

"Okay. Now to see what these boys used as their password."

English's fingers flitted across the keyboard, and screen after screen appeared on the monitor. A fan in the laptop whirred into life as numbers and digits scrolled in boxes on the monitor.

"How long will this take?" said Macca.

"No clue. Depends on how high the encryption is on the

laptop. Given its purpose, I'm going to guess huge. If you want to take a nap, go ahead. I've got this covered."

Macca dropped onto the sofa. "Nah, it's good to watch a master at work."

He reached into his pocket and pulled out the wallet. A driver's license sat inside a plastic pouch at its front.

"Niall Cox. He doesn't look like a Niall, does he?"

"He looks like a dick," said English. "What else is in there?"

Macca flipped through the leather slits. "A couple of credit cards. Surprisingly, no library card. I guess the modern assassin doesn't get time to read much."

He flipped the first card over. "With fraud being so prevalent, it baffles the life out of me that most Americans never sign the back of their credit cards. You'd think they'd get ripped off all the time."

"Most of them carry loaded guns next to their cards," said English. "I dare you."

"Excellent point."

He flipped over the second.

"Hang on, this one's got tape stuck to it. Weird."

English held out a hand. "Let me see that."

Macca passed the card. English held it up to one of the lights. A strip of adhesive tape ran across its back. Where it met white plastic, it appeared clear, but over the dark brown of the signature strip a small pattern of whorls was just visible.

"Since no one mentioned the dead guy missing his thumbs, I did wonder how Cox thought he'd get into the laptop. The password is part one of a two-part process. Now I know. This could be his buddy's fingerprint."

Macca stood and clapped. "Excellent. So, once your machine cracks the password, all we have to do is press that tape to the laptop sensor thing and we're in?"

"Not quite."

"Oh. Shit."

"Cox would still have failed. For one, the scanner won't recognize regular ink and, two, if it's as high-end as I suspect it is, a flat image isn't going to cut it, either. It'll need to be a conductive, 3D image."

"What language is that because I could swear you spoke English? You've still lost me."

"That's okay, mate. Leave it with me and I'll give it some thought."

Macca slumped back onto the sofa. "So now what?"

English pointed to the monitor. "I say we go join the others and get our heads down for a while. We let that program do its thing and hope it can crack the password."

"And then?"

"Then, we cross the next bridge when we get to it."

"Mate, last time I crossed a bridge as important as this I went airborne for about ten seconds and lost three tires."

"Yes, but did you make it?"

"Well, yeah. The Jeep was destroyed but I'm still here, aren't I?"

English turned back to the monitor. "Then, there you go. Have some faith. Just be sure to stay away from my car."

Chapter Fifteen

"Pump the gas. I'll take a leak and then go pay."

Sam listened as the car bounced again and the passenger door slammed shut.

"Fill her up?"

"Yep, might as well. We still have plenty of driving to do. You want anything?"

"Sure, grab me some Fritos and a soda. With plenty of ice."

"Got it. Check on the bitch."

With a whimper, Sam rolled to face the trunk and gripped the tire iron until the metal dug into her skin. The part in her hand was warm and slick with sweat. She wiped it against her pants leg and checked that the bent end was pointing where she'd aim. There might only be one chance. The first swing had to be good.

"Screw her, she can have Fritos, too."

"I don't mean that, dumbass. You don't feed stock that's ready for slaughter, that's a waste of good food. Make sure she's still breathing. If we don't get her there in one piece, we're as good as dead."

Sam screwed her eyes closed to hold back tears as her body shivered. Her grip tightened further still, and she tried to imagine the feeling of the metal connecting to skin. She dry-heaved and sobbed.

Dumbass managed a grunt, and then the car body rattled as he removed the filler cap and thrust the pump nozzle into the opening.

She shuffled into as close an upright position as possible. Her head and shoulder pressed against the trunk lid, and the spare wheel dug into her knees. An insistent cramp returned and tugged at her calves.

After a few minutes, steps moved to the rear of the car.

She jerked and almost dropped the iron when something slammed against the lid.

"Damn you, woman. He's gonna be pissed when he sees what you done to the taillight. That's real inconsiderate. Anyone would think you're trying to get us pulled over by law enforcement."

The lid popped and light flooded into the trunk space through the opening crack.

Inch by inch, it raised and slowly revealed a pair of faded jeans with scuffed knees.

Sam crouched, held her breath, and waited while her heart rate increased to send blood pounding like chanting whispers through her ears. When his crotch area appeared, she acted on instinct and took her chance.

She flipped both her plan and the tire iron, took a breath, then cupped the blunt end against her palm and thrust and lifted the pointed end forward, out of the trunk and into the guy's most vulnerable parts.

He buckled with a groan.

Without waiting, she pushed up with her shoulders and barged into the trunk lid, sending it into the underside of his chin with a dull thud.

He windmilled backwards as his teeth crashed together, lost his footing, and landed heavily on his butt then rolled onto his side and curled into a fetal ball.

Sam swung her legs over the trunk's edge and stood upright. Her knees screamed a protest as they straightened, the base of her spine cracked, and she gripped the side of the car for support.

Theirs was the only car on the forecourt. She was alone.

The green light came from an enormous neon sign which showed today's gas price and a two for one offer on sodas.

Behind her, the other guy stood with his back to the window while he browsed the chips aisle. The dark and deserted highway stretched either side of her while, across the road, a wall of thick trees bordered the road for as far as she could see.

In a moment of panic, when she needed to run, Sam froze.

Surprisingly, the trunk plan had worked.

One guy was preoccupied, and the other was groaning in pain and trying to unfold himself from a painful position.

But now what? Again. Think like Evie. Options.

One. She could run along the highway and flag down a passing car, but that would be suicide. With her recent run of luck, she'd no doubt get run down or picked up by the bad guys.

Two. She could burst into the store and scream like a crazy lady for them to call the cops. These guys were prepared to kidnap and were probably armed; the other guy would shoot the attendant, and she'd be back to square one.

Three. The car.

She slammed the trunk shut, scrambled around the side,

and yanked open the driver's door. Damn it; Fritos boy had the keys.

Which left option four. Across the road, branches swayed in a slight breeze. The moon peeked through gaps at fleeting intervals, and a million bogeymen lurked in the misty shadows.

The woods, as terrifying as they were, were her only choice.

In the station's lights, her purse still glittered under the driver's seat. She snatched it, ran toward the road, then stopped and turned to the guy on the ground. Something cracked when she summoned all her strength and smashed the blunt end of the tire iron into his leg, and she shouted over him as he screamed.

"You're a bad man. Didn't your momma teach you anything? Boys shouldn't call girls bitches. It's like, literally, one of the worst things you can say to a girl."

She threw the iron under the car and, as it clanged against the concrete, she raced across the road and disappeared into the darkness of the woods.

———

Evie tied off the boat and held out one hand to help Carina step onto dry land while she juggled the phone in the other.

"Okay, Penny, what's next?"

"Time to hustle, Evie. If you head away with the water behind you, you should hit highway I-80 in about a half mile. It looks like Sam's car is stopped on the roadside."

"What, like broken down? How ironic would that be? Explaining a kidnap victim to the breakdown guy. A double rescue. Do Triple A even practice for that?"

"I doubt it. Hard to say, but I'm trying to get satellite to zoom in and see what's going on. I'm having issues with the software. English isn't picking up, but it's early morning where he is so he may be sleeping. I'll figure it out by the time you get to the road."

Evie broke into a jog, and Carina kept pace beside her.

"It's much appreciated, Penny. I'll hang up to preserve my battery. I don't have a charger with me, and I don't know what we're up against yet. I'd hate to lose contact."

"Not a problem," said Penny. "Numbers and I are taking turns to allow for nap time. Don't get too tired yourself, you know that's when mistakes happen."

"I hear you," said Evie, "but the mistake already happened. These guys have my sister. Their mistake."

"Be careful, Evie. Don't underestimate them. I'll give you a call if I find anything new."

"Gotcha. Evie out."

She disconnected the call and slipped the phone into her jeans.

"Do you always talk like that?" said Carina. "Evie out? Sounds like you should have enlisted."

"I sort of did," said Evie. "Came with the wedding."

Her breath came easily as they weaved through the trees.

"When you marry a military man, you marry into it all, the discipline and the lifestyle. And you gain family. I love my extended family. We'd do anything for one another."

"Clearly," said Carina. "Might have to get me one of those."

They parted to pass a thick trunk and rejoined without missing a beat.

"You should get you one of those. So what's your story, anyway?" said Evie. "You know, man-wise? You're a good-looking girl. How come you're not out on a shopping spree with Mr. Carina?"

Carina took in a deep breath through her nose and let it pass through her lips slowly. "Those three pesky little words."

"Oh, oh," said Evie. "I know those."

"Yep. Work, work, and work."

"Ah. I know those, too, but not in this context. I thought you meant…"

"Nope. I know those, too, and I can only wish. I spent every waking minute making sure I was as good as I could get at my job. Notes for breakfast, PowerPoint slides for lunch, conference calls for dinner. Don't get me wrong, I got offers. Lots, in fact. Especially from guys at work. But once we sat down for a date and got talking, work took over. I never found the off switch."

"Not cool."

"Not at all. Then, one day, I woke up with mid-life looming. Damn, I don't even have a cat."

"I was ready to shoot you, earlier today."

"That's nice," said Carina.

"Yeah, but now I want to fix you up with any single friends I have."

"That's nicer."

Evie pulled up as light flickered through the tree line.

"Looks like we found the highway. I'll call Penny."

Penny answered on the first ring. "Everything's working. I have satellite view. Can you see a green light?"

"Hang on," said Evie.

They pushed through the last few yards and came out at the side of the road. To the left lay nothing but immediate darkness, with the peaceful twinkle of town lights in the far distance. To the right, the road rose in a steady incline, but a halo of green bounced off the clouds a few hundred yards away.

She gestured right, and they jogged up the rise.

When they reached the brow, the neon glow of a gas station broke the night on the far side of the highway.

"Yep. Got it."

"Okay. Now, I need you to be careful. Is there still a car on the forecourt?"

Evie strained her eyes and picked out the silhouette of a sedan parked at the side of a pump. "There is. Just one."

"Cool. I wondered if there was a delay on this image, but it seems to be live. Okay, Evie? Sam was in that car."

Evie felt her stomach churn. "Penny, did you say Sam *was* in that car?"

"Evie, Sam's a badass."

Evie let out a snort. "Sure, with a hairdryer, a flat iron and some foundation."

"No, really. I think this was a tire iron. She got away and took out one of the guys in style while she did it."

Evie lowered the phone and glanced at Carina, who shook her head and shrugged and then raised it again.

"Penny, you've got to be shitting me. What did she do, lipstick him to death?"

"I shit you not. I'll share the gas station camera footage when this is all over but, for now, I can't get close enough to see what's going on. The guys didn't move for about five minutes, then they took off into the woods you just ran through. They're trying to find Sam."

"Can't you go thermal?"

"Dammit, Evie, I really need to wake Numbers. He'd have called that one. Hang on."

While Penny switched modes, Evie sprinted to the car.

Carina stuck at her side.

She gestured to the attendant when none of the doors opened.

He shrugged and gestured across the road, toward the woods.

Penny came back. "She's in the woods across the road. Those guys have split up. One is headed in the wrong direction, but the other is getting close. It's like watching the predator. Damn, I wish she could hear me, I could direct her."

"No matter," said Evie. "Direct us instead."

She tilted her head toward the road, and Carina followed.

Once off the forecourt, Evie pulled the gun, checked the clip, and crossed the road into the tree line.

"Isn't your phone lit up?" said Penny. "You'll look like a firefly going through the woods. They'll see you coming a mile away."

"Shit. Yes, it is. I'll have to turn it off. Okay, Penny, point me in the right direction and then I'll disconnect."

Evie paused while Penny either worked out direction or cursed the impending lack of contact.

"If the road is directly at your back, Sam is about thirty degrees to the left of you."

Evie visualized a compass in her mind, spun, and began to walk.

"Okay," said Penny, "you're headed in the right direction, give or take. Just one problem."

"Okay, and what's that?"

"Well, I can't accurately work out distance with this thing but, if you're a half mile from Sam, there's a bad guy almost breathing down her neck."

Chapter Sixteen

It took a moment for Anneka Ergström to work out what had woken her.

The rhythmic thrum of helicopter blades cut through the sea air and beat waves of percussion against her window. The facility's helipad was a few hundred yards away, but powerful winds sent the buffeting sound much farther than it would normally travel.

She slipped out of bed, pulled on a fleece robe, and wandered over to the porthole window.

In the distance, the blazing sun peeked over the horizon, a semi-circle of powerful orange. The sea rippled, unusually steady and calm.

She must have beaten her alarm by mere minutes.

Floodlights lit the deck outside and made the fluorescent yellow walking areas glow in the morning hue.

The helicopter made its graceful descent, silhouetted against the dramatic dawn backdrop, and rested easily on its rails. The rhythm slowed until the blades came to a stop and sagged.

Dahl strode across the causeway toward the helicopter, ignoring the yellow markings, trailed by two men.

Anneka squinted her eyes to try to pick out detail. Dahl had mentioned a small security detail, but this was the first time she'd seen them.

The pilot climbed out and disappeared behind the craft, and shadows moved inside it before Dahl reappeared, followed by the men.

They flanked a figure that resisted and squirmed between them. An outside light flashed across his face and, for a moment, she thought she recognized him but, based on some of Dahl's stories and the things she'd read, there was no way Thomas Fraine would come anywhere near their facility. At least not voluntarily.

Tabloids and journals alike documented the relationship between them as volatile. The two scientists were the academic equivalent of having college basketball teams in the same city. Bitter rivalry.

They pulled him forward in the direction of the living quarters and disappeared out of sight. The pilot climbed back into the craft and nodded to an unseen person, and the whine of the helicopter's engine rose until the rotors spun into a blur once more, and the craft lifted from the helipad in a cloud of vapor, spun to face the ocean, dipped its nose, and faded away into the sunrise.

As it blinked out of sight, her alarm sang its morning song.

Ergström silenced it and shivered, stripped off her robe and stepped, deep in thought, into the shower.

———

A gentle nudge shook English from a deep sleep.

The silhouette of Sarge's cap blocked out most of the glow from the orange overhead light.

"Morning, buddy. Rise and shine. Your fellow Brit has some good news and wants you in the Situation Room."

Instantly, English's faculties snapped awake and he rolled from the makeshift bed and stood.

"Surprisingly comfortable," said Sarge with a nod to the fabric bed. He turned and led them from the room.

"Yep. Despite the temperature and leg cramps, it beats sleeping on the shit we had in Desert Storm. The sides of tanks, concrete doorways, you name it. Thank God we didn't spend too much time there."

They turned a corner and walked past Cox. He glared, puffy eyed and silent, as they strolled past him.

"Buddy, you have no idea. I've slept on forest floors with all kinds of wildlife for company. We ate most of them. I'll lie on anything these days, except that memory foam junk. Only thing that crap remembers is the exact shape of your body. Then, you end up stuck in your own foam valley. Can't even turn over properly without rolling back to where you started."

"That's all about the advertising," said English. "If it's a model with brunette hair and a cool accent, buy that one. Otherwise, sleep on your grill or the lawn."

"I hear you," said Sarge. "Back to important stuff, what's the plan? I feel a little out of the loop."

"Sorry about that, brother, you were taking a well-earned nap. As you know, we have the bad guy. We just need to work out what the bastard was up to. Or, more importantly, who sent him."

"Macca might have something to say about that."

They rounded a few more turns and ducked under a low arch into the Situation Room.

English nodded a 'morning' to the rest of the team, then gazed at the screen.

An urgent red border flashed around its edges, with a combination of letters, numbers, and symbols splashed across the center.

English smiled. "Is that my password?"

Tony turned from the desk and nudged Macca.

Macca smiled. "I reckon so, mate. Now what?"

"Now what? Let's key it in and move on to phase two. I feel like a kid at Christmas."

Tony moved aside as English flipped open the laptop and waited for the screen to appear. As soon as the cursor blinked, he copied the password from the screen, checked each entry as he keyed it, crossed his fingers, and hit enter.

The screen flickered and an hourglass appeared and spun end over end. A small glass circle below the mousepad glowed red.

"Bugger. Still, I expected that. Step two. We need a thumbprint."

"No problem," said Macca. "I'll go chat with our friend back there. I'm sure he'd oblige if I show him the shears."

"Don't bother," said English. "I've not tested it, but I don't think he's the brains behind their operation. I reckon Sarge took care of those back at the pub."

"Oh. And chances are, he's not where we left him anymore."

English picked up the wallet and pulled the card. "Potentially, we have his print, it's just not in the format we need."

Tony stepped forward. "Potentially? Mind if I see that?"

English passed it over.

"If our friend kept it like that, it has to be what we need, but the reader won't pick it up as a flat image."

"No problem," smiled Tony. He walked over to the glass

box and patted its top. "3D printer. Like I said, I supply all kinds of things from here, and this is not my first rodeo."

"So you can produce a fingerprint?" said Macca. "Tone, I'd kiss you, but…"

"Yeah, but no. I have a thing about kissing Scottish men. First things first, we need a decent scanned image, and I doubt the scanner will pick up anything where the card is white. I've got no nails, so someone will have to peel the tape off. Carefully. We can't afford to smudge it. One chance, and one chance only."

"I'll do it," said Marbles. "I've got the hands of a surgeon. Comes from working on all manner of machinery."

Tony passed the card. "Go for it, mate."

Marbles picked at the tape until he raised a corner then peeled it back until it left the card with a quiet snick. He held it up to the light and smiled. "Even with one eye, that looks good to me."

Tony took the tape and pulled a small wooden box and a brush from the rack. "Pressie from a friend at CSI Glasgow. Fingerprint powder."

"Thought that was your blusher brush, mate," said Macca.

"I keep those upstairs," said Tony. He leaned over the desk, laid the tape flat, and dipped the brush into the powder. After he tapped the brush against the edge of the box, he stroked it across the tape.

"Easy does it. Start light and work it in. The powder will stick to the tape in thicker quantities than to the oily fingerprint, which will…"

He lifted the tape and held it to the light. The whorls of a perfectly formed print sat at the center of the tape.

"…produce this work of art."

"I'm impressed," said Sarge.

"I'm disturbed," said Marbles. "You've done that too many times."

Tony sat at the desk and lifted the scanner lid. "Only for the brothers, mate. Right, now to take an image that I can send to the printer."

After a moment of whirring and bright light, the print appeared on the monitor. He tapped in a series of commands before the printer hummed into life.

"Give it a minute and we should be good to go. Hopefully, the final product should be thin enough to be pliable, but we'll soon see."

The printer carried out its work in silence until the print head settled to a stop and Tony peeled a piece of molded plastic from the printer's metal base and handed it to English.

"There you go, mate. Stick that on your thumb and give it a go."

English laid the plastic across his thumb, sent up a silent prayer, and pressed it to the laptop's scanner.

The hourglass continued to sift its imaginary sand, end over end.

"Damn it," said Macca. "And we were doing so well."

"Hang on," said English, "I think it slipped. Let me try again."

He fiddled with the plastic and supported its edges as he lowered it again onto the scanner.

The screen cleared and a series of boxes appeared.

"Bloody hell, mate, we're in. Okay, now to see what we can find."

He placed the laptop on the desk and sat before it then checked out each box. "Encrypted, obviously," he said, "but that shouldn't be an issue. If I can read the president's emails, I'm sure I can tackle this."

"You can read the president's emails?" said Tony. "Can you read the Queen's? Only, I've always been curious."

"I'm sure her spelling is much better," said English as he moved the mouse over various icons on the main screen and clicked. "I need to see where the last incoming signal originated from. That would be a good place to start. Then, as Macca said, we can shake the chain and find the weakest link."

Another box opened on the main screen, which quickly filled with a series of numbers.

"That's not this Saturday's lottery numbers, is it?" said Dud.

"Sorry, mate, but no. Those are IP addresses. This thing is visiting more locations than the world's most popular hooker. There are VPNs galore."

"Is VPN something to do with hookers, too? Sounds like one of those itchy diseases I really don't want."

"False addresses. They make you think the signal originates somewhere random like Holland or Germany rather than where you're at. Then, the next one moves it from the original fake location and sends that to another false location. It's like me asking the wife to get my wallet from the dresser when I've moved it from the loo, to the kitchen, to the dining room and out to the shed, when it's really in the loft."

Dud stepped back. "It's all yours, mate. Good luck. And don't ask me to get your wallet."

The numbers continued to scroll until, one by one, they disappeared.

Finally, one row remained.

English clicked again, copied and pasted the numbers into another box, and then sat back and waited.

Seconds later, an address appeared onscreen.

After a few more key taps, a map replaced the address. One more, and vertical and horizontal crosshairs swept across the screen until they stopped, and a red dot appeared, floating in an ocean of blue, next to two sets of numbers.

He stood and clapped his hands.

"Okay. Now we're talking."

He turned to face the group as Macca raised a hand.

"Those co-ordinates look familiar. Hang on a second."

He reached into a plastic tote beneath one of the racks, pulled out a folder, and fanned out its contents onto the desk.

"I kept Knowles' work here for safety. I'm sure—"

After a firm tap on the desk, he pointed to the screen.

"Unless my training has failed me, that location onscreen is about ten miles from the area Knowles found. Directly east of Aberdeen. The area where the boats would turn off their transponders."

"That can't be a coincidence," said Sarge.

"I don't believe in them, mate. Everything for a reason and all that. So whoever wants me dead…"

"…and hired our friends from the pub," said Marbles.

"Yes, is in the same place as whatever's going on with the boats. And here's the kicker; remember me saying that it happened once a week, regular as clockwork?"

The group nodded as one.

"Tomorrow would be that day. At about twelve o'clock noon, to be precise."

"Sounds like we have a mission," said Sarge. "We're going to need some gear."

"And a good boat," said Marbles.

Macca smiled. "Agreed. Let's head back to my place and snatch some sleep, then call back here, eat, and get kitted out. Then, we can all go for a wee swim."

Chapter Seventeen

Sam rested against a tree and waited for the insistent stabbing against her ribs to ease.

Every reckless step she'd taken crunched against damp leaves or sent a dry twig snapping sharp sounds like a gunfire crack back toward the highway, but a solid three-minute sprint placed her precious yards from the road. For perhaps the first time, she blessed flat shoes.

After another two minutes of steady jogging, her strength deserted her. Adrenaline fueled a final, desperate sixty seconds.

Her heart hammered triple time, her calves and thighs ached, and the soles of her feet throbbed from one too many hard landings against an uneven surface.

She spun a three-sixty to find a vast darkness broken by the occasional flicker of moonlight that broke through tree boughs that swayed ghostly arms. The light from the highway seemed miles away.

With the heat of the fabric-lined trunk already a distant memory, wafts of fall night air nipped at her arms. Goose-bumps rose against her cooling sweat.

And everything creaked and cracked. From the tips of the trees to the ground beneath her feet. Away from the rush of the highway, every sound doubled in volume and echoed like a clap in a canyon.

Even her breathing sounded like a loud whisper. She jumped when something rustled to her right. Did coyotes live in the woods? Or snakes? God, what about wolves or wild dogs?

Or worse, had the bad guys already found her?

With a small whimper, Sam straightened and considered her next move. Without heat, she'd soon struggle to even move. Familiar cramps already threatened to return to tug her calves. Every breeze cut through her thin top to send her shuddering into fresh shivers, while her shoes were already damp and cloying and sucked at her feet.

She was in the middle of God knows where, with nothing but a purse and whatever wits she had.

The purse.

With it rested on her thighs, she sifted through its contents and counted them off, one by one, in terms of usefulness.

Lipstick. Useless. A pack of tissues. Same. Her wallet. Dangerous in a mall, useless here. A pack of gum. An emery board. Hair spray. On a scale of one to ten, a whole bunch of zeroes. Everything useless.

The heaviest thing to hand was the can of hair spray. She hefted it in her palm and practiced a jabbing motion then closed the purse and took another look at her surroundings.

Again, the standard crisis question, What would Evie do? Evie would probably climb a tall tree, Katniss Everdeen style, get some height, and see what the options were from a bird's eye point of view. She'd totally do that.

In the dark, all the trees looked the same. Sam strained her eyes to try to pick out one that might be climbable.

To her left, a cluster of low-hanging branches held possibility. Not only could she reach the lowest branch, but it was in the opposite direction to whatever had made that sound.

Still crouched, she tiptoed across a small clearing and was almost at the tree when a voice shouted behind her. She cleared the last few steps at pace and ducked behind the tree.

"Any sign?"

The shouted question sounded as if it came from a few feet away.

Sam gripped her purse and the hairspray, placed a hand against her hammering chest, and swallowed down a whimper that threatened to betray her.

"Nothing. Keep looking. Unless she got lucky and hitched a ride, she's around here somewhere. We don't take her back and we're as good as dead."

The other voice barely reached her, quite a distance away, but someone had no idea of stealth and came toward her, crashing through the woods.

Now, she could hear every word.

"Damned woman gonna cause me a whole world of pain. Why didn't I listen to—"

The sentence remained unfinished as the guy stumbled into Sam's path. His mouth dropped open as their eyes met.

She panicked while he fumbled at his waistband and she acted on instinct and slammed the can of hairspray into his face.

Her stomach lurched as the metal base connected with his nose, and then the plastic lid buckled, popped off the can, and fell to the ground.

"Bitch, I'm gonna make you wish—"

Another sentence remained unfinished as Sam flipped the can, felt for the spray release, pressed the plunger, and unleashed a torrent of fine mist into the guy's face.

He gagged for air as the chemicals clogged his throat then clutched at his face and screamed when his eyes began to smart.

Before he could say a word, she aimed a swift kick that connected solidly with his groin and dropped him to his knees to leave him writhing and moaning on the damp ground.

"I already told you about your language," she hissed.

She tried to tune him out and listened. His partner must have heard the scream.

She ran. With no idea of direction, she scrambled and slipped between trees, ducking branches that clawed and scratched at her arms as she fought to stay upright.

Moonlight peeked through gaps like camera flashes to bathe the woods in strobes and fans of light. Her breath came in increasingly ragged gasps as her heartbeat pounded again and, after a short sprint, she pulled up breathless and leaned forward with her hands resting on her knees.

The wind dropped as clouds covered the moon. A blanket of darkness swept over the woods.

Then, a metallic sound clicked in front of her.

She lifted her head as a barely formed silhouette stepped out from behind a tree.

"Stop right there, bitch."

———

Fraine massaged the stiffness from his wrists and studied what appeared to be, at least for the time being, his new quarters.

Clinical didn't begin to describe it.

Steel-gray tile covered the floor, while the walls were sprayed in a white plastic coating. Two porthole windows took up one wall and looked out to sea. A spray of wash lashed them every time the wind gusted.

A metal-framed bed butted against the next wall, basic with no headboard, next to a white laminate bedside cabinet topped with a chrome lamp and a digital clock.

A similar wardrobe and a wide chest of drawers took up the third wall, along with a small desk and a chair, while the fourth contained nothing but a door, which had no handle.

His view through the window was useless; a corrugated metal deck with the sea beyond it reaching up to the horizon.

What the hell was Dahl thinking? It was sheer craziness to kidnap an eminent figure in one of the richest neighborhoods in the world. Cameras outnumbered dropped litter in Beverly Hills and the whole event was bound to have been recorded.

Then, he remembered the graffiti, crude but effective. The logo that swept across the entrance wall. And probably the camera. Was the rest of the security system on that level of the garage similarly treated?

Nausea writhed in his stomach. With everything blacked out, perhaps no one knew he was here.

With his head covered in thick fabric, he had no clue how long they'd been traveling. The van ride ended at what sounded like a small airport, where he was bundled into a cold cargo hold. Cramps contorted his body as the plane cruised, until the almost welcome rumble of wheels on a runway was replaced by a rush of colder air, and he was dropped to the ground, only to be lifted by strong arms and folded into a helicopter.

From the van ride to his destination, no one spoke a word until the pilot requested permission to land. Every one of his terrified pleas went unanswered, and he finally gave up talking and huddled in silence.

The journey might have taken four hours, and it might have taken ten.

He gazed once again through the window. Solid metal

walls stretched out from either side of the windows to create a small tunnel that led out to the helipad. Beyond it, his only view was an expanse of treacherous-looking sea and a sky filled with bruised clouds, hopeless in terms of working out where he was, but definite in terms of quashing any hope of escape, especially if the view behind him was the same.

He turned at a light rap on the door to see Dahl enter the room. As it clicked shut, he stormed forward.

"What the fuck do you think you're doing? Are you insane? You know exactly who I am, and you can rest assured I'll be pressing every charge in the book against you."

Dahl perched on the corner of the bed, blinked slowly, and gestured toward the chair.

"Don't you just love a situation where the tables are turned? Thomas, please take a seat."

"I'll do no such thing. Let me out of here, right now. How the hell do you think you can get away with this? On what planet is this acceptable? Kidnapping?"

"Only in your mind, Thomas. And it's not kidnapping if you decide to stay, but merely encouragement. Please, be patient and bear with me, I have a proposition for you."

Fraine scoffed. "Propositions are usually offered over drinks or food, you maniac, not after blindfolded helicopter trips."

"Oh, I'm sorry. I can get you a sandwich if it would make you feel better? Cheese and onion?"

He seethed and clutched the back of the chair while Dahl smiled.

"Coffee?"

"Dahl, I'll…"

"Oh, well," said Dahl, "you can't say I didn't try. Thomas, if it's okay with you, I'll cut to the chase. I've brought you to an incredible facility. Don't be concerned about the location, it's quite safe. We have loads of safety systems, fire extinguishers in each lab, you name it. We're working on some breakthrough technology, cutting edge, but we seem to have reached a hurdle that my guys are having difficulty in clearing. It's smack bang in your area of expertise, and I think you could help. I remember you firing me because I was a threat to your position, but I'm prepared to let that go and give you the chance you never gave me. Thomas, how would you like to become part of an amazing team?"

"Jesus Christ, you are insane. What in the name of all things holy would inspire me to help you? Dahl, we've been at either end of the spectrum concerning our careers. We're mortal enemies. Black and white. I'd sooner die than progress yours any further."

Dahl laughed and rose from the bed. "Who said anything about careers? And death seems a little severe, Thomas. You're no good to me dead. But you can still work from a wheelchair."

Fraine waited for another reaction at the end of the sentence. When none came, he roared and flung the chair across the room. Its metal legs clanged against the wall before the chair settled with a bounce and clattered beneath the windows.

"Feel better?" said Dahl.

He fought to hold back frustrated tears. "Damn it, Dahl, where the hell have you brought me? And what do you want? God knows, you seem to have everything. With that award, you are considered the best in our field. Clearly, money is no issue, and I assume you have a partner. What else is there? Why are you doing this?"

Dahl sauntered across to the door, looked him in the eye, and tapped it. It clicked, open an inch.

Fraine tried to see through the crack to who or what lay

beyond but was met with nothing but the glare of fluorescent light and another soulless white wall.

"Okay," said Dahl, "I'll make you a deal. Work for me and I'll tell you exactly what I want. I'll tell you everything. And, of course, I'll pay you. Handsomely. Though there would be one condition; no one in my team can know that you're working under anything but your own volition. I have a happy team. If they suspect that you are here under duress, the results would be very painful for both you and everyone you know."

"Go to hell."

Dahl shrugged. "Okay. Or, you can work for free and I'll have both your legs broken and, while you're screaming, I'll whisper what I want in your ear."

Chapter Eighteen

"I imagined we'd have to limbo under miles of yellow crime scene tape," said Sarge as Macca led them across the small entry to the pub's empty doorway.

"We take care of our own around here," said Macca. "While you guys were eating, I made a quick call to Tony. Most of the customers had left by the time Cox made his last move, and the one instance of social media coverage that leaked has been blocked. And Clarence is made of stern stuff; he's battered and bruised but ready to get back to work. Mrs. Clarence stitched up the nastier wounds. The only major upset is Ken, but the coroner informed the family of his traffic accident, and he'll get a closed casket funeral. No autopsy."

"Seems cold," said Sarge. "A good man gave his life, and no one but us will know why."

"It is cold, but it's the way of things. Always has been, always will be. How many men have you stood beside that didn't go home? People go about their lives and have no idea of the sacrifices being made for their security. And a bad man gave his life to balance the books. I'm not saying it's the right way, but our friend won't be bothering anyone else."

"I was about to ask," said English.

"Tony made it quick," said Macca. "It seems that, as tempting as it was to exact revenge in a big way, Cox said that Ken didn't suffer. He repaid the favor."

The door latch clicked as they approached the pub, and the somber-looking landlord beckoned them inside.

Macca gripped him in a hug. "Appreciate this, mate. Sorry for the early morning call. And I'm deeply sorry I brought this crap to your door. Hope you're holding up okay."

"I'm always up at the crack of dawn, mate. Old habits. And mourning another fallen comrade. Each one is one too many. Don't worry about bringing anything to my door, though, it's always open for the brothers. I didn't call this place The Billet for nothing, it's what I made it for. Come on, follow me."

They made their way past the bar, through the employee entrance, and down into the vaults.

Sarge offered up a silent prayer as he passed the empty room which had held Cox then followed them into the cooler corridors.

"I researched Aberdeen," said Tony. "Can't comment on the football team, West Ham have never played against them, but the town itself is pretty busy. Lots of cameras about, assuming you're still taking precautions. The good news is there are plenty of boatyards to choose from since I can't get you a boat. You have the skills to sort that out?"

"I've got that covered," said Marbles. "I'll be sure to skip the dinghy and pick something larger."

"What else will you guys be needing, then?" said Tony. "Where exactly are you headed?"

"North East is about as good as it gets," said Macca. "All

we know is it's somewhere out in the North Sea. Could be a stationary platform, or it could be something floating and tricky to isolate. Cannae be sure until we get there."

"Either will be frigid." Tony pointed toward another corridor. "Ignore the door panels, I've cleared access to all the rooms so you can wander in and out at leisure. First one is menswear, backpacks, and belts. It has a closet full of winter and wet-wear. I suggest you get well wrapped up; it's beyond freezing on the water, especially if you get soaked. And you will. Once hypothermia sets in, it's all over bar the chattering teeth and shivers."

"Appreciated mate. Pardon the pun, but these are uncharted waters. How about hardware?"

Sarge, Dud, and Numbers leaned into the conversation.

"Second room has sidearms. Hate to dictate, and I'm sure you guys know the drill but, since you don't have a clue what you're getting into, I'd recommend picking up the Kimber Compacts. They're stainless, plus I had them coated. In a pinch and a tight space, I love to shoot a Glock, but I don't remember them being big fans of salt water. Depends on how long you're planning on being out there."

"As long as it takes," said Macca, "but I'll take your advice. Again, it's appreciated."

Tony nodded. "Third door is the bigger stuff. I don't know how much you want to carry, but if you want long range weaponry, then it's in there. Semi-autos, rifles and scopes, shotguns. Help yourselves. Fourth door I call the Q room. Named it after the bloke off the James Bond films. Blades, grenades, mines and the sexy stuff you see on the telly. Plenty of cool gadgets for the discerning man."

"I'm lost for words," said Marbles, "and that's rare. You sure know how to kit out a guy."

"It's what I do," said Tony. "Dive in and give me a shout when you're done so I can lock up."

He turned to go, then stopped.

"Oh, and womenswear and lingerie are on the second floor. Behave yourselves if you go up there, but there are plenty of mirrors and I think I've got your size."

———

Sam squeezed her eyes shut as tears trickled down her cheeks.

"Please, I don't know what I'm supposed to have done, but—"

"But nothing, you've caused enough trouble. We can't go back empty-handed, so you can either come quietly, or I'll beat the shit out of you and dump you in the trunk."

Moonlight threw up the shadow of a gun. He waved it from side to side.

"Now, direct us to my buddy. And he'd better be—"

The guy dropped to his knees as another shadow appeared behind him. And then another.

The first shadow twisted until the clearing echoed with the sound of a dull thud.

The guy grunted then pitched forward to lie, face down, on the ground.

Sam screamed, squeezed her eyes closed again, and jumped up and down as a bright light lit up the surroundings.

"Omigod, omigod, omigod."

"Sam. Sam! Calm down. It's me, Evie."

Sam opened her eyes to see Evie toss away a large tree limb.

They met in the center of the clearing, and Sam sunk into the warmth of Evie's hug.

"It's okay, I've got you. You're safe now."

Tears dripped from her chin before she peeled herself away. "Evie, we've got to move. There's another guy back there. I kicked him where it hurts the most, but he could be here any minute."

"That's okay, Carina's getting directions on her phone."

"Carina? Purse thief?"

Carina stepped forward. "Hey, I heard that. Sam, there's a lot you don't know. How about we fill you in on the way back to the road?"

Evie leaned forward, rifled the guy's pockets, and came away with a set of keys. "How about on the way back to the car?"

Carina picked up the pistol. "What about this?"

"I already have one. Stick it in your purse."

Five minutes later, Evie gunned the engine and drove back in the boat's direction.

Sam yelped when Carina reached into her purse and handed over a phone.

"It's not what you think," she said as she rummaged again and held up her own phone.

"See? I thought your phone was mine. I didn't steal it; it was an honest mistake. Unfortunately, my mistake has dragged you into my trouble."

Sam powered up her phone. "I have to call Daryl; he'll be worried sick."

"Shit." Carina held up her wallet to show an empty slot. "They have my driver's license."

"That's okay," said Sam, "you can get another."

Carina looked at Evie and shook her head. "My license has my address on it."

"Oh, crap," said Sam. She reached into her purse.

"And my picture and date of birth," said Carina. "It won't take long for the guys we're dealing with to find me again."

Sam whimpered. "They have mine, too."

Evie pulled the car over and slammed on the brakes. "Sam, call Daryl now and tell him to get out of the house and go to a friend. Tell him to stay there and wait until you call again. And for God's sake, don't tell him why, you'll freak him out."

"Freak him out? Crap, Evie, it's all I can do to string together a sentence."

"Call him."

"Okay, okay, I'm on it. Jeez."

Sam dialed as Carina slipped her phone back into her purse. "I don't have to call anyone at home," she said, "but don't you think we should call the police?"

"Check the glove box," said Evie. "See if there's anything in there we could share with them. Right now, the only evidence we have is this car and a gun, and our prints are all over both of them. If they were professionals, the police might get the wrong idea, especially if either is stolen."

Carina reached into the console and pulled out a single sheet of folded paper. She flipped it over to read something handwritten on the back.

"Well, that was easy. This is the entire contents of the glove box."

"And?"

"It's an address with a zip code I don't recognize. Hang on a sec, I'll key it into my phone and see where it is."

A few key taps later and she looked up as Sam disconnected her call.

"Son of a gun was already at a friend's house. Playing cards and drinking beer. He didn't even realize I was missing. Anyway, I said that I was with you but that there was a gas issue with the house, and he should stay put."

"Good," said Evie. "That gives us time to work things out." She glanced at Carina. "Where's it at?"

"New York."

"Really? You don't think…"

"Bad guy's address?"

Evie nodded.

"Wow. That would be something for the police."

"But do we trust them?" said Evie.

"The police? I would hope so, they maintain law and order. Serve and protect, and so on."

"But you read so much about corruption and whether the cops are paid off and involved."

"So what are you saying?"

"What if we tell the cops and they're involved? They'd silence us to keep the whole operation going since there's so much money at stake."

"You think?"

"Hang fire," said Evie, "and let me make a call."

She stepped outside the car, closed the door, walked away with her phone to her ear, and returned after a few minutes.

"He's not impressed, but I reckon it's the way to go."

Sam leaned forward from the rear and rested an elbow on each front seat. "Who's not impressed, and what's the way to what? Clue me in here, Sister, I feel like a spare part."

"Numbers isn't happy, but he and Penny can cover us. They have the tech in Kentucky to monitor us and step in with help if we need them."

"Help and monitor what?" said Carina. "I mean, with all due respect, you're speaking English, but you're not making much sense."

"The bad guys know who you are, right?"

"Yes."

"And where you live."

"Yes."

"And Sam, too."

"I don't like that," said Sam through the gap in the seats.

"Neither do I," said Evie. "So before we call the police, and since we're almost halfway there already, why don't we drive to this address and see what we find?"

"Death, probably," said Carina. "At least some form of torture."

"Don't underestimate The Old Farts Club," said Evie.

"Evie, we're not The Old Farts Club. We're three women; one unemployed, one who loves shopping too much and, admittedly, one who's bad-ass."

"Are you forgetting about the plates?" said Evie.

Carina huffed a huge sigh. "No."

"What plates?" said Sam. "Like, dinner or dessert?"

"Like counterfeit," said Carina.

"Cool. You know about counterfeit plates?"

"Unfortunately, yes. We really need to tell you everything, Sam."

"And did you forget about the gangs," said Evie, "tearing apart towns and killing people to find them?"

"No."

Sam's eyebrows shot up. "Say what? What gangs?"

Evie continued. "So, to my mind, they won't stop until you either tell them where they are, or they stop you from telling anyone else. Either option is going to end in a bad way."

Carina folded into her seat and crossed her arms. "Well, when you put it like that, we don't really have much of a choice, do we?"

"We should at least check it out," said Evie. "Like I said, we've already traveled this far. And anyway, what's the worst that could happen?"

Sam held up both hands and fanned out her fingers. "I got

called a bitch and I broke three nails. The worst has already happened."

"Okay, Sam, we have to tell you everything. But first, Carina, do you know where we are?"

"Definitely not Disneyland."

"No, but we aren't a million miles away from the big prize."

"Okay, you've lost me. Stop speaking in tongues and put me out of my misery."

"Carina, we're right outside of Pittsburgh."

Carina went pale and said nothing, while Sam looked back and forth between the two.

"And we know what's in Pittsburgh, don't we boys and girls?"

Carina nodded.

"Okay, kids," said Sam. "Enough of this crap. Like, spill the beans. What's going on?"

"Sam, the plates we mentioned?"

"The ones they want to kill everyone for?"

"The very ones. They're here. Hidden in Pittsburgh. I reckon we should go and get them."

Chapter Nineteen

A liquid digital display over the lab door morphed from eight fifty-nine into nine o'clock as the entrance snicked open, and Thomas Fraine stepped through, followed by an inrush of sterilized air.

As the door closed, Anneka Ergström studied the enemy.

Dahl loathed him. His methods, his papers, even his dress sense.

Fraine could have been a model, with a rigid stance, square jaw, and bulges in all the right places. His usual wardrobe of gleaming black shoes and a sharp-pressed business suit had been replaced with faded denim jeans, brown slip-ons, and a baggy lab coat.

And he still looked like a model. Along with his immaculate dress sense, he was also known to be acerbic. Pedantic. Impossible to work with. An absolute dictator.

But the man before her seemed timid. Broken, like a caged circus animal. Dark curves underlined his eyes, and his pristine shirt held a form that seemed bent and submissive.

She frowned and waited for him to speak.

Instead, he made brief eye contact and walked past her to the farthest bench. The clock read 9:10 before she plucked up the courage to speak.

When she did, he flinched.

"Mr. Fraine, it's an honor to have you in my lab. I've read all your papers. I have to ask, what brings you here? I'm surprised you'd set foot anywhere near our work."

She could almost hear the digital clock ticking as Fraine seemed to search for the right words to answer.

Finally.

"This subject is important," he said. He waved his hand back and forth to emphasize his words. "This thing we do? Lives depend on it, and yet we fight one another to find the best results in a quicker or cheaper way. Don't you think it's time we stopped this ridiculous bickering and thought about the contribution we make?"

He paused and gripped the bench. Compared to the man she knew, he was unrecognizable.

"It's time for us to join forces, as it were. Enough competition. Dahl approached me and asked for my help, and I'm willing to give it. Apparently, you are having problems identifying AB-negative blood with a form of paper strip?"

Ergström took a breath to compose herself.

Facing her was one of the greatest scientific minds of her time, someone she suspected Dahl still looked up to, someone she'd studied through college and all the way through every school she'd attended.

Someone who, most times, seemed arrogant and unapproachable. Standing right across from her. Offering help.

Initially, she stuttered and then pulled herself together to tell him of the problems concerning the one blood type, the rarest, that could change the world if they could work out how to test for it instantly. How Dahl was committed, regardless of cost, to help humanity. How precious hours could be shaved from donor testing, to supplying that lifesaving liquid; hours that would save countless lives.

He listened and nodded in all the right places. Said the right words to reassure and encourage. But something seemed off.

The confident and assertive man from the many online videos and conferences was missing, replaced by someone who shuffled, gazed at the floor, and seemed to search for the easiest answer.

"So it's you and I against the world," he said after a pause.

"Well, I don't know about that," said Ergström. "We have an incredible team here, committed and resilient. It's much more than just us. Of course, we have supply issues, but Dahl is taking care of that."

"I don't doubt that. Dahl is nothing if not persistent."

Ergström frowned at his comment before he continued.

"You have worked out how to identify most blood types with a paper swab? Like a blood litmus test?"

"Yes," she said. "It's an instant read. No need for invasive blood-draws and the frustrating wait for lab results."

"But AB-negative refuses to show itself."

"Correct. It's elusive, to put it mildly."

"Do we have a decent supply of AB-negative blood? It's difficult to come by."

"We will," said Ergström. "Supplies will arrive soon. Dahl is sourcing more for us to utilize."

His eyes clouded over before he recovered.

"I don't doubt that, either. And God help the donors. For the record, I'd prefer to never know where it comes from, given the quantities we might need."

Before Ergström could speak, Fraine strode around the bench and stood beside her.

She flushed as his sleeve brushed against hers.

"Still," he said, "like it or not we're in this together. If you've solved the other types, you must be on the right track. Why don't you show me your work so far and we'll go from there?"

———

What should have been a two-and-a-half-hour drive from Edinburgh to Aberdeen took almost three as Macca wound his vehicle around smaller side roads to avoid the camera covered main roads that skirted the Scottish East coast.

They passed signs that pointed to castles, golf courses, and numerous inns, and the Jeep made short work of grassy banks and rock-strewn roads and avoided herds of uncontrollable sheep, until he pulled into a small marina at exactly nine o'clock.

Marbles threw open the door and stepped out onto crunching gravel. Steam left his mouth as he took deep breaths of the cold morning air.

Macca stood beside him. "It's a wee bit brisk, isn't it?"

He nodded as English lifted the rear hatch of the Jeep and sifted through the vehicle's contents.

"Never been any different, in my limited experience. It's always freezing up here. Give me a baking, dripping humid, oxygen-depleted Kentucky summer day any time."

Sarge and Dud slung wax coated gym bags over their shoulders as Marbles glanced out into the marina.

"We have an hour before these guys open shop, but they'll probably be here earlier to prep everything so we can't hang around. I'll wander up to the shore and check out our transport options."

The boat yard sat alongside a small bay. To the left, rolling hills, browning with the season, wound up to a huge cliff tipped with a castle, balanced against nature, that looked out over the ocean. To his right, the ribbon of road they'd avoided on the drive here twisted and turned away and disappeared into the horizon.

Inside the yard, six feet tall piles of brown, rusted anchor chains sat beside the store like coiled snakes. Salt gritted the store's small windows, and all but obscured its interior. Marbles cupped a hand to the glass and peered into the dark. When he saw no movement, he strode across old wood, out onto the jetty, and glanced along the water line. Fishing boats bobbed beside him and bumped against a tethered row of old tires, while larger private vessels swayed with the tide a half mile away. Between them, a burst of orange flashed each time the wind gusted to dip them into the water.

He turned at the sound of footsteps to find English, Dud and Sarge walking up behind him. At the entrance, Macca reversed the Jeep into a parking space and locked it.

"We packed binoculars, right, guys?"

Sarge dropped a bag to the ground and rummaged inside.

"Everything but the kitchen sink, buddy. Here you go."

Marbles took the lenses and trained them on the distant jetty. Beyond the larger boats, the orange flashes turned out to be the starboard side of a mid-sized fishing boat.

"There's nothing here that I'd trust in the choppy waters Macca mentioned, but I did spot something in the next bay. You guys up for a hike?"

Ten minutes later, they stood beside the boat.

"So we're borrowing this one?" said Dud. "Can you drive it?"

"I can sail it," said Marbles with a smile, "and maybe even steer or helm it."

"I guess the first thing is can you start it?"

Marbles placed a foot against a thick rubber band that circled the vessel. "Only one way to find out. Shall we board?"

Dud held out a hand. "After you, captain."

Marbles saluted, grabbed a rope that hung from the cabin, and hauled himself up on deck.

He ducked into the cabin while the others stowed the equipment in containers that sat beneath benches at the rear of the boat.

Varnished wood gleamed on every wall, and a white plastic seat sat before a chrome wheel that punched into a panel on the right. A red, plastic lifebuoy hung beneath the seat, next to a fire extinguisher stored behind a glass panel.

Sarge appeared at the side window, the beck of his cap poking through the opening. "Found the spare keys yet?"

"No keys for this bad boy, Sarge. There'll be a dead man's switch to override, then some battery banks and an electric ignition to deal with. Before I do that, I want to be sure I know where the engine coolant system is. It wouldn't do for us to be out in the middle of nowhere and the engine overheat and die on us."

"Nope, let's not do that and just say we did," said Sarge. "And there are no alarms?"

"It's considered dangerous to hotwire a boat, Sarge. Not quite as simple as boosting a car, so most folks don't bother."

"Okay, well we're about to don life vests, buddy, you should do the same. Leave you to it."

Another ten minutes later and the boat sputtered to life. Gray smoke belched from the stern as Marbles took the helm, reversed the vessel from its dock, and pushed its bow out into the marina.

English sat on a ledge inside the cabin. "I don't see too many signposts. Know where you're going?"

"Nope. Just figured I'd get us out of harm's way before

whoever owns this boat turns up and sees a random bunch of geriatric military guys commandeering it."

"I like how you say commandeering as opposed to borrowing. And less of the geriatric, if you don't mind."

Marbles smiled. "English, when you borrow something in the States, you usually give it back. Can't speak for you Brits. Given the expected conditions we're sailing into, something tells me this trip might be a one-way affair for this poor boat."

"That would be a shame. And I noticed you changed your glass eye. Wasn't it smiling earlier?"

A golden sun blazed from Marbles' left eye socket, replacing his favorite smiling emoji.

"Yep. Figured I'd counter the elements. If we're headed into rough waters, perhaps a little sun might make things easier. Let's say it's a call for luck."

They cleared the marina and left the bay behind. The harsh expanse of the North Sea took up the entire front window. A dull wash of angry water roiled and rocked before them.

"You might be right," said English. "Macca has the coordinates for our destination keyed into a sat phone. With luck we'll keep a signal for the entire trip and get there under our own steam."

"That would be nice, and satellites are everywhere, although these boats have their own GPS, too. We just have to program what we need into it since we don't really know where we're going."

"Well, we're heading for the point where Knowles said the transponder signal drops. With luck, again, that's a deliberate thing and not something we're forced into."

"Forced into?"

English shrugged. "Well, you know, shit keeps disappearing."

Marbles hid a smile. "What, you mean like the Bermuda Triangle type disappearing?"

"You superstitious?" said English.

"Heck, no."

"Good. Then, we're certain it's the bad guys turning the signal off, right? Not something otherworldly?"

"Dude, only an English guy could say the word otherworldly and still make it sound cool and not lethal."

"But you're certain. Right?"

"English, is there something playing on your mind? You sound a little concerned."

"No. No, I'm cool. I just…"

"How about you go pray to the god of single malt or craft beer or whatever and let me take care of getting us there."

"I can do that," said English.

He stood and patted Marbles on the back.

"Pleasant chat, mate. Catch you soon."

Chapter Twenty

Sam fanned her face with both hands and took a deep breath.

"Damn it, I think I'm, like, totally hyperventilating. And I still don't have my inhaler. Okay, let me get this straight. You want us to grab some hidden counterfeit plates that only Carina knows about and that people are dying over and then drive to New York to see if we can settle an issue with some crazy gang that knows Carina saw their operation, knows about and suspects that she has their plates, and wants to kill her?"

Carina and Evie shared a glance, grimaced together, and joined Sam at the rear of the car.

"Not sure we should have told her everything," said Evie.

"In a nutshell?" said Carina.

"A nutshell would be nice," said Sam. "Dang it, I feel hives forming."

"Yes. Only, there are two gangs."

"Crap-a-doodle. Okay, what's a bit less than a nutshell?"

"A nut?" said Evie. "Or a shell. I don't know. Sam, these people know where you live. If we can get to them and sort this before they knock on your door, it protects your family and saves a whole bunch of explaining."

Sam turned with a scowl. "Is that the best you've got, Evie? It saves a whole bunch of explaining?"

"Did you miss the entire 'protects your family' part?"

"No, but we're not built for facing gangs. Most days, I struggle to pick a nail varnish color. What the hell am I supposed to do with a whole gang?"

"Two gangs," said Carina.

"You're not helping," said Evie. "Be constructive or be quiet."

"Sorry."

"What are we supposed to do if we find them?" said Sam. "Hairspray them to death? Cos I've tried that, and they keep moving."

Evie threw an arm around her shoulders. "Sam, we have resources that most people can only dream of. The guys might be busy, but Numbers and Penny will have our backs and can tell us everything we need to know about who we're up against and where they are. They've got drones and imaging software and communications stuff out the butt. Heck, they've got satellites."

"Well, then why the heck am I paying for cable? Get Numbers to sort that out. If I'm doing this, I want my reality TV for free."

Evie gnawed her lip and continued. "Okay, I'll talk to him about that. In the meantime, can we get back in the car and see if we can resolve this together? If it looks too dangerous, I swear I'll take a step back and call the police."

"On Dud's life?"

"You learned his nickname. Finally."

"Yes, I did. On his life?"

"I swear. On his life."

"All right, but damn it, Evie, if I break another nail, there'll be hell to pay."

"I'll foot the bill," said Carina. "Hell is affordable. Heck, I've had a mortgage, I've already been there. Can we please go now?"

The girls crowded into the car. Carina took the driver's seat, Evie buckled herself in beside her, and Sam took the back seat.

With her purse.

Evie put her phone on hands free and dialed.

Numbers answered on the first ring.

"Evie, are you sure about this? As promised, I've not mentioned it to Dud. They're on radio silence, to be fair, but if anything even remotely bad happens, I'll never live with myself. Please, I'm begging you, call the authorities."

"Don't have time, Numbers. I already promised to be super careful and, push comes to shove, I'll come live with you. Speaking of the guys, do you know how they're doing? Dud did say they'd have to be radio silent."

"They're fine, Evie. In fact, they don't seem to be in as much danger as you. Knowing your husband as I do, I suspect you're a chip off the old block and you have a plan?"

"Sure do," said Evie. "We're going to find some counterfeit printing plates then drive to an address in New York. We're going to see who lives there and then sort things out so that Carina can relax and not fear for her life every day."

The line was silent for a while.

"That's your plan?" said Numbers.

"Yep. Just came up with it."

"You're killing me. You are not a chip off the old block, Evie Wilkerson. Counterfeit printing plates? On a positive note, I do have good news. Penny showed me an app that

English has. Well, when I say app, more like a hacked link into some major databases. To the authorities."

"What, police, fire, and such?"

"Nope, much deeper. For us, the FBI. For England, the CIA. For Israel, Mossad. For Russia, the Federal Security Service. I could go on, but it's a long list and I'm sure you get the picture."

"Holy crap, so English has a link into the intelligence agencies of different countries?"

"Yep, and not just a link. He has full, disguised access. I can pull and download files from anywhere, anonymously. I don't know how he's done it or where he got it from, and I've loaded up another Glock since it makes me nervous to even look at it, but it's pretty amazing."

"And I assume you found something?"

"Yes. This was easy, first level stuff. Those guys you're chasing in New York? They're badass, with records that stretch for miles. The Feds have been watching them for a while but have never made a move."

"Really? I wonder why?"

"No clue. Lack of evidence, maybe? Evie, please reconsider. Take everyone home and let the professionals deal with this."

"It's too late now, buddy, we're on the way. Carina knows where the plates are. They're vital evidence. Promise me you have us covered, though?"

"That goes without saying, but gosh darn, Evie, if I didn't, it would be a hard-fought battle between Penny and Dud over who'd make me pay first."

"Good to hear. Okay, we'll hit the road. Keep us in your

sights, or whatever that computery thing is, and I'll get back to you as soon as we get close to where we're going."

"Evie?"

"Yes?"

"Please be safe."

"Consider it done, Numbers. Don't worry, I'm ready to get back to my husband. I miss him." Evie disconnected the call and pulled up the GPS.

"So, really," said Sam, "what's the plan?"

"We're driving to Pittsburgh and then to an address in New York."

"Oh, crap. That's the entire plan? Against a bunch of the FBI's Most Wanted? That's no plan."

"Numbers never said they were the most wanted. They're just under observation. First level. And yes, I figure we get the plates, get to New York, then get Numbers and Penny to let us know what we're up against. Then, we can decide whether to get involved or call the authorities. With what Carina knows, plus the plates, that might be the evidence the Feds need to reel them in."

Sam let out a breath. "Okay. That sounds a bit more like a plan. Let's go; I want my cable. Oh, there is one thing, though. Where are the plates?"

———

Sarge watched as Marbles maneuvered the boat into deeper waters. Five minutes into the trip, and his stomach had settled to accommodate the rolling waves but, the farther out they got, the choppier the water became.

"All good, buddy?"

Marbles checked the destination coordinates he'd punched into the GPS panel and waited for the display to refresh.

"Yep. Cleaned out the bilge pump and checked the gas. We're in good shape, even for a return trip, as long as things go our way."

"It feels strange. I normally have a plan and an idea of what I'm headed into. Can't say that I like this not knowing."

Marbles nodded at the group outside the cabin. Dud, Macca, and English huddled along one side of the boat, seated on a bench that ran around the edge of the deck. At intervals, shallow sheets of water washed over them then trickled off their waterproof clothing.

"You feeling okay about this? English seemed concerned, too."

Sarge swiped a drop of water from his nose. "Well, there's normally advanced recon, or at least an idea of what lies ahead. This time, we don't know how many guys are waiting, or even if there are any guys waiting. We don't know what we'll find, other than probably a big-ass boat. And even then, we might have to search for that if it turns off its transponder."

"A lot of variables," said Marbles.

"That can, invariably, go wrong."

Marbles nodded again to the team.

"We've got it covered, Sarge. This is a stellar group of people with a massive range of skills. And Macca certainly adds something unique to The Club."

On the benches, the three men laughed and joked, standard practice when headed into a tense situation.

"What do you make of him?" said Marbles.

"Macca? Seems okay to me. Maybe a little rougher around the edges than the rest of us. He didn't flinch at the thought of doing some dirty work on our friend beneath the pub. That's not something I'd justify, but then he has saved English's life a few times so perhaps there's a balance."

"Defusing IEDs. You got to have solid nerves to do that."

"Or no concern for your life."

"True, but either way I'd sooner be charging toward something I could control than clipping away at wires, wondering which one was going to dismember me the quickest."

"So," said Sarge, "all in all, a good guy to have along for the trip. Brothers in arms, and all that. I'm surprised Tony didn't join us."

"I mentioned that to English. He's staying behind to make things seem as normal as possible. And he's helping to arrange Ken's funeral. It might be an empty casket, but no one else knows that."

"Not cool. I didn't know the lad, but this wasn't his fight. Hate when civilians get involved."

Marbles coughed a cynical laugh. "Sarge, we're all civilians now, but I know what you mean."

"True, but at least we signed up for this. How much longer until we reach our destination?"

"If we can maintain this speed, GPS says we'll get there around eleven o'clock."

"And Macca said the transponder dies at noon."

"Which only gives us an hour to play with. I don't think he counted on the drive taking so long, but I know you'd have set off earlier."

"We work with what we have, buddy. Can we go any faster?"

Marbles gestured through the front window. "Yes, we can go faster, but we really shouldn't. I can steer this just fine, but the water is going to get rougher the farther we leave the shore and, to be honest, I'm beginning to think we should have borrowed a bigger boat. I can't lie, given how fast the sea is changing, I'm concerned about how severe conditions could get."

"Appreciate that. At least we can all swim."

"Yep, but there's nowhere and nothing to swim to. And I don't know if you've checked your phone, but I have no signal. No one knows we're here, dude, since we didn't check in with Numbers before we left. No one is watching. We're on our own out here."

Sarge felt his stomach take a rare tumble.

"We don't have our own transponder?"

"Nope," said Marbles. "We're too small. Like I said, we probably needed a bigger boat."

Dud ducked into the cabin and slid onto the bench next to Sarge. He rubbed his hands together as icy water dripped from his clothing.

"How's it going, guys? Are we on track?"

"We are," said Sarge, "just about. But we need a bigger boat."

Sarge wiped his face again as Dud shook off his sleeves, sending spray across the windows.

"No shit, Sherlock. It's getting too rough and cold out there for me. The others seem to be enjoying it."

On the deck, Macca and English slid around on the slim bench and continued to laugh.

"They're sharing war stories," said Dud. "Did you know English almost got married in Afghanistan?"

"I recall Macca saying something about that when we met," said Sarge.

"Yep. He met this girl over there on one of his tours. Apparently, she was beautiful, worked for a news agency just outside the base. They kept bumping into each other until it became more than just a thing, and they dated for months. Obviously, this was way before Penny."

"Goes without saying," said Marbles. "She'd have killed

him then brought him back to life and killed him again in a different way."

"No doubt. Each time English finished his shift, she'd go back to his place, and they'd hang out until she either went to work or he went back on duty."

"Seems harmless enough," said Sarge.

"Yep, it seemed that way. Macca watched the whole thing develop and noticed that they never went back to her place. Don't forget that, at times, English would have struggled for privacy. When she hinted at wanting something more serious, Macca followed her home one night and found where she lived. The next time she was with English, he called in and had a look around, just to be sure he was in good hands."

"And?"

"She'd been turned. She worked for ISIS."

"Bastards. A honey pot. Oldest trick in the book."

"Yep. Macca took plenty of pictures and got back to him later the same night. Got him out and showed him everything. They reckon, since he pretty much ran the IT set-up on base, it made him the perfect candidate for information on channels, frequencies, you name it. With a hack on the base's communications, the consequences could have been horrific. Weapons movement, troop deployment, who knows? If she couldn't get it from him using her womanly charms, there was always the possibility of a romantic evening of girlfriendly kidnap and torture along with a nice glass of wine."

"Damn," said Marbles, "I'd prefer an IED. At least you'd go out with your pants on."

"What happened to her?" said Sarge.

"The base sent a party to her place the next morning and found it empty. She disappeared from the news agency, too. Editor said she was a brilliant researcher, and he'd miss her."

"He had no clue, either."

"Nope. Scary times, guys. Just glad I met Evie."

"You got a good one there," said Marbles. "How is the boss after your Jamaica trip?"

"All good, dude. While we do this, she's gone to Ohio for some down time and shopping with her crazy sister."

Dud gazed through the windows at the churning slab of grey ocean that stretched out into nothing more than even darker grey.

He shook his head.

"We're out here, almost surfing without a board, and I'll bet she's having a whale of a time."

Chapter Twenty-One

"They're where?" said Evie.

Carina focused her eyes on the road and kept to the highway's speed limit. "In the middle of Pittsburgh Zoo."

"They're in the butterfly enclosure, aren't they?" said Sam. "I'm getting a warm and fuzzy feeling about it."

Carina gripped the wheel a little tighter and nudged the accelerator. "Actually, we buried them at the bottom of the shark tank."

Only the secure snap of a seat belt held Evie in place. "You've got to be fucking kidding me. You buried the plates in the shark tank?"

"Evie," said Sam, "if Mom heard your potty mouth…"

"Mom can dive to the bottom of a fucking shark tank for some printing plates. How about that, Sam? Or maybe you can, as long as it doesn't mess up your nail varnish."

The car fell silent for a few seconds.

"Stressed much?" said Carina.

"Jesus, Carina, the shark tank? What were you thinking?"

Carina turned to glare at Evie. "Do you fancy diving in there and getting them?"

"Hell, no."

"Precisely. Where better to put them than somewhere no one wants to go."

"Except, now we need to," said Sam from the rear seat, "and I have a question."

"Only one?" said Evie, "I've got a list."

"Well, you said that the shark tank was where we buried them. Who's we?"

The car fell silent again, and it took a full minute before Carina replied. "Okay, I know I said I was single and unemployed, and I am. But previously, I was engaged and almost unemployed. My fiancée saw everything, too. When we realized what the plates were, we moved on impulse, grabbed them and hid them in the best place we could think of. Drew worked at the Zoo. He knew its layout back to front."

"Knew?" said Evie. "Carina, I'm so sorry. I hate when things don't work out. I had no idea."

"Why would you? I should have said something earlier." Carina still glared at the road, but her eyes welled with tears that hung and waited for permission to fall.

She blinked, and they fell.

"Things were working out. Drew went missing about three months ago. He's never been found. I reckon everyone's given up looking for him."

Sam let out a huge sigh. "Damn, Carina, I thought you guys had just split up. I don't know what to say."

Carina swiped away the tears. "There's nothing to say. I gave up expecting good news after a few weeks and tried to get back to normal life. It's not been easy. Shopping helps."

"I can relate to that," said Sam. "What did Drew do?"

"He worked with the sharks. He knew them well, so he

distracted them while I dived and buried the plates. I haven't been in there for a while, but you can see the burial spot from the tunnel."

"The tunnel?" said Evie.

"The glass tunnel beneath the tank. Where the sharks swim, a round glass tunnel goes right through their area. People walk through it while the sharks swim around them. It's relaxing."

"Behind glass, I'm sure it is. How the hell do we get the plates in a tank of sharks? And how many sharks are we talking about?"

"Last I knew, thirty."

"Say what?" said Sam.

"There are thirty sharks. Obviously, they're not all dangerous."

"Obviously," said Evie. "Richard Dreyfuss probably said the same thing filming *Jaws*; there are thousands of sharks in the ocean, but it's okay because they're not all dangerous."

Carina huffed. "Sarcasm is the lowest form of wit."

"Trust me, I can get much lower."

"She can," said Sam. "I've heard it."

"So, come on, Carina," said Evie, "what's the new plan?"

"Well, the good news is that it's off-peak season. There won't be as many visitors to the attractions. That should make it easier to mingle and then dive in when the opportunity arises."

"Dive in," said Sam. "Okay, another question. Who's doing the diving? Only, I'm not that good at swimming. I struggle with widths and lengths. I'm, like, excellent at depths, but only on the way down. I have issues getting back up again."

"So basically you're not a strong swimmer," said Carina, "but you're great at sinking."

Sam blushed and glared at the car's foot mat. "Er, yeah."

"Well, that narrows it down. Evie, you have two options. You can either distract the sharks or dive and retrieve the plates."

Evie cracked her knuckles and banged her head against the headrest. "Are you a good swimmer?"

"Top of my class," said Carina.

"Okay. Since you know where the plates are, I'll distract the sharks. How do I do that? Do the "Monster Mash" along the edge of the pool? Because, let me tell you, that worked a treat in high school."

"I can tell you're nervous," said Carina, "but we're about fifteen minutes from the zoo, so you'd better get your shit together. As far as I'm aware, sharks don't react to bad dancing, but then I've not seen you dance. More good news is, they rarely bother with humans unless they're curious or confused. If you keep them busy with a fish-fest, we should be okay."

"So Sam can stay out of the way and look pretty."

"Yes."

"And I just have to feed them?"

"Yes."

"I can cope with that. Cunning plan."

Carina held the wheel as they stared through the windshield and sat in nervous silence.

"Well?" said Evie. "What are you waiting for? Times a-ticking."

———

True to her word, Carina pulled into a space on the zoo's asphalt parking lot fifteen minutes later, beckoned everyone from the car, and locked it with a beep.

The usually busy lot had plenty of vacant spots, the black

strips standing out between randomly dotted vehicles like dominos.

"So how are you guys going to do this?" said Sam as they sauntered up a winding path and past a bamboo stand with a large welcome sign tacked to its center. "Are you going to climb a fence like a pair of ninjas and sneak through the bushes?"

"We're not ninjas, Sis," said Evie, "or criminals. If English's program searched for us, it'd find we have too many clothes and that's about it. I'm sure we can walk right through the main doors."

"We may be able to do better than that," said Carina. She pointed to a small door to the side of the main building. "I know a few of the people who work here. Let me see if I can get us in through the employee entrance."

"That'd work," said Evie. "Sam, while we do our thing, why don't you hang around inside that tunnel and watch from there? You could be our lookout."

"I can totally do that. Will there be any penguins? I love penguins."

"Sorry, Sam," said Carina with a pained expression. "The sharks ate all the penguins."

As Sam's mouth dropped open, Carina landed a friendly punch on her arm.

"Just kidding, girl. The penguins are in a separate enclosure. They prefer the temperature to be a little cooler than our finned friends. Give me a sec and let me have a word. Be right back."

She jogged toward the entrance, while Evie and Sam sat on a concrete step.

"I'm not sure about this," said Sam. "These are real sharks, Evie. I get nervous when I charge more than fifty dollars to my store card. What if something goes wrong? I only just met Carina but, now I know she didn't steal my purse, I kinda like her already. I don't want to watch her get bitten in half."

Evie wrapped an arm around her sister's shoulder and pulled her close. "Don't forget that Carina's partner worked with these sharks. You can bet she spent plenty of time here. She's probably on first-name terms with most of them."

"Ha. Like Dave The Shark," said Sam. "That's funny."

"And I've already figured out that Carina can be pretty mean. There's a good chance the sharks could get food poisoning."

Sam hugged her back. "I like it when you're not being all military."

"Make the most of it, Sis. I'm not having bad guys turn up at your house. This is the first part of a two-stage mission. Once we get the plates, we're off to New York."

"And I guess a trip to Times Square is out of the question?"

"As you'd say? Totally."

Sam stood as Carina appeared at the employee entrance. She planted a kiss on top of Evie's head.

"Smartass. Love ya, Sis."

"Love ya back," said Evie. "Don't worry, we'll be ultra-careful."

"Totally. Come on, Carina's waving us over."

The girls met at the entrance, and Evie and Sam stifled a giggle as a greeter with a name badge that said *Dave* ushered them through the entrance and into the zoo courtyard.

"I'd love to give you a bunch of Zoo-Bucks to spend," said Dave, "but they come with the entrance tickets."

"Honestly, it's not a problem," said Carina, "you've helped more than enough. And thanks for the kind words about Drew. I'll let you know if I hear anything."

They hugged, then Dave sloped off to the main entrance and Carina turned to face them.

"More good news," she said. "The shark enclosure is closed for maintenance, so we don't have to worry about people watching from the surface. And they fed the sharks about an hour ago so, hopefully, they'll also be a little more docile than usual."

"Is there such a thing as a docile shark?" said Evie.

"Sharks have a bad rep. They're not that bad if you respect their space. Five of the ones here are Sand Tiger sharks. Their eyesight isn't brilliant, and they swim in a pattern so, as long as you steer clear of them, or in this case, I steer clear of them, we should be okay. Four more are called Dark Shysharks. If they feel threatened, they curl up and wrap their tails over their eyes."

"That is, like, totally cute," said Sam. "They sound like the sleeping cats I've seen on Facebook."

"But they still have huge teeth," said Carina.

"And I'm still staying topside."

"So, in effect, we're only concerned about the other twenty-one, carnivorous man-eaters?" said Evie.

Carina offered a grim smile and led them into the zoo. "Well, when you put it like that. Truth be told, they eat mostly fish. Bull, Tiger, and Great White sharks are the guys with the reputation for a bad attitude, but none of those breeds are here. Plus, since the year 2000, there have only been twenty-two shark attacks recorded in the US. Dogs attack more people. I feel pretty safe."

"That's recorded attacks," said Sam. "And dogs don't bite off your head so you can't record."

"And now I'm concerned."

"Sorry. I'll shut up now."

"You should," said Carina, "or you're going in first."

They walked in silence until they reached a fork in the path.

Carina directed Sam onto another path to take her to the public viewing area and the glass tunnel, and then she and Evie strode to the entrance of the enclosure. Dramatic pictures of sharks in action bordered the open doorway that led to a concrete expanse that surrounded a vast pool.

Construction signs meant that no one else had ventured this far off the path that skirted the zoo's exhibits. Evie looked left to right, and then at the clear water before them. Gray shapes moved under the surface with a swaying motion that generated unease and respect in equal measures. Everything from strategically placed rocks to sea life fauna was visible through the clear water. Occasionally, a fin split the surface and sent tiny ripples to the pool's edge.

"Shit, my hands are shaking, and I'm just standing here. So now what? I see them in there. Huge, human-eating machines. I don't assume you're jumping in wearing just your underwear."

"Heck, no. Not that thick leather or even thin metal would make much of a difference, but there's a room at the far end of the pool where they keep the swimwear and refrigerated fish. We should stick to what they're familiar with. I vote we don't antagonize them any more than necessary. I'll suit up, you get fishy."

"I second that. Lead the way."

As Evie scooped pound after pound of slimy fish into plastic buckets, Carina disappeared into a small locker room and re-emerged in a shiny black nylon and Lycra swimsuit. Evie couldn't help but admire the way the material clung to her curves.

"Don't look at me like that," said Carina, "I already feel like a ready meal."

"Sorry. Just makes me realize that I need to get in shape. Dud and his buddies are all so health conscious. They're called The Old Farts Club, but I suspect they could all lap us if we got together on a track."

"What can I say? Benefits of a single life and a half healthy diet. Come on. Are you ready?"

"As I'll ever be, watching a friend dive into a pool of thirty sharks that I have to distract."

Carina cocked her head and smiled. "I'm already a friend? That's cool. I'll try to resurface uneaten."

"That would be greatly appreciated," said Evie.

Carina positioned herself at the edge of the pool as Evie rolled the tubs of fish beside her.

"So how's this going to work?"

In an instant, Carina slipped into the water like a seal. The surface hardly moved as she adjusted and turned to face Evie.

"I've counted it out. It takes about thirty seconds to get to the bottom of the tank. We hid the plates under a replica shipwreck. I can hold my breath for about two minutes, give or take, dependent on my heartrate and other factors."

"Now is not the time to tell me this," said Evie. "Calm your heartrate, and don't even mention other factors since I don't know what they are."

"Sorry. What it boils down to is this; either I'll be back in a couple of minutes, dive in after me if it's longer than that, or go home and bolt the doors."

"In terms of reassuring," said Evie, "that's not. How about you just get down there and do your thing? Speaking of which, do I just dump these buckets into the tank."

Carina gripped the edge of the pool. "For the love of all things holy, don't do that. You'll create a feeding frenzy. Toss the fish out one by one. As the guys get to see them, you'll create interest, and they'll form a kind of circle. Like the line at a gourmet buffet, but more civilized."

"When you say that, it sounds equally cool and bat shit crazy. And I love how you call them 'the guys'. I hope they feel the same way about you."

"Who knows?" said Carina, "Maybe they call me 'the food'. I'm going to dive and drop to the left, okay? You toss fish to the right and watch for them to gather. There's a hierarchy in here, but everyone gets a turn. The key thing is to be sure that everyone gets a turn. If one of the boys misses out and feels hunger pangs, he may look elsewhere."

"I thought they'd just been fed?"

"Yep, an hour ago. But they're predators. They never know when the next meal's coming. Better to eat now and starve later."

"I can relate to that. Okay, say when."

Carina turned and dropped, and Evie watched her arch her body and dive. Her heels broke the surface before her form cut through the water like a knife to merge with the rocks.

"Okay. I guess that's when."

She grabbed a fish, turned to the right, and tossed it into the pool. It splashed into the water, sank and rested against a rock.

"Well, shit."

She grabbed another and muddied the water with it, then grabbed another and tossed both into the same place.

It took a few seconds, but the first curious shark rose to the surface to check out the commotion.

"Come on, boys," she said. "Dinner is served, and it's not wearing nylon and Lycra."

Another fish splashed into the pool and another gray shadow joined the other. Then two more.

Evie checked left to find no trace of Carina. She must have dived beyond the surface and out of sight. How long had it been now? Thirty seconds. A minute? Had she already reached the shipwreck?

Four sharks now circled the latest introduction of food.

That only left another twenty-six in the tank. Seventeen, if you discounted the shy guys and the blind guys.

————

Sam followed the path away from the shark enclosure and came upon another set of signs. After a moment, she worked out which way to go and wandered through random people that passed her way until she reached the glass tunnel.

Carina was right, the view was spectacular.

The sharks drifted by close enough to touch, almost bouncing off the glass. The water seemed to ripple around them, as if you could see where they cut through it. Everything was effortless, and they glided, twisted, and turned in the water as if they owned it.

Beside her, a class of around ten children gazed through and thumped against the glass. Their teacher begged for them to behave.

A few feet away, she could she a shipwreck. A faux wooden ship, with its sides stripped away, its masts tilted.

Tiny boxes littered the ground around it, waiting for an intrepid adventurer to find them and share them with the world.

A dark-clad figure writhed and slipped into position and squatted beside the boat.

Carina.

Sam waved, impressed with her form in the skin-tight suit.

Carina responded with a thumbs up and a wave of her own.

The kids went ballistic.

A small boy with his nose pressed against the glass, pointed and turned to the teacher. "Miss, there's someone swimming with the sharks. Can we do that?"

Sam watched Carina lift the display and thrust her hand beneath it. A tiny bead of air bubbles escaped from her mouth, and the water muddied and agitated as she dug and rummaged. A few feet above her head, sharks circled.

"She's probably there to clean the water," said the teacher. "It's important for the sharks to have a nice home."

"There's one," said the boy. "Cool, he's coming closer. It looks like he wants to see what she's doing."

A lithe shadow cut with confident ease through the water. Starting as a silhouette, a sweeping tail drove a pointed nose and a powerhouse body down through the water until the gray became solid.

"Children," said the teacher, "step away from the glass. I don't think he's supposed to get that close."

Carina glanced up and waved a cloth covered bundle as the shark closed in.

Sam screamed and hammered against the glass.

Chapter Twenty-Two

English and Macca joined the others in the now cramped cabin as waves lashed the side of the fishing boat. The vessel rose and fell and rocked from side to side and fought to stay upright against the constant pummeling.

"Horrendous conditions," said English as they crested another wave and then dipped, rollercoaster-like, back into the ocean. "Should have picked a bigger boat. And we should have checked in with Numbers and Penny. I don't like this."

Marbles stood with his feet wide apart for balance, glared through the front window, and gripped the wheel. His white knuckles blended in with the chrome.

"You don't say. I figured the boat thing out about a half hour ago. Give me a sleek speedboat or a full-sized cruiser any day."

"Why don't you take a seat, buddy?" said Sarge. "It looks like a piece of cheap plastic made for a child, but standing like that can't be easy on the legs."

Every window offered the same view; a raging wash of violent gray that tossed the boat around like a toy.

"Vision's not great as it is, Sarge. I'll manage. If the GPS is accurate, we shouldn't be much longer. Speaking of which, how are we doing for time? We must be getting close to transponder switch off hour, and we haven't seen anything that might have a transponder."

Macca glanced at his watch and then the GPS.

"Minutes away, mate. And, based on our position, we should be seeing something any moment now. All I can see is weather wild enough to freak out a God. I cannae even work out where the water ends and the sky begins, it's just one gigantic mass of nasty."

Marbles continued to crane his neck and shout over his shoulder. "Is it too late to say I regret our lack of planning?"

"Yep," said Dud, "but there's no turning back now, brother. Still, say it if it makes you feel better."

"I regret our lack of planning. Did anyone consider how we'd drop anchor? The water is way too choppy, and the GPS says the ocean floor is three hundred and twelve feet beneath us. Call me negative, but I don't see our anchor falling that far and my belt loop's not going to make up the difference."

"I'd call you realistic. Plus, it never entered my head, so don't beat yourself up. We're okay for fuel, right?"

"So far. We've burned through about a third of the tank, so we should be okay to bounce around for a while. It'll take a while longer to turn us back to shore in these conditions, but that's nothing I can't handle."

Marbles eased back the throttle a few minutes later and set the engine to idle.

"Okay, guys, we're here. For obvious reasons, I can't kill the engine. We'll be at the mercy of the waves for a while, so keep your eyes peeled and let's hope we spot something."

Each man took a different window and gazed out into empty miles of nothing.

"This is useless," said Dud, "it might as well be dark." He gestured toward the open deck as another wave crashed across it and rocked the boat. "There are binoculars in my pack, but it's stashed out there. I'd get washed overboard before I could get to them."

"Well, this is the spot," said Marbles, "I just . . ."

"I see something," said English. "Or at least I think I do, it's hard to tell. Is that a light?"

He pointed through the window. A white pinprick flashed through the gloom and then vanished.

The team grouped at the starboard side of the boat.

"There it is again. And again."

"What is that?" said Sarge. "Morse code?"

English concentrated his vision. "No, that's a constant light. They probably see us in the same way. It's a combination of our boat and that one rising and falling in the water. We're both dropping out of sight of one another."

"The motion of the ocean," said Macca, "only last time I heard that statement it was preceded by 'it's not all about the size of the boat'."

"Never had that issue," said English with a smile, "but let's hope that's our target. I wish I could call Numbers; he could check the area and let us know what's out there."

"Like you said, it's too late for that. What's the plan? We need to know what that thing is."

"The lifebuoy," said Dud. He pointed to the red ring strapped beneath the helm's plastic chair. "I'll hang on to that, you guys hold the rope, and I'll belly crawl onto deck and get the binoculars."

Wood and metal creaked and groaned as another wave lifted and dropped the boat. Dud yanked at the straps on his life jacket and tugged them tight.

"You sure?" said Macca. "If Hell was water and not fire, it's out there on deck."

"We need to know what we're up against."

"I like it," said Sarge, "as long as I'm in here."

He unhooked the ring and held it as Dud threaded an arm through it then handed over a six-foot length of corded rope.

"Hold me like you hold your girls, guys. I don't fancy taking a dip in this."

The men stood like a tug-of-war team and gripped a section of the rope as Dud dropped to the floor and slid out onto the deck.

Water lashed his body the moment he left the confines of the cabin and forced him sideways. Each time he slid, he dug in with his toes and inched back. Time and again, he shook stinging water from his eyes to look forward, only to find himself sliding back on an inch-thick raft of saltwater.

"Go on, buddy," shouted English, "you're almost there." He turned to the others. "I don't know why I said that, I can barely hear myself."

"Affirmation," said Sarge. "It's what we do to make ourselves feel better."

Inch by inch, Dud crawled along the deck until he was able to unhook the clips that held the storage container closed. The moment he sat up to reach inside, another wave crashed into his chest and sent him flying backwards. He dropped on to his back and spun as he slid along the deck and slammed his feet into the edge of the boat while his head missed the side of the wooden bench by a hair's breadth. With a quick glance inside the cabin and a rueful shake of the head, he shimmied back to the container and arched an arm to rummage inside.

The first dip grabbed a pistol. Dud tucked it awkwardly into his waistband and delved again. After a moment, he looped a finger inside the straps of the binoculars and tugged until the lenses appeared and dropped over the edge.

He turned to the cabin and shouted an instruction that faded into the crash of another wave.

He shouted again, his lips moving silently. "…me back."

"Pull him back," said English.

The team yanked on the rope to send Dud sliding back down the deck toward them. One more wave slammed him into the entrance before he lay, breathless, beside the cabin chair.

"I try not to curse," he said between gulps of air, "but, fuck me, that was intense."

"Good effort, mate," said English. He took the binoculars. "I see them. It's definitely a boat."

"Well," said Macca, "after all that mayhem, it wasn't going to be a frigging unicorn, was it? What kind of boat? Any sign of life? Do they look mean? Is there a pirate flag? Give us details, man."

Dud stood and massaged his ribs. "Most important of all, does it look large enough to have a transponder?"

English focused the lenses again.

"I'd say so. It looks like a large fishing boat, much bigger than this. Probably the type we should have grabbed."

"Carry on," said Marbles, "and I'll pitch you over the side. They'll never find your body."

"No sign of life on deck, but there is a light in the cabin as well as the one on the mast."

"So it's manned," said Macca. "No flags to signify purpose or country of registration?"

"Nothing. Bare bones, as far as I can tell."

"So, they're here," said Sarge. "The right place and the right time. Now, what's the plan?"

"You guys seen *Pirates of the Caribbean?*" said Dud. "You think we should board them?"

As he spoke, a horn sounded that vibrated every piece of glass in the cabin. Each man turned away from the mystery vessel and looked through the windows on the opposite side of the boat.

A solid black shape blocked out both the sea and the skyline.

"What the hell is that?" said Marbles. "It's frigging huge."

Above the black shadow, trails of rope and cable and the arm of a crane stretched across its width. The boat floated backwards on a growing swell of wake as the oncoming vessel scythed through the water sixty feet away and headed right for them.

Macca scrambled to the front of the cabin and glared defiantly through the window as Marbles raced to open the throttle.

"Shit, it's a reefer."

"The fish offloading boat thing?" said Dud.

Fifty feet away.

"One and the same."

The smaller boat rose on the ocean, its throttle useless, as over three hundred metric tons of steel bore down on them. The wake from its bow rose higher than the boat.

"So now what do we do?"

Forty feet.

"I can't move us," screamed Marbles, "and it sure isn't going to stop. Pull the tabs on your vests, it'll activate the beacons."

"You're kidding?" said Sarge. "Jump? We won't last five minutes out there."

Thirty feet.

"We won't last five seconds in here. Pull the tabs and jump. With luck, the other boat will spot the lights and fish us out."

With all planning gone, the team rushed out onto the deck.

Twenty feet.

"And all of our equipment-"

"Can be replaced. For God's sake, Sarge, now."

Ten feet.

Macca dove first, followed by Dud.

English watched their bodies hit the water. The waves swallowed them in an instant.

Sarge followed, then Marbles.

He glanced up once more to see the bow of the reefer in stark detail.

As the sharp edge of steel plowed into the rear of the fishing boat, he jumped to the sound of wind and splintering wood.

Chapter Twenty-Three

Carina felt the shark before she saw it.

Despite Sam's frantic but silent hammering on the outside of the glass, the change in water pressure was all she needed to know that a colossal weight was cutting through the tank behind her.

The crowd of small children who watched her descent became a blur as they stepped back and, in a heartbeat, Carina registered her situation and remembered everything that Drew had told her. She turned to face her attacker.

Even with its mouth shut, curved teeth protruded at all angles, each one capable of tearing a deadly hole. A Sand Tiger shark.

Despite the adrenaline that mingled with the rush of blood in her ears, Carina gave a slight sigh of relief. Sand Tiger sharks rarely attacked humans, and the number of fatalities they caused was minimal. Given the other occupants of the tank, this could have been much worse.

But the shark kept coming until they were almost face-to-face.

She moved quickly and swung the plates upwards until they connected with the shark's nose. It veered to one side, but not before a tooth nicked a cut in her arm.

As the shark sashayed away, blood clouded the water until it turned pink.

Blood in the water was a hunting call for sharks, and another twenty-nine of them circled overhead. Still, the fact that they could smell it from a mile away was a myth. Drew said that scent in the water traveled on the current. Best not to make waves.

Carina shook the plates free from the canvas cloth that held them and used the cloth to bind the wound. As she completed the last turn, a bump from behind took her breath.

Air bubbles rose before her as the shark glided past, and she fought the urge to breathe to replace the lost oxygen.

No one was visible through the glass. Hopefully, Sam had gone to the surface to tell Evie about the attack.

She turned again to see the shark's approach. Drew also said, 'Stay big, sharks respect size and strength'.

Carina planted her feet at the bottom of the tank, giving the shark only one angle of attack. She clutched the plates and waited until it was almost upon her and then thrust the metal out and into its nose.

Again, it angled off to one side. She knew the element of surprise was all but over. The next sweep wouldn't be as placid.

Why had the shark acted this way? The kids tapping on the glass? Her muddying of the waters while she dug?

Her heart hammered, while her lungs began their own survival process and instructed her brain to take in oxygen.

Only training stopped her from sucking in deadly water.

The next approach would be the important one.

The shark came again, a controlled mass of sharp-toothed

violence. But, this time, others followed at a distance, finally aroused by the scent of her blood.

She remembered yet another Drew lesson. God, she missed him. In defense, go for the nose, gills, and eyes.

It was feet away when she launched off the base of the tank. She rose and, as she passed the shark, slammed the plates into the nearest eye.

Most sharks had protective membranes to protect their eyes. Sand Tiger sharks didn't.

There was no audible sound, but the shark darted away in apparent pain while the others continued their patrol.

Carina tucked the plates into her waistband and pumped her legs to get to the surface. Every inch felt like a mile. She jerked to swerve past one shark that came close then twisted and swam beneath another that moved in. Her smaller form gave her the edge in terms of movement, but a lack of oxygen brought dark shadows to the edge of her vision. Pressure pounded in her head, and her legs grew heavier and pumped slower the higher she rose.

The surface of the pool glinted diamonds above her, and she stretched for the lights before a colossal blow from behind smashed the rest of the oxygen from her lungs.

Dark shadows washed like ink over her final stream of air bubbles, and her body went limp as everything faded to black.

———

Sam slalomed through the herd of frantic children, out of the tunnel, and along the path up to the enclosure's entrance. Her feet slammed against the concrete until she gripped an entrance post and spun, breathless, into the enclosure.

In the tank, other than the occasional fin that sliced ripples into the water, nothing moved. No Carina. And no Evie.

She stormed forward to the water's edge and dropped to her knees. Silhouetted by the tunnel lights, two forms pushed for the surface with ominous shadows turning and curving above and below them.

Sam fanned her face as tears of panic formed in her eyes.

"Shit, shit, shit, shit. Where's my inhaler? Okay, no time for that. Think, Samantha."

She looked around the enclosure. To her left and behind lay row after row of plastic bleachers, waiting for peak-season spectators. The tank glistened before her, and the main complex sat off to the right.

Two long poles rested in a corner, each reaching at least two feet above the height of the complex roof. Next to them, glistening heads and tails lolled from a half empty bucket of fish that lay toppled onto its side.

Sam grabbed one of the poles, raced back to the tank, and thrust it into the water.

She almost fell in when someone grabbed the other end and pulled. As the grip weakened, she stood and walked backwards, dragging the pole alongside her.

Evie's head broke the surface in an explosion of spray and droplets. She coughed and shook her head before she spotted Sam.

Her voice fought for breath. "Quick, Sam. Help."

Sam dropped the pole and sprinted to her sister. Carina's motionless body floated in the water beside her while, across the tank, another gray fin cut through the surface and moved toward them.

"Another's coming," shouted Sam. "What can I do?"

"Fish. Throw the fish."

It took Sam a moment to work out Evie's instruction, and then she raced to the complex, picked up the bucket, and tossed fish toward the approaching shadow. Each sank with a frustrated plop.

Evie dragged herself from the water onto the concrete, gripped Carina's wrist, and pulled.

The owner of the fin was now close enough to see. Sam glared into beady eyes that stared back.

"Sam, she's too heavy. Help me."

A cut in Carina's arm dripped blood into the water. The tiny red rings morphed and grew into pink circles.

"Shit, that's not good. Sam, where the hell are…"

"I'm right here, Sis. Hang on."

Sam reached into the water until she found Carina's other arm.

The shark had sensed the blood and now wake washed from its fin as it plowed toward them.

"Pull," shouted Sam.

Together, they braced themselves and pulled. Carina's cheek grazed the edge of the tank as her body slid from the water.

She caught as the plates snagged.

Evie whimpered. "Come on, Carina, stop being so frigging difficult."

Sam leaned farther and tugged until her back popped.

Carina lurched and then moved again. Her feet cleared the rim as the shark appeared, snapped at thin air, then turned to send an angry wave of water onto the concrete. It whirled away and dived out of sight.

The girls collapsed together.

Sam spoke first. "Carina. Is she…"

"Not on my watch," said Evie. She rolled upright and rested her head on Carina's chest. "Nothing. Okay, CPR."

Evie handed Sam the plates and then linked her fingers.

Carina's body rose and fell with each compression, while she maintained an even rhythm.

After thirty compressions, she leaned forward, pinched Carina's nose, and blew two breaths into her still body.

Sam watched as she repeated the process. At the sixth round of actions, Evie's breathing grew heavy.

By the eighth, she slowed.

Halfway through the ninth, Evie fell backwards as Carina coughed up a shower of spray. As Evie took breaths, she rolled onto her side as more coughs racked her body, until she curled into a fetal ball and sobbed.

Sam hugged Evie, then rested a calm hand on Carina's shoulder.

"Carina? Are you okay?"

"Yes?"

"Cool. Can you not die again? I don't have my inhaler, and you totally freaked me out."

Carina's sob sputtered into a laugh. "Sorry," she said. "I'll do my best."

Chapter Twenty-Four

Sarge woke to the grating sound of metal on metal and rolled in the bunk to face the door just as it opened. A young, blonde head peeked through the opening.

"You are awake?"

"Yes," he nodded. "Barely."

The door creaked open farther, and the youth took a tentative step into the room. Sarge estimated his age to be somewhere between twenty and twenty-five.

"How are you feeling?"

"Old," said Sarge, "for the first time in a long time. I feel like I went ten rounds with Mike Tyson."

"Who?"

"Never mind."

He swung his legs off the bunk and winced as his bare feet connected with cold metal.

"Sorry," said the youth. A strong accent lent a strange lilt to his well-formed English. "Your socks and shoes are drying. We find nothing worse than wet feet. Can lead to all kinds of complications."

"Been there, done that," muttered Sarge. "Trench foot is a bitch."

"And I'm also sorry that I don't introduce myself. I am Elias, but the others call me New Guy. I have only been aboard for three weeks. They still give me a hard time."

Sarge stood and stretched. Bones and joints cracked and popped, and a nagging pain throbbed down his left side.

"I'm surprised you can stand so well," said Elias. "When they fished you from the water, you had been under for too long. It is lucky they spotted your tiny boat. Not so lucky that we were unable to stop in time. It takes a while, with us being so, how you say?"

"Frigging huge?" said Sarge.

"I don't know the first word but, yes, huge. It takes a long time to stop, and we were not able to. I am sorry, but at least we were able to get to all of you before the cold did. It was crazy for you to come here in such a small boat."

"We know. Now. Should have gotten a bigger boat. They'll carve that onto our headstones. So you managed to save us all?"

Elias grinned. "Yes. The captain can be hard, but he made sure we got all of you."

"And my friends? They're here?"

"They are. You are, as you say, in adjoining rooms."

Sarge felt the burden of potential grief lift as he sat again to massage his calves.

"Any chance I could see them?"

"Of course, although, at the moment, they also sleep. You have been through a huge, frigging ordeal."

Sarge smiled as Elias seemed impressed with his use of the word. "That we have. Still, if I could look in on them, it would help me relax a little. I worry about them."

"I understand. They are your friends. Wait right here."

Elias stepped out into the corridor, the door clanged shut, and the bolt engaged with a shriek.

"Damn it," said Sarge. "He better come back."

He checked out the room, saw his baseball cap looped onto a post at the end of the bed, and placed it back on his head.

The room was nothing more than a sailor's cabin. Basic and barely functional. From the depth of the dust on the laminate table, it hadn't been used in months.

How long had he been here? He remembered activating the light on his life vest, and the stinging cold of the North Sea as he said a quick prayer before he dived into its bitter waters. He remembered clutching a floating piece of wood, probably part of their destroyed boat, and he remembered hearing voices. Through the wind, there was no way to know if the voices were friend or foe.

Still, here he sat. Warm. Dry. And alive.

He jumped as the door screeched again. Elias appeared and thrust a clean pair of socks and a pair of faded shoes through the gap.

"I'm sure Erik will not miss these," he said, "and he looks to be about your size."

The footwear thumped to the ground as Elias dropped them, stepped back, and waited.

Sarge smiled, scooped them up, and slipped them on.

He stepped from the room into a painted metal corridor. Everything was white, with the odd teardrop run of rust from old rivets.

"Am I on the reefer?"

"Yes, you are. And I apologize, I am still being rude. Welcome to the SS Depression."

"Seriously? That's the name of your vessel?"

"It is," said Elias. "Something to do with a time period, although the captain sometimes calls it SS Grim Reefer."

"That does seem more apt," said Sarge, "although it might be too much of a close call." He gestured to the door of the next cabin. "So all of my friends are here?"

"Indeed."

Elias gripped the door lever and opened it an inch at a time.

"They have not used these cabins in a while," he whispered. "Do you have WD-40 in your country?"

"Yes, we have it in America. Seems like your vessel could use a WD-40 shower."

Elias laughed as the door cracked open. He stood back and waved Sarge forward.

"Please, I am sure he would prefer to see your face to mine. He seems a little angry."

Sarge nodded and pried open the door enough to set a foot inside the cabin. When he saw the empty bunk, he stopped.

"Buddy, it's me. Sarge."

"Shit, Sarge," said Dud, "I almost smacked you."

Dud stepped out from behind the door as Sarge entered.

"Seems I slept a little deeper than you," said Sarge. "This guy came into my room and he's still standing."

Dud glared through the opening and into the corridor.

"It's okay," said Sarge. "Dud, this is Elias. Elias, meet Dud."

The young man gestured through the doorway.

"He's on our side," said Sarge.

Dud poked his head out into the corridor. "Where are we, Sarge?"

"We're humble guests of the captain of the SS Depression."

"You're shitting me."

"Nope. Would you prefer the SS Grim Reefer?"

"Heck, no," said Dud. "Are we all present and accounted for? And in one piece?"

"According to Elias, we are. Care to check?"

Dud followed Sarge's outstretched arm and stepped into the corridor.

"All of your friends are here," said Elias. "One moment."

He walked to the next door, dispensed with pleasantries, and yanked it open.

A Scottish accent yelled, "What the fuck?" and Macca's face appeared in the doorway, fists raised and ready to swing.

"Dud," he nodded as he stepped out of the cabin. "Good to see you. Sarge, many apologies. Forgive the profanity. And how come you have shoes and I'm barefoot?"

After brief explanations, Elias strode forward to the next door.

"I learned from the first time," he said. He nudged open the door with his foot and stepped back.

Marbles stuck his head through the opening, one eye blue, the other a blazing fire. "What the actual hell? Where are we?"

"I like his eyes," said Elias, "but he was not happy last time."

"Long story short," said Dud, "we're aboard the reefer. Don't ask about its name, it'll just freak you out. This fella here is Elias, and he's one of the good guys. Turns out the lights on the life vests worked. They spotted us and were able to fish us all out."

"That's good news," said Marbles. "Even my glass eye got cold. I thought we were done for."

"Me, too," said Sarge. "Thanks to these guys for plucking us out of the mayhem. Okay, Elias. On to the last one."

Elias stopped. "The last one?"

"Yeah, English. The other guy that talks funny."

Elias frowned. "I don't understand."

"You said you had us all. English is the other guy."

Elias took a few steps back and held up his hands. The temperature in the corridor rose a few notches. "Guys, please stay calm, but this is it. We got all of you. There is no one else."

———

Sam sat in the back seat and cradled the plates on her knees.

"So there's like, eight of them? Must take ages to print a load of bills. Good job they don't cost anything."

"Four sets," said Carina, "Two fronts and two rears. And it doesn't work that way, Sam, they run long rolls of paper through them to produce lots of bills."

"It's weird. They seem the exact same size as a dollar bill, but they look like they're for, like, printing twenties."

Evie shook her head as Carina held in a snicker.

In the mirror, her face looked battered, with angry, yellow bruising blending in with the red scratch that covered her cheek.

"They are the exact same size. They use different inks and then use those plates to print the actual bills, so they have to be the same size."

"Yeah, but aren't twenties…oh, yeah, they're all the same size."

"Hello, Sam, and welcome to the show," said Evie. "On a more sensible note, thank you for your help at the zoo. Honestly, I didn't think you had it in you." She reached back, gripped Sam's shoulder and squeezed. "I'm so proud of you."

"Yes," said Carina, "you guys saved my life. Literally. If I were a cat, I'd only have about four left by now."

"It's fine with me if we never do that again," said Sam.

"Now I've had time to calm down and take everything in, that was some of the most intense stuff I've been through. Even the finale of the first season of the Kardashians wasn't that intense. And trust me," she said with a shudder, "that was totally, like, fricking intense."

"We live in different worlds," said Carina, "thank God. Sam, okay if I take those and keep them safe?"

Sam passed the plates between the seats. "You nearly died so you could get these. So you should hold on to them because they must be really valuable to you."

"Sam, I did die. You were there, right? And honestly? If they serve to keep us safe and put some bad guys away, some really evil bad guys, it will be worth it. And, of course, stop them paying us a visit."

The car fell silent for a moment.

"Okay," said Carina, "so now we're all alive and kicking, and battered and bruised, what's next? A road trip to New York?"

Evie held up her cell phone.

"Yep. Let's check in with Numbers and Penny, and then we'll hit the road." She hit dial and put the phone in speaker mode.

Penny answered. "Hi, guys. Numbers is taking a break, so you're stuck with me. Truth be told, he's gone home for a couple of hours to remind his wife he's still alive. Are you getting close to New York?"

"We're about to set off. The was an incident with a shark."

"Sounds interesting," said Penny, "but, moving swiftly on, is everyone okay?"

"Carina died," said Sam from the back seat, "but Evie brought her back to life."

"Don't ask," said Evie. "It's better not to know. I figured you'd be tracking us?"

"Nothing surprises me anymore. I'll let you tell me about that when you get back. And, yes, I am, but I have you on a different screen. Honestly, it's been such a long time since the guys checked in, I'm scouring all of their phone signals for signs of life and I'm getting nothing."

"I wouldn't worry too much about that. Dud said they'd be going off grid for a while."

Penny huffed down the line, causing the speaker to crackle. "I know. And I know they can look after themselves, I'm just sitting here trying to be a good wife."

"And a magnificent job you're doing. Have faith in the boys, okay? They're a team to be reckoned with, and they all have one another's backs."

"You're right." Penny adopted a cheerier tone. "So what's up with you girls?"

"We have some counterfeit printing plates," shouted Sam.

"Nice," said Penny, "although, given the subject matter, you might want to keep that quiet."

Carina leaned toward the phone, as if getting closer would bring her into the conversation.

"They're the evidence the Feds might need to bust open this counterfeit ring. But, since they know where both Sam and I live, we figure we'll head over there and check out the lay of the land. I don't like the idea of bad guys turning up on my doorstep unannounced. Can we count on your support, Penny?"

"One hundred percent. Anything you need, let me know. Could you just do a couple of things for me?"

"Sure," said Evie. "Name them."

"Well, first off, if the situation looks any more than, say, thirty percent dangerous, stop and call the authorities. You've got the evidence; let them do their job."

"Deal. And you said a couple of things?"

"I did. Carina?"

Carina leaned forward again. "Yes?"

"Please don't die again. It would be incredibly inconvenient."

"At the risk of repeating myself," said Carina, "I'll do my best."

"Much appreciated. Stay safe, guys." Penny hung up.

Evie dug out the New York address and punched it into the GPS. "Buckle up, girls," she said, "it's time for a road trip."

Chapter Twenty-Five

English squinted his eyes to see through a haze of blinding white.

The presence of an overhead light fixture convinced him that at least this wasn't Heaven.

As his eyes grew accustomed to the glare, he looked around and heaved a sigh of relief. He lay in a bed.

To one side, an IV line snaked from a chrome stand and into his arm. The word *Saline* ran around the front of a half-empty bag of clear liquid that hung from a small hook and dripped with a steady rhythm into a small glass tube before making its way into his bloodstream.

Chrome siderails on the bed. A miserable gray sky through a small letterbox window high in the wall. White corridor walls through the small pane of wired glass in the door. Hospital.

A panicked thought had him sit upright, only for a searing pain to rip into his shoulder and across his temple to drop him back to the comfort of the pillow. "Jesus, that hurt."

His fingertips traced a prickly line of stitches that ran from his cheek, past his ear and up to the shaven middle of his right temple. The guys. If he was here, had someone also picked up the rest of the team? Were they close? And the boat.

The last thing he remembered was watching the last of the men, Marbles, disappear into the violent froth of the sea. Then, the bow of an enormous vessel smashed through the back of the boat, to send a huge piece of the deck hurtling toward his head. Then darkness and nothing.

And now light and pain. Had they flown him back to a hospital on the Scottish mainland?

A figure breezed by the door.

By the time it registered, English ran out of time to summon the strength to shout. Instead, he scoured the wall behind the bed and searched the sides for a panic button. When he found nothing, he leaned sideways onto an elbow and levered himself upright.

As soon as his bare feet touched the tiled floor, a wave of nausea knotted his stomach. The stitches pulled and his head throbbed as a jet of vomit splashed the ground beside the IV stand. "So that's what the North Sea tastes like," he groaned.

Thigh muscles complained when he rested his hands on his knees and pushed but, with help from the side of the bed, he managed to remain standing. Skirting the pool on the floor, he pulled the IV stand behind him and walked to the door.

The handle wouldn't budge.

English frowned and tried it again.

Locked.

Did hospitals lock the patient's room doors now? Military hospitals didn't. Asylums did.

Perhaps the Scottish had different rules.

A glance through the small window showed nothing but a larger stretch of clinical white corridor.

The first pangs of concern nipped at his mind as he

dragged the IV back to the bed and slumped onto the edge of the mattress.

With no clock on the wall, there was no way to know either the time right now, or the time of day. And with no pictures or decoration of any kind in the room, the place felt soulless and empty.

He stood again to check out the small closet. It contained his clothes, cleaned and pressed, with his shoes sitting side by side beneath them. The small set of bedside drawers contained nothing.

Another figure walked past the door.

"Excuse me!"

A face reappeared in the window, the lock turned, and the door swung open.

A tall man in a white lab coat and denim jeans stepped into the room. "Sir, I'm sure you should be in bed resting. You've had quite an experience."

"No kidding," said English. At once, a barrage of questions flooded his mind. "Could I trouble you for painkillers? Where am I? And are my friends here, too?"

"Of course. Let me find out when you had the last dose. I'll need to see who's taking care of you. Hop back into bed and give me a moment."

The man stepped back, closed the door and locked it, and then walked away.

With nothing else to do, English followed instructions, climbed beneath the sheets, and closed his eyes.

When he opened them again, no daylight shone through the high window. A three-quarter moon hung in the sky to bask the room in a beam of dull yellow glow. Light still burned through the small window in the door.

Now piqued, concern slithered its way to the front of his mind. The ache in his head worked at half its earlier strength, but his empty stomach grumbled. Any food that might have been in his system was lying on the floor beside him.

How long had he been here?

The muscles in his legs felt looser and more relaxed, and the saline would prevent dehydration, but his body demanded solid food. He glanced up at the bag and jumped.

A full bag dripped with the same steady rhythm into the same clear glass tube. At the side of the IV stand, the floor gleamed, with all traces of his stomach contents vanished.

Someone had entered the room while he slept, cleaned the floor, and changed the empty bag.

Using the same method, he slid out of bed, grabbed the stand, and strode to the door. He tried it again to find it still locked. Nothing moved beyond the window, and he balled his hand into a fist and pounded on the door.

"Hey. Can anyone hear me? I demand to know what's going on. Someone, talk to me."

Silence.

He hammered again and again until the edge of his hand ached. "What the hell is going on?"

Five minutes ticked off in his mind, until the lock clicked, and the door opened.

The same guy walked in, followed by a stunning blonde woman. The tall guy moved to one side as she breezed past him. Impeccable clothing and perfect makeup emphasized a natural beauty that took English's breath away.

He shook off the feeling. "Where am I?"

The woman strode forward to sit at the foot of the bed. "I apologize for leaving you here for so long. You must be starving."

"Where am I?" said English.

"All that matters is that you're safe. A fishing vessel spotted you in a treacherous place. Apparently, you were floating on your back, which probably saved your life. If not for that, they might not have seen the light on your life vest." She gestured toward the closet. "I'm afraid we had to cut off the vest, but your clothes are washed and pressed."

She stood and moved to sit beside him. A mixture of shampoo and expensive perfume washed over him. "You are fortunate to be alive. My team has repaired your right shoulder. It was dislocated. And you've gained eight stitches at the side of your face where you had a large gash. I can't guarantee they did as good a job as an expert plastic surgeon, but they do have plenty of experience in stitching up people. You also lost valuable blood, but nothing that your body won't be able to regenerate."

English jumped again as she slapped her thighs and stood.

"How rude of me. I'm waffling on and you're probably ready to gnaw off your own arm. Let me get someone to bring you food. I'd recommend something light to begin with, perhaps a sandwich. We did pump quite a bit of seawater from your system. The saline will have taken care of the salt, but we don't want you to throw everything up again."

She laughed to show a row of perfect teeth. "Your stomach probably thinks your throat's been cut."

"How long will I be here? And are my friends here, too?"

"I'm sure you have a million questions, but let's get you fed first. I do have one question for you. I'm told that there was no identification with you. We have no idea who you are, and we'd like to notify your next of kin that you're here and are not harmed. What is your name?"

English thought for a moment.

The woman seemed friendly enough, but something about the situation didn't sit right. If everything was okay, then it wouldn't matter. If something were off, he'd need strength to tackle it.

Food brought strength and, right now, there was too much he didn't know about his surroundings.

"Keith," he said.

"Keith." She turned her head coyly and smiled. "Okay, does Keith have a second name?"

"Smith," said English.

She laughed again, a sexy, throaty burst of humor.

"Smith, such a typically English name."

"Absolutely," said English with a smile of his own. "As common as muck."

"Of course. I've heard that saying."

She strode to the door. The tall guy turned to leave when she spun back and laughed again. "I'm so sorry, I'm exceling at being rude today. I didn't introduce myself."

She moved back to the bed to thrust out a hand.

English shook it and admired a set of perfect nails and flawless skin.

"I'm Marte. Marte Dahl."

Chapter Twenty-Six

Dud backed Elias into a metal stairway.

"We have to go back."

"That is impossible," stammered Elias, "the captain keeps the ship on a tight schedule. We must now deliver some of our cargo and then move on to our next stop. They are waiting for us. Plus, we are miles from where we found you. Even if a part of your boat still floats, your friend would not last long in the water." He offered a bleak smile. "Perhaps another ship picked him up? I am sorry, but I will report this to the captain. He can alert the Coast Guard, and other vessels in the area could do a search."

Macca pushed through. "Unacceptable. You need to—"

Sarge placed a hand on Macca's shoulder. "Easy, buddy, it's not this fella's fault. Elias, why don't you take us to your captain? While I understand the situation, we know people who may be able to search the area via satellite. If we could use your communications, we can check in with them and report our friend missing."

"Again, I am sorry," said Elias, "but the captain insisted

that you remain on this side of the ship." He gulped. "I'm not allowed to let you leave this area."

"Are you saying we're prisoners?" said Macca.

At Macca's tone of voice, Elias took one step back onto the staircase. "Of course not, you are guests. But we have important stops to make. Many people rely on us. And the captain doesn't like to have anyone but the crew move around the ship. There are sections even I'm not allowed to enter."

"That's fair enough," said Macca as he stepped forward. "I understand."

In one fluid movement, he spun Elias on his heels, wrapped an arm around his throat, pulled him close and held him tight.

The youth's soft hands clawed at Macca's forearm for a while until his efforts grew weaker and his oxygen deprived arms dropped limp and heavy to his side.

"Sorry, guys, but I cannae be messing around. Don't worry, Sarge, I was as gentle as you can be while you're choking someone. He'll nap for a short while and wake with a sore throat, but he'll be fine. Nothing a good whisky won't fix."

They carried Elias into one of the rooms, frisked him for weapons, tied him to the bedframe with his shirt, and locked him inside.

Dud led the way up the staircase to another solid door. The wheel at its center turned easily, and he opened it as Macca, coiled and tensed for action, waited for any surprises on the other side.

When nothing moved, they stepped into an identical corridor with another door and a staircase at each end.

"Does everyone agree that the captain will probably be front and center on the top deck?" said Marbles.

"Agreed," said Macca. "Standard positioning. It would be nice to know which end was bow and stern, though."

Sarge twisted his cap. "Soon find out, I guess. I say, if anything, this corridor rises on the right. Stands to reason the front of the boat will be taller to ride the waves, so perhaps that way is the bow. Listen, does anyone else have an uneasy feeling about this? Elias seems like a nice enough guy, but he said that even he doesn't have access to the entire ship. Is that normal? It's not like we're on a military vessel. And he mentioned that we need to stay on this side of the ship, so what's on the other side? And I smell rust and salt, but no fish. I thought this was a reefer. Shouldn't it reek of fish?"

"Good point," said Marbles. "although I get the impression that maybe this wing is for accommodation since it's where they put us. Still, we've not seen anyone else and, so far, both corridors are enclosed compartments. Perhaps that'll change as we move up. As for access to the rest of the ship, he's just a kid. Maybe he still has to earn his stripes? I'm too old to remember those days."

Dud smiled and moved to the right. "I'm not. I agree with Sarge, this way feels slightly uphill. Let's keep climbing, deck by deck, but we should err on the side of caution, the next guy might not be fresh out of school."

The following door opened onto more of the same, but the layout changed at the next.

A staircase and a door with a porthole window lay at one end of the corridor, but a cage of propane tanks sealed the other.

Dud led the team to the door and peered through the glass.

"I don't see anyone. This corridor continues onwards, past the door to another rising staircase at the end, but there's also a sharp turn left."

"You reckon that turn takes us to the balls of the ship?" said Macca. "This section is about half the length of the others. What if this is like a central hub where we can split off either way?"

"Sounds good," said Dud, "but did you say, 'the balls of the ship'?"

"Aye, you know, the nuts and bolts of the operation. The nitty gritty. Where they allegedly keep the fish. If we have doubts, and I'm starting to think I could piss and shit doubts by now, maybe we should head that way and check out the other side. Make sure it's legit."

"Check out the balls."

"Why not? Then we'll know for sure."

"Never thought I'd utter this statement," said Dud, "but, okay, let's go check out the balls."

As the door swung open and Dud stepped through into the turn, another door in the corridor on the left also opened.

A crewmember stepped out and stopped, his hand rested against the doorframe. His eyes shot wide with surprise as he pointed.

"*Hvem er du?*"

"Sorry, brother," said Dud as he prepared to duck back around the corner to safety, "but I don't speak whatever language that was."

The guy vanished through the doorway and reappeared in seconds with a pistol.

Dud lifted his hands.

"Shit, you're fast. Okay, so you don't speak English, you seem to be alone and you have me at gunpoint."

He stepped forward from the door, turned to face the others, and dropped to his knees.

"I'm all yours, buddy. Come and get me."

The guy crept forward, his breath held, with a shaking gun trained on Dud, until he drew level with the other corridor.

Dud watched as he stepped into space.

Hunched against the wall around the corner, Macca leaned back and then, as he appeared, put all his weight into a punch that caught the guy square on the chin.

His legs folded and he dropped to the ground with a thud.

Macca heaved a sigh of relief. "Appreciate the play-by-play," he said as he crouched to pick up the pistol. "Made things a little easier."

"Appreciate the boxing skills. A one-shot knock-out. Academy?"

"Worse. Local disco in Edinburgh. Rough neighborhood and just out of school. It was do or die in those days."

"Fair enough. Well, at least we know we're not among friendlies. And now we're partially armed."

"We should search his room. You never know."

Marbles checked and appeared moments later with another nine-millimeter and handed it to Sarge.

"Tucked under his pillow. Now what?"

"Well," said Sarge, "you know the game where you get warmer or colder? Since this guy is the first sign of life we've seen since we met Elias, I reckon we just got warmer, so I say let's continue in this direction."

"I'm with you," said Marbles.

They followed the corridor past other open doorways until they reached a different door.

A large horizontal bar replaced the wheel that opened the other doors. Macca and Sarge knelt with their pistols aimed as Dud reached past them and wrenched the lever upwards.

He shivered as a blast of cold air raised goosebumps over his arms. Finally, the familiar smell of fish wafted over them, and the door creaked open to reveal a dark room, hidden behind an apron of thick, plastic strips that hung as an overlapping curtain.

"I think we've hit the jackpot, gents," said Macca. "Something fishy this way comes."

He slid an arm through the curtain and held it open for the others to creep through. The floor vibrated with the steady hum of a bank of refrigerators, and Dud rubbed up and down his arms.

Breath appeared as he spoke. "Damn, this is freaky. Cold, weird and very frigging stinky. That's a strange smell, like there's more than fish."

In the emergency lighting, each outside wall of the room seemed lined with white doors, locked with thick chrome handles.

Other than a faint, blinking red light over another door, nothing else stood out.

Dud popped the magazine from the pistol, checked the rounds, and slid it back into place with a comforting click. The moment he stood, the blinking red light turned to a solid green and fluorescent lights buzzed and blinked into life overhead.

He dropped again as bright light bathed the entire room.

"Shit. Sorry, guys. Motion sensitive lighting."

With nothing to lose, he swept the pistol from side to side and entered the room.

"If Elias's cooler brother wants to turn up around now, I'm down with that."

"So far, we've not been that lucky," said Macca. "Let's continue to expect the worst."

"Agreed," said Sarge, "but what's that smell?"

"Fish," said Marbles, "although not good fish. Maybe some produce a few days past its sell by date?"

Dud drew in another breath of frigid air. The expected smell still pulled at his nostrils, but something else mingled in the scent. Something familiar, from a bad time.

"I get it, too, Sarge. What the hell is that?"

Macca shuffled forward. "I remember that smell, from not that long ago."

Marbles joined the group. "Smells like fish mixed with copper pipe."

Dud stood and marched into the room. "Blood? Let's check out these fridges."

He tugged open a door to find a mound of fish covered with chips of ice.

"Nothing here."

The next door revealed the same. And the third.

As he wrenched open the fourth, he stopped, staggered back and gagged.

"Guys," he said. "Come here and check this out." He swung the door wide. "This accounts for the smell, but what the hell is it doing here?"

Chapter Twenty-Seven

The GPS set their drive time from Pittsburgh to New York at a little under six hours.

At the three-hour mark, Evie spotted a small diner at the side of the highway and pulled into the lot. As the car nosed into a vacant space by the entrance, a small group of youths stepped outside and lit cigarettes behind cupped hands.

With the car locked, she held the entrance open for Carina and Sam, then followed them inside as a wolf whistle crept through the closing door behind her.

"Did those kids just whistle you?" said Carina.

"Scary, isn't it? They're barely out of diapers. I'm not sure they should even be smoking."

"Hey, these days, and in the rare times that it happens to me, I straddle the line between being offended or being flattered."

"How about not bothered?" said Evie. "All of them together wouldn't equal the man I have at home. Or wherever he might be at this moment in time."

They took a table by the window that looked out onto the

highway.

"Still heard nothing?"

"No, although I don't expect to. I didn't know him for a lot of the time he served, and I've decided that I prefer it that way. Dud can look out for himself, and he's always had other guys beside him, but I don't think I could cope with not knowing for weeks at a time if he was okay. A few days is long enough."

"And I assume he no longer serves?"

"Yes and no. He's no longer on active duty, if that's what you mean, but, given recent events, he still serves, just unofficially. Once a soldier, always a soldier. The Old Farts Club is on a much smaller scale, but it's not civilian life, either. We barely touched ground from the vacation from Hell and he's dived right back into the thick of it. I'll tell you about it sometime. Jamaica is beautiful, but where there's beauty, there's also danger."

Sam butted in. "That's very cryptic and all, but I'm, like, thirsty and totally starving. My stomach has developed its own language. Can we save the talking for in the car like normal people and order food?"

"Sorry, Sam," said Evie, "just missing my man."

"Lucky you. Mine's probably drunk by now."

Carina slid menus across the table as the youths stumbled back into the diner and slinked over to a bottle-covered table next to the restrooms.

"Fancy a beer, myself. Are you okay to continue with the driving duties, Evie?"

"Yep, I'm in the groove now, you dive in."

The girls ordered food. Sam and Evie drank water while Carina poured a bottled beer into a frosted glass.

Sam placed her glass onto a cardboard coaster. "That sucks. I just realized that I don't miss him."

"Who, Daryl?" said Evie.

"Yeah. I mean, this trip's been like, totally crazy and super dangerous, but for the first time in years, I feel like I'm doing something. I'll be fifty, soon. Fifty. That's half a decade. And what have I done?"

"Half a century," said Carina, "but much respect to you, you don't look a day over forty. Is that good genes or good living?"

"Oh, I only wear Wrangler's," said Sam, "they have that relaxed fit that shows off all your curves, but I drink gallons of water. I put it down to the water."

"Or the fact that Daryl does everything for you," said Evie. "I don't know what goes on behind closed doors, but Daryl seems like a good catch to me."

"Live with him. You might find he's more catch and release than a keeper. And you know what's worse?"

Carina took another mouthful of beer. "I dread to think. Go on, what's worse?"

"I broke nails today," said Sam.

She laid her hands, palms down, on the table. One set of nails had thin lines of dirt beneath them, but they were intact. The other had chips and breaks on every finger but the thumb.

An enormous diamond gleamed in a silver setting on her wedding finger.

"Did Daryl buy you that?" said Carina. "That's probably worth more than my house."

"Yes, he's fine with the material stuff, it's just the, you know, the good stuff."

Another mouthful of beer.

"Screw that, they have plenty of substitutes for the good stuff. Doesn't get tired or drunk, either. He's a keeper."

"Okay," said Sam, "I totally have to pee before food comes. I'll be right back."

Carina watched Sam walk past the rowdy table and into

the restrooms.

Four pairs of eyes followed her every step.

She turned to Evie. "I think your sister is going to be beneficial on this trip. At first, I had her pegged as a prim and proper girly-girl, but she's grown into the role of team member."

Evie placed her elbows on the table and leaned toward Carina. "My sister is a special case, without a doubt. But I love her to death. I won't have her anywhere near danger if that's what this comes to. If it heads that way, it's me and you. Okay?"

Carina held up her hands. "Absolutely. I didn't say I was going to have her take out some dude. I'll leave that to you."

"There will be no taking out any dudes," said Evie. "Like I said before, we'll assess the situation, make sure no one has any of our information that might result in unwanted house calls, and we'll pass them off to the authorities."

"I can live with that."

"Good. No, in a pinch, it's me and you. And I don't know about taking out dudes, but if Sam breaks another nail, we'll have to take her out."

———

Sam chatted with her reflection in the bathroom mirror.

"For the love of Pete, what a hideous sight. Girl, you look like you spent the day rolling around in a field."

She giggled. "Well, I guess you kind of did, after you spent hours in the trunk of a strange car."

She ran her fingers through her hair. "If Daryl could see you now, this would put a little gas in his tank. Talk about rough and ready."

Despite the aches that flowed through her body, she felt

good. No. Alive. For the first time in a long time, she felt alive.

She turned and entered one of the cubicles. Her purse fit nicely on the back of the toilet, and she unzipped her pants then sat and stared at the small space beneath the door.

Today, she thought, *I defended myself against a guy. And not any guy, but a proper bad guy. A gangster. Note to self, you need more hairspray. And a bigger purse. With maybe a small gun?*

Damn, where were these thoughts coming from? This was Evie territory, and she totally did not belong there. To live there meant you had to do that funny military speak where everything sounded like a command or someone saying the time using the numbers past twelve.

Her work done, Sam grabbed some paper, dabbed, then stopped as a shadow passed beneath the door.

"Evie? Is that you?"

Silence.

"Carina?"

She shook her head, stood, and zipped up. This crazy day was giving her crazy thoughts.

"Anyone there?"

Nothing.

Sam picked up her purse and considered checking its contents for something heavy then shook her head again at her own paranoia, unlocked the door, and stepped into the bathroom.

Empty.

Just her and a slightly more beaten reflection of herself in the mirror.

With her purse to one side, she ran the water and pumped foam soap onto her hands.

"Time to get what's left of these disgusting nails clean, girl," she said as she studied her hands in the basin.

"Your hands are fine," said a voice behind her, "just like

your ass. I want a piece of that."

She spun to find a cubicle door swinging shut. One of the youths towered over her.

"Saw you walk in," he said. "You're not from around here, are you?"

Sam didn't wait for another word but lunged and slammed her palms into his eyes.

He screamed as the soap stung. "Jesus, you bitch."

She felt the heat rise before her body trembled with anger. Three times in one day, guys called her a bitch. Enough.

"Oh, you didn't go there, did you? Of all days, not today, kiddo."

Her knee connected with his groin, and he dropped with a groan.

"Can you see me?" she said.

"Shit. My eyes…"

She fumbled in her purse and pulled out a hairbrush, then pressed it to the back of his head. "Know what that is?"

"Don't hurt me," he said, "the guys put me up to it. I didn't mean any harm."

"Sounds like you boys need to learn a lesson."

Sam frowned and smiled at the surge of confidence that raced through her. Old Sam took a back seat as New Sam strode forward. "Do you feel lucky?"

The kid relaxed his fetal roll enough to mumble, "What?"

"I said do you feel lucky?"

"Isn't that in a film?"

She pushed the brush harder into the back of his skull. "Do you?"

"No. Shit, no. I just want to go back to my friends."

"I'll make you a deal," said Sam.

"Anything. Whatever you want."

"Good. You and your friends need to leave."

"Okay."

"Or I'll paint this bathroom with your brains."

He whimpered.

Sam saw tears trickle down his face. A small part of her felt guilty, but she also felt liberation for a day of abuse, paid back in kind. From this day forward, no one else would step on this girl.

"Please, don't kill me," he said.

"You'll leave? With no trouble?"

"Yes. Yes, I'll tell everyone we're done here."

"Okay," said Sam, "but we're not done yet."

"Please, God, I just want to go home."

"And that's what you'll do. Go home and hug your mom."

The guy tried to open his eyes then squeezed them shut when the brush forced his head forward.

"Hug my mom? Is that it?"

"Do you love your mom?" said Sam.

"Who the hell are you? Of course, I love my mom."

"And what do you think your mom would say if she knew how disrespectful you are to women old enough to be her?"

"I don't know," he said, "she'd probably be pissed."

"I totally guarantee it," said Sam. "Now, you're going to lock yourself in a cubicle for two minutes while I finish washing my hands. Then, you're going to get your buddies, pay for our meal, and go home. If you deviate from this course of action, I will blow a hole in you big enough for your buddies to piss through. Are we clear?"

Sam cringed as the guy's crotch darkened and he sobbed.

"Yes. Just let me be."

"Get up."

She guided him into a cubicle and waited for the lock to engage then washed and dried her hands and walked back to the table.

Chapter Twenty-Eight

English licked his finger and dabbed it across the plate to pick up the remains of a sturdy cheese and onion sandwich then slid the empty plate across a laminate tray table that hovered over the width of the bed.

Two more gulps finished off a glass of freshly squeezed orange juice, and he placed the pulp lined glass on the tray and laid his head back on the pillow.

So far, so good. Marte Dahl promised food, and she'd delivered. Or, rather, the tall guy had. Since their conversation, almost two hours ago, she hadn't returned.

Her beauty stamped an imprint on the back of his mind like a negative but, despite everything so far, something about her didn't sit right.

His test of the still locked door didn't help to calm his concerns.

Despite the care, he still had no idea where he was. There was no contact with the outside world, and no suggestion to offer it. No one had answered any of his questions and had, in fact, skillfully avoided them with diversions and distractions.

It was like trying to interview a politician.

The good news, if the news were accurate, was that this was the last bag of saline he'd need.

Once this bag is empty, said Tall Guy, you should be in good shape.

Which was great, but in good shape for what?

As if by magic, Tall Guy walked past the door.

Now well-practiced, English leapt from the bed, avoided the tray, and planted his bare feet at the door, with the IV stand behind him, in seconds.

"Hey! Sir?"

Tall Guy stopped, spun, unlocked the door and cracked it open.

"Can I help you? Was the sandwich satisfactory?"

"I, er," said English, caught off guard by the politeness, "yes, the sandwich was gorgeous. But, honestly, I'm a little confused. I'm not a prisoner here, am I?" He finished the sentence with a nervous chuckle.

"Of course not," said Tall Guy, "but Ms. Dahl takes most things seriously. If you are here under her care, then she will ensure that it is the best care available."

"That's great," said English, "and much appreciated. But I want to know where my friends are. There were four other people on that boat with me, four of my best friends. I need to know that they're okay. Are they here, in the same condition as me?"

"I wouldn't know about that. This is my section. I only know my section."

"So who would know? Could I speak with Ms. Dahl again? I hate to sound ungrateful, but I need answers. I'm not comfortable hanging out in this room while my friends might be suffering."

"I understand," said Tall Guy. "Let me see what I can do."

He pulled the door closed and locked it.

"And why am I locked in here?" shouted English through the glass. "I'm hardly dangerous."

At least not right now, he thought, *but if this continues, who knows?*

Tall Guy walked away, oblivious to the rest of the conversation.

English climbed back onto the bed and stared at the ceiling. "And it would be nice to have a proper window. Now I know why hotels charge more for rooms with a window; it's not cool being unable to see outside."

He glanced at the prison-like slit, high up and out of reach in the wall. Through it, a cloudy sky absorbed the warm glow of an impending sunrise.

"Guys, where are you? I hope to God you're all okay."

The sun rose before Marte Dahl reappeared.

The lock clicked, and she entered and strode with an assured confidence to his bedside.

Before the door closed, another woman entered. Shorter, and dressed in lab whites, but with the same chiseled cheek bones and blonde hair. The new woman marched into the room with a clipboard and stopped on the other side of the bed to check out the IV stand.

"Mr. Smith," said Dahl.

"Please," he said, "call me Keith."

"Very well. Keith, it's time I told you a little more about your situation."

Dahl noticed as English's skin crawled. "I'm sorry, I didn't phrase that well at all. I understand that you are disoriented, and unsure of a number of things, so I intend to put your mind at rest."

English nodded. "Thank you, I'm listening."

"You are in one of my facilities. It seems you do not know

me but, if you followed my area of expertise, you'd find that I am well known in my field. We are researching ways to help increase the speed in gathering information for the blood type requirements of blood donors. That might not sound too interesting to you, but if you'd had, say, a motorcycle accident, and you were hemorrhaging blood at the roadside, precious seconds are wasted where the first attenders ascertain your type to speed up the organization of a transfusion. We are working on a way to make that instantaneous."

"I commend your work," said English. "I've been in situations where that kind of information would have been, literally, lifesaving."

Dahl smiled and English relaxed into the mattress.

"Then, we are on the same page." She gestured to the other woman. "I'd like to introduce you to Anneka Ergström."

"Pleased to meet you," said English.

Dahl continued as the girl smiled. "Anneka is my chief lab assistant. My name may be on the awards, but Anneka does the legwork. She is my third hand, the action to my thought. I wanted her to meet you because, Keith, you have a special quality that she is interested in."

English's skin crawled again.

"Really? You still haven't mentioned my friends. Are they here?"

"Ah, your friends," said Dahl.

As she spoke, the sun rose through the narrow window. Despite the wash of warm color, English shivered as the room temperature seemed to plummet.

"No. Your friends are not here. A colleague of mine rescued you from waters that no sane person had a reason to sail in. You are here alone."

English stiffened and sat up then felt something sharp sting the side of his neck.

"Thank you, Anneka," said Dahl, "you can leave us now. I'll explain everything later."

The young girl pulled the door closed behind her as Dahl circled the bed.

"While my team stitched up your wounds, we found that your blood is something we've been looking for. Keith, you have AB-negative blood. Do you have any idea how difficult that is to acquire?"

English blinked as the closet doors swayed from side to side. The room seemed to float in water as the slitted window wafted against the wall.

When he spoke, his voice sounded muffled, with each word barely formed.

"I'm aware of that. I had to carry cards each time I was on duty to let the medics know."

"That would be expected," said Dahl. "but the average person doesn't do that. I've been trying to get a steady supply of your blood type to further my research. Talk about a stroke of luck."

English gripped the edge of the mattress, but his fingertips plucked at the material and fell to the side.

"Anneka has administered a sedative. Something to help you to relax. We have big plans for you, so we'll need to keep you sleepy. It wouldn't do to harm you."

"What the hell have you done?" said English. "My friends..."

"I know nothing about your friends," said Dahl, "but I know all about you. It wouldn't be practical to list your name in the credits for what we're doing, but I'll be sure to remember you when I lift the award."

English felt drool soak his pillow as his head lolled. "What are you..."

Dahl leaned in close. Her eyes pierced his, a scathing

beauty that only cover models could manage. A beauty so cold it numbed his entire body.

"You're my personal blood bank, Keith." She smiled and, to English's drugged mind, it looked like a pose for a photo shoot.

"We're trying to find an answer, the final link in the chain, a way to detect your blood type instantly."

She smiled and, suddenly, the beauty vanished, replaced by ruthless efficiency.

"And now we have a limitless supply. You are alive and healthy and, regardless of what we pull from you, we will ensure that you remain that way. It may take weeks, maybe months, to find our solution, but now we can inflict a thousand cuts, whenever we like, until we get there."

Chapter Twenty-Nine

Dud opened the refrigerator door wide then stood back as Sarge leaned in and pulled out a frosted glass jar through a haze of frigid air.

Other than a barcode stuck to its metal lid, the jar had no markings.

Marbles stepped forward and craned his neck. "Is that what I think it is?"

Sarge shook the jar and watched as a meaty object slid side to side through a red slush to bounce with a dull thud against the sides. "If you think it's an organ of some sort, you'd be right. Do you reckon it's human?"

Dud grabbed another jar from the next shelf. Its contents slithered to the side of the glass.

"I've seen enough TV to know that this is a heart. Couldn't tell you if it's human, but it looks about the right size."

"And I have a kidney," said Sarge. He placed the jar back in its place with a careful reverence. "Don't ask me how I know that; those days are long gone."

Macca opened another fridge to find the same shelves,

tightly packed with the same glass jars, all about the size of a small paint can, filled with a red slush. A barcode covered the shelf face in front of each jar, next to a letter and a number.

"Holy crap. This looks like a freaky library. Do you think we've landed inside an organ farm? Maybe we found what Knowles stumbled upon. From what little I know about organ harvesting, these fridges are filled with product worth more than any drug on the market."

"And this might explain why they won't let our buddy Elias roam the ship. I wonder how many more rooms there are like this?"

Dud replaced his jar and closed the fridge door. "We can check out the ship later, but first let's go talk to the captain. We need to find English and radio this in. We know it isn't going to be friendly, so I hope you guys are ready for action."

"I'm ready to find our comrade," said Sarge. "Lead the way."

Dud inched open the other door and then quietly closed it again. "We have to hide, company's coming our way. Two guys with a cart."

They retreated and ducked into the shadowy space behind the hanging plastic strips.

A few seconds later, the lights blinked out.

Moments after that, the door creaked open, and they clicked on again.

"This room freaks me out," said a voice. "It's thirty minutes to the next stop. Let's get what they need and get the hell out of here. I didn't sign up for this shit."

"No," said another, "me neither, but you know that now we're in, there's only one way out."

"Exactly, and I don't want to end up like Jonas. Erik says parts of him might be in some of these jars."

"Bastards. I hope they killed him before they started chopping. Come on, you read the locations, I'll scan and pack the product. The sooner we start, the sooner we're done."

The first man read off a list of numbers and letters, each combination followed by a beep and the rustle of ice. As they got into a rhythm, Dud parted the plastic curtains an inch.

One man gripped a clipboard and stood against a tall cart with his back to the curtain. An open fridge door hid the other.

Macca followed and threaded his fingers through the plastic. "You want Fridge Guy," he whispered, "or Cart Guy?"

"Fridge Guy. You do your thing with Cart Guy."

"Try not to kill them," said Sarge, "sounds like they don't want to be here any more than we do."

Sarge and Marbles held the plastic strips apart to prevent them from slapping together, as Macca and Dud crept forward.

From two feet away, Macca lunged. The side of his palm scythed an arc from overhead and into the artery at the side of Cart Guy's neck.

At the same time, Dud charged and slammed his shoulder into the fridge door. As Cart Guy dropped, he stepped around the door and landed two punches into a surprised and bloodied face.

Fridge Guy landed unconscious beside his colleague.

The others stepped from behind the curtain as Dud rifled the prone bodies and found two pistols. "Now we have one each. I feel better already."

Sarge picked up the clipboard.

"This thing looks as clear as a crossword puzzle. It's the list he was reading from. Letters and numbers. No names or clues to what or who this might be for. The address section has one of those weird boxes you find on food packages."

"No surprise there," said Macca. "No one is going to put a

name or address to an order for potentially human body parts." He glanced at the sheet. "That's a QR code, Sarge. Quick Response. If your phone wasn't resting on the seabed, its camera could scan and read that and bring up all kinds of information. Take the paper; where there are codes, there are normally scanners. We should put these boys somewhere safe and then move on."

Five minutes later, with the fridge guys secured with Elias, Dud pried open the door for a second time.

"We're good to go. It would make sense that, the farther up we go, the more folks we'll find. There are no hiding places in this corridor, just a staircase and another door at the end. Sarge, since you're the best shot and all we have are these pistols, do you want to lead the way?"

"Be my pleasure, buddy."

He popped the clip and checked his pistol.

"Glock 17. These boys are accurate, and this one has the standard seventeen rounds, all present and accounted for. I could do much worse, I just hope not to."

"Understood, Sarge," said Marbles, "and we'll be right behind you."

With the clip snapped back into place, Sarge stepped out into the corridor. Every footstep clanged and echoed like a peeling bell, but they made it to the staircase unnoticed.

"Now what?" said Dud. "The cart guys were headed somewhere and, if our footsteps made that kind of noise, we'd have heard that cart coming down the stairs from a mile away. That door leads somewhere, maybe a loading bay or a separate storage area."

"Maybe," said Sarge, "but if we get to the bridge and neutralize whatever the heck this is, we can check the rest out at our leisure. Let's face it, a ship carrying body parts can't possibly be up to any good. I say we plan on getting control of the vessel, and then we can check out the rest."

"I'm with Sarge," said Macca. "I'm also wary of the other fella saying we were thirty minutes from the next stop, wherever that might be, but at least that gives us plenty of time. Let's press on and speak to the main man."

They climbed the staircase and finally saw the ocean.

Through another porthole window, the sea heaved and slapped its colossal weight against the ship.

"We're almost on deck, guys," said Sarge. "I'm amazed we haven't met anyone else, but I'll take it. Does someone want to look and see what lies beyond this door? Then we can formulate the next phase of the plan."

"I love this guy," said Macca, "I've never met anyone who said shit like that. It's awesome."

Sarge fixed him with a glare. "It's real. Lives may depend on it."

Dud sensed the tension and stepped up. "It's all good, guys. I've got this. Give me a sec." He opened the door and stepped out onto the blustery deck.

He returned minutes later, panting and wide eyed and drenched in water. "Weird. I expected a militia, given what's on board and all, but I still don't see many folks about. The main cabin is maybe thirty seconds ahead of us. The windows are fogged and streaked, so I can't see inside, but there's a light on, so someone is home. There's a frigging huge crane above us. God only knows how this thing stays afloat with that thing perched up there, and there are crates tied down with cargo netting along one side of the deck. Other than that, and a shit-ton of freezing water, it's pretty bare out there."

"I expected more," said Marbles. "This is a refueling vessel, right?"

The team nodded.

"So where's all the fuel? We found the crew quarters and the seriously dodgy storage area but, other than a few propane tanks, I haven't seen a hint of fuel storage."

"You think it's a cover?" said Macca. "For illegal trading?"

Marbles nodded. "Has to be. We haven't covered that much of the ship, but liquid fuel takes up a lot of space. Huge tanks. And I can't imagine there being enough space left on this ship to store fuel for a few fishing vessels, let alone a fleet, unless it takes up the entire other side. Plus, I expected more resistance. Where is everyone? I thought they'd be lined up, ready for us."

"No clue," said Dud. "Maybe the cargo is too valuable to allow too big a crowd to see it? Cuts and percentages and all. All the more reason to hit the main cabin. Too many questions and too few answers. We need to speak to a dude."

"Agreed," said Macca. "Okay, same formation to the cabin?"

"Makes sense," said Sarge with a sigh. "On me."

He pushed open the door to the whistling scream and harsh blast of the North Sea.

As one, they crouched, stepped into the open, and moved along, step by sluggish step, as strong winds and blasts of freezing mist rocked them and pinned them to the bulkhead.

Dud tried to communicate then gave up. He stared into a never-ending view of seething gray sea. Howling wind and the slam of water against the deck washed out any other sound. The wind bit into his cheeks and forced him to squint as he tried to work out if anyone occupied the cabin that lay ahead.

Only light filtered through the rainstorm view. Nothing moved in the dim glare.

Dud's shoulder hugged and brushed the bulkhead as he inched forward, pistol leveled, through the battering of the ocean. One step after another brought them closer to the glow of the cabin.

For the entire trek, nothing moved.

He held up a fist, and the team stopped and gathered.

"I don't like this," he shouted over the crash of waves. "That shit back there is too valuable to have no security. Where is everybody? We're almost at the cabin. There should be people. It all seems too easy."

A few feet away, the light of the cabin still fought to cut through the constant spray, but it remained steady and unblinking.

"So what?" said Macca. "The cabin's not that big. How many men could they fit in there?"

"That's not my point. Not all security carries a gun."

"So what? You talking about landmines and shit?"

"On a boat? No, that's suicide. But something doesn't add up. Who controls the ship? There should be a whole crew. Either they never expected any company, which is possible given the terrain, or we're missing something."

Dud pointed to the cabin. "Only one way to find out and, since we're a million and one miles past a plan B, I say all we can do is either go for a swim or head to the cabin."

"Agreed," said Sarge. Water dripped off the front of his cap, but it remained jammed in place. "I'm soaked, I don't like swimming; we need answers, and we need them now. Let's move on. Regardless of what Elias said, we don't know if English is here, or even if he's alive. We have to find out. We leave no man behind."

"That goes without saying," said Macca. "And we'll get to that. Let's go. Let's hit that cabin. If it's full of men, I don't care about collateral damage, just make sure the captain is still standing when we're done. He needs to answer some questions."

After a somber nod, the team moved forward until they reached the main cabin door.

A single latch held it closed.

"Ready?" said Sarge.

Everyone nodded.

He yanked on the latch and leaned a shoulder into the door. It gave instantly and Sarge almost fell into the room.

The others stepped over him, pistols raised.

Mist fogged every window in the room except the two at the front of the vessel, kept clear with two hardworking wipers that swept a constant arc back and forth against an equally constant spray whipped up by an angry ocean.

Beneath them, radar screens and depth readers flickered and blinked green and red. A chrome wheel, larger than the one in the now destroyed fishing boat, sat unmanned and turned in fractions, one way and then the other, as if controlled by a ghost.

The captain sat in a seat and glared at them.

His first mate sat beside him.

As Sarge tumbled into the room, the captain frowned, anger burned in his eyes, and he slammed his hand against the wheel.

"What the fuck are you doing here? I knew we should have left you. Damn it. You'd be fish food by now."

Dud stepped past Sarge and swept the room. Other than consoles and digital maps, the two men up front were the only occupants.

"Where is everyone?"

"How should I know?" said the captain. "It's not a fucking school night, is it?"

"With the size of this vessel, you must have a crew. You're the captain. Where are they?"

"Look around. This is it, me and the first mate. Other than

some help down below to keep the engines running and to take in and offload supplies, this is it."

"What supplies? What are you carrying?"

"Fish. This is a fishing vessel."

"And the other stuff? What the hell is in those fridges?"

"Different fish," said the captain. "And it's none of your business. Who are you, the sea police?"

Dud stepped forward until the pistol rested inches from the captain's head.

The captain smiled. "Honestly, son, I've been in much worse situations than this. Is that supposed to intimidate me?"

"So have I," said Dud, "and no, it's supposed to put a hole in your head. But I'm hoping it won't come to that. Where's our friend?"

The captain shook his head as his colleague followed suit.

"Which friend? You're going to have to help me out because we picked up everyone we could see and, I got to tell you, it was hard going. Shitty weather."

The rest of the team filed into the room.

He pointed a finger at the group. "There, that's everyone. I swear. And I'm beginning to wish I'd never fucking bothered."

"We have to go back and search," said Dud. "Now."

"Impossible."

"You're hardly in a position to say that."

The captain leaned forward until his forehead wrinkled against the gun's barrel and pushed it back into Dud's palm.

"Is this position any better? I said impossible for two reasons, dipshit. One, if there was another man on your boat, he's long gone. Hypothermia would have finished him ages ago. You're fortunate that our engines stop for a while where we hit you. Can't be too early for the next stop. We shone a searchlight into those waves for almost half an hour. Everyone we found is on board and, unfortunately, standing here."

Dud tried not to show any emotion. "And second?"

"Second, can you see me gripping and fighting with this wheel under these insanely treacherous conditions?"

Dud said nothing.

"No, you can't. And do you want to know why?"

"Enlighten me," said Dud.

"Because someone pays a ridiculous amount of money to have this vessel's course pre-programmed. I have no control over where we go. Do you think we rammed your boat for a laugh? You weren't supposed to be there, you fucking idiot. Nothing else sails on this course. I would have tried to miss, but I couldn't if my life depended on it. A computer steers this ship, not me."

Macca, Marbles, and Sarge stepped up to the bridge, their pistols trained on the two men.

"So where are we going?" said Marbles.

The captain glanced to his colleague, who reached back and handed him a clipboard. He held it up so that the team could see a manifest, identical to the one Sarge already had.

He tapped a finger on a swirly square in the top corner. "There. No names or addresses."

"QR code," said Macca. "Been there, done that."

"Whatever," said the captain. "Everything runs on these things and barcodes. They don't tell me where it is. I just go there and unload and, when I get back to land, I get paid and go for a beer. Simple as that."

He gripped the wheel and jiggled it from side to side with a wide smile.

"And since you're stuck here and the sea's too rough, deep, and cold to jump into, it looks like you're coming with us."

Chapter Thirty

Thomas Frain sucked in a deep breath of filtered air and slid an iPad across the counter until it bumped into Ergström's fingertips.

"Look for yourself. You've been relying on two markers to pinpoint the blood type, but there's a third. How did you not see it? And, if you run a sufficient amount of blood through the process at the slower rate I'm proposing, you'll eliminate the outside factors and all you'll be left with is the data you need to produce your test strip. You can tweak the review factors as the blood flows across the test area until you reach the desired effect on the strip. No more guessing."

He slid his hands across the smooth surface of the work area.

Ergström studied the tablet and then looked up. "I never considered using such a consistent supply. But that's a lot of blood flowing at a constantly slow rate. Surely, if you directed a blood supply at this rate across the sensors, it would coagulate and render itself useless before we could reach a conclusion. At that rate, blood doesn't remain in a fluid state long enough to produce the results we're looking for."

Frain held up a finger and began to pace the room like a university lecturer.

Suddenly, his importance and stature returned.

He huffed out his chest.

"True. But it you applied an anti-coagulant to the blood supply at the same time, and at the same rate, it would allow the procedure to maintain its rate and achieve the required results."

Ergström thought for a moment, a million variations on the same theme racing through her mind.

Finally.

"It could work. There's only one problem that I see."

"And what's that?" said Frain.

"Where do we get such a consistent supply of blood? We've already been struggling to get enough pouches to further our research. We'd need a much more consistent supply to even attempt this. One that could almost replenish itself."

"Doesn't your lord and master supply everything?" said Frain. "God knows, she gets everything else she wants."

"This might be a little out of even her league," said Ergström. "There are more people working with the same type, drawing on the same resources. AB-negative blood doesn't grow on trees."

"But it can turn up in most unexpected of places."

They turned to find Dahl standing inside the doorway.

"Sorry to snoop," she said, "but then I do own this facility, so maybe not. Am I correct in thinking you need a steady supply of AB-negative blood to complete the research? Excuse my ignorance, but I came in at the tail-end of the conversation."

Ergström nodded while Frain chewed his nails.

"I'll take that as a yes," said Dahl with a smile. "You think that, with a steady supply, you can solve the strip problem?"

"Yes," said Frain.

"How consistent are we talking?"

"A steady flow," said Frain, "over a few hours. A sort of IV drip type of supply to run over our core sample. Something that we could easily regulate."

Dahl smiled.

"And how opposed are you to ethics?" she said, "saying that, perhaps, I could supply such a thing but perhaps not necessarily one hundred percent ethically."

"How unethical are you talking?" said Ergström. "Like breaking the law?"

"How much do you want these results?"

"You know that I've worked on this for years. I'll bend the rules, but I draw the line at breaking them."

"Have you heard the phrase 'ignorance is bliss'?"

"I have."

"And could you cope with that?"

"If I never knew?" said Ergström. "Possibly."

Frain shook his head and whispered 'brainwashed' as Dahl continued to speak.

"Well, then sit tight. I have just the thing."

———

Carina buckled her seatbelt as Sam climbed into the seat behind her and Evie started the car.

"That just goes to show that you should never judge people by their appearances," she said. "Those guys looked so mean when we passed them, and yet they paid for our meal. How nice is that? Do you think they realized they were a little intimidating and wanted to make it up to us?"

"Yep," said Sam, "totally that. Setting a good example for the young folk."

"They did leave in a hurry, though," said Evie. "One of the guys was nursing a damp crotch. Maybe he knocked over a drink. His face was fluorescent with embarrassment. Still, we have full tummies, all paid for, and we're ready for the rest of the trip."

She reset the phone's GPS and zoomed in on their destination. "Best I can tell, it's a bunch of industrial units by a subdivision. The satellite view looks like a load of boxes stacked side by side."

"Check in with your phone guy, again," said Carina. "See if he can spot more."

"No point. He'll have the same view. I'll call when we get closer and can pick out a building. Then, he can see who's about and give us an idea of what we'll be up against."

"Or if we need to call this in. Don't forget what you said, if it looks crazy dangerous, you'll call the authorities."

"And I will."

Sam leaned through the gap in the seats. "But if it's just, like, a couple of guys, we can take care of that, right? My nails are already ruined, so I say in for a penny, in for a pound."

Evie craned her head to look at Sam. "Who are you, and what have you done with my sister?"

"Like you said, we've come this far. And they kidnapped me. We should totally do this if we can."

"And they kidnapped me, too," said Carina. "So we're all agreed. Come on, Evie, girl power. Step on it."

"Jeez, I feel as if I'm riding with Charlie's Angels." She clipped the phone onto its stand and pulled out of the lot.

Just short of three hours later, they passed the New York State sign.

Sam pointed to it as it blurred past the car. "It says 'Welcome to The Empire State', but I don't see it anywhere. It's, like, one of the tallest buildings in the world, right? What the heck?"

"There's my sister," said Evie. "She's back."

Carina flashed her a sly smile. "Want me to take the phone and guide us in? According to the GPS, we're only a few miles away."

"Good idea. Get me close and I'll call Numbers to see what we're dealing with."

They turned off the highway and weaved through a maze of backroads that took them in the direction of a large river.

Carina pointed to a small sideroad that ran between two rows of three-story houses. "Pull in over there. The address we need should be on the other side of those buildings."

Litter crunched beneath the wheels as Evie pulled up behind a battered SUV and killed the engine.

"Pleasant neighborhood. Part of me thinks we should just call The Feds and pass everything to them."

She climbed out of the car, pushed the door shut, and slipped the pistol into her pocket. She wrinkled her nose at the stench of decay that filled the air. "But most of me thinks, despite the smell, we should at least snoop around a little. Let's get closer and then I'll call Numbers."

They stepped over an overgrown grass verge and skirted the side of the buildings.

Evie pulled up short as they turned into the next street.

"What the hell is that?"

Only one building remained of the next row, but it spanned the width of six of the other houses.

Through layers of creeping ivy, beige wooden slats shored up broken windows, concrete crumbled from disintegrating steps, doors hung open, and the entire structure looked ready to fall in on itself.

"Looks like the Addams family decided to rent out apartments," said Carina. "Are you sure this is the right place?"

Evie checked her phone. "Yep. This is it. I'm tempted to call Numbers right now. Something feels off about this. I expected a fortress, not the set from a horror movie."

"Agreed," said Sam. "This is, like, the creepiest place I've seen since the sewers with the clown in them on that real creepy movie."

"That almost makes sense," said Evie. "Give me a sec and I'll find out what's going on."

Numbers answered after the first ring. "Evie, you're in New York."

"Still tracking us," she said. "Nicely reassuring, and yet strange at the same time."

"Your husband would disembowel me if I didn't," said Numbers.

"Not a pleasant thought, Numbers, I prefer your bowels where they are. We've reached the address we had, and it looks like a block of apartments that had a bomb dropped on them. Can you do the thermal thing and let me know what's here?"

"Of course. Give me a minute or two and I'll see what I can find."

Twenty seconds later.

"Okay, you're in a pretty dense neighborhood. Miles from the suburbs. Easy to move around, blend in, and not be noticed. That building has more than a few heat signatures, but the surrounding area looks normal. Just a few folks at home, trying to stay safe."

"And when you say more than a few, exactly how many is that?"

Evie waited as Numbers counted aloud.

"I count sixteen heat signatures, but I'm not able to pinpoint exactly what or who they are."

"Are you shitting me?" said Evie.

"I shit you not, I'm still learning this program. Can I offer some advice?"

"Absolutely. Offer away."

"Call the authorities," said Numbers. "Six would have been pushing it. Sixteen is more than the guys could handle, and they're trained. Call it a day, Evie. Let the experts do their thing."

"I don't suppose you have their number?"

Numbers reeled off the number.

"Damn, you're good. Thanks, Numbers. I'll give them a call."

Evie disconnected and turned to the others.

"But not yet. I want to see what's going on here. This is all too weird. I mean, what the hell is that place and what is this operation? Slumlords R Us? This building is the head of a counterfeit money operation? I don't get it."

"I'm with you," said Carina. "Like we said earlier, I want to be sure I can go home and not worry about unwanted company knocking at my door. The only way to do that is see this through."

"Agreed," said Sam, "for totally the same reason. I'm ready to kick ass and take names."

"Sixteen names?" said Evie. "Sam, have you ever fired a gun."

"Sure. Not a real one, obviously, but like one that fires little metal balls. I hit a tree once."

Evie shuddered. "Okay, let's take a careful look and go

from there. Like Numbers said, even the guys would struggle with sixteen bad guys, and we're not even remotely on their level. At the first sign of real danger, we retreat, meet back at the car and call The Feds. Deal?"

"Deal," said Carina.

"Okay," said Sam. "Let's go get 'em."

Chapter Thirty-One

When the captain and first mate refused to answer any more questions, Macca and Dud marched them downstairs and secured them in the same room as the others. They returned to the bridge to find Marbles studying the ship's control panels.

"He's not the kind of guy I'd go for a beer with," he said, "but the captain seems to have been telling the truth. Perhaps about everything. I hate that English isn't here, and that we aren't in busier shipping lanes. You reckon someone else could have picked him up?"

"Damn, the kid just joined the club," said Sarge. "He'll turn up, I'm sure of it. And I've said a prayer. The big guy sees everything. I only hope he managed to find someone close enough to grab our boy. Seems to me, all we can do is see this through and then use everything at our disposal to find him."

"We'll definitely do that," said Marbles, "and we'll have plenty at our disposal once we get back on land. No point worrying about shit we can't control. Speaking of which, we're at the ship's mercy in terms of direction. The captain said they stopped for a while to kill time, which leads me to believe that everything about this is automated, including when we get there. We're going to end up at the delivery point at the appointed time, whether we like it or not."

"Which means they'll know we're coming and could be waiting for us. And we stopped in the region Knowles had found," said Macca. "If those fridge contents really are human organs, then we're dealing with a big money operation. Plenty big enough to have people silenced. Maybe we'll find answers when we get there. We need to prepare."

"But we still don't know who gave the order," said Sarge. "Or where we're going."

Marbles jiggled the wheel.

"And I can't change that. This wheel might as well be a prop. It's useless and here for show. In fact, I've only found two things that aren't controlled, and one of them is the seat."

"The other?" said Sarge.

"Is the radio. I'm trying to get it to a place where we can contact Numbers and find our location. English could do this in a heartbeat, but it's a little outside my skillset. You've noticed that no one on board has a phone, right?"

Macca sat in the captain's seat. "Even if they did, I'm certain they'd have to patch into the ship's signal. Something tells me this is the bad guy equivalent of a black ops effort. I'd be surprised if they allowed communications."

"I think it's like the captain said, a get out, do the job, get home and get paid kind of gig," said Dud. "No outside eyes or ears. Radio silence from start to finish."

"So we're still none the wiser," said Marbles. "I'll keep tinkering with the…what the hell?"

He paused as the boat leaned.

The wheel remained stationary but, through the window, the ocean swept by them from one side to the other.

Sarge swiveled his cap. "Okay, so I guess this is the naval equivalent of banking. Looks like we're making a tight turn."

"But why do that?" said Dud. "We're in the middle of the frigging ocean. We have all the room in the world to make a controlled turn."

Sarge pulled his cap back and pointed through the window as the boat righted itself.

"Maybe so we'd come up on that at the right angle."

The team moved forward and crowded the window.

After a moment's silence, Marbles spoke first.

"What the hell is it?"

The hum of the ship's engine died to leave no other sound than howling wind and crashing waves.

"Looks like we'll be coasting up to this to make our special delivery," said Dud.

Macca ran fingers through his hair. "I should have known. The North Sea is a huge oil mining region. Guys, it looks like we've reached our destination. It's a bloody big oil rig."

He gazed at the vast structure.

"And the lights are on. Someone's home."

———

English woke in a different room and instantly tugged at restraints that cut into his skin. A gleaming metal cuff held one arm to the chrome siderail of the bed, while thick plastic ties held the other rigid to a wooden board that lay secured to the other rail, level with the mattress.

A familiar smell stung his nostrils. Clinical. Sterile. Then, it registered. Hospital disinfectant.

Gone was the room with the closet and the small prison-like window, replaced with another with a larger window that looked out into a brightly lit laboratory.

A row of narrow fridges lined one wall. The opposite held a long bench fitted out with boxes of latex gloves, empty plastic pill bottles, and small racks that supported dangling metal cylinders.

From this distance, they looked like shining test tubes.

A bank of monitors replaced the IV stand, and a tall plastic console sat at the side of the bed. The gray console beeped with his vitals and held two large syringes with their plungers raised to the highest level. The first held a clear liquid, the second glowed a vivid pink.

A metal disk hovered above each syringe, held in place by small hydraulic arms.

Plastic tubes led from each into his arm and pierced his skin next to a third tube that snaked away under the bed rail to a white box that punctured the wall between the two rooms.

Two figures stood with their backs to the window, both in lab coats, both studying paperwork and oblivious to his presence.

The door clicked open and Dahl breezed into the room. "Keith. Excellent, you're awake."

English tugged again at the cuff and achieved nothing more than a clanging noise.

"What the hell…"

"Now, now," said Dahl. "Don't behave like a child, you'll do nothing more than hurt yourself."

He spoke through gritted teeth. "What the fuck is this? Where am I? And what are these syringes?"

Dahl tipped back her head and laughed. In any other situation, the sound would have brought goosebumps to most men.

To English, it was the sound of the devil laughing.

"So many questions and so little time," she said. "Let me see. First, you are a part of, at least potentially, history in the making. Congratulations on being here, commiserations on any chance of having your name attached to it. Secondly, you're in a type of operating theater set up. Not exactly by the book, but close enough to serve our purpose. And third, the syringes are a means to help us to work out how to save many lives. Sorry about yours."

"If you're doing legitimate research," said English, "I'd probably help willingly. You don't need to restrain me."

Dahl held up a finger and paced the room. "A long time ago, I was actually that trusting. Then, my parents and I had a disagreement. Can you believe they were going to cut me out of their will over my decision to take a career path they didn't agree with? Of course, I had to take corrective action to make sure that wouldn't happen, and then I dedicated my life to helping others. Which is where you come in."

"Again," said English, "I'd possibly be willing."

"Under the right circumstances, I'm sure you would. Problem is, we're undertaking quite a risky procedure. I'm not sure you'd agree."

English swallowed as his stomach dipped.

Dahl continued. "When people ask, 'what do you want', it should be a hard question to answer, especially when you have everything. I don't have that issue. I want my name to live forever, and I'm on the brink of that. After all, history only remembers the winners."

"And the nut jobs," said English. "What are you trying to be, the next Adolf Hitler?"

"Oh, good grief. That man and his ridiculous mustache. He was insane. No, nothing like that. Keith, you have an exceedingly rare blood group."

"Yes, you said. More than once."

"I did; it's exciting, and it's hard to come by. At least legally. And then, by some cosmic alignment of the stars, you fell into my lap. Well, you fell into the ocean, but who's being romantic, right? Anyway, back to your questions. The syringes. One has a chemical to keep you relaxed and to keep your heart pumping at a steady rate. The other contains an anti-coagulant to keep your blood thin."

English swallowed again, this time gulping down a throatful of bile. "Why do you need to keep my blood thin?"

"Excellent question and the source of some bad news, I'm afraid. Truth is, I'm taking your blood. I didn't think you'd just let me, so the third tube in your arm leads to a pump that will push your blood over some equipment my colleagues have assembled. I'm quite sure that, before we run out, we'll achieve our required results."

Plastic ties bit deeper into his skin as English struggled to free himself. "You crazy bitch. Before we run out? You're going to drain me?"

"Keith, after what you've seen here, I can't possibly let you leave. There's a possibility that we'll strike gold quickly. If that happens, you'll have lots of blood left. If it takes a while, then not so much. The whole thing will be painless for you, I've taken care of that with some outstanding sedatives. I've also taken the precaution of setting a kind of booby trap just in case you're resistant, get resourceful, and find a way to free yourself. The plate that your arms rests on, and the tubes that run into your arm, are wirelessly connected to a frequency driven pump."

English glared in silence.

"There's an awful thing called hypercalcemia. Too much calcium in the blood causes all manner of nasty illnesses. Do you see the clock above your heart rate?"

English glanced at the plastic console and saw 0:60 in glowing green above his jumping heartbeat.

"I've modified the chemicals here to induce a severe case.

Should you try to mess with my machinery, the pump will trigger, and the pink syringe will dispense its entire contents into your bloodstream in around sixty seconds. It would be a terrible waste of rare blood, but I'm confident my ties are good enough to avoid it.

"The syringe contains a heightened form of potassium EDTA. My own carefully crafted recipe. Should you receive the full dose, your blood will basically calcify in a further sixty seconds. Human to chalk stick in two minutes. I consider it thoughtful that I've left you a timer to watch, should that happen. Everyone enjoys a countdown. Can you imagine running a vehicle without oil? Similar thing. You'll dry out and die the most painful death when everything seizes. Best to lie back, relax, and let my guys do their thing. I'm sure you understand."

"You're crazy."

"Well, sensible might win awards, but it never changed history, did it?"

Dahl walked over to the window. "Mirrored glass. This is our blood supply room. Normally, a pouch would hang by this window and filter through the aperture in the wall to provide a steady test source, but I managed to improvise in your case. My esteemed colleagues have no idea you're back here. I soundproofed this room, too. Don't be fooled by the window. Scream and shout as much as you like, all you'll do is raise your heart rate and waste the chemical I've provided to keep you relaxed. It might be prudent to reserve that just in case it does take a while to get the required result. You'll thank me in the end. Well, you won't, you'll be dead, but you know what I mean. And the tubes in your arm are fortified. A special blend of plastic and metal. No knife will cut through them. Just in case that thought crossed your mind."

"If I ever get out of here," said English, "I'll…"

"Buy me dinner? Sorry, Keith, you're not my type."

She strode to the bed. Her perfume washed over him before she leaned to kiss his forehead and then opened the door. "Now, be a good boy, relax and enjoy the chemicals. It's time to get this show on the road."

Chapter Thirty-Two

The girls ran in a ragged, hunchbacked formation until they reached the left side of the building to slam their backs into the wall.

"Gosh darn," whispered Sam, "my heart is pounding like a hammer."

"You can still go back to the car," said Evie. "You're not made for this, Sam."

Sam gripped her pistol, racked back the slide, and studied the brass that gleamed back at her. "The heck I'm not. I'm tired of being the go-to girl. Those days are done. This is the new me, and I'm totally ready to kick some ass. The next guy that asks me to get him a beer will be wearing the can between his teeth. And I'm not going to mention what will happen if it's a bottle."

Carina glanced at Evie, who stared, slack-jawed, at Sam.

"And the guy in the restaurant? The one who peed himself? I did that. When we get done here, there's going to be, like, a ton of changes at home. Big changes."

"Crap," said Evie, "I'd better call Daryl before I call Dud. He's in deep shit."

"The deepest," said Sam. "There's a new girl on the block."

"Okay," said Carina as she gestured to the nearest doorway, "does the new girl want to take the lead?"

"The new girl will get the next one," said Sam. "After you."

Carina slipped to the front, leveled her pistol, and toed open a door that hung by one hinge. Its corner ground in dirt and the sound echoed inside the building.

"Shit," she said, "sorry. Did not mean to do that."

She crouched and ducked under the leaning door and waited for her eyes to adjust to the darkness. Light shot through the gloom in thin sheets that bled through wooden boards nailed across broken windows.

"It looks like an eighties disco," whispered Sam, "but one for zombies. I expected people."

"Me, too, but there's still a lot of space to cover. Stay close and stay alert."

The first room held nothing more than a broken chair and a six-month layer of dust. They moved forward into the next, to find the same thing. A staircase hugged the far wall, its carpet caked in grime. A closed door stood beside it.

"I guess it's the cleaning maid's century off," said Evie. "How about you two guard the bottom of the staircase while I check out upstairs."

The girls nodded as Evie climbed the staircase.

She returned two minutes later.

"Nothing. Not even any furniture. This place looks abandoned."

"That's how they'd want it to seem," said Sam. "What

better disguise. Let's check through this door. I guess it goes into the next building."

Evie trained her gun on the center of the door as Carina tugged it open. An identical scene lay ahead.

"I don't get it," said Evie. "Numbers said sixteen signatures. Where the hell are they?"

They moved into the next space then froze as the sound of moving stone clicked across the room. As a team, the girls dropped to their haunches and sighted pistols at the unknown threat.

The other side of what used to be a lounge lay in shadow, with streaks of light slashed across the staircase.

A scratch echoed in the empty room.

"Shit," said Sam, "this is totally uncool."

Dust motes floated through the shafts of light, but nothing else moved. After a minute, Carina stood and led the way as they cleared that room, then the next and, finally, upstairs.

"By my reckoning," she said, "that's two down and four to go. I don't like this one bit. Even the air feels cloying. It's bone dry in here, but it's like wearing a cloak. I say we get out and call The Feds."

Sam shrieked. "Oh, holy shit, crap-a-doodle, what the actual fuck was that? Something ran over my foot."

Evie looked around.

"Sam, it's just us. What the heck…"

Evie jumped, too, and looked down in time to see a black tail dart into a dark corner.

"Okay, girls, it's just rats."

Carina marched to the door. "Screw that. Bad guys I can cope with. Rats? I'm out. Call the Feds."

"I'm with Carina," said Sam. "I'll deal with dudes. Rats and their freaky tails? Not a chance."

They congregated at the car, and Evie pulled out her

phone and dialed the number that Numbers had given her.

The call was patched through to an agent. "And you say you're where?"

Evie gave them the address.

The reply was instant.

"Stay right there. We'll send a team to meet you."

———

Sarge stepped out onto the deck, followed by Dud, then Marbles.

Macca hung back in the bridge doorway and peered over their shoulders.

"I've lived in Scotland for years, knowing that loads of these things are planted in the ocean, but I never thought I'd see one up close. Jesus, it's massive."

A colossal metal column plunged into the water, surrounded by four towers of faded yellow iron, criss-crossed and held together by rusted rivets the size of a fist. Perched above them stretched a vast platform. A low handrail stretched around its perimeter.

"They're closing them down," he said. "Decommissioning them. Some still run today, but a lot are empty or repurposed."

"This one looks like it has a purpose," said Sarge.

The ship's engines fired up, the boat shifted slightly to one side, and the engines died again.

"Course correction," said Marbles. "We're definitely stopping here. I reckon it's safe to assume that we'll coast up to a dock of some sort."

Dud walked up to the rail and strained his eyes to focus through the wash. "Other than the ironwork, I don't see anything but daylight beneath this thing. If we're making a delivery, where do we drop it?"

The others joined him.

"No idea," said Marbles. "I'm half expecting…"

The engines burst into life again and the ship lurched.

"…a small reverse thrust," finished Marbles, "to slow us into the final approach."

Dud pointed into the ocean ahead of the ship. "In a few days of major surprises, I can't believe I'm still finding reasons to say what the hell is that?"

Thirty feet from the front of the ship, a red eye glared and pulsed through the water.

"Is it moving?" said Sarge as he pulled his pistol. "It seems to be drifting from side to side."

Dud gripped the rail and focused.

"No, that's the water washing over a lens. Guys, I've fired enough rounds through red dots to know a laser when I see one."

The eye drifted to the left. The engines fired again. The ship shifted again until its prow lined up with the red beam.

"It's guiding us in."

"To what?" said Sarge. "We can't stop on a laser."

They watched as the ship grew closer until the red glare became blinding. Then, as they prepared to look away, it moved.

Inch by inch, the eye rose from the water, lifted by a huge black rubber buffer.

"You've got to be shitting me," said Marbles.

The buffer rose three feet out of the water until a V shape sat and glistened like whale skin above the waves.

"I keep expecting Sean Connery to appear. This is all very James Bond."

The engines fired once more, and the ship bobbed gracefully into the buffer and stopped with a jolt.

"Just like hitching a fishing boat to a trailer," said Sarge.

"Only bigger. Much bigger. And scarier."

"And I guess now they'll be waiting for a delivery," said Macca. He pointed to the rig.

"Except we're too far away. What are we supposed to do? Launch the containers quarterback style and hope someone catches them?"

"That's got to be over a hundred feet away," said Dud. "Your arm isn't that good. Maybe we have to wait for something else to rise out of the water."

Overhead, gears shifted and hummed, and a platform hugged the rear of the nearest column and began a steady descent from the underside of the rig.

"Or not."

After two long minutes, it slammed to a halt around a hundred feet above the sea level.

Nothing moved but the swell and crash of waves. The ship vibrated in place as they buffeted its sides.

"Okay, there's a dock, but I'm still none the wiser," said Sarge. "I expected people. And how do we get aboard?"

Marbles pointed behind them and over the bridge.

"The crane. That'll reach. I'll bet the fridge guys load up a container and then crane it across to the platform."

"What?" said Sarge. "You're thinking that we should…"

"We can do that, right?" said Macca.

"Ride the crane?" said Marbles. "Sure, we've done worse."

"You can work it?"

"Dude, really? Give me five minutes."

Marbles scrambled up a small ladder and climbed into the crane's cockpit.

Three minutes later, the boom extended and began a slow swing from the prow of the ship to its starboard side. A huge hook lowered from its tip and swung slowly two feet from Macca's face.

"No one likes a smartarse," he shouted then gripped the hook to stop its sway and pushed it toward Sarge. "Want to go first, mate?"

Sarge stepped back. "Don't want the glory. After you, buddy. I'll let you try it first."

"Dud?"

"Have at it, Macca. We'll be right behind you."

Macca straddled the hook and gave Marbles the thumbs up. "Ready when you are, just go steady. No sudden jerks on the old groinal area. I don't think I'll need it again, but you never know."

The hook rose and hoisted Macca from the deck. Wind ruffled his hair as he cleared the ship's rail, and the boom swung him out over the ocean.

Still, nothing moved on the platform as he climbed thirty feet, then fifty, then a hundred, while the boom extended further.

Sarge strained to hear Macca's next words, but the wind whipped them away.

"I suspect he's saying that he'd prefer a parachute jump without a chute, but I could be wrong."

The boom stopped and Macca hovered over the platform and looked around. When he gave another thumbs up, Marbles lowered him and swung the boom back to the ship.

Dud followed, and Sarge gulped as the hook returned and dangled before him. He climbed up onto it, wrapped an arm around its width, and held on as Marbles lifted him up and out into thin air.

Icy wind whipped his clothing, and Sarge gripped tighter as the feeling of an unpredictable rollercoaster ride stirred his stomach. He opened his eyes to risk a glance at the churning water below, grabbed his cap to stop it flying away, then closed them again until the wind died as he grew closer to the rig.

Macca held out a hand and pulled him over the edge of the platform, before helping him climb down from the hook.

No sooner had he gathered himself it swung back once more to the ship.

"I never considered how Marbles is going to get here? Is he staying aboard or coming with us?"

"When this is over," said Sarge, "we really need to brush up on communication protocols in situations like this. I guess all we can do is watch and wait."

The boom swung back but didn't retract and didn't descend. It stopped at the prow. The hook swayed back and forth.

"What the heck is he doing?" said Dud.

The team shrugged as the boom began to spin its slow circle again. Marbles stepped out of the cockpit and waved before he turned out of sight. He reappeared moments later, straddled across the boom.

"Surely to God he's not going to climb the thing," said Macca. "The man's a maniac."

On his stomach, Marbles shuffled along the length of the boom. The hook passed the platform when he was almost halfway along its length. By the time it passed again, they could see the strain on his face. On the third pass, Marbles balanced himself on the tip.

He yelled from a few feet away. "Get ready to catch me."

"I'll say one thing about you guys," said Macca, "your balls seem to be about the same size as your brains."

"I'll take that as a compliment," said Dud as Marbles launched himself off the boom.

For a moment, a gust of wind seemed to hold him motion-less in mid-air, and then he crashed between them onto the platform.

Macca wrapped him into a hug and dropped to the ground with a heavy thump.

The boom continued its swing back toward the ship as Marbles stood and dusted himself down.

He took a moment to catch his breath.

"Thanks, guys. I've jammed the lever with a length of wire, so it'll just keep spinning. I also pulled a careful selection of wires to kill any chance of the engine starting again, but I couldn't tell you how long that boom will spin before it dies. I'd happily say let's never do that again, but it might be our only way off this thing."

"Can't wait," said Sarge. "Now what?"

"You know what they say," said Marbles. "What goes up must come down. If they want this delivery, the reverse must apply. We sure as hell can't climb."

The sea crashed against the metal columns, and gusts of wind whistled around the fixtures. The sharp smell of seaweed and salt cut through everything. And nothing else moved.

"Or we could come up with a plan B before we all freeze to death."

The same gears clicked and whirred, and the platform began a steady climb.

As one unit, the four men pulled pistols, checked rounds, and formed a spaced-out line, two standing and two kneeling, to face the upper level.

"Consider plan B now in operation," said Sarge.

The higher the platform rose, the harder the wind blew. By the time it reached the top, the breeze swirled in dangerous spirals that threatened to tug the men into the ocean.

The upper level consisted of a large block of single level buildings, a concourse, and a helipad. Lights burned in random windows but, again, nothing moved.

"This is starting to freak me out," said Dud. "Do you think

we have the right place? Someone here killed Knowles, wants Macca dead, and oversees an operation to trade in organs. I'd expect even a little robot dude to come and grab this delivery. Where is everyone?"

"Let's not make assumptions," said Sarge. "Break for cover. Up against the wall and below the window line."

They scurried across the concourse and ducked beneath the windows.

"What are we up to? Plan C?"

"Something like that," said Dud.

"Okay, plan C; I reckon we circle the area, try to see what we're up against. Points of entry and exit and, if possible, a number count of potential bad guys. That thing didn't bring us here to see the sights. Something is going on, but without any input from Numbers, we're going in blind. At this point, we don't even know what this place is, let alone what might be waiting for us."

"I like it," said Macca. "Let's split up, I'll go to our left with Sarge. Marbles, you and Dud circle right, and we'll meet back here to compare notes."

The team nodded and started to move then stopped as another sound bled through the white noise of their surroundings.

Sarge adjusted his cap, and Macca raised a flat hand over his eyes to peer into the bruised cloud base.

"I know what that sounds like," said Marbles, "but at the risk of repeating myself, are you shitting me?"

"That can't be a coincidence," said Sarge. "We turn up disguised as a delivery in the middle of nowhere, and suddenly we have company?"

"Yep," said Macca. "Gentlemen, to complicate things a wee bit more, it seems we have an incoming helicopter."

Chapter Thirty-Three

As the lab door swung open, Frain turned to watch Dahl swan into the room, absorbed in her own self-importance. Her beauty couldn't be denied; the way her cheekbones cut the air, the sparkle of her stunning eyes, and a body that curved and hugged every part of a tight-fitting suit.

He also knew that her beauty hid the personality of a sociopath.

He looked away as he felt Ergström's eyes burn into his. Behind them flashed a list of questions, every one of which would be awkward to answer.

Dahl gestured to a clinical white box mounted to the wall beneath a large mirror. "You wanted a good supply of test blood?"

"Yes," said Frain, "although I can do without seeing every imperfection in my damned skin while I'm working. Why the hell do we have a mirrored wall? This is hardly a catwalk."

"This room is at the center of the installation, Thomas, and our blood supply room lies on the other side of the mirror. Don't think for a second that I care about your vanity; this is just the best place to carry out a historic event. When we're done, I'm sure you'll agree."

Ergström watched him again as he held back a barrage of abuse.

"You have approximately ten pints of blood to play with," said Dahl, "which will flow from the unit in the wall and through your equipment at the rate you suggested. Hopefully, ten pints will be enough. It was quite an effort to secure it."

Frain couldn't help but notice Ergström's eyes again. This time, they barely concealed a flash of alarm. Ten pints was a telling number. The average blood supply of an adult human being.

The moment was broken by a sound that sent chills through his entire body. A thrumming and beating, the sound of a machine that defied physics to do what it did.

The machine that brought him to this place.

"Is that a helicopter?"

Dahl flapped a hand.

"It's delivery day. Erick is always on time. He's our man to transport product to the mainland. Thomas, we run a tight ship, pardon the pun. And I might as well fill you in since you're now part of a small team. This facility supplies human organs to people prepared to pay the right amount for them."

Ergström glanced at her white tennis shoes as he frowned.

"Human organs? What, like trafficking?"

Dahl smiled. "I hardly think that's fair. Supply and demand are the principles that make the world go around, right? Some people want something, other people can supply it. It's basic economics."

"Okay," said Frain as his head spun, "but why here? And where do these organs come from?"

"China," huffed Dahl with a shrug, "like everything else. They seem to have the lead on everything, don't they? Still, this product doesn't come with that nasty plastic seam that you have to pick off with your nails if you want your purchase to look good. There's nothing molded here, Thomas, just quality product."

His legs grew weak, and he gripped a workbench for support.

Ergström still wouldn't meet his gaze.

"This can't possibly be legal." He turned to Ergström. "You know about this?"

"Anneka is paid very well for what she does," said Dahl. "To be fair, she is not directly involved in that aspect of our work. However, she is here to change the course of medicine, as are you. Now, enough distractions. Erick knows how to load the deliveries; we can leave him to do his job. It's time to do yours. As soon as you start the program, the blood will flow from the storage vessel, through the panel in the wall, and across the test strip. I've set the flow rate to exactly the speed you recommended, so you'll know how much time you have until you exhaust the supply. I strongly suggest you achieve your objective before your supply runs out."

"And if we don't?" said Frain. "What if I refuse?"

Dahl slunk across the room and rested her body against his. "Thomas, how well do you think you know me?"

Her heat and perfume distracted him for a moment until he felt the tip of a knife press into his spine. Pins and needles shot up his torso as she twisted the blade.

"Well enough," he said.

Dahl stepped back and flashed a dazzling smile. "Good man. Well, go on, then. History's waiting. Press the button."

———

Erick Gundersen gripped the cyclic stick between his thighs and quickly massaged the bridge of his nose then retook the stick and made a slight adjustment before the craft veered off course.

A late night in Oslo, combined with a tense visit at a nearby refueling rig, had raised his blood pressure enough to cause a steady throb behind his eyes. Despite agreements that had stood for years, some idiots still had to go through the ancient ritual of puffing out a chest or strutting like a prize cock.

Pedersen, second in command at the rig, was a prize cock, but Erick had managed to refuel to capacity and get airborne before the standoff about fuel allowances escalated.

He was in no mood to kill anyone.

Not today.

The crack of a gunshot would only elevate a dull throb to a pounding migraine.

And, since she'd signed off on it, he'd ask Dahl about the allowance.

After just over four hours of flight time, he dipped the blades to take the Sikorsky S-92 from just below the cloud base, to center his view on what he called Dahlington Palace.

A lot of the North Sea oil rigs had been taken over by private corporations. The others either still operated or were listed to be taken down by their owners.

Dahl's rig sat in a geographical no-man's land.

In a deal that should have involved inspections, referencing and real estate legality, Dahl had paid off any outside eyes so that her purchase had been between her and the corporation that had previously owned the abandoned rig. Another chunk of cash disappeared a whole set of paperwork and a mind full of memories.

From the air, the rig looked like a large ship. Other than a strange blip on Google Earth, the site didn't exist. And who scoured Google Earth to check out the North Sea?

In the distance, the grim color of the crashing sea shot through the faded yellow of the ironwork and made the rig look like a floating bee. Without a decent GPS, the place might be a myth and yet, in the middle of nowhere, it practically glowed against its grim backdrop.

And then there was the woman herself. Marte Dahl. Simply stunning. Cheekbones to cut paper, the eyes of a model, and the body of a goddess. A woman worthy of coaxing affairs from the happiest of married men. And, after a night of unforgettable passion, cold enough to kill them without a thought.

Erick had been tempted. And had resisted.

He knew of the bodies that floated in the ocean, he'd just never worked out if they were men or women. Or both.

He adjusted the pitch and nosed the helicopter forward then leveled and dropped until the huge yellow *H* painted on the helipad rested between the skids of his craft.

Moments later, he killed the engine and pushed open the door, with a superstitious glance at the empty co-pilot seat.

Over a perilous winter eight months ago, he and Peter collected drops from Dahlington Palace and split the proceeds equally.

Then, Peter had suggested that the flights were worth more than what Dahl paid.

Seconds after the waves swallowed Peter's body, Dahl told Erick to learn to fly alone. A co-pilot, she said, was there to check and correct mistakes. Make no mistakes and you don't need a co-pilot.

Erick shuddered and pulled his jacket closer around him as the wind bit into his body.

Somehow, Dahl's deliveries were never late. Despite the

volatile mood of the ocean, and the reliance on other people to supply product, not one delivery had gone missing or turned up late. Weird, but useful.

A simple stop to strap a few canisters into the passenger seats of the craft, and then an even simpler flight to Scotland to offload and let the Scots deal with distribution.

Refuel and home.

As always, despite being lit up by the cold glow of fluorescent light, none of the outside windows showed any sign of life. From experience, Erick knew that whatever went on here happened at the center of the installation.

Away from prying eyes. Despite her public persona, the woman who worked here remained intensely private.

He paused as a shadow moved beneath the windows of the front wall before another wave crashed against the structure and he passed it off as the movement of water thrown by wind.

The sheer size of the rig still took him by surprise, even though it seemed that little of it was used. The delivery platform lay perhaps a hundred yards ahead, still shrouded in shadow.

His eyes seemed to be playing tricks. Through the side rail of the rig, the platform appeared to be empty.

Erick snickered.

Dahl never missed a delivery. It was there somewhere.

He put his head down against the wind, pulled up his collar, and strode onwards.

———

English licked his lips to recover saliva before it rolled from the sides of his mouth.

I can't drool, he thought. *Never have and never will. At least not sober.*

He turned to look at the one-way mirror. His eyes reached the wall, but the blurred image took an extra second to catch up. When it did, his stomach tumbled, and he swallowed down bile.

Whatever this sedative was, regardless of the side effects, it did a good job. A tornado could tear the room apart, and he'd be able to do nothing but watch.

Was it two IEDs? Mist fogged his brain as he fought to recall how many times his life had been threatened and saved. Rocket propelled grenade attacks, running zigzag to avoid sniper fire, streaks of hot lead keening past his ears, and his life was about to be ended by a tall supermodel with a comfortable bed and a syringe.

He fought the urge to pull at the board beneath his arm as a thread of his blood snaked along the plastic tube, to disappear through a hole in the wall. Another clear tube added the anticoagulant and sedative that Dahl had mentioned.

The pull of the device cramped his arm, and the site where the needle punctured his skin itched but, knowing the consequences of movement, he lay back and closed his eyes.

An image of Penny played against the backs of his eyelids. Walking around the grounds at their home; wine tasting on hay bales at a vineyard in Indiana; talk of children.

A helpless tug at his right arm achieved nothing but a pinch of skin against his ties.

He took another breath, opened his eyes and studied the console.

———

Dud watched as the pilot covered up against the elements and moved toward them.

The blades of his helicopter hung like limp branches waiting for spring, with the wash of the ocean sending waves of droplets to cascade down its front screen. The craft sat on the helipad like a snake in a trap, coiled and waiting to pounce to life.

After the initial shock of the thrum of blades, the team raced around the nearest corner and hunkered against the wall.

From this angle, the delivery platform was still visible, but shadows kept them hidden.

Marbles was the first to exclaim surprise that the good-sized helicopter had landed with only one pilot. It took a few visual checks to try to spot a silhouette before they accepted that the guy was alone.

"I feel guilty," he said. "If this guy is flying an S-92 solo, he's as good a man as me. We can't hurt him, he has skills."

"Depends on his motivation," said Macca. "If he's picking up the fucked-up delivery that we screwed up, we'll soon see if he's as good a man as you. I suspect he's going to be a very pissed man who will kill kittens to get his way."

"Dude," said Marbles. "Leave kittens out of this. That's just mean."

"What's the plan?" said Dud.

"Hard truth is, we've got to take him out," said Sarge. "The fact that he's even here makes him a potential bad guy. The harder fact that he has the key to our way out of here makes him a valuable bad guy. I say we incapacitate him and go from there. Keep our options open."

"I like the way Sarge thinks," said Macca. "And I agree. If the shit hits the fan and we need a quick getaway, that helicopter looks good. Marbles, can you..."

Marbles rolled his eyes. "Really? Have you not got the message yet?"

"Sorry, pal," said Macca. "Message received. Disarm and take down, but make sure we can still get the chopper working. In other words, get the keys."

"There are no keys," said Marbles. "You go and do what you do. When it's time, I'll do what I do."

Macca nodded as the pilot stepped onto the empty delivery platform.

"Seems fair."

The pilot turned again, arms raised in question, as if another circle would magic the inventory into reality.

As he completed his circle, Macca stepped before him. His eyebrows raised and then creased in the dim light before a hard punch caught him on the jaw.

He swayed as the blow blurred his senses and clenched his fist to retaliate before another from the opposite direction rocked his head and turned out the lights.

"Grab what you need from his pockets," said Macca, "and make him secure. I cannae take any more of this bullshit. It's time we went inside to see what's going on."

With the pilot secured to the guard rail, they pulled open the door to the facility.

The door opened onto an interior that resembled a hospital. White walls led to white doors, that opened onto more white corridors.

The team moved forward and cleared one empty room after another.

"Does anyone work here?" said Marbles. "I feel like the dude that got to the wedding a half hour after the end of the cake cutting ceremony. There has to be more."

"Agreed," said Sarge. "Keep moving forward. Too many

coincidences brought us here. We just haven't got to where we need to be."

The first corridor ended in a T.

"Left or right?" said Dud.

"Right," said Macca. "Seems instinctive for some reason."

They turned right and moved along an identical corridor. Nothing moved behind the small glass panes in each door, each room bathed in the cool glow of nightlights.

"Where's the action?" said Sarge. "It all seems too quiet."

"You saw the size of this thing," said Marbles. "Probably, the outer row of rooms gets too much of a beating by the weather. The action will be in the center, where it's quieter and warmer."

"Okay, then let's head to the center."

A few turns later, they ducked and filed past a window that looked into a room filled with wide desks.

Four lab technicians sat hunched over microscopes, each with long, dark hair tied back to hang over their lab coats like a tail.

"What is this place?" said Dud. "Deliveries of body parts, scientist type people, helicopter pick-ups. I've seen some weird shit on my travels, but this tops the list. The whole thing freaks me out. Give me something I can shoot or fight with; I doubt those guys could punch their way through a wet paper bag. I'd feel guilty tackling them."

"Then let's not," said Macca. "The only bad thing about them is their posture. Let's keep moving."

Another turn put another wall between them and the ocean. The constant crashing of water and whistle of arctic winds died to background noise, but the scenery remained the same. Clinical white.

The next turn changed things.

Dud wrinkled his nose. "You smell that?"

"Yep," said Sarge. "Came across it many times and, regardless of the time or location, it always smells the same."

"Hospital disinfectant," said Marbles. "I hoped I'd never come across that again. After a few minutes, it feels as if you're chewing it rather than breathing it."

"So we're getting close to the nitty gritty," said Macca. "Come on, I don't know what's waiting for us, but I'll be glad to see the back of it."

The next corridor seemed long enough to stretch the length of the facility.

Lights burned through windows at the far end.

Dud led the way and checked each room as they reached it. Each seemed built for storage, and they saw nothing of value until they reached the farthest room.

In a crouch, Dud peered around the next corner and, once confident it was clear, raised himself until he could peer through the window.

Two people hunched over a desk that faced a huge mirror that filled most of the far wall. A set of numbers flashed on a monitor before them, while a reel turned in a sealed glass cabinet beside them and threaded a thin tape into a small box.

"What the hell is this?" he said. "It looks like bingo night for nerds."

Macca joined him. "It's the first meaningful sign of life we've seen. Reckon we should check it out?"

"We need answers," said Dud. "What's the worst that could happen?"

He turned the handle and pushed open the door.

Chapter Thirty-Four

Something in her peripheral vision seemed out of place.

It took a moment for Dahl to realize that the empty helicopter still sat on the helipad, its blades drooped like underwatered flowers.

Then, her stomach lurched.

Erick had shown an interest in Ergström during their last conversation. Nothing serious, more of a testing of the water, but it was clear he had eyes for the assistant. If he ventured into the facility and came across Frain, the shit wouldn't just hit the fan but spray over an area the size of the ocean. And Frain would know that there was a means of escape.

No need for paranoia, she thought. *He's outside, battling against the elements that seemed to have upped the ante in the last few hours.*

She dropped the latest organ requests, leaped to her feet, and powered through the corridors to the entrance nearest the delivery bay. Outside pressure forced her to lean into the door to open it, and a blast of icy wind swept back her hair as she squinted to check out the bay. Empty.

So he was loaded. Why wasn't he flying?

While she smoothed back her hair, she turned on sharp heels and marched through corridors she'd know with her eyes closed.

So many steps to this turn, this many to the next. She knew every last one. And every room.

All the outside rooms bar two were empty.

One of the two was the room Ergström had requested as her quarters. Apparently, the sound of Mother Nature at her worst lulled Ergström to sleep.

The other was at the far end of the facility, away from everything. The room where Keith Smith was secured.

She passed storage rooms, control rooms, and rooms that held the equipment to filter air and supply heat. She glanced through windows at the small research team hard at work and turned the last corner to reach the rooms at the center of the facility.

Instinctively, she reached for the handle to open the door into the room where Ergström and Frain worked and then stopped when she saw the view through the wired glass pane.

She slammed her back into the wall to the side of the door, reached into her jacket pocket, and pulled out a small, snub-nosed pistol.

Ergström and Frain faced the door, but hadn't seen her, because between them stood a small team of men.

She steadied the pistol and opened the door. "The first person to move dies."

Frain's eyes widened as the group of men raised their arms.

"I don't know how you did it," said Dahl, "but congratulations, you found me. You can all lay your pistols on the ground, then turn to face me."

———

Dud turned to find a gorgeous blonde woman standing in the doorway, facing him along with the jet-black circle of a pistol barrel.

Macca spoke first. "It's four against one, lady. You reckon you're quick enough to take out all of us before one of us reaches you? How about you put your pistol on the ground?"

She paused for a moment, as if she were weighing up her odds, and then smiled. "Well, well. Wait, and fate will provide. I know who you are, John MacIntyre. Do you know me?"

Dud glanced at Macca, whose demeanor somehow remained the same. He carried on as if she'd said nothing.

"We've already had a chat with these fine folks," said Macca, "and this fella is not at all happy about being here." He gestured to Ergström. "And I think she might have a wee crush on you. But go on, I'll bite. How do you know me, and who are you?"

"John MacIntyre," she said. "The nasty thorn in my side, finally here in the flesh."

She paced beside them until she rested a curved hip against a desk. "The two people in white are Anneka Ergström and Thomas Frain. I'm Marte Dahl."

"Congratulations, I'm happy for you. Should I be impressed?"

"You should be concerned," she said. "After all, I hired the teams that caused your friend's head to explode all over the street in Scotland. You were getting too close to my operation. Shame how those teams ended up. Clearly not up to the job, since here you are."

"You hired the kill teams?"

"Well, you stuck your noses into business that didn't belong to you. You were the cats that got curious, and you know what they say about that."

"This cat is still kicking," said Macca, "and ready for revenge. Jason Knowles was a good man with a family."

"Shame. Still, if I were you, I'd control that temper, Mr. MacIntyre. It seems to me like the gang's not all here."

"And what the hell is that supposed to mean?" said Marbles.

"Aren't you missing someone? An English guy?"

As one unit, the team tensed and took a step forward.

"You'd better start talking," said Sarge with a snarl. "What do you know about our buddy?"

"He has the most interesting of accents," she said, "and the rarest of blood types. He's nearby, if that piques your interest."

Dud controlled his emotions but couldn't halt the rush of warmth that washed over him. "English is alive?"

Dahl laughed and sauntered back toward the door. "You call him English? How cute. Yes, he is alive. At least, for the time being."

"Meaning what?" said Dud.

Dahl mocked a yawn. "Meaning whatever. I'm bored with this. You want to see him again?"

No one moved.

"I'll take your ignorance as a yes, so I'd suggest you all behave before you really offend me."

Still no movement.

"Or he can die where he lies."

Dud frowned as the guy named Frain glanced between him and Dahl and then at the box with the tape and the plastic tube that carried a thread of blood. A tube that ran through a box into whatever lay in the next room. A room hidden behind a huge mirror.

As the others talked, he lifted a paperweight from the desk and thrust it backwards into the corner of the mirror.

The crashing sound shocked everyone into silence. Shards of lethal glass shattered on the floor, leaving a chasm that looked into another room.

A prone figure lay zip-tied to a bed. Tubes pierced his arms from a double IV, with another tube that ran through the wall and drained his blood over a paper tape.

The two lab techs watched, slack jawed.

The smaller girl blanched and steadied herself against a desk.

"When she said supply vessel, I had no idea…"

Macca was the first to react, followed by Sarge.

They leaped through the opening as Dud and Marbles turned to face the woman.

The door clicked shut.

She was gone.

"Take care of English," said Dud. "Marbles, how about we go and sort out the crazy woman?"

"That would be my pleasure," said Marbles. "Macca, Sarge; fix up our buddy. We'll be right back."

———

Macca looked back and forth between the plastic tubes and English's glazed eyes.

"Mate, can you hear me?"

"Plate," said English in a drunken drawl. His eyes fluttered, and he took a breath before he was able to speak again. "Trap. Don't."

Sarge joined them.

"He's pumped with sedatives. I've seen that state plenty of times. Pull the tubes and stop that crap flowing into his bloodstream."

He reached toward the IV until Macca put a steady hand against his arm.

"Hold fire, Sarge, something's not right here."

Sarge pulled back.

"Go on then, buddy. What's going on?"

Macca kneeled at the side of the bed and studied that board that held English's arm.

"This is not the first time I've heard him say 'trap'. He had a stupid habit of stepping on IEDs in the Middle East. It always seemed to be me who turned up to bail him out. He hasn't stepped on one this time, but something is definitely not right with this picture."

He pulled at sheets and peeled the bedding away.

"Jesus Christ, someone sutured the tubes into his wrist. I don't know how deep the stitching goes. There's no pulling them out without potentially yanking his veins through his skin. I could kill him as soon as save him."

"I have a drug to combat the sedative."

The young lady, Anneka, looked through the open window.

Frain glanced helplessly over her shoulder. "I'd like to help, too," he said, "and then bring this psycho bitch down."

Anneka cleared broken glass with a clipboard then climbed through the opening. "I had no idea she would resort to this. I want to help. Your friend's blood is draining slowly, he's in no danger there. But those syringes look like something altogether different. I wouldn't put it past Dahl to put countermeasures in place."

"Countermeasures?" said Macca. "Are you one of us?"

"I wanted to do good things, although I'll admit to bending rules, but this is too much for me. Dahl is a genius, but she's insane. If she thought there was any threat to this procedure, she'd have taken precautions to keep your friend placid. And the color of the chemical reminds me of a drug she's used before. I suspect the syringe contains something to calcify his blood. Wait here and let me help."

"I've no idea what that means," said Sarge, "but do we have a choice?"

The girl had already left the room.

She returned moments later and carefully injected a fluid into a vein at the crook of English's elbow.

"It'll take a few minutes for this to counteract the effects of the sedative. Then he'll be more coherent, and you'll be able to talk to him. Your other friends picked up their guns and went after her."

Sarge sat at the foot of the bed.

"Then, I guess all we can do is wait."

———

As the exterior door closed, Dahl tipped back her head and screamed.

Wind washed away the rasping sound.

MacIntyre was right. The odds of her hitting four moving targets before one reached her were not worth the risk.

Still, it would have been fulfilling to put a round between his eyes to finish the job.

She considered her options.

Assuming Erick was still alive, he could fly them to the mainland. Other than automated deliveries, nothing and no one else visited the facility. If she could take out communications, it would be easy to leave everyone here for a few weeks. Once the food ran out, they'd turn on one another. The survivors would starve soon after. She could return, pitch the bodies into the sea and put a new team together.

She ran to the helicopter and yanked open the nearest door. Empty.

MacIntyre would follow her once he realized his friend was dead, so the main entrance was a no go. She turned and raced across the concourse to the other side of the building. As she rounded a corner, something fluttered in the shadow. With her weapon raised, she crept forward until she grew close enough to recognize the pilot slumped against the delivery platform rail.

A strange whirring noise blended in with the familiar crash of water and whistle of wind.

She squatted beside him and lifted his head by the hair. A trickle of blood ran from the side of his mouth, but twin jets of breath plumed from his nostrils. "Erick!"

Three hard slaps to the face brought him around.

Dahl cut him from the rail and helped him to stand.

"Do you have a gun?"

He held onto the rail as he spoke. "In the chopper. Under the seat."

"Get it," said Dahl. "Help me resolve this, and I'll pay you more money than you could ever spend."

The pilot gripped the rail harder as he swayed. "Give me a minute to gather my senses. I can barely see straight."

"Do you hear that? What is that sound?"

He tilted his head as she leaned over the rail.

Beneath them, the reefer still sat against its buffer, its crane spinning in a slow circle.

"So that's how they got here. Bastards."

Dahl tugged at him and dragged him behind her.

"We don't have time. I was going to have you fly me away from here, but they're probably still confused. Between us, we can deal with them before they realize what's happening."

They moved across the back of the facility, past a small entrance, and turned the corner to the helicopter.

"You have no idea how much money I could spend," said Erick.

"Don't worry, I've got you covered. Do this and I might offer you more than money."

Shapes moved in the shadows by the helicopter.

Dahl hushed his reply and ducked as two figures walked away from the chopper and made their way back to the facility.

"Excellent, they've split up. I've taken you to my supply room before, can you remember how to get there?"

Erick nodded.

"Good. I'm going to use the other entrance and come at them from the rear. The communications room is just inside. I'll take care of that and those two. You head to the supply room and use the door before it. There are two armed men in there, and another strapped to a bed. Kill them all. Anneka and another man might also be there. Kill him too and do what you like with her. Just do it quickly and make sure they all end up in the ocean when you're finished."

Erick nodded again and crept up to the helicopter. Moments later, he emerged with a blocky pistol and made his way toward the main entrance. Once he vanished around the corner, Dahl turned and slipped back into the building through the rear door.

Chapter Thirty-Five

Marbles slammed shut the chopper door.

"Seemed like the common sense move to me, but then the pilot is tied up on the delivery dock. Still, perhaps she can fly, too."

Dud looked around the platform. Violent sea chopped and churned at every turn.

"Unless she's prepared to jump onto the crane you used, she's still here somewhere. She didn't look the flying type to me, so I say we head back inside and search the place room by room."

"Agreed," said Marbles, "but let's check around back. There must be another door. The windows are all sealed units, so there has to be a second entrance, an escape in case of fire."

"Good call. Let's go."

The two men raced across the side of the building and turned the corner. Three quarters of the way along the rear wall, a small handle protruded from the flat sweep of the wall.

"As if by magic," said Dud.

He yanked open the door as Marbles trained his pistol and swept the open space.

"Clear. Looks the same as out front. Okay, I hate up close and personal, but door to door it is. Ready?"

Dud nodded.

Before them, white corridor stretched to a T. The same cold, fluorescent light lit the space.

Two doors sat in the first wall, one on either side.

"Okay. I'll breach, you cover."

Dud nodded once more, and the men moved forward.

———

"English? Are you back with us, buddy?"

Sarge spun his cap as English batted his eyes and stretched until his back popped.

"Bloody hell. If I feel like this, what does the truck look like?"

"That bad, huh?" He spun back the cap. "Listen, lie still and tell us everything you remember. There's a weird board set-up beneath your arm that Macca seems to think could be a problem."

English turned his head with a whiplash jerk to look at the console beside them. "The clock's not ticking. Thank God."

"Meaning what?" said Macca.

"Sorry about this, mate, but it looks as if you're going to have to defuse another bastard for me."

"Thought as much. You're a pain in the arse, mate. What am I dealing with this time?"

English explained Dahl's trap as Anneka shook her head in disbelief.

"She wanted you to watch a countdown to your own death? I honestly thought I knew her and had no idea she'd do this. All she's ever wanted is to get her name in the history books, but I never thought she'd do it in this way."

"It's no surprise to me," shouted Frain from the open window. "The crazy bitch kidnapped me to work with you. She's pure evil."

"One thing at a time," said Macca. "You know the drill, English. Perfectly still, mate. Let me take a look at this. Anneka, do you have a pair of scissors?"

She opened a closet door above the row of shining test tubes and pulled down a plastic tote. "Of all things," she said, "a first aid kit. You know, because my boss cares about our welfare."

She handed over the scissors, and Macca cut away the sheets around the board before handing them back.

Anneka moved to the other side of the bed. "What am I thinking? I can at least remove this tube and patch up one arm."

She knelt, eased the plastic cannula from English's arm and applied antiseptic and a band aid. They watched as the remaining blood snaked through the tube and vanished.

"I much prefer your bedside manner," said English. "Very refreshing."

"And much less lethal. Can I apologize for her? I'd have done more had I known she was using you as our supply. I've already tried to radio for help, but the system is down, and I can't get a signal on my phone."

"I had my suspicions about everything," said Frain, "but I was too scared to talk."

"No apologies necessary," said English. "Get me off this thing and then deal with her."

Anneka stood and moved aside then stopped and turned as the door in the other room slammed open and bounced back off the wall.

Erick stepped into the room, lifted his gun, and fired.

The first round caught Frain in the face. Blood sprayed across the room and the impact spun him and sent him backwards to leave his lifeless body draped across the window space.

Anneka screamed and dropped to the ground.

Sarge lifted his pistol as another round thumped into the wall behind them.

Macca returned fire first, and the pilot ducked behind the door.

"Quick," shouted Sarge. "The bed. English is a sitting duck. Help me flip him."

They grabbed one end rail each and overturned the bed, leaving the underside of the mattress facing the door.

English grimaced and gripped the side rail as his body dropped and his weight pulled at the tie.

Another shot pinged off the metal rail and buzzed past Sarge's ear. The next thudded into the mattress.

The console beeped.

Macca lifted his head enough to see over the top of the bed as Sarge moved toward the door.

"I'll flank him," he whispered.

Just as Sarge opened the door, the pilot reappeared.

Macca shot twice, hitting the man in the chest. As he staggered backwards, a third shot punched a hole between his eyes, and he slid down the outside wall.

Macca heaved a sigh. "Don't bother, he's down. Grab the bed, quickly, English is holding on for dear life."

With a lurch, the bed clattered upright and shook on rubber casters.

As he settled back into place, English gestured toward the console.

The countdown clock read fifty-five seconds, then blinked

to fifty-four as the plunger over the pink chemical began to move.

"Oh, shit," he said.

———

Dahl paused as the sound of a crashing door echoed along the corridor, followed by a muted, "Clear."

That was quick, she thought. *Professionals.*

No point trying to outrun them, and she may not have the skill to deal with them together. It might be simple to pick off one as he rounded the corner, but the other would soon rally and make life difficult.

The strongest survived by adapting quickly to ever-changing situations. So, on to Plan B.

If she could delay them long enough, she could give Erick time to finish off MacIntyre and the others, meet up with him, and still leave the facility. Or even team up with Erick to deal with the lot.

Dahl felt a tiny pang of guilt about Anneka's fate, but she had revealed herself to be softer than expected. Nothing good ever came easily and, with Anneka unprepared to commit fully to the cause, she'd left her with no choice.

She peered around another corner then paused to visualize the layout of the facility.

In the next corridor, the secondary lab sat on the left, the lab where she and Anneka had discovered so much.

Plan B formed in an instant.

Dahl took the corner and scurried into the lab and emerged with a CO_2 fire extinguisher. Every lab had one. Safety first.

She ran back along the corridor, cracked open an inviting

door, laid the extinguisher on the blind side of the corner, and retreated to wait.

Another door slammed.

Another, "Clear."

The process repeated until the crash of slamming doors grew close enough to vibrate her ears.

After a moment of silence, faint whispers drifted toward her from the other corridor.

They were discussing the cracked door bait.

She leveled the pistol and focused the sights on the center of the extinguisher as they crept around the corner. Before they had time to glance down at the metal cylinder, she put a nine-millimeter shell through its casing.

The extinguisher slid backwards from the impact then rocked and bucked as a concentrated stream of gas poured from the wound, expanded, and sprayed a blistering jet of pressurized ice into the air.

A scream cut through the freezing mist.

Dahl chuckled, turned, and ran deeper into the facility.

————

"We'll achieve nothing in a panic," said Macca as he looked around the room. "Think, people."

A hydraulic lever pushed the plunger down, fraction by fraction.

English lay wide eyed as the pink fluid entered his blood-stream. "But panicking does get people moving," he said.

The countdown timer read fifty-one seconds.

"And, since I'm strapped to a fucking bed, I'd really appreciate it if people moved."

Sarge sat transfixed as Anneka recovered, leaped to her feet, and began to cut at the tubes with the scissors.

"They're fortified," said English. "Dahl said that a knife wouldn't cut them."

"And we can't yank them," said Sarge, "not without pulling bits of English out all over the sheets."

"You could cut me free, though," said English.

Anneka snipped the ties that held him to the bed rails.

English flexed his free arm and stopped. "Guys, my joints feel as if they're seizing up. My elbow just ground as I moved it."

"It's started," said Anneka. "He's calcifying."

The timer read forty-eight seconds.

"Wait," she said. "I'll be right back."

She leaped through the open window space as Sarge looked on.

"You'd best be back soon," he said.

"It's just like an IED," said Macca. He rapped his knuckles against his head. "Think, man."

He looked again at the console, and then around the room, then snapped his fingers. "Got it."

He grabbed one of the metal test tubes from the rack on the wall. "We can't touch the tubing, but we can touch the console." He slid the tube beneath the plunger. "This should stop it delivering any more of the chemical."

A quarter inch still stood between the bottom of the plunger and the top of the tube.

"Give or take. But God only knows if it'll stop enough of the pink shit being pumped into his system."

"His system?" said English. "Bloody hell, mate, I'm right here."

The countdown read forty-two seconds when the plunger finally met the top of the tube.

For a moment, the tube rocked, and the machine groaned

and emitted a long, solid beep before the plunger ground into the metal and stopped.

English sighed and blinked. "Guys, my eyes feel like I've washed them in grit. In fact, everything feels as if it needs oiling."

Anneka climbed through the open window with a syringe. "Trust me?" she said.

"Do I have a choice?" said English. "A few more minutes and I suspect it won't matter one way or another."

She nodded, steadied her shaking hands, and slipped the needle easily into his vein. "It's a mixture of magnesium and vitamin K2. I'm only guessing, but the combination should hopefully reverse the effects of the agent in your bloodstream."

"Sounds cool," said English, until a bolt of heat shot through his body. He slammed against the mattress as his eyes watered and he drooled for a second time. Then, his body relaxed. His joints eased and his eyes opened and closed freely.

"I think you got it," he said. "Thank you, Anneka."

He turned to look at Macca.

"Again?" said the Scot. "How many more times have I got to save your life? You owe me a beer and a good meal."

English smiled and studied his arms. "Consider it a date, mate. First, though, can we get this shit off me?"

Anneka walked to the cupboards on the wall and returned with a small, curved blade. "I can do this," she said.

One by one, she cut the sutures holding the tubing in place, until she was able to free the tubes enough to pull them from English's arm.

Another dose of antiseptic and a larger band aid and he sat up in bed and gently massaged his arms.

"Thank you, again. I hate to say it, but now I owe my life to two people. I'm sure one of them will be humble."

"But not this one," said Macca. "We have a date. First, let's go find the others. That crazy bitch is around here somewhere. All the noise has been in here. I expected fireworks from outside."

"I'm coming with you," said English. "The sedative has pretty much worn off. I might be a bit sluggish, but I owe that woman some pain."

"You sure you're okay, buddy?" said Sarge. "You know we can take care of this."

"Don't doubt that for a second, Sarge, but this got personal. I'll feel better once I'm up and moving."

Macca and Sarge helped English through the window space and made their way outside as Anneka began to gather the tubing. She stopped when the door behind her opened.

Dahl stepped into the room and paused when she saw Frain's body draped over the open window then gasped when she stepped farther into the room and saw the bloody smear on the outside wall above Erick's crumpled body.

"Well, isn't this a shit show." She huffed an exaggerated sigh as Anneka retreated into a corner.

"Anneka, my flight out of here seems to be gone but, somehow, you're still here. You and I have a little catching up to do."

Chapter Thirty-Six

The girls watched as a gleaming black SUV with tinted windows glided into the street and parallel parked perfectly opposite the car.

A tall man in a dark suit climbed out of the driver's side and slid a pair of sunglasses over his eyes. A tall brunette appeared from the passenger side and did the same.

"Hubba, hubba," said Sam. "Who is that?"

Both walked forward with an air of total confidence.

"That's the FBI," said Carina, "or possibly the Men in Black, it's hard to tell without ID. Either way, I'd suggest showing them some respect. From experience, they can be assholes."

"One of you girls called the field office," said the guy as more of a statement than a question.

His partner eyed the girls up and down.

"Yes," said Evie. "I did. It seems we're in a situation where we thought we'd take care of some bad guys but got railroaded by rats."

"Rats? I'm sorry, but you've lost me."

She led them back along the street and pointed to the row of houses.

"Long story short, we've been tracking a gang of counter-feiters who've kidnapped and threatened us in one form or another."

The guy's eyebrows raised. "And something led you to this building?"

"Yes."

"Can I ask how?"

"Threats to me," said Carina.

"And kidnapping for me," said Sam. "And I kicked a guy in the balls and got this address."

"Okay," said the Fed. He lifted his sunglasses, reached into his pocket and pulled out a wallet. It dropped open to reveal a badge.

"I'm Agent Willis, and this is my partner, Agent Shepherd. For the sake of my sanity, can we start at the beginning and try to make some sense?"

Evie took them through the time from Carina's purse snatch up to the present.

"And there's nothing in the buildings," she said, "except rats. Probably sixteen of them, and I'm going to kick Numbers' ass when I see him."

"Numbers?"

"How could you confuse the heat signature of a rat with that of a gangster? Never mind. Anyway, we wanted to put an end to a threat that left us scared. They know where we live, and we couldn't let that be."

Willis folded his arms and smiled. "And by 'they', you mean the gang that used those buildings?"

"Used?" said Carina.

"They're all behind bars," said Shepherd. "We rounded up the leadership a couple of days ago. We've been watching this place for months, waiting for the evidence to bust them. Then, one of them was stupid enough to use his own fake bills to buy a new car. Nothing like that gets past us. With the help of CCTV and a little shadowing, we were able to find this place, break up the operation, and take everyone into custody. The car guy told us where to find his bosses in exchange for a lighter sentence. The plates they used had a tiny flaw in the print, which was picked up on the bills. It was as good as a fingerprint."

"This place is deserted," said Sam, "like, totally empty. Except for rats."

Willis smiled again. "It is now. I'm guessing you didn't find the door to the basement."

The girls stared in silence.

"Rats got to you first, huh?" said Willis. "There's a staircase in one of the buildings. The gang knocked through the entire lower level. It's basically a huge printing plant; rows of machines that churned out the bills."

Carina reached into her waistband and pulled out the plates. "You'll be needing these, then. I've had them for long enough. They seem to attract trouble, so be careful with them."

"So this is why they used the faulty plates," said Willis, "you had the good ones, and they grew impatient and greedy. How did you come to possess these? And what kind of trouble?"

"I saw them and thought they'd be better off with me," said Carina. "But they attract sharks. It's never pretty where sharks are involved."

"Loan sharks?"

"Gray ones. With slippery skin and big teeth."

Willis and Shepherd glanced at one another then shrugged.

"I gather from the accent that you're not from around here," said Willis as he glanced at Sam.

Sam flushed. "Kentucky. Is it that obvious?"

Willis smiled and showed a row of perfect teeth.

"I've always liked that southern drawl," he said. "The way it takes the pace from words, I like that pace. Slow and steady."

"Do you need to get my married sister's contact details?" said Evie, "or are we free to head home?"

"This case is closed, bar the sentencing," said Shepherd, "although leaving your contact details would be a good idea. We have witnesses and footage galore now we can match the bills to the gang, but it couldn't hurt to have you girls on the end of the phone. Just in case."

Ten minutes later, Willis and Shepherd climbed back into their SUV and drove away in a dramatic squeal of tire smoke.

The girls slumped into the car and clicked seatbelts into place.

"Well, that was a disappointment," said Carina.

"After what I've been through recently," said Evie, "I might agree. But, if not for this, we'd never have met. We make an excellent team, not that I'm planning on doing this again. But we'll stay in touch, right?"

Carina smiled. "Of course. How about you, Sam?"

Sam held up a business card. "I beg to differ, too. Carl gave me his number," she said.

"Carl?" said Evie. "You're on first-name terms with the FBI guy? What about Daryl?"

Sam tucked the card inside her sparkling phone case. "Of all the things I thought I might find at the end of this, I totally didn't expect to find myself. But I did. I'm tired of being the one to fetch Daryl's beer on game night. I love him but, gosh darn, I'm done with being the one who cooks the meal and then gets left to do the dishes, too. I've found me, I've got skills and attitude, and shit's going to change."

She held up the phone and waved it in the air.

"And I've totally found alternatives. Damn, underneath that suit, I reckon that dude's muscles had muscles. You can imagine them, like, rippling when he moves. Daryl's whole stomach ripples when he moves, and not in a good way. If FBI guys are into me, Daryl better get his shit together, because Samantha is back. And she means business."

———

"You okay?" said Dud.

Marbles blinked a few times.

A glowing red weal slashed across his face, a ribbon of swollen skin with a gleaming emoji at its center.

"Damn, that's sore as a crack across the ass, but thank God it was this side of my face. A few inches across and I'd probably be blind."

"First time you've been grateful to have a glass eye, right?"

"I've been grateful plenty of times, pal," said Marbles. "There are plenty of folks worse off than me. How about you?"

"The stream went across my body," said Dud. "This clothing protected me."

Marbles gave a reassuring nod, kicked the empty canister away, and pushed himself up off the floor.

"Come on, we can't let her get away. It's not like we can call for help. Again, we don't know if she can fly, but if she can and she gets to the helicopter it's over for all of us. She takes off and we're literally dead in the water."

Dud led the way.

"Don't you find it odd that there are so few people here?

You'd think someone paranoid enough to put out a hit team, make that at least two hit teams, would have a ton of security. Other than the nerds in that lab, we've come across more resistance on the reefer. And that was negligible. I've had tougher fights out of a bar."

"The fewer people know what's going on, the less people can talk," said Marbles. "And we're in the middle of nowhere. Who's going to visit? And then, even if someone does and they're not as crazy as us, the only way to get up here is by helicopter and you'd have plenty of time to defend that. Why waste the money or take the extra risk?"

"Makes sense. Dude, I don't think she's going to be in any of these rooms. That extinguisher trap was to slow us down. I reckon she's making a beeline for the helicopter."

"Agreed. Up the pace, but let's not underestimate her."

They turned another corner and stopped. Ahead, something shuffled around the next turn.

Dud held up a fist and Marbles stopped, lowered himself to the ground and trained his pistol on the corner.

Dud stood over him and did the same.

Another scuff sounded, closer.

As the first figure rounded the corner, Dud shouted. "Stop, or we'll shoot."

Macca raised his hands. "Whoa, steady on there, mate. None of that friendly fire malarky."

They relaxed as Sarge appeared. With one more scuff, a pale English dragged himself into view.

"It's good to see you up and about," said Dud, "but we heard you coming from a mile away. You should rest up, brother, you look like an extra from *Twilight*."

English nodded. "Appreciate that, mate, but I can still shoot. We can't let them get away with this."

"And we won't, buddy," said Sarge. "The pilot's been

permanently grounded and, other than the nerds in the other lab, we haven't seen anyone else but the young girl, Anneka, and our attractive lunatic friend. Anneka saved English's life, so I reckon we only have one more issue to deal with."

"You obviously didn't pass her?" said Marbles.

"We passed no one," said English. "Place is deserted."

"So there's only the young girl left. You reckon psycho bitch would want to clear the slate? Leave no witnesses?"

"I wouldn't put it past her," said Sarge. He turned and stormed away. "Come on, we owe our new friend."

———

Dahl ran a manicured nail across the smooth top of the bed's side rail. The opposite side had a crease where Erick's bullet had connected a few inches too high. A plastic tie and the tubing plate lay on the mattress.

Anneka cringed in the corner.

"I assume you helped?" said Dahl.

"Of course I did." Anneka spat out each word. "How did you think you could ever get away with this? Are you crazy?"

"You poor child. So naïve. I've been getting away with things like this for years. How do you think we maintain our lifestyles? Some must suffer for the greater good. It's been that way since time began, but you've ruined it. As much as I loathed Frain, he had the intelligence to solve our final problem. His brains are no good to me all over the floor."

She pointed through the open window space as her voice rose from calm conversation to a violent whisper.

Her face twisted and her body shook with rage.

"And Erick, he sacrificed so much to serve us," she said as her voice warped once more into a full-throated shout, "and he was my ride out of here. Now what? We're stuck."

Anneka shrunk farther into the corner and reached slowly behind her back.

"And you fucking helped," screamed Dahl.

She lifted the pistol and fired with shaking hands as Anneka dived to one side.

A ragged hole appeared in the wall as Dahl turned and fired again.

Frain's body jerked as the round tore a hole in his jacket.

Anneka pushed off the bed and lunged with her scissors.

Dahl screamed as the blades punctured her shoulder.

The gun clattered to the ground, and she swung one punch after another.

The blows dazed Anneka and rocked her backwards onto the mattress. Dahl towered over her, yanked out the scissors with a scream, and threw them across the room.

"You're going to pay for that, you scheming bitch."

Anneka yelped as Dahl leaned forward, grabbed her hair in one hand, and yanked her upright. She gagged as the other wrapped coils of plastic tubing around her throat and pulled.

In seconds, her temples throbbed.

"Ironic, don't you think?" hissed Dahl. "These tubes were destined to kill someone." She yanked even harder. "It's almost poetic."

Anneka tugged at the tubing then tried to gouge Dahl's eyes. Black spots danced in her view, while a dark ink spread in from the edges. Her panicked fumbling rested on the wooden platform, English's pressure trap. She clutched an edge and swung the board.

Dahl grunted and released her grip as the wood connected with her head, and Anneka turned the board and slammed its narrow edge into Dahl's throat.

She gasped and dropped to her knees.

Anneka unwound the tubing from her neck as a light

glinted from the console.

Dahl looked through bloodshot eyes as Anneka approached.

"You don't deserve to live. Evil has no place here." She reached past Dahl to grab another tube. Remnants of pink chemical still clung to its inside.

"You want to talk about irony?" said Anneka. She thrust the tip of the tube into the hole in Dahl's shoulder and pushed it deep then swiped away the metal test tube that held back the console's plunger. With two fingers, she forced down the plunger.

Pink filled the tube and coursed into Dahl's body.

The blonde tried to scream, but her crushed throat stopped any sound. She thrashed with her arms and tried to stand, but Anneka braced her shoulder and held the tube in place. "Didn't you say sixty seconds?"

Dahl's arms slowed until her movements became jerky and they dropped to her side. Color washed from her face as a glaze formed over her eyes and her rasped breathing slowed.

"But that was with an anticoagulant. And you don't have any of that. I'd give you twenty seconds at best."

Dahl caught her gaze and blinked slowly as her breaths grew even shorter. Her piercing eyes faded as icy cataracts spread across them, and she blinked once more before they froze open and the breathing stopped.

Dahl's body remained upright, posed like a plaster doll, with her fingers splayed in one last attempt to move.

Anneka stepped back and slid down the wall, unable to take her eyes off the mannequin-like figure, half expecting it to come back to life.

She jumped as the far door opened and the men filed into the room, then lay down, hugged her shoulders and burst into tears.

Chapter Thirty-Seven

Chapter Thirty -Seven

Evie closed the front door, and she and Sam filed along the hallway, past the living room door, and into the kitchen.

Daryl's voice came from behind them, raised over the sound of a sport commentary.

"Is that you, babe? Grab me another beer, would you?"

Sam turned toward the fridge before she stopped herself. "Wow, that is, like, totally a habit. Those days are gone. Do you think he even realized we've been missing?"

In the background, a loud cheer erupted from the television.

"I guess it depends who's playing," said Evie. "Only one way to find out. Look, I'll leave you guys to it. I'm not looking forward to another few hours of driving after that trip, but I'm ready to be home."

Sam stepped forward and wrapped her in a hug.

"Let's do this again. Well, not what we just did, but let's hang out more."

"I'd like that," said Evie.

"And I need someone to teach me how to shoot properly. I heard the world can be a scary place, but I've, like, seen scary up close. I don't like it. And I love Daryl, but he's about as useless as a chocolate fireguard. One of us needs to know how to defend ourselves."

"Dud told me about a poster he saw that said nobody likes to fight, but someone needs to know how to."

"That's cool," said Sam. "I'd like to know how to. If you have any more missions, I'm totally on board. This whole thing has woken something up in me. It's turned me into a me that I like. No more wimpy Sam."

"I'm not planning any more missions, but with Carina only a few miles away there's nothing stopping the two of you getting together and heading to the range to let loose a few rounds."

"Yeah, I like her. Now I know she didn't steal my phone."

"Babe," shouted Daryl. "Beer."

"One minute," shouted Sam. "Is it wrong that a tiny part of me wants Agent Willis to call?"

"If those kidnappers ever turn up, he said that he would. You're a key witness."

Sam clapped her hands and jumped up and down on the spot. "Yes, I am. It's, like, the coolest thing that's ever happened to me."

"Babe."

"Don't kill him," said Evie. "And if you have to beat him, go with body shots. No visible marks."

"Really?" said Sam.

"No, of course not. Go talk to him. It's going to be an adjustment, but you've got this."

They hugged again.

"Love you, big sis," said Sam. "Don't be a stranger."

"Love you back," said Evie. "Don't kill him."

Sam took a beer from the fridge. "The last 'on-demand' beer he's getting from me."

They walked back along the hallway.

Evie closed the front door as Sam stepped into the living room.

———

"Why is there a turd on my taters?" said Marbles.

Tony laughed as he pulled out a chair and joined the others.

"Give a man what he wants, and he still bloody moans. That's haggis, mate. Trust me, unless you're vegan, you'll like it."

"And what did you call this meal?"

"Haggis, with neeps and tatties."

"Sounds borderline pornographic," said Dud "What exactly is it?"

"A Scottish staple. Neeps are like turnips, boiled and pureed. Tatties are obviously mashed potatoes. The shots are a good malt."

"And the haggis?"

"I'll let you try it first. It comes in different shapes and sizes, but the recipe is similar wherever you go. Believe it or not, they make some that are used in sport. For throwing."

"You say us Americans are crazy," said Sarge, "while you throw good food and tree trunks for sport."

Macca glanced around the inside of the pub, then lifted a shot glass and raised it.

"A toast. First, to Tony. You've been nothing short of exceptional, pal. We couldn't have done this without you. Our apologies for losing the gear you gave us. Over time, we'll make it up to you."

"Lost in battle," said Tony. "Easy come, easy go."

"Second, to fallen comrades. Knowles and Ken. We knew them, we'll remember them, and they will not be forgotten."

A chorus of respectful murmurs rose as each man tapped his glass against the table.

"And, finally," said Macca, "to The Old Farts Club. I would never have believed it had I not seen it for myself. I'm forever in your debt."

He slammed the shot, enjoyed the aftertaste, and then addressed his plate.

"Tuck in, fellas."

They spoke over the clinking of cutlery.

"So Marbles flew you back in the bad guy's chopper. Where did you land?"

"About a half mile from here," said Marbles. "It's secluded, and I don't think anyone saw us. Feel free to take a helicopter as a down payment on what we owe you. I doubt it's registered anywhere."

"Seems a bit severe," said Tony, "but I'll take it. Cheers. How did you leave everything?"

"English got comms up and running," said Sarge, "and we checked in with the people who count."

"Apparently, Evie's had an adventure," said Dud, "and made a new friend. She said she'll tell me all when we get home."

"And Numbers said he felt redundant and insists on joining

us next time," said Marbles. "He and Penny almost took up knitting."

Sarge continued. "The young girl on the rig, Anneka, said that she'd wait until we got back before she reported everything to the Coast Guard. With a little rearrangement, it'll look like the crazy woman went postal and took everyone out."

Marbles took up the story. "The Coast Guard will also take care of the reefer. There's enough evidence there to convict the captain and his first mate of illegal trafficking. I don't know about the young lad below deck; he seemed oblivious to what they were up to. I guess the justice system will deal with him."

"And what about the young girl?" said Tony.

"When she finished shaking," said Sarge, "she realized there's enough of a team there to continue research of the genuine kind. She found access to the bad guy's offshore accounts; they contain enough cash to last a lifetime, and she has a desire to use it for good. The rig's paid for, all she has to cover are the utilities and salaries, so she's going to stay there and use her own ties to recruit and keep it going. Once the authorities complete their investigations, she should be in the clear."

"Nice and tidy," said Marbles. "So, come on, Tony, what's this haggis made from? I'm pleasantly surprised. It's a gorgeous blend of some kind of meat and spices."

Tony smiled. "Indeed, it is, mate. Sheep's pluck."

"I'm sure they do, but I'm none the wiser."

"That's what it's called, sheep's pluck. They take the heart, lungs and liver of one sheep—"

"The what?" said Marbles as he swallowed, heavily.

"Did you give him the throwing kind?" said English, "because it looks like he's about to."

"And they mince it with onion, suet, oatmeal, some stock,

and a bunch of other stuff and spices and, traditionally, wrap it in the animal's stomach and boil it."

Marbles leaped to his feet. "Oh, crap, I think I need your bathroom."

"Haven't got one, mate," laughed Tony, "but you're welcome to use the gents."

Acknowledgments

The without whom bit...

I used to imagine authors sat in front of a blazing fire with a glass of wine, typewriter clicking away, churning out my favourite books. Type the words, get them printed, wrap them in a nice cover, job done. Easy peasy.

But it's not like that at all.

For too many reasons to mention, 2019 was our personal 'annus horribilis', and we went into 2020 with a 'fresh start' mentality, not knowing that there was a pandemic on the horizon. 2020 has been especially testing, and definitely not the best time to make life changing decisions like re-emigrating to Kentucky! If not for some folks, it would not have been possible. That, combined with writing *The Old Farts Club* #2, made this another year to remember.

So many people have been involved in getting the thing you hold in your hands into the shape it's in.

In no particular order, this is what they did...

Michelle, Bella, Phil, Liam, and Chris at The Royal Exchange were always gracious enough to get me a table and keep me watered and fed while I tippy-tapped away on the laptop. I love and miss this place more than I ever thought I could. If you're ever in Stone, Staffordshire, The Royal Exchange has the best beer and the nicest people. Pay them a visit.

When the words were done, others needed to check them out for typos, plot holes and military mishaps. Julie Cox is the best pre-edit editor I know. Kerry Parsons and Steph Lawrence have keen eyes and run two of the best book blogs that you should check out (chataboutbooks and steflozbook-blog respectively). Steve Jackson knows more about helicopter types and militaryness than I do, and Kenneth Morris has always had the eyes of a hawk. Without them, this wouldn't have made anywhere near as much sense as it does!

My son, Rob Williams, fills me with more pride than one man can handle, but he still manages to take care of my website (mickwilliamsauthor.com) while he juggles a family and work and makes me look way better than I feel. Love you, #1 son.

Sean and Melonie Sullivan, along with Gary and Missy Platt, made our move to KY possible and as painless as it could be. I'll be forever in their debt. I love my American Framily more than they know.

Back in England, John Pye, JF Burgess, and Phil Hodgkiss kept the writer light burning. I'll miss our curry night get togethers, although you should all know that they have curries in America! Just saying.

And in the US, folks like Tony Acree, Stephen Zimmer, Holly Phillipe, and a whole host of names (a lot in the Kentuckiana Authors group) were eager to take me back into the fold and offer the same support as always. It's good to be back and it still feels like home!

My family on both sides of the pond, #1 Son and Rach,

Steve and Max, Lynn and Andy, and my Mum in England, along with Zack and Lexie, and Chase and Liz in the States, who have always kept me pushing.

The people that put the Sparkle in my life. You know who you are and what you do. I wish there were twenty-nine hours in a day so that we could talk more. When we don't, I still think of you.

And Cathy. The strong and amazing woman who keeps the cats at bay and lets me pursue this dream. Let's see where we are when #9 comes along.

About the Author

Mick Williams moved from Stoke-On-Trent, England to Kentucky, USA. Then, after almost a decade, he moved back to England. Then, after three years, he moved back to Kentucky again.

This time he's staying.

He writes in multiple genres, but each story contains the same action, adventure, and comedic banter – and always has a dash of romance. His readers say that, if you like one, you'll like them all.

In between reading, writing, and listening to good music, he still watches proper football and, for his sins, follows his local team, Port Vale. He does also still cheer for the Indianapolis Colts.

He was adopted by two cats, Crash and Thud, and resides with his patient wife (who is also tired of moving) in Kentucky.

Also by Mick Williams

A Reason to Grieve

A Guy Walks Into a Bar

Whatever It Takes

Exodus; The Old Farts Club Book One

Callie's Eyes

Hope's Game

Final Clearance

Available from www.mickwilliamsauthor.com,
www.hydrapublications.com, and the Amazon

site in your country.

www.ingramcontent.com/pod-product-compliance
Lightning Source LLC
Chambersburg PA
CBHW070624260626
47161CB00007B/2570